SABBAT WORLDS

THE SONS CAME at them from all sides in the twilight. Drumming was the only sound Gaunt could hear. Feygor, Caffran and Corbec slammed off shots as they came in, and Bragg followed on, blasting with his cannons. He mowed them down. The Sons of Sek were so many, he didn't have to try again. Gaunt's sword swung and struck. He emptied his bolt pistol four times.

He thought they would be overwhelmed. He thought they weren't going to make it, but they were fast, and they were good, and they had surprise on their side, despite the incredible ferocity of the Sons of Sek.

They were Ghosts. They were five of the best Guardsmen the Imperium had ever produced.

They covered one another. They checked and turned with expertise. They watched the flanks, they plastered the angles, they fired in turns to stagger reloading. At any given point in the action at least three of them were shooting.

They cut through the Sons like an elite strike force, because they were an elite strike force. They were immortals. They were gods of war.

They reached the bridge.

A WARHAMMER 40,000 ANTHOLOGY

SABBAT WORLDS

Edited by Dan Abnett

BLACK LIBRARY

A BLACK LIBRARY PUBLICATION

First published in Great Britain in 2010
Paperback edition published in 2001 by
The Black Library,
Games Workshop Ltd.,
Willow Road, Nottingham,
NG7 2WS, UK.

10 9 8 7 6 5 4 3 2 1

Cover illustration by Stefan Kopinski.

A CIP record for this book is available from the British Library.

ISBN: 978 1 84970 083 2

Distributed in the US by Simon & Schuster
1230 Avenue of the Americas, New York, NY 10020, US.

See the Black Library on the internet at
www.blacklibrary.com

Find out more about Games Workshop
and the world of Warhammer 40,000 at
www.games-workshop.com

Printed and bound in the US.

IT IS THE 41st millennium. For more than a hundred centuries the Emperor has sat immobile on the Golden Throne of Earth. He is the master of mankind by the will of the gods, and master of a million worlds by the might of his inexhaustible armies. He is a rotting carcass writhing invisibly with power from the Dark Age of Technology. He is the Carrion Lord of the Imperium for whom a thousand souls are sacrificed every day, so that he may never truly die.

YET EVEN IN his deathless state, the Emperor continues his eternal vigilance. Mighty battlefleets cross the daemon-infested miasma of the warp, the only route between distant stars, their way lit by the Astronomican, the psychic manifestation of the Emperor's will. Vast armies give battle in His name on uncounted worlds. Greatest amongst his soldiers are the Adeptus Astartes, the Space Marines, bio-engineered super-warriors. Their comrades in arms are legion: the Imperial Guard and countless Planetary Defence Forces, the ever-vigilant Inquisition and the tech-priests of the Adeptus Mechanicus to name only a few. But for all their multitudes, they are barely enough to hold off the ever-present threat from aliens, heretics, mutants - and worse.

TO BE A man in such times is to be one amongst untold billions. It is to live in the cruellest and most bloody regime imaginable. These are the tales of those times. Forget the power of technology and science, for so much has been forgotten, never to be re-learned. Forget the promise of progress and understanding, for in the grim dark future there is only war. There is no peace amongst the stars, only an eternity of carnage and slaughter, and the laughter of thirsting gods.

CONTENTS

INTRODUCTION

IT SEEMS I can add 'world builder' to my CV.

Actually, that comes as no great revelation to me. Anyone who works in what's loosely known as 'genre fiction' (ie SF, fantasy, horror, comics, a great deal of gaming etc. etc.), is used to the process. What's basically meant by the phrase is the deliberate and artful construction of a consistent fictional background, setting or milieu for your story or stories to operate in. There are some singularly achieved examples (Middle-earth, Arrakis, Gormenghast) and there are some spectacularly piecemeal yet inclusive examples too (the continuity of *Doctor Who*, the Marvel Comics Universe). I've personally done it many times, often without even consciously realising I'm doing it, as I create the background for a story or series of my own. This happened with the city of Downlode in my *2000AD* series *Sinister Dexter*, and it happened every time I invented a planet setting for a *Star Trek* or *Legion of Super-Heroes* story. Sometimes it means literally inventing a world, sometimes it means something more figurative. What you're basically setting out to do is establish a playing field that is logical and stable and doesn't start suddenly contradicting itself.

When I was first asked to write for Warhammer 40,000 (as memory serves, this would have been around about 1996), the basics of the 'world' I would be working in were already well built. Like many popular and long-running intellectual properties, 40K is a 'shared universe – lots of individuals work within, and contribute creatively to, the whole. But the universe was truly vast, and there was a great deal of room for 'micro-invention' within it.

I don't mean this to sound like a criticism of Warhammer 40,000 at all: the inclusion of huge scope for individual development was a deliberately designed aspect of the universe. This was an adventure you were being invited to join in with, and contribute to. As anyone who's played the game or built his own army (and its mythology) from the ground up will testify, that's the appeal. There is room for that invention.

As I've written novels for the Black Library, in excess of thirty and counting, I'd like to think I've contributed in two particular areas of the world building process (maybe it's not really my place to review this but, hey, I've got the mic right now). The first area is what might be called small-scale texture or domestic detail. With various books, but particularly the *Eisenhorn* trilogy, I wrote about the 40K universe away from the front line of eternal war. I created a lot of words, phrases and ideas that have been adopted as part of the basic vernacular (*vox*, anybody? *promethium*?) and used by other writers, by players, and by game designers alike. That gives me a huge warm feeling inside.

The other area is an actual area. It's called the Sabbat Worlds.

One of the first (not the very first, but one of the first) short stories I wrote for the Black Library's *Inferno!* magazine was about a bunch of Imperial Guard called the Tanith First and Only. Along with their commander, Ibram Gaunt, they have gone on to feature in fourteen novels. They have a vast, dogged and devoted fanbase, and they represent my most monumental creative achievement (even if you simply measure it in words).

I had no idea how far the Gaunt's Ghosts stories would take me when I wrote that first tale (or the handful that followed, or even the first few novels, if I'm honest), but I did know I wanted some kind of backdrop. I wanted Gaunt and his men to be fighting in a particular campaign, and so I created names (in a loose and scattershot way) for the small corner of the vast 40K galaxy that they were fighting in. I called it the Sabbat Worlds. I don't know where that name came from (I don't know where any of the names came from, actually, except that I deliberately went for 'Celtic' names for the Tanith). 'The Sabbat Worlds' sounded exotic and atmospheric. I made reference to events that had happened just prior to the first story, and mentioned other places. It gave the stories a little meat, a little context.

As the novels took off, the background developed. It grew flesh over its bones. By the fourth book, *Honour Guard*, we had a real sense of what the Sabbat Worlds were all about and why they were important. These elements have become more and more significant as I've progressed. I find it very satisfying that those early, almost throwaway references to places and events are becoming increasingly important. The series as a whole is broken down into discrete story arcs (the first three novels form the first arc, *The Founding*; the next four form the second arc, *The Saint*; the next four form the third, *The Lost*). The latest arc, the fourth, is called *The Victory*, and only the first of its four novels has been published at the time of writing. Even in this book, *Blood Pact*, readers will see how the setting is coming to drive the action more and more. Those flyaway bits of colour text I decorated the story with in 1996 are now monolithic parts of the epic.

So partly through my own deliberate efforts, and partly through a spontaneous creative process, the Sabbat Worlds have evolved. At one point, we produced a wallchart of them, and a campaign overview book that is now rarer than hens' teeth. I never imagined that this corner of space (called, by the cheeky BL editors, 'the Daniverse') would get so big. But there are, as I said, thirteen Gaunt books, plus the air combat novel *Double Eagle* and the Titan novel *Titanicus*, both of which are set in the same crusade. All told, that's something over a million and a half words worth of Sabbat adventuring.

I suppose the real test of a piece of world building is how well it stands up to the visits of guest creators. In late 2009, just as I was due to begin work on the sequel to *Blood Pact*, I was pole-axed by late-onset epilepsy. It was a freaky time, not least because it took a while for the condition to be diagnosed, and there were a good couple of months where the seizures could have been the consequence of something... how can I put it? *Final*.

When I discovered at last it was 'just epilepsy' (*there's* a phrase you don't imagine yourself saying) I was incredibly relieved. I've been picking myself up since, learning what I can do, and what I can't. There is a period of adjustment while you get your meds balanced, for example. I'm now settling down to a new lease of life that I'm very content about. But while the crisis was happening, boy did some deadlines get screwed.

The Gaunt novel, *Salvation's Reach*, had to slide back and miss its expected autumn slot. There was just no way it was going to happen. But Black Library editor Christian Dunn got chatting to me to see if we could devise a stonking hit of Sabbat Worlds loveliness for the readers to tide them over.

This book is the result. I've invited other Black Library writers whose work I admire to contribute stories set in the Sabbat Worlds, perhaps even touching on strands or characters established in or suggested by the storylines in my books. I've also added a brand new Gaunt's Ghosts novella to round things out.

I am blown away by the stories various writers have given back to me, by the sheer creative energy they've poured into bits of my haphazard world building. It is a great honour and privilege to commend them to you, the reader.

So, join me for a Sabbat Worlds road trip. I call shotgun. Believe me, we're going to need one.

Dan Abnett
Maidstone, May 2010

Graham needs little introduction to Black Library readers. The author of the Ultramarines series and of Horus Heresy epics including the New York Times bestseller A Thousand Sons, he is the master of 40K hugeness and fury, and a writer I unfailingly refer to as 'mighty' when I talk about him in my blogs. Graham and I have evolved an enjoyably close way of working in tandem for the Horus books, which he described as me 'knocking shots into the air for him to smash'. This seemed to pay dividends with Horus Rising and False Gods, and will again with the parasitic twins A Thousand Sons and Prospero Burns.

Graham has taken as his starting point Double Eagle, the air combat novel I wrote a few years back. I had a splendid time writing it, and it was something I'd wanted to do for a long time. Unashamedly, I set out to do a sort of 'Battle of Britain' in 40K terms. It has earned a lot of fans (including, I'm delighted to say, some Luftwaffe crewmen, from whom I have a standing invitation to visit a German airbase – must get around to doing that), to such an extent that I've been planning a sequel for a long time. I know what *it's called (Interceptor City, since you asked) and I know what happens, I just haven't had the time to write it yet. It keeps getting pushed back. When Graham said he wanted to write something involving the characters featured in* Double Eagle, *I was all for it. I think this story will go some way towards soothing the jonesing of* Double Eagle *fans.*

Double Eagle *principally featured the Phantine XX squadron, flying Thunderbolts in defence of the Sabbat World Enothis, but we also met the elite, privileged squadron of combat aces called the Apostles. Larice Asche, once of the Phantine, managed to win a place in this exclusive club. But exactly how long will she last? And how much glory is there when battle honour and status comes with approximately zero life expectancy?*

Dan Abnett

APOSTLE'S CREED

Graham McNeill

THE THUNDERBOLT CUT through the frigid air like an ivory
dagger, trailing white contrails from the leading edges of its
wings. Following the manoeuvres of Apostle Seven, Larice
Asche executed a perfect quarter roll before inverting and
pulling into a shallow turn. She took her time, not pushing
the aircraft. After three months strapped down in the hold
of a Munitorum mass conveyer, it was never a good idea
to ask too much of a plane until you'd given it some time
to stretch its wings and get used to being in the air again.

She watched the crisp movements of Apostle Seven
through the canopy, a cream-coloured Thunderbolt that
hung in the air like an angel basking in the sunlight.
Dario Quint was at its controls, his flawless stickwork
apparently effortless. Larice knew that wasn't the case.
Quint had logged thousands of hours and flown hundreds of sorties to hone his skill.

'Level flight, Apostle Five,' said Quint. 'There's mur-
derous shear coming off the Breakers, so use vectors to
compensate if you go in close.'

'Understood, Seven,' responded Larice. It was the longest single sentence Quint had said to her since Seekan had invited her to join the Apostles back on Enothis. She'd tried to engage him in conversation aboard the *Rosencranz*, en route to Amedeo, but he'd always ignored her. Not in a way she could get mad about, and not with any rudeness. More like he chose not to engage because he didn't know how to.

Despite Quint's warning, the air at nine thousand metres was calm, and it was a simple matter to stay on his wing. Larice scanned the auspex inbetween craning her neck to look around for the telltale glint of sunlight on metal that might indicate a hostile contact.

Nothing. The skies were clear. She was disappointed.

They'd already made kills today, an intercept with some Tormentors returning from a bombing raid on Coriana, foremost city of the Ice, but that tussle had been too easy to be properly interesting. The bombers had already shed their payloads, but that didn't matter. Bombers that didn't make it back to their base wouldn't return with fresh ordnance to crack the Ice.

Cordiale had always said it was bad luck to tangle with the enemy on a shakeout flight, but his luck had run out over the Zophonian Sea, so what did he know? In any case, a Thunderbolt was a weapon of war, a lethal sabre that, once drawn, needed to taste blood before being sheathed.

The Tormentors had been rushing through the valleys of the Breakers, hoping their speed, low flight and the lousy auspex bounces from the peaks would hide them from Imperial retribution.

No such luck.

Apostle Seven had found them, though she had no idea how, since they were running with their auspex silent, and had to rely on Operations to guide them to intercepts. Seekan once told her that Quint, the ace of aces, had an innate sense for where bats were hiding, and she hadn't questioned it.

The bombers had top cover, a trio of Hell Talons, enough to give most pilots pause, but they were the Apostles. Quint took a line on them before firing up his auspex.

'Turn and burn,' he said, his clipped, economical tones muffled by his mask.

His Thunderbolt stood on its wing and dived for the deck.

Coming in high from the east, she and Quint pounced on the Hell Talons, and Larice had relished the panic she'd seen in their desperate scatter. Quint had splashed two bats before they even realised the direction of the attack. He raked the Talons with las before punching through their formation and leaving the last for Larice.

The bat broke high and she turned into it, anticipating its next move and mashing the firing stud on her stick. She had a good angle of deflection, and her bolts tore the bat to burning wreckage. Hauling on the stick, she pulled into a shallow dive to engage the Tormenters themselves.

Quint had already gutted the first bomber and was lining up on his second, viffing and jinking to avoid the turret fire that seemed unable to pin him in place. Larice turned into the third bomber and raked it end to end with her quads. It dropped from the sky, almost cut in two. Pulling a high-g turn, she closed on the last bomber. The pilot was heading for the deck, trying to gain speed, but that was just stupid. There was no way he could outrun her.

It drifted into her firing reticule, and Larice gently lifted the nose of her plane. Quad-fire hammered from her guns and the Tormentor obligingly flew into the lashing bolts. The pilot's canopy bloomed glass and fire, and the ponderous bird described a lazy arc towards the ground.

It slammed into the mountainside, leaving a blackened teardrop of fire on the snow.

She'd pulled up and they resumed their patrol circuit

as though nothing had happened. Seven kills between them, not a bad outing for one day. It had been an easy intercept. The bats hadn't seen them until it was too late. The glaring white of the ever-present ice and snow made it hellishly difficult to spot incoming craft until they were right on top of you, a situation that had served them well here, but cut both ways.

Looking down past her port wing, Larice saw a dappled black line of giant ice floes detaching from the coastline where the frozen sea had loosened its grip on the land. To her right, the Breakers reared like gleaming white fangs, a jagged rampart of mountains keeping the worst of the razor-ice storms that swept down from the northern polar wastes from ravaging the southern cites.

Archenemy land forces were moving in on those cities from the west, but lately waves of bombers and ground attack fighters had opened up a new flank, striking from the heart of the northern ice wastes. Though it had been declared impossible, it seemed the enemy had managed to establish a base somewhere on the frozen surface of the ocean. Orbital auspex had been unable to locate this base, and the existence of a mass carrier on the ice had been ruled out.

After the war on Enothis, Larice knew that anything high command decided was impossible had an inversely proportional chance of being true.

'Apostle Five, hold my wing,' said Quint. 'You're drifting.'

Larice returned her focus to her instruments, making a visual check on her positioning.

Quint was right, she had drifted. By a metre.

At first she was irritated – a metre was nothing when you were flying in such an easy pattern – but she cut herself off. She was an Apostle now, and a metre *was* a big deal. Leave lazy flying to other pilots. The 101st Apostles were the elite flyers of the Navy, and she was better than that.

'Sorry, Apostle Five,' she said.

Quint didn't answer, but she didn't expect him to. Instead, he rolled and pulled his plane in a steep turn to the north. He was heading out over the frozen surface of the ocean. Larice followed automatically, matching Quint's turn and keeping tight to his wing.

'What's up, Seven?' she asked.

'Getting a vector from Operations,' said Quint. 'There's an intercept going on. Indigo Flight from the 235th. They need some help.'

'Where?'

'Fifty kilometres over the ocean ice, a thousand metres off the deck.'

'Auspex?'

'Yes, light them up,' voxed Quint.

Larice did so, but all she got was a hissing wash of backscatter from the mountains. The tech-seers had blessed her auspex before takeoff, but it looked like it was still sluggish from its time inactive. She cursed, heightening the gain, and immediately saw the engagement. It looked like a bad one. Four Navy machines, with at least nine bats swarming them.

'Got them?'

'Yeah, nine of them,' said Larice. 'You sure you want to tangle with that many?'

'There's two of us,' clarified Quint. 'And we are Apostles. *They* should be asking that question.'

'Good point.'

'Afterburners,' said Quint. 'Hit it.'

Larice flipped up the guard on the afterburner trigger, and braced herself for the enormous power of the Thunderbolt's turbofan in her back. She eased the stick forward, just enough down angle to take them into the upper reaches of the fight.

'Grip,' she said, and thumbed the trigger.

A sucking machine breath. A booming roar of jets. A monstrous hand pressed her hard against her seat. The airframe shuddered and the few clouds blurred as the plane leapt forwards like an unleashed colt. The sense of speed was intoxicating. She held the stick, keeping her body braced in the grip position as she felt the blood being forced from her extremities. She held course, feeling the plane straining at her control.

'Incoming contacts, twelve thousand metres,' said Quint. 'Cut burners and go subsonic.'

Larice cut the afterburners and immediately felt the blood return to her hands and feet with a painful prickling sensation. She glanced at the auspex, taking in the shape of the fight in a second. The four Navy flyers were in a dirty scrap, using all their skill to dance out of weapons locks and converging streams of las-fire.

'Hell Blades,' said Larice, recognising the enemy flyers' flight profile. She felt a tremor of excitement. Fast-moving, highly manoeuvrable fighters that could easily match a Thunderbolt in a vector dance, Hell Blades were a far more fearsome prospect than Tormentors.

The vox crackled in her helmet, the voice of a controller in Operations.

'Apostle Flight, be advised we have nine hostiles north on your location,' said the controller. 'Speed and flight pattern indicates–'

'Hell Blades, yeah we know,' snapped Larice. 'Way to keep up, Ops.'

EVEN WITH THE planes of the 235th, they were outnumbered two to one, but Quint was right. They were Apostles, the best flyers in the Navy. She flew with the ace of aces, and her own Thunderbolt boasted no shortage of kill markings on its cream-coloured nose. She checked her dials, noting her fuel and armament status. Aerial combat manoeuvres burned fuel at a terrifying rate, but there was enough in the tank for this one fight.

With Quint at her side, Larice was confident they'd turn the bats into dark smudges of wreckage on the sea ice. With relative closing speeds in excess of a thousand kph, the gap between the two forces was shrinking rapidly. It was going to get real ugly, real quick.

There! Nine lean darts with tapered wings like the fins on a seeker missile. The sky filled with light as the bats opened up. The Navy birds, painted a brusque camo-green, were twisting and diving with desperate turns and rolls, using every trick in the book to shake their pursuers. In an evenly matched fight, that might work, but not against so many bats.

One Thunderbolt exploded as a flurry of shots from a darting enemy fighter found its engines and blew it apart.

'Indigo Flight, Apostles inbound,' said Quint, and it was the only warning anyone got.

Larice and Quint slashed down into the fight, coming in high and fast. She slipped in behind a Hell Blade taking his sweet time in lining up a shot. Too confident of the kill, the enemy pilot was making the first and last mistake most rookies made.

She squeezed her trigger and the bat flew into her streaming las-bolts, coming apart in a seething fireball. She slipped sideways and barrelled past the dead Hell Blade's wingman as Quint tore up the fuselage of another bat.

A wing flashed past her canopy and Larice yanked the stick right. She rolled, pushing out the throttle and inverting. She deployed the air brakes and viffed onto the tail of the aircraft that had nearly hit her. A crimson Hell Blade, its tapered nose spiralling as it slid back and forth through the air.

'Too easy,' she said, sending a hail of quad-fire into its tail section. The wounded Hell Blade shuddered as though invisible hammers pounded its engine until it ruptured in a spewing blaze of fire.

'Five, break, break!' ordered Quint.

Larice sidestepped, viffing up to let the enemy fire paint the air beneath her. A Hell Blade had broken from attacking the Navy flyers and turned into her.

'He's good,' she said, dancing through the air in a dazzling series of rolls, banks and vectored slips. He stuck with her, firing bursts of las as he tried to anticipate her next move. She put her plane into a shallow climb, and slammed the throttle back as the air brakes flared. She was risking a stall, but her manoeuvre worked and the bat zipped past her port wing. She took a snap shot, jinking sideways and ripping her fire along its wing and hull.

Its wing snapped off and it rolled uncontrollably, spinning down towards the ice and leaving a plume of black smoke in its wake.

Five on five, suddenly the odds were evened.

Or they would have been if Quint hadn't already splashed another two bats.

Two more Navy birds were down, and Larice didn't see any chutes. Not that the odds of survival punching out over the ocean ice were much better than going down in flames. She'd hit the silk once before and it wasn't an experience she cared to repeat.

A las-round smacked her Thunderbolt. She jinked low, rolling to bring her guns back on target. She had a fraction of a second to act. Her quads barked, and booming thunder spat from her craft. The deflection was bad and her shots went over the bat. Correction, another burst. This time the bat blew apart in a shredding flicker of mauve and crimson.

She turned hard, pushing the envelope in the race to get behind the last bats. She grunted as heavy g-forces pressed on her, despite the grip position supposed to make it easier to bear. The rubber of her mask flattened against her face, and she tasted the metallic quality of her air mix.

She rolled and pulled hard, feathering her air brakes and flattening out as she caught a flash of a Hell Blade's vector flare.

'Got you,' she hissed, unleashing a brilliant salvo. The Hell Blade blew apart, its engine exploding as her bolts blasted it from the air. Her guns coughed dry, the battery drained, and she switched back to her quads.

'Apostle, break, break!' shouted a voice she didn't recognise.

Larice hauled on the stick and threw out her tail rudder, twisting her plane into a tight loop. A blitz of tracers flew past her port side, a single shell kissing the rear quarter of her canopy and crazing the toughened glass.

She snapped left and right, hunting the bat that had her.

'On your seven,' said the voice.

'I see it,' she said, pulling into the Hell Blade's turn and opening out the throttle as she viffed in a jagged sidestep. The bat matched her turn, pushing her outwards, and she knew there was more than likely another aircraft waiting to take the kill shot. Instead of playing that game, she threw her plane around, using the vectors to pull a near one-eighty and reverse her thrust. The pressure pulled the cracks in the canopy wider.

The pursuing Hell Blade filled her canopy and she mashed the trigger, feeling the percussive recoil from the heavy autocannons mounted in the nose. The Hell Blade viffed up over her burst. It had her and there was nothing she could do.

A camo-green shape zipped over her canopy, quad cannons blazing.

The bat ripped in two. Black smoke and a blooming fireball blew outwards. Larice threw her Thunderbolt into a screamingly tight turn and inverted to take the brunt of the explosion on her underside. Air was driven from her lungs, and her vision greyed at the force of the turn. Her fuselage lurched, and hammering blows of metal on metal thudded along its length as debris from the Hell Blade struck her bird.

Warning lights and buzzers filled the canopy. She flipped over, restoring level flight.

Larice loosened the throttle. Her breathing eased and she screwed her eyes shut for a second to throw off the greyness lurking at the edge of her vision. She tasted blood and pulled off her mask, spitting into the footwell.

A dark shape appeared off her starboard wing. She looked up to see the last surviving Navy flyer of Indigo Flight.

'You okay there?' said the pilot. 'Your bird's pretty banged up.'

'Yeah,' she said, though the stick felt sluggish and unresponsive in her hand. It galled her that she'd needed an assist, but it had been a hell of a move coming in over her to take out that bat. Only a pilot supremely sure of himself would try something that risky.

One wrong move from either pilot would have seen them both splashed.

Quint pulled in on her port wing, the ivory of his aircraft untouched and pristine.

'Indigo Flight, identify,' said Quint.

'Flight Lieutenant Erzyn Laquell, 235th Naval Attack Wing,' said the pilot with a thumbs-up. 'You're the Apostles. It's an honour to fly with you.'

'You're not flying with us,' said Quint. 'You just happen to be sharing my sky.'

'Of course I am,' returned Laquell. 'I'll be sure to tell my pilots to steer clear next time one of your high and mighty Apostles needs an assist.'

Though a glossy black visor and rubber air-mix mask covered Laquell's face, she just knew he was grinning a cocksure grin.

'Keep talking like that and I'll make sure you never fly again,' promised Quint.

Before Laquell could answer, a flurry of winking lights appeared on the auspex and Larice blinked away moisture to be sure she was seeing what it was telling her correctly.

'Seven, are you getting this?'

'Affirmative.'

The auspex was a mass of returns. From their speed and height they were clearly fighters. They weren't squawking on any Imperial frequency, and that made them bad news. Razors most likely. Or more Hell Blades.

'Ten more bats,' she said. 'High and coming in fast. Too many to fight.'

'Agreed,' answered Quint. His plane dipped below her wing before coming level once more. He chopped his hand down towards the belly of her Thunderbolt.

'Five, you're leaking fluid,' he said 'Check your fuel status.'

Larice scanned her gauges, watching with dismay as the numbers unspooled like an altimeter in a power dive. She tapped the dial with her finger, but the numbers kept going.

'Frig it! I'm losing fuel fast. Must've taken a hit to the feed lines.'

'Do you have enough to return to Coriana?'

'Negative, Seven,' said Larice. The airfield where the 101st were stationed was way beyond her range now. 'At the speed I'm losing fuel, I'll be lucky to get down in one piece, let alone back to Coriana. I'll need an alternate.'

'I'll get your wounded bird down,' said Laquell, doing a passable job at keeping the smugness from his tone. 'Rimfire is only a hundred and ten kilometres east.'

Rimfire was the designation for the airbase set up to face the Archenemy's newly opened flank. It was a rush job, hardened hangars cut into the ice and honeycomb landing strips laid out on the Ice by Munitorum pioneers. Its tower facilities were mobile command vehicles and its auspex coverage came from airborne surveyor craft originally designed to hunt for ground minerals. Flyers based at Coriana joked that the pilots based at Rimfire were either too dumb or too reckless to be based anywhere else.

'Will you make it that far?' asked Quint. 'That's a valuable piece of machinery you're flying and we need all the aircraft we have.'

'Thanks for your concern,' replied Larice. 'I'll be flying on fumes and the Emperor's mercy by then, but, yeah, I think I can make it.'

'Then head for Rimfire. I'll see you back at Coriana if you live. Seven out.'

Quint's plane peeled off, leaving a slick of vapour-white fumes in his wake. His plane surged back towards the Breakers and within seconds it was lost to sight.

'Friendly sort, isn't he?' said Laquell.

'He's earned the right to choose his friends with care,' said Larice.

'I guess he has.'

'Okay, Laquell. Lead on,' said Larice. 'In case you hadn't noticed I'm losing fuel.'

'Sure thing. Make your bearing one-six-five and start climbing.'

'I know how to extend,' she snapped, pulling around and aiming her Thunderbolt towards Rimfire. She pulled her stick back, putting her plane into a fuel-efficient climb. When her tanks ran dry she'd be able to glide some of the way in if she had enough altitude.

'Just trying to help,' said Laquell. 'Listen, you know my name, but what do I call you?'

'Apostle Five,' said Larice.

'Yeah, I got that, but what's your real name? You know, what your friends call you?'

'Asche,' she sighed. 'Call me Larice Asche.'

'Pleased to meet you Larice Asche,' said Laquell. 'Follow my wing and I'll get you down in one piece. I promise.'

LAQUELL WAS AS good as his word, and they crossed the Breakers high and with a favourable tailwind that gifted Larice a thousand metres of altitude. There was a nasty squall of ice crystals swelling out over the ocean ice, a skin-shredding storm of frozen blades that would do no end of damage to an aircraft, but the luck of the Emperor was with them and it blew west before reaching the mountains.

Though she tried to keep her flight smooth and level, Larice watched her fuel reserves dwindle like she was in the midst of the most furious engagement imaginable, viffing, pulling high-g turns, escape climbs and power dives. The shear Quint had mentioned clawed up from the wind-sculpted cliffs, buffeting her plane as though an invisible leash tethered to her fuselage was being pulled and tugged.

Then they were over, and the landscape fell away from them, tumbling to the flatlands of Amedeo, a bleak tundra of browns and muted greens. It wasn't the most welcoming world, but then what she'd seen of Enothis had been mostly desert and swamp, so at least it offered a different view from the canopy.

Located in the trailing arc of the crusade to liberate the Sabbat Worlds, Amedeo had been largely ignored by both the Imperium and the Archenemy, but then the forces of Magister Innokenti had fallen on Herodor. Though the tactical significance of Herodor was, at best, debatable, the soldiers' rumour mill had it that Innokenti himself had descended to that world's surface.

And that made Amedeo important. Perfectly positioned to allow a flanking thrust to hamstring the Imperial defence, the planners of the crusade were swift to recognise the danger to Herodor. Naval wings and Guard regiments were deployed with unaccustomed swiftness, alongside, so the rumour-spinners went on to claim, a detachment of Adeptus Astartes.

Larice had seen nothing of any Space Marines, but Amedeo was a big theatre of operations, and entire campaigns were being fought out of sight of the aerial duellists.

Her fuel warning light, which had been hypnotically blinking throughout the crossing of the Breakers, now assumed a more constant aspect. Her engines flamed out and the rpms of her twin turbofans spiralled south.

'I'm dry,' she voxed to Laquell. 'I'm flying fourteen tonnes of scrap metal unless we're close to Rimfire.'

'Yeah, we're not far,' replied Laquell, his voice calm and reassuring. 'Switch on your transponder and key it to this frequency or else the base defences will tag you as hostile and shoot you down.'

A data squirt appeared on her slate and she keyed in the corresponding frequency, thumbing the activation switch. An answering light appeared on her tactical plot, thirty kilometres out. Rimfire. But was it close enough? Her altimeter was unwinding fast, and she did a quick mental calculation. It was just within reach.

'Stay on my wing,' said Laquell. 'Keep the nose up and fly steady.'

Larice nodded to herself, holding the stick tight and trying to keep any unnecessary movement from her path. Every second she spent in the air was a few hundred metres closer to safety.

'You're doing great, Larice. That's it, steady and smooth. Gradually ease around to two-seven-seven.'

'I don't have time for manoeuvre,' she said.

'I know, but there's some crazy thermals that come up from the southern rift plains. They'll give you some extra lift. Trust me, I've used them before when I'm coming back with a tank of vapour.'

Larice adjusted her course, the stick feeling leaden in her grip and the plane responding like she imagined a tank would manoeuvre. They came down through a light dusting of clouds, and there it was, a down and dirty collection of air-defence vehicles, ad hoc runways, quick-fire launch racks and fuel bowsers clustered around a random scattering of landing mats strewn across the ice.

Rimfire was around three kilometres away, but at the rate she was shedding height it might as well have been three thousand. She wasn't going to make it.

'I'm short,' she said. 'I don't have enough–'

A slamming wind hoisted her higher, the spiralling tunnel of warm air Laquell had promised her. Her descent slowed and she saw it might be enough. Her Thunderbolt could transition to vertical landing, but without fuel that wasn't going to be possible.

'Rimfire Tower, this is Apostle Five, requesting emergency landing clearance.'

'Apostle Five, confirmed. You are clear to land on runway six-epsilon. Directing now,' said an echoing voice that sounded like it was coming from inside a small metal box. Looking at the haphazard collection of vehicles gathered beneath arctic camo-netting at the edge of the runway, Larice decided that was exactly where it was coming from.

'Emergency vehicles are standing by, Apostle Five,' said the controller.

'Thanks for the vote of confidence, Rimfire,' snapped Larice, wrestling with the stick as vicious crosswinds and random vector gusts bounced up from the ground. She lowered her claws at the last moment, and fought to bring the nose up before she ploughed straight into the runway.

Her wing claws bit and the nose slammed down a second later. Her speed bled off and the ice-crazed surface of the runway threw up a blinding flurry of ice and snow. She was pretty much blind. Larice threw up her arrestors and slammed on the brakes, feeling the Thunderbolt turn in a lazy skid. The plane slid around until it was pointed back the way it had come, and Larice let out a shuddering breath.

On a runway next to hers, she saw Laquell's plane touch down and make a point-perfect rollout, managing the slipperiness of the runway with the aplomb of a veteran flyer. He taxied over the ice and parked up ten metres from her starboard wing.

Fitters and emergency ground crew ran over to her plane. One drew a finger over his throat, and she nodded, shutting off her armaments panel and disconnecting her fuel lines – not that there was any fuel left to ignite. She popped the canopy and the cold hit her like a blow. Her breath caught in her throat, the raw ice of it like a full-body slap. Fitters propped a ladder against her plane and she unsnapped herself from the cockpit and climbed down. Someone wrapped her in a foil-lined thermal blanket and she took an unsteady step away from her cream-coloured Thunderbolt.

Long and heavily winged, the Thunderbolt wasn't an elegant flyer, but it had a robust beauty all of its own. The ivory paint scheme was scarred and smeared with oil and scorch marks where her fuel lines had ruptured. She waved away a medicae, watching as red- and yellow-jacketed ground crew milled around her plane, eager to work on a plane belonging to one of the Apostles. She felt a stab of protectiveness towards her damaged bird as fitters began appraising the damage, wincing at the sound of whining power-wrenches and pneumo-hammers.

Armoured plating hung like scabbed skin from its underside, and dribbles of hydraulic fluid and lubricant spotted the ice beneath its belly. A tow rig rumbled towards the planes from a hangar buried beneath ten metres of snow and ice.

She heard footsteps and Laquell's voice said, 'Took a beating, but she'll fly again.'

'You talking about the plane or me?' she said without turning.

'The plane, of course,' said Laquell. 'You look just fine.'

She turned and saw him, like her, wrapped in a thermal blanket. He sipped a mug of something hot that steamed in the cold air. He was striking in an Imperial-recruiting-poster kind of way: angular chin, high cheekbones and eyes that radiated trust and courage. His dark hair was cut close to the skull, and he was smiling at her.

'You want one?'

'One what?' she said.

'Soup,' said Laquell, holding up his mug and making it sound like a joke. 'You don't want a caffeine, you'll get the jitters, even though the Munitorum actually make a pretty decent brew around here. Soup'll warm you up and won't have you bouncing off the flakboard.'

Larice nodded, feeling the strain of her sortie settle upon her. 'Sure, soup sounds good.'

He handed her his mug and she took a grateful sip. It tasted of hot vegetables and game.

It was the best thing she'd drunk in months.

'Come on,' said Laquell, leading her towards the buried hangar. 'The mess facilities here don't look like much, but you can get a halfway decent meal and a hot shower.'

'Now *that* sounds better,' said Larice, disarmed by his easy manner and winning smile.

They passed his plane, and Larice saw the kill markings painted on the nose.

'You have thirty-seven kills,' she said.

'Yeah, it's been a busy day.'

'You're a frigging ace,' she said.

'So they tell me,' said Laquell, as if it was nothing.

'How long have you been flying?'

'On Amedeo? Two weeks, but I bagged my first kill about six months ago.'

Larice found herself re-evaluating the cocky young flyer, now seeing a combination of skill and natural ability in his flying.

'And you've thirty-seven kills to your name? Confirmed?'

'Every one of them,' he said. 'One's even on pict-loop in the officer's quarters.'

'Nice work,' said Larice, impressed despite herself.

Laquell nodded, pleased with her compliment, but too much of an aviator to look too pleased. They stepped into the hangar. Out of the winds whipping across the isolated base, the temperature was at least bearable. Inside, a dozen Thunderbolts in the camo-green paint scheme of the 235th sat in a herringbone pattern, attended by an army of servitors and fitters in orange jumpsuits. Gurneys of missiles and heavy boxes of shells threaded their way between the planes, and a robed priest of the Mechanicus, together with his cybernetic entourage, attended to the guts of a partially disassembled aircraft. Its nose was wreathed in fragrant smoke and hot unguents dripped from an exposed turbofan.

As they walked between the aircraft towards the crew quarters, Larice knew she was attracting stares. Word that one of the Apostles had landed at Rimfire had circulated through the base with a speed normally reserved for the pox after a tour of shore leave. Her jet-black flight suit, compact form and girlish good looks didn't hurt either.

They looked at her and she looked back, counting no fewer than seven aircraft with kill markings indicating that their pilots were aces. And the rest weren't too far behind. None of them had thirty-seven kills, though. She saw Laquell notice her appraisal, but said nothing.

There was clear order and discipline to the work going on throughout the hangar, a sense of purpose that was common to most air wings, but which was even more focussed than usual. This far out from support, everyone's survival depended on keeping these aircraft ready to fly and fight at a moment's notice. Far from being the dumping ground for reckless or deficient pilots, Rimfire was a base where only the best survived.

'That was a hell of a piece of flying you did up there,' said Laquell. 'You and that other Apostle really pulled us out of it.'

'Quint's a hell of a flyer,' she said.

'That was Quint?' said Laquell. 'The ace of aces? Maybe I shouldn't have cheeked him.'

'Maybe not,' agreed Larice, already wondering what Seekan would make of this young, cocksure colt of a pilot. She looked at him and he returned her gaze with a frankness she found unsettling, like she was a target in the reticule of a quad gun sight.

I remember that look, she thought, and that made her mind up.

'So tell me about that kill, the one on pict-loop,' she said.

'Why?' he said, faintly embarrassed. 'It's not that good, and it's over too quick.'

'Sounds like a lot of lovers I've had,' said Larice.

'Seriously, why do you want to see it?'

She smiled and said, 'Because if I'm going to recommend you to Wing Leader Seekan, then I'll need to know I'm not going to be making a damn idiot out of myself.'

THEY ALWAYS PICK *the places that used to be magnificent.*

The Aquilian had once been the toast of Coriana's wealthy gadabouts apparently, a grand folly built in opposition to a rival's hotel further down the city's main thoroughfare. Which of the two had come out on top was a mystery now, for Archenemy shock troops had destroyed the other hotel in the opening stages of the war. High command had been using it as their lodgings and strategic planning centre, and only an accident of timing had seen them elsewhere when the blood-masked enemy troopers attacked.

Since then, the brass kept on the move.

Which meant the next grandest structure in Coriana was free for the taking.

Processional steps led up to its columned entrance, the space between each column draped with a gold and black flag of the Imperium. Larice led Laquell up the steps and through the cracked marble-floored vestibule, following the booming sounds of martial music. She recognised the tune, *Imperitas Invictus*, a rousing tune said to have been written for Lord Helican's triumphal march through the Spatian Gate. It wasn't a tune played much any more.

'I can't believe I'm going to meet the Apostles,' said Laquell, and Larice was amused at the star-struck quality to his voice. His eyes were bright and his features eager.

'Then be prepared to be disappointed,' she said. 'They're just pilots.'

'You don't see it because you're one of them,' said Laquell. 'They're more than "just pilots": they're legends, warriors of the air, killers of enemy aces. They're the best flyers in the Navy. And they want me. I think that's pretty damn fine.'

'Hold on there, pilot,' warned Larice. 'All I'm doing is putting you forward for consideration. It'll be Seekan's decision whether to take you or not.'

'Come on,' he said, puffing out his chest and tapping the service ribbons on his chest. 'Look at me. How could they not want me? I expect they'll offer me a place on the spot.'

'I wouldn't bet on it,' said Larice as the music swelled as a door opened and shut.

'Are we missing a party?' asked Laquell, straightening his dress uniform jacket, a deep russet colour with tasteful silver frogging over the shoulders and a stiffened collar of lacquered leather.

Larice didn't answer.

Her former commanding officer, Bree Jagdea, had told her about the habits of the Apostles, and she knew there was only one reason her new squadron mates would gather like this. She crossed the chequerboard floor and swept down a wide corridor towards a set of walnut-panelled doors. She pushed through them into what had once been a grand ballroom, but was now an echoing empty space hung with blast curtains. Almost every item of furniture was draped in dustsheets, cobwebs laced the spaces between the chandeliers and a faint smell of mildew lurked below the hot crackle of the fire and scent of burning sapwood.

A group of people clad in cream-coloured frock coats gathered around an enormous fireplace. Seven of them, the best and luckiest damn pilots in the Navy.

The Apostles.

They looked small; diminished and alone in a vast space that normally held grand revelries and magnificent dances. The ballroom echoed with unloved music and drunken debate.

Seekan was the first to notice them, turning and favouring her with a quizzical smile. His dark hair was swept back and oiled, his uniform crisp and gleaming with row upon row of medals.

'Larice,' he said, crisp like a cold morning. 'We weren't expecting you.'

'Why not?' she said, glaring at Quint, who perched on a stool opposite Jeric Suhr. A regicide board sat between them. 'Did you think I was dead?'

'Not at all,' said Seekan. 'We heard the chatter that an Apostle had landed at Rimfire. We knew you were alive.'

'So why the drink and the dress uniforms?'

'Because the *Rosencranz* is gone,' said Ziner Krone, pushing away from the fire surround and making his way to an isolated drinks cabinet. His dark-skinned cheeks were flushed with amasec and heat. The scar on his cheek twitched and he poured a drink, which he promptly downed. He poured another and thrust it towards Larice with a lascivious grin.

'Drink it,' he ordered. 'Drink to the lost souls of the *Rosencranz*.'

Larice didn't want the amasec, but took it anyway. Krone watched her sip it, making no attempt to hide his lingering glance at her chest and hips. He'd propositioned her in the crew barracks aboard the *Rosencranz*, but Larice had told him where to get off in no uncertain terms. Those days were behind her.

'The *Rosencranz* is gone?' said Laquell. 'How?'

Krone ignored his question and turned back to the drinks.

Larice had last seen the Munitorum mass carrier when she'd flown her Thunderbolt from its cavernous hold to the planet's surface. Kilometres long, the mass conveyer was a city adrift in space, a landmass capable of interstellar flight. Bulky and ungainly, it seemed inconceivable that anything so colossal could possibly be destroyed.

'Who gives a shit?' snapped Jeric Suhr. He waved his balloon of liquor, spilling some on the board. Quint scowled at Suhr as his wiry opponent rose unsteadily to his feet. Suhr's chest seemed too narrow to contain all the medals he'd won, and his sharp features were thrown into stark relief by the firelight. 'Warp core failure, a plasma meltdown, fifth columnists in the dock crews, infiltrators? Who cares, it's all the same in the end. We're one carrier and a shitting load of planes and pilots down.'

'And who the hell is this anyway?' said Krone, finally acknowledging Laquell's presence and pouring another drink. 'This is a private party. For Apostles only. Get out before I throw you out.'

Larice felt Laquell bristle and said, 'Krone, this is Flight Lieutenant Erzyn Laquell of the 235th Naval Attack Wing.'

'Ah, the Navy flyboy who hauled your backside out of the fire,' said Suhr, slumping back onto his stool, though he'd plainly abandoned interest in the regicide board.

'Shut your mouth, Jeric,' said Seekan.

'Well he did, didn't he?'

'Flight Lieutenant Laquell came to my assistance, yes,' said Larice. 'He has thirty-seven confirmed kills in less than six months of flying time.'

'Ah, I see,' noted Seekan, turning away towards the fire. Saul Cirksen, the pilot he'd recruited on Enothis, stood there, nursing his drink. He'd been an Apostle for only slightly longer than Larice, but had already adopted the disaffected mannerisms of his adopted wing. He didn't look at Laquell, as though he didn't want to acknowledge his presence, like he was someone who'd go away if only they pretended he wasn't there.

Likewise Owen Thule and Leena Sharto, the two pilots Seekan had recruited at the very end of the war on Enothis, ignored him. Thule was a big-boned flyer from the 43rd Angels, a pugnacious man with heavy jowls and bushy sideburns. Leena Sharto had been tagged from the 144th Typhoons, and affected an air of disinterest that she couldn't quite pull off. Larice had tried to get to know them, seeking solace in the solidarity of their shared newness to the Apostles, but none of her overtures had been returned, and she had eventually given up.

'Larice, am I given to understand that you have brought the Flight Lieutenant here as a potential candidate for elevation to the Apostles?'

'Yeah, take a look at his jacket and you'll see what I mean.'

'I am quite familiar with Flight Lieutenant Laquell's record.'

'You are?'

'Of course he is,' slurred Krone. 'You think he's not always on the lookout for flyers that've slipped beneath fate's gaze? Some lucky bastard who's fallen off death's auspex?'

'I don't understand,' said Larice. 'If you know his jacket, you must know that–'

'He has the highest flight to kill ratio on Amedeo, greater even that that of Quint here?' said Seekan. 'Yes, I am well aware of that.'

Quint looked up from the board at the mention of his name, but said nothing.

'Then why wouldn't you invite him to become an Apostle?' asked Larice.

'Because the Apostles are a unique group, Larice,' said Seekan. 'Even to those newly promoted to its ranks. And every new member dilutes that exclusivity, makes us less select. I know, I know, it makes no sense, of course.'

Seekan turned to his fellow flyers. 'After all, of the Apostles that went to Enothis, only four of us survive, and by the end of this crusade, I do not expect any of us to be alive. Death is, at heart, a tallyman, and all the books must balance eventually.'

'He's a hell of a flyer,' pressed Larice. 'I've seen cap-
tures from his gun-picters.'

'As have I, Larice, but I sense there is more to this than
simply Flight Lieutenant Laquell's skill in the cockpit.'

'What's that supposed to mean?'

'He means you like him,' snapped Suhr. 'And we
don't need anyone likeable in the Apostles. Only odious shits like me, lechers like Krone or misery magnets
like Quint.'

Seekan sighed and said, 'I'm thankful I was left off
that list, but for all his boorishness, Jeric is right. I told
Commander Jagdea this, and I'll tell you too, Larice. It
doesn't do to have friends when you've flown as long
as us and seen as much death through your canopy as
we have. It's a liability, a weakness that slows you down
and clouds your judgement. And you know as well as I,
that anything that keeps you from the top of your game
in the air gets you killed.'

'It doesn't have to be like that,' insisted Larice. 'It
wasn't like that in the Phantine XX, and they exceeded
your combined kills on Enothis.'

'Then why don't you go back to them?' said Krone.

Larice hesitated, suddenly missing the easy back and
forth of the crew dorms perched on the rock above the
Scald or the card schools Milan Blansher used to run in
the hold of whatever Munitorum transport they were
travelling within.

'I don't know where they are,' she said, now realising
how much that hurt to say.

'You're an Apostle now, Larice,' said Seekan. 'I know
it's hard to adjust to our way of thinking, but if you want
to survive, it's the best way.'

'It's the only way,' said Quint, surprising them all. 'It's
the Apostles' Creed. Live by it or get the hell out.'

Laquell returned to Rimfire and Larice took her place in
the rotation as the war on Amedeo continued at its brutal
pace. The flyers at Rimfire found themselves under ever

more pressure as the attacks over the Breakers increased in frequency and the cities of the Ice were hit by more and more bomber waves. The Apostles flew a dozen intercepts in three days, splashing sixty-eight craft between them.

As expected, Quint took the highest tally. Larice was a hair's breadth behind him.

Nothing more was said of the night Larice brought Laquell to the Aquilian, yet it festered like a splinter of rotten wood beneath her skin. In the short period between flights she checked the Operations logs for any mention of Laquell, and was gratified to see his kill count climb steadily.

Eight days passed before she saw him again, amid a furious intercept in the skies ten kilometres north of Coriana. A huge wave of bombers and fighter escorts, two hundred and ten aircraft in total, appeared without warning over the snow-lashed Breakers, and the Lightnings and Thunderbolts based at Rimfire had only moments to scramble.

Less than three-quarters of the planes managed to get airborne before the first bombs hit, flattening the makeshift runways and obliterating what little infrastructure there was. The Imperial aircraft immediately tangled with the bombers' escort planes, a mix of Razors, Talons and Hell Blades, and a furious engagement began.

The Thunderbolts danced with the escorts while the faster Lightnings powered through the low-flying formations to target the slow movers above. Like wolves in the fold, the Lightnings savaged the packs of bombers, sending twenty to the ice in palls of smoke and fire, before the Archenemy escorts could break from the fight below to come to their aid.

The Thunderbolts followed them up, but before the two groups of fighters locked horns, another forty enemy fighters screamed down from the north. Operations at Coriana screamed a warning to the pilots, unable to believe that so many bats had simply popped into existence on their auspex.

The arrival of so many enemy aircraft forced the flyers from Rimfire to disengage.

And with their base now a volcanic crater in the ice, they turned south for Coriana.

LARICE YANKED THE stick hard right, viffing down and barely avoiding a drifting stream of cannon fire from a diving Hell Talon. The pilot had misjudged his deflection, and she rolled back and deployed her air brakes, coming in around behind the bat as it slashed through the formation. She pushed out the throttle, lining up her shot, when she heard the shrill warning tone of a weapons lock.

'Five, break left!' shouted Leena Sharto.

Her target forgotten, Larice pulled left and down, driving the engine to full military power and weaving in and out of the morass of duelling planes. A Razor flashed in front of her, a Navy bird in hot pursuit, and she squeezed off a short burst of las. The pilot's canopy disintegrated in a shower of diamond splinters as it spun away.

Larice didn't watch it die. She twisted left and right, trying to locate her pursuer. It was still locked on to her, but she couldn't see it. An eye-wateringly bright blizzard of las-fire flashed over her and she threw her aircraft down, finally catching the blaze of light from the enemy guns.

Larice flew like a flock of Killers were on her tail, jinking and viffing through the air like an aerial acrobat. Her pursuer stayed with her, but there were few who understood how a Thunderbolt danced as well as Larice Asche, and it couldn't match her turns.

'You're fixated,' she said, grunting as a high-g turn drove the breath from her. 'And that's gotten you killed.'

She hauled back on the stick and flexed her plane through a screaming hammerhead turn, pulling vertical before rolling her tail section over and aiming her aircraft straight down. It was a risky manoeuvre, bleeding speed and leaving her hanging in the air. The Razor was right below her, lining up its shot, but Larice fired first.

Her quads banged and thumped, and the Razor split open in a storming burst of debris. Larice dropped through the flaming wreckage, her canopy awash with fire and the fuselage thumping with impacts. Nothing flashed red and she pulled out of her dive, coming level and increasing speed in case any other enemy craft were waiting to pounce.

None were, and she rolled back into the fight. The sky was thick with bats, swarming, razor-winged darts that flew aggressively and protected the slower bombers with the tenacity of a mother grox defending her offspring.

They outnumbered the Imperial aircraft, but that advantage wasn't counting for much. Larice knew the Archenemy were careless with their craft, preferring overwhelming numbers to skill and talent in the air. With every passing minute, the bombers were getting closer to Coriana, but their numbers were thinning as they went. The Apostles and sixty other planes were dancing with them at low altitude, screaming over the ice and outlying industrial complexes surrounding the city.

Larice saw a stretched V of aircraft taking the low-level approach to Coriana and thumbed the vox.

'This is Five, seven plus heavy bombers with escort going in low over the refineries.'

'I see them, Five.' Seekan.

'Take the lead, Five. I'm right behind you.' Suhr.

'Lead us in, Larice,' said a familiar voice and she smiled as she recognised the laconic tones.

She smiled. 'Good to have you on board, Laquell.'

'I've got Schaw and Ysor from Indigo with me,' voxed Laquell. 'On your left wing.'

Larice looked over, seeing Laquell's trio of fighters, and pushed her stick forwards and surged power to the afterburners.

'Five on lead,' said Larice, switching to quads.

'Bear in mind that we're flying over incredibly volatile structures,' advised Seekan as though informing them of light cloud cover. 'Short, controlled bursts only.'

'Diving in now,' said Larice. 'Stoop and sting those escorts!'

Almost as soon as she'd armed her guns, the two groups of aircraft were tangled up in a madly spinning, close-range dogfight. Larice rolled hard left, catching sight of a Razor's tail section, and followed it down.

Every move the Razor made, Larice was with him, the planes spinning around the sky like insects in a bizarre mating ritual. The plane spun right, but Larice was waiting for it. It flashed across her gunsight and she pulled the cannon trigger.

'Got you,' she hissed as bright laser bolts tore into the enemy plane's fuselage and ripped the darting craft in two. The plane spewed smoke and flames, tumbling downwards, and Larice caught a glimpse of the blood-splattered pilot as he struggled weakly with his doomed aircraft.

She rolled out of her attack, turning back into the fight. Aircraft swooped and dived around her, and she watched Seekan saw the tail off a Tormentor with a precise burst of las-fire. Owen Thule peppered a Hell Blade with his quads and lit up a Razor seconds later as he viffed over the wreckage and stood his plane on its wing to shred a spinning Hell Talon.

A diving Razor slotted itself in on his six and gunfire punched holes in his right wing.

'Eight, break right!' yelled Larice as her threat board lit up. She slammed the stick right and feathered the engines as a white rocket contrail speared past her canopy.

Red metal suddenly filled her vision and she swore, pushing the plane down and left as the belly of a Hell Blade screamed over her canopy, so close she felt she could reach out and touch it. Its jetwash threw her around for a moment until she was able to bring herself level again and come back on Owen Thule. She breathed deeply, amazed at how close the near miss had been.

'He's stuck to my six!' shouted Thule.

'I'm on him,' shouted Laquell, spinning his Thunderbolt into a rolling S to come in on the bat's five. His deflection was perfect and the bat flew straight into his storm of shells, blowing apart as its engine detonated.

'Thanks,' voxed Thule, turning into another engagement.

'Laquell! Heads up!' called Larice, 'You got one on your high six!'

Cannon shells spat from a Hell Blade's guns, a couple raking the topside armour of the Thunderbolt. Larice saw it was armed with underslung rockets too.

'Damn! Bad guy on my tail! Schaw, get him off me!'

'I'm on it,' replied his wingman.

The rear of Laquell's Thunderbolt spat brightly burning flares in an attempt to prevent the enemy rocket from locking onto his engine emissions. He threw the plane into a series of wild manoeuvres to try and shake his pursuer.

'Damn, this guy's good!' swore Laquell as the bat matched him move for move.

'Rocket away!' shouted Schaw.

'Breaking left!' answered Laquell, rolling hard and down.

'Come on...' prayed Larice, kicking in the afterburner and diving hard. She felt her vision greying under the pressure of the increased g-forces. Her flight suit expanded and she felt the composition of her air-mix change as she pushed the craft to the edge of the envelope.

She mashed the cannon trigger and filled the air behind Laquell's plane with las-fire.

The missile detonated prematurely as one of Larice's shots clipped its warhead. She felt the shockwave of its detonation and laughed in relief.

Laquell spun his plane round in a screaming turn

and chopped the throttle, almost stalling the craft. The
pilot of the Hell Blade tried to stay with him, but the
explosion had concealed Laquell's survival, and its pilot
couldn't match the Thunderbolt's turn.

The cocky pilot of the 235th rolled inverted and pulled
in behind the red aircraft, slotting it neatly between his
gunsights. Quad-fire banged from the nose guns, shredding the bat's tailpipe and blowing the aircraft apart in
a spectacular orange fireball.

Laquell hollered his triumph over the vox and flew
over the debris.

Larice checked the auspex and saw the remaining five
bombers had broken through the fighter cordon and
were heading towards the civilian areas of Coriana. A
screen of twelve bats lingered in their wash, ready to
turn on any pursuit.

'Apostle Five in pursuit,' said Larice. 'Who's with me?'

'Apostle Lead,' said Seekan.

'Indigo Lead,' replied Laquell.

'Apostle Nine,' said Ziner Krone.

'Apostle Six,' said Saul Cirksen.

'Indigo Two,' said Schaw.

'Rise to Angels minus five hundred and dive on burners,' ordered Seekan, asserting his natural authority over
this ad hoc squadron. A flight's destination altitude was
never given in the open, and 'Angels' was a set altitude
that changed every day. In this case it had been set at a
thousand metres.

The Thunderbolts, a mix of camo-green and cream,
snapped up in a sharp climb before aiming their guns
down upon the bats.

'Turn and burn,' ordered Seekan.

Larice hit her afterburners, closing the distance to
the bombers and their escort in a matter of moments.
The bats broke into a combat spread and the Thunderbolts slashed through their formation. Larice tagged
one plane, shearing its left wing off with her quads. It
tumbled end over end into the ground, and ploughed a

fiery gouge through a maze of pipework extending from
an aluminium-skinned structure.

Laquell splashed another and each of the Apostles
claimed a kill before they vectored back into the fight.
Now it was one on one, and Larice shot her quads
at a crimson Hell Talon with bloody teeth painted
on its swept wings. The Talon threw itself into a low
dive, sweeping under an aqueduct of pipes, and Larice
followed him down. The bat slashed through the air,
jinking past flame-topped towers, around vast, portal-
framed fabriks and between enormous cylindrical
ore-silos.

Larice kept to her quads, loosing a sharp burst every
time she got weapons lock, but the bat was good. He
kept her at arm's length, always anticipating her deflec-
tions and viffing out of the way in time.

'Stand still, frig you,' she hissed, deploying air brakes
and vectoring right to sidestep around the tall lifter der-
ricks of a Leman Russ assembly yard. Swaying pallets
of building materials flashed past her canopy and she
caught the terrified 'O' of the derrick's crewman, passing within a metre of her wingtip. The bat spun around
a blazing plume of venting gases from a promethium
refinery and a host of las-bolts exploded around her. She
felt the hammer blows on her fuselage and jinked down.

Whip aerials on the roof of a manufactory snapped off
on her underside and she snagged a trailing cord from
a Mechanicus banner. It burned up in her heat bloom,
and Larice couldn't decide what kind of omen that was.
The bat arced past her canopy, and she stood her plane
on its end, rolling inverted and hitting the burners again
to get on its tail.

The gases from the refinery surged in her jetwash
and punched her after the bat like she'd been launched
from the rails with her rocket assist. The acceleration
slammed her back in her seat, but seconds later she was
right on the bat's tail. Larice cut her burners and mashed
the firing trigger. A stream of autocannon shells ripped

into the bat's engines and sliced through its entire
length. Literally sawn in two, the shorn halves of the bat
fell out of the sky in flames.

Larice pulled up, hearing triumphant shouts from the
other pilots as they splashed their targets. Only Schaw
failed to take down his bat, misjudging a turn and ending up with a bat on his tail instead. Seekan shot down
the bat, and the Imperial planes roared after the rising
bombers as they started their attack runs.

Too slow to evade the Imperial pursuit, the Tormentors unloaded their bombs early and aimed their aircraft
towards the ground. Each one ploughed into the tangle
of pipes, bridges and construction yards of Coriana's
industrial hinterland, leaving a trail of devastation
hundreds of metres long. Fires raged in the swathes of
burning jet fuel wreckage, and Larice pulled up through
banks of shimmering thermals and buffeting winds of
exploding ordnance.

It wasn't pretty, but looking towards the untouched
hab-stacks, residential sprawls and commercia districts,
she knew it could have been a lot worse.

TWO MORE ATTACKS came in over the mountains, again
with little warning until they'd crossed the Breakers,
and the Apostles flew round-the-clock sorties with the
regrouped diaspora of aircraft from the forward airbases.
It was brutal flying, the Archenemy planes battering at
the gates of Coriana as though it were the ultimate prize
in the war.

Larice supposed it was, looking up at the map pinned
to the wall of the market hall. The air carried the taste
of spoiled fruit and dairy products, of decay and aban-
donment. She sat on a camp chair with her booted feet
resting on a packing crate that had once contained Mark
V magazines for lasguns.

Pilots on the rotation hustled back and forth between
mission briefings and Munitorum supply depots where
cold caffeine and hot food were on offer. The abandoned

market hall now served as a makeshift Operations centre. At the far end of the vaulted, echoing chamber, a heaving mass of cogitators and logic engines were hooked up to a series of coughing generators. A gaggle of uniformed officers and tech-priests surrounded an illuminated plotting table. It bathed their faces in a bleaching light, and a fug of incense hung over their deliberations. Runners sped back and forth, updating senior flight officers on developments over the Ice, and commands were barked into vox-horns to scramble this flight, divert that flight or assist another. One particular flight officer, a fat man in a voluminous robe, seemed to be the centre of attention, and Larice wondered how he'd ever managed to fit in the cockpit of an aircraft.

Seekan stood next to him, taking animatedly and using his hands a lot. He seemed to be demonstrating air combat manoeuvres and gesturing over to where the Apostles waited.

Larice had never thought much about the men and women who directed her in the air, assuming they were sitting in a calm, ordered command centre. Watching the chaos surrounding the plotter and hearing the barked flood of information gathered by the ground-based and aerial augurs, she found a new respect for their skill in juggling so many variables.

Ziner Krone lay sprawled in a cot bed, arms crossed over his chest like a body in a funerary parlour. Jeric Suhr and Quint played a bad-tempered game of regicide, and Larice wondered if it was a continuation of the one they'd been playing in the ballroom of the Aquilian. She looked over at the duty roster, confirming that she wasn't on the rotation for another two hours.

Larice knew she should rest, but she was too wired to sleep, and the noise from the freshly hammered-down runways and launch rails beyond the walls of the market hall made it too difficult to sleep. Some aviators found a natural rhythm in flight operations, snatching sleep when they could, eating on the run and flying in the spaces inbetween. Larice always found it took time to settle into any kind of routine, and they'd flown out of three different bases already.

In any case, she'd hooked up with Laquell, whose squadron was deployed in the same hangars and runways as the Apostles. They'd taken to spending their downtime playing cards and talking of particularly memorable intercepts, and Larice found herself warming to the handsome flyer. Seekan still hadn't offered him a place in the Apostles, which Larice found baffling. Laquell's kill count had climbed steadily, now standing at an impressive seventy-three, and he'd provided assists to no fewer than six of the Apostles.

Leena Sharto, Saul Cirksen and Owen Thule were in the sky, running air superiority missions over the Imperial Guard. Three regiments, two Mordian and one Vostroyan, were engaged in a bitter land war two hundred kilometres west of Coriana. Larice had flown on such missions before, finding it hard to imagine waging war without being strapped to the awesome power of a Thunderbolt. To face the guns of the enemy without its speed, armour and powerful guns seemed like a sure-fire way to get yourself killed.

The medicae convoys pouring into Coriana and the number of facilities converted to deal with the dead appeared to back this up.

'Busy I see,' said Laquell, returning with a pot of caffeine and two battered tin mugs.

'Just keeping an eye on things,' said Larice, accepting a mug and taking a sip. She grimaced.

'Yeah, I know,' he said, sitting next to her. 'I sure do miss the caffeine at Rimfire.'

'It was that good?'

'No, but it was better than this. So how's it going?' said Laquell, nodding towards the map. Junior flight officers moved coloured tacks around the board as intercepts developed and fresh intelligence became available.

'A map tacked to the wall isn't the most efficient way

of hearing what's going on, but it's better than nothing,' said Larice. 'I think something big's on the way. All the runners got called back to the table and the tech-priests nearly had a frigging fit.'

'Any idea what's up?'

'Not a clue,' said Larice. 'You know we're always the last to know what's happening.'

'Looks like Seekan's in amongst it.'

'*Wing Leader* Seekan,' corrected Larice.

'Yeah, sorry.'

'You think he's putting you in harm's way?'

'Him or someone with more medals on their chest.'

Laquell nodded and looked over at the map. 'Looks like the Guard are getting hit hard.'

'Not as hard as they'd be without us watching over them from above.'

'True.'

'When are you up?' she asked.

Larice checked her wrist chron. Every pilot had one. They delivered a warning note and a mild electric shock when an alert came in, and were universally hated.

'Two hours,' he said. 'You?'

'The same.'

'Looks like the Apostles and Indigo will be flying together again.'

'Good to know,' she said, draining her caffeine as Seekan strode from the plotting table towards them. His crisp demeanour was animated and his face flushed with excitement, like a junior pilot after his first kill. Larice didn't know whether to be amused or scared.

Krone came awake as Seekan approached, but Suhr and Quint continued their game.

Larice took her feet down from the packing crate and said, 'We've got a mission?'

'That we have, Larice,' said Seekan. 'And it's rather a big one.'

* * *

AS THE BREAKERS passed beneath her Thunderbolt, Larice began to appreciate Wing Leader Seekan's gift for understatement. As part of Winter Spear, the name given to the attack force heading out over the ocean ice, the Apostles had been tasked with the toughest job of the sortie. Two hundred and sixty-six aircraft filled the air, a mix of vector jets, ground attack craft, air-superiority fighters, heavy bombers and a pair of converted Marauders equipped with souped-up auspex gear. Designated Orbis Flight, these last two planes would attempt to provide mobile command and control over the coming battle.

Forty Marauders, comprised of aircraft from the 22nd Yysarians and the 323rd Vincamus, growled behind the fighter screen. Their bomb bays were fully laden with armour-penetrating warheads so heavy it seemed like the aircraft might not make it over the peaks. Together with the slower, prop-driven Laredo-class bombers, seventy-two slow movers shook the mountaintops clear of snow, wallowing in the jetwash of the racing fighters.

Ranging ahead of the bombers, the Apostles formed the tip of the spear, eight cream-coloured Thunderbolts flying at seven thousand metres. Fast-moving Lightnings from the 39th Buccaneers prowled the bombers' flanks, and squadrons from the 666th Devil Dogs and 42nd Prefects provided low and top cover for the formation. Two dozen locally-produced fighters, known as Y-ten-tens but which the Navy flyers had christened Die-ten-tens due to their lack of manoeuvrability and slow speed, flew alongside the bombers. Everyone knew that if it came to these planes defending the bombers, then the assault was as good as defeated.

The three pilots of Indigo Flight cruised behind and below the Apostles. Larice had given Laquell the traditional Navy send-off before a mission.

'Good hunting,' she'd said on the hardstands of Coriana.

'You too,' he'd replied, and she'd smacked his arse as he climbed the ladder.

'What was that for?' he said, climbing in and strapping himself down as the fitters pulled the arming pins on the hellstrike rockets mounted on the pylons beneath his wings.

'For luck.'

'Don't I get to give you one?'

'When we get back, Laquell,' she'd said, turning and jogging over to her own plane.

Seekan's voice crackled over the vox, pulling her back to the present, and she checked her spacing and gripped her stick with hands that were sweating inside her textured gloves.

'Coming up on Initial Point,' he said. 'Combat spread and drop to Angels minus five. The enemy will have been watching for us, and will undoubtedly have their bats airborne by now. Expect contact any minute.'

One by one, the Apostles acknowledged and Larice thumbed her auspex into active search mode, watching as the scope began filling with rapidly ascending contacts. High-speed interceptors, slower close-in defence craft, and heavy ground contacts.

But in the centre of the slate one contact overshadowed all the others, a monstrous return that was far too large to be a flyer. This was what they had come to destroy. This was how the Archenemy had launched their attacks over the Breakers without warning.

This was why their aerial armada was sweeping down over the mountains.

Though it was over ten kilometres away, Larice saw it clearly; its stark blackness a stain on the ocean ice. It was locked in the ice by the rapidly freezing water and huddled, though it seemed impossible that something so vast could huddle, in the midst of ice spires pushed up from the water by undersea volcanic activity.

Nearly two thousand metres long and glossy black with a flat topside bristling with crooked towers, sloped takeoff ramps and jet blast deflectors, the Archenemy mass carrier swarmed with bats.

And Larice saw how it had evaded detection for so long.

It was a *submersible* mass carrier.

'APOSTLE LEAD, THIS is Orbis One. We are reading strong auspex bands low on the ice, five kilometres from your position,' said the monotone voice of one of the tech-priests. 'Identification: six outlying super-heavies on the ice equipped with surface-to-air rockets between Winter Spear and its objective.'

'Understood, Orbis One,' said Seekan. 'The Apostles will clear the way.'

Seekan's plane dropped from the formation and the seven cream-coloured Thunderbolts followed him down towards the ocean ice. As the Apostles dived, the fighter element of Winter Spear surged forward, ready to engage and destroy the enemy screen of bats before they could splash the bombers.

Target information from Orbis inloaded onto Larice's armaments panel, the target of her Thunderbolt's wrath blinking a taunting red. Six multiple rocket-launching batteries surrounded the mass carrier, each capable of throwing up a lethal screen of seeker rockets. They had to be taken out before any slow movers could reach the carrier.

'You all heard what I heard,' said Seekan over the vox to his pilots. 'Switch your targeting auspex to ground engagement. We will be going low and fast. Pair off. Odds will be on unmasking duty, Evens on termination.'

He spoke with crisp authority, and as Larice heard the confirmations coming over the vox she was again struck by the machine-like obedience of her fellow Apostles. There was no verbal roughhousing like you'd find in most Navy wings, no wishes of good hunting or bene-dictions to the Emperor. The Apostles were all about the task, anything else was a liability.

'You and me, Asche,' said Jeric Suhr, sliding into view on her port wing. 'Let's go.'

Larice nodded and pushed the stick straight down, diving for the ice. No point in giving the rocket batteries an easier target until it was time to kill them. The ice roared up to meet her, and she found herself relying on her altimeter to gauge her pull-out. The immensity of the glaring pack-ice filled her canopy, a blank vision of emptiness that made it next to impossible to judge exactly how high she was.

The numbers unspooled, and when they hit two hundred metres, she yanked back on the stick and feathered her engines, viffing her vectors hard and flaring out with a thunderous boom that split the ice. She shot off at ninety degrees to her dive, and a slashing V of ice crystals ripped up from the ice in her flashing wake.

She flew a mere twenty metres above the ocean ice with Suhr a hundred metres behind on her starboard wing. Such flying required the coolest of hands on the stick as the slightest miscalculation would send her plane ploughing into the ice.

Nap-of-the-ice flight was necessary if they were going to take out these rocket batteries. Thunderbolts and Lightnings could outrun missiles and outfly gunners, but the Marauders would have no chance against them.

Larice had trained in fire suppression missions, but had never actually flown one before.

In theory it was simple.

The aircraft worked in pairs. One pilot would fly their plane into the arc of anti-aircraft fire and allow the rocket battery to acquire him. Once the battery had 'unmasked' itself in this way, the second aircraft would swoop in to attack the gun battery and blow it to pieces.

In theory.

Flying fire suppression was one of the most testing and dangerous missions a pilot could undertake. Playing chicken with streams of shells and missiles was a task few had the stomach for, requiring the most fearless, skilful and, some would say, reckless flyers.

Truth be told, Larice was thrilled to be flying into harm's way.

As a native of Phantine, she was, literally, born to fly. Any moment she wasn't in the cockpit of an armed aircraft was a moment wasted.

'Apostle Six,' said Larice.

'Six here,' replied Suhr. 'Go ahead, Five.'

'You ready to do this?'

'Of course,' replied Suhr, sounding insulted she'd even asked.

The Thunderbolts were fast approaching the mass carrier and its ring of protection. Her low-level approach would make it difficult for the enemy gunners to achieve weapons lock. The auspex feed from Orbis showed the rocket battery, but Larice didn't need it to see the ugly construction of black metal, blades and the rearing templum-organ of its launch tubes fastened to the ice by extended clamps like a raptor's claws. A number of armoured vehicles and stalk tanks clustered around the battery, and red-armoured warriors with raised rifles spread out from it. Larice ignored them. Only the rocket battery mattered.

She thumbed the vox.

'Apostle Five inbound and ready.'

Larice armed her quads, pushing the throttle out and dropping her fighter suicidally close to the ice. Meltwater blasted from the pack-ice flashed by her canopy as she flew at high speed along her approach vector.

'Asche!' cried the normally unflappable Jeric Suhr. 'You're too low!'

'Shut up, and don't frigging miss,' snapped Larice, hauling violently on the stick, pulling the Thunderbolt into an almost vertical climb. Her ivory plane roared into view above the rocket battery, flashing its underside and largest surface area. She eased into an unforgivably lazy banking turn and waited on the *shoom, shoom, shoom* of smoke from the battery.

A bloom of yellow-stained propellant exploded from

the battery's rear and a trio of seeker warheads leapt from the launch tubes. Slaved autocannons followed her passage, banging high explosive shells in a near-constant stream into the air.

She rolled over and dived for the ice as shots blasted around her. She twisted and looped the plane like a lunatic. The autocannon shells were well wide and Larice grinned as adrenaline dumped into her system, keeping the effects of her high-g turns at bay.

She pulled the Thunderbolt into a long, slow climb, allowing the rockets to close before throwing the aircraft into a dazzling pirouette, hammering the throttle and pumping out clouds of decoy flares. The Thunderbolt shot away at almost ninety degrees to its original course and two rockets overshot, exploding as their seeker warheads fell for the flares.

The third rocket twisted round and followed her down, the gap closing. Jeric Suhr's Thunderbolt overflew the battery and fired two of his hellstrike missiles. Even as the Archenemy crew realised that they were now the hunted, the missiles slammed into the rocket vehicle's topside.

The battery exploded in a searing white fireball, burning fuel and wreckage flying in all directions. Three other vehicles detonated, caught in the blast and veering across the ice to crush the soldiers gathered around them. Lumbering stalk-tanks fired their heavy guns, but the Thunderbolts were too quick for the gunners and every one of their shots missed.

The rockets in the battery's magazine cooked off explosively. Warheads blew in a string of roaring booms. Razor-sharp fragments sprayed out and enemy soldiers ran from the destruction, their grossly misshapen bodies twisting in agony as they burned.

Larice let out a yell of exultation as the explosions lit up the ice and flew through the expanding mushroom cloud of fire rising from the destroyed battery. Flames rippled over her canopy like liquid orange light and the last rocket followed her into the fire. It detonated in the midst of the explosion and Larice pulled her Thunderbolt into a looping, inverted climb.

'Good shooting, Suhr,' she said, feeling her heart rate climbing down from its rapid tattoo.

'What else did you expect?' replied Suhr, closing on her wing. Larice called up the auspex feed from Orbis and tallied off the destroyed rocket batteries.

One, two, three, four, five...

Before she could get to six, the live feed flickered and died.

'Orbis Flight is down!' shouted the voice of a panicked Marauder pilot. 'Orbis is down!'

Larice looked up, seeing a sky thick with swarming bats and Imperial craft. A major air battle was going on above their heads and it wasn't clear who had the upper hand. Slashing red Hell Talons and Razors filled the air with las and the dance of fighters above was a blazing free-fire zone.

Larice switched vox channel, and the cockpit was filled with the frantic chatter of pilots screaming at each other to break, dive, roll, cover and eject.

Seekan's voice cut through the babble.

'Apostles,' he said, 'take back the sky.'

Larice stood her plane on its tail and hit her burners, melting a ten-metre-wide crater in the ice as her Thunderbolt leapt skyward.

LARICE PICKED HER target, a spiralling Hell Talon flying an aggressive pursuit against one of the 42nd Prefects. The Lightning was dancing through the sky, but the Talon was stuck to it like glue. Larice waited until the Lightning rolled over on an escape turn and the Talon bled off speed to follow it round. A spurt of las tore a wing from its body and the madly spinning craft looped down towards the ice. She broke off and fanned her aircraft down after a flash of a crimson wing. A Hell Blade swished past her wing, its speed a match for hers, and she looked into the cockpit of the enemy pilot.

His helmet was a carved, daemonic leer and hellish red light lit his masked face. A long, reptilian tongue slid from his mouth, and Larice recoiled as she realised the pilot wasn't wearing a helmet. She punched her air brakes and cut her thrust, viffing in behind the enemy plane. He broke right and stepped down with a flutter of vector thrust. Larice angled her plane down, knowing he would surge forward.

Her quads banged, the recoil fierce and loud.

Shells streamed from the nose guns and tore up that damnable cockpit, erasing that monstrous visage from existence. Her breathing stoked shallow, spiking pulse rate high. A pilot never normally saw the face of the enemy, and to know the hideous things they were flying against had shaken her. It took her a moment to regain her calm, but in an aerial fight, a moment can be too long.

Heavy fire thumped her wings and fuselage, tearing over the armour behind her canopy. Red icons winked to life and she threw the Thunderbolt into a looping roll. A sidestepping viff put her back level and she twisted in her seat, hunting her hunter.

'Larice, break right!' shouted a voice over the vox. Laquell.

She hauled around, narrowly avoiding a collimated blaze of las-fire. Left, right, up, roll left. Her attacker was still with her. She saw it behind her, a gleam of purple and gold. Hell Blade. She saw a flicker of camo-green and the enemy plane lit up like a sunflare shell as Laquell's guns shredded it and its engine core went critical.

'Thanks, Laquell,' said Larice, rising up above the engagement and getting her breath back under control.

'You all right?' asked Laquell, pulling out alongside her.

'Fine.'

'Where's your wingman?'

'Suhr? I don't know. Where's yours?'

'Ysor got tagged. A bat tore up his wings and his missiles cooked off on the pylon.'

'Damn,' hissed Larice.

'Yeah,' agreed Laquell. 'I'll watch your wing if you watch mine.'

'Deal,' she said, turning her aircraft back down into the madly swirling engagement.

Their aircraft slashed down through a wedge of attacking Razors, splitting them and blowing two to fragments. Larice pulled wide and splashed a Hell Blade as it lined up a shot on Apostle Eight.

'You're welcome, Thule,' she said as his aircraft zoomed back into the fight.

The two mobs of fighters were well and truly enmeshed now, like starving hounds locked in a cage, the battle an impossible-to-follow tangle of explosions, missile contrails, air-bursting flak, las-fire and vector flare. Larice and Laquell danced through the battle with muscular turns and delicate spins, dancers in the midst of a stampede. They made a good team, instinctively understanding how the other flew, matching turns and viffs with the accuracy of flyers who'd fought together for years.

Larice lost count of how many kills she took, mashing the firing trigger on the stick until the battery of her las coughed dry. She switched to quads, claiming another three kills. This engagement alone would make every pilot an ace in a day.

Flashing wings, speeding tail sections and spirals of engine noise. Snap shots and desperate breaks. Larice was sweating and her body ached from gripping on hard turns. Every muscle burned and she was in for a hell of an adrenal comedown when she put her plane back on the deck.

A shadow shimmered over her canopy, and she saw a trailing formation of bombers coming in, diving and looking like a flock of migrating birds coming into nest.

Seekan's voice came over the vox. 'Apostles, this is Lead,' he said. 'The door is open, so while the Lightnings have the bats' attention, we'll escort the Marauders in.'

'Laquell,' she voxed, aiming her Thunderbolt towards the mass carrier. 'You want to fly with the Apostles?'

'Sure, Larice,' replied Laquell. 'I could do with another heart attack today.'

Larice flipped her aircraft over and pushed its nose down. The two fighters spread out and increased power, diving for the deck at high speed. She saw the enormous carrier was wallowing in the ocean, industrial-grade meltas flaring around its edges to melt the ice and allow it to escape beneath the water. The bats in the air would have nowhere to land if it submerged, but that didn't seem to matter to the Archenemy commanders.

Autocannon shots burst around them and Larice grinned as she jinked the Thunderbolt up and down, avoiding the flak as though it was coming at her in slow motion. She flew instinctively, not even consciously aware of any decision-making process, just flying as though she knew, just *knew*, where the streams of tracers would be.

'There's too much fire!' shouted Laquell.

'You might be right,' agreed Larice, calmly lining up her cannon's gunsight on the command spire of the mass carrier. Her quads opened up, and drifting blooms of fire erupted across the surface of the black tower like orange-petalled flowers with every impact.

'We've got to pull up, Larice! We're too close!' screamed Laquell, hauling his plane away in a desperate climb that cost him valuable speed.

Three rockets leapt from the deck of the carrier as Larice pulled the trigger on her control column again. The quad-mounted autocannon thundered and blazed, the noise like a roaring chainsaw. The shells impacted ten metres in front of one of the carrier's launch batteries before tearing into it and ripping it messily in half.

She pushed out the throttle to full military power and

executed a tight, rolling spin, flipping up and over the deck of the carrier. Masked warriors fired pistols and rifles at her, and the rockets streaked across the deck in pursuit of her furnace-hot turbofans. Booming waves of icy water surged up from the carrier's sides as it began to submerge.

Her auspex screamed warnings at her. She pulled a recklessly tight turn around the carrier's command spire, spitting a string of incandescent flares as she punched the engines.

The rockets couldn't match a vector turn and two of them slammed into the control spire of the carrier, gutting its upper levels with fire and high explosives. Its top section keeled over drunkenly, falling slowly, like the tallest tree in the forest. It slammed into the deck as Larice pulled higher and aimed her Thunderbolt towards the heavens as the Marauders swooped down like sharks with the scent of blood.

She saw the first bombs shedding from their bellies, falling like black raindrops towards the carrier. A few streams of close-in defence fire licked upwards. Some of the bombs would be caught in the flak storm, but nowhere near enough of them to make a difference.

Larice turned away from the doomed carrier, bleeding off airspeed in time to see the last rocket explode five metres from the engine of Erzyn Laquell's Thunderbolt.

The blast sheared off his aircraft's port wing and tail section, sending the aircraft into an uncontrolled downward spin.

'Punch out!' screamed Larice, 'Come on, damn you! Eject!'

But the Thunderbolt continued to fall. It smashed into a spire of ice, cartwheeling end over end in a brilliant fireball. It slammed into the ice in a blizzard of silvered shrapnel.

'Damn you, Laquell, I told you to punch out!' she yelled at the wreckage of the burning aircraft. She cut her speed as low as she dared, flying over the crash site even though she knew there was no way anyone could have survived so fierce an impact. Hot tears pricked her eyes and she pulled up and away from the carrier as thunderous detonations rocked the air with hammerblows of searing air and percussive shockwaves.

Behind her, the Archenemy mass carrier shuddered like a dying beast as the Marauders spilled their load of iron and fire upon it. Bombs punched through its decks and exploded in the hangars, the dark temples and the slave pens. They vaporised the engines, the ballast tanks, the supply halls and the torture cells.

Blazing columns of tar-black smoke coiled from its ruptured innards, hundred-metre flames roaring from its wounds like elemental blood. The air went phosphor white as a collection of incendiaries, dropped from a Marauder of the 22nd Yysarians named *Give 'em Hell*, sailed through the cratered deck of the sinking carrier and exploded in the midst of its ruptured engine core.

Larice didn't see it break in two and didn't watch as it came apart in cracking splits of unclean metal. She didn't watch it upend and spill its thousands-strong crew into the freezing water beneath the sea. She didn't watch the greatest victory any of the men and women on Amedeo had ever seen.

She flew with her wings dipped over the remains of Erzyn Laquell's Thunderbolt and felt her heart turn as cold as the ocean ice below.

'GET UP,' SAID Seekan.

'Get out,' replied Larice.

'I said get up, Apostle Five,' said Seekan. 'And if it makes things clearer, that's an order.'

Larice rolled over, seeing Seekan silhouetted by the door of her room with a suit bag slung over his shoulder. Dressed in his heavily-medalled cream frock coat, dress blue trousers and polished boots, he looked every inch the Wing Leader of an elite squadron of Navy flyers.

His hair was immaculately oiled and his thin features were almost expressionless.

Almost, but not quite.

Seekan came into the room and sat on the edge of the bed, laying the linen fabric of the suit bag across his lap. One of the advantages of taking the Aquilian as their billet meant there was plenty of space for each pilot to have their own room. What would once have housed wealthy off-world socialites now sheltered weary Naval aviators. In case of flash alerts, all their rooms were on the first floor, and Larice heard the booming strains of *Laude Beati Triumphia* coming from the ballroom. Clearly Krone was in charge of the music again: he favoured rousing marching tunes.

'Another carrier destroyed?' she asked, pulling the bed sheets around her naked body.

'No,' said Seekan. He didn't elaborate.

'Then what? None of the Apostles died.'

Winter Spear had been an unqualified success, with a combined tally of three hundred and ninety-six enemy bats accounted for in the air, together with however many were aboard the mass carrier when it sank. A total of one hundred and six Imperial craft were shot down, mostly the Die-ten-tens and Laredo bombers, but none of the attacking squadrons had come through without losses.

No squadron but the Apostles.

'None of the Apostles died, that's true,' agreed Seekan. 'But one of them learned a valuable lesson.'

'That's why you didn't offer Laquell a place, isn't it?'

Seekan nodded. 'I'm not as unfeeling as I appear, Larice. We don't have the camaraderie of other Naval wings, and now you know why. We can't afford to be friends with the people we fly alongside. Out of all the wings that fought in the attack on the carrier, we are the only ones to escape loss. Fate's wheel has turned, and once again we escape its notice. The galaxy isn't ready for us to die, and you need to show it that you don't care one way or another. You need to show it that you don't fear it, to spit into the darkness and say that nothing it can do will make the slightest bit of difference.'

Larice bunched the sheets in her fists. 'I don't know if I can.'

'You have to,' said Seekan. 'The minute you start to care, that's when they get you.'

'They?'

He shrugged. 'Fate, Death, whatever's out there in the darkness.'

'And that's what you do? Not care?'

'I do what I have to. I drink and I sing and I rage at the stars, whatever really. Each of us has his own way. You've seen that.'

'Does it help?'

'It makes it easier. I don't know if that's the same thing, but it means I can climb into the cockpit of a Thunderbolt and not care if I come back.'

Larice felt tears brimming on her eyelids, but forced them back with a swallow and grim nod. She reached for the suit bag draped across Seekan's lap.

'Give me it,' she said. 'I'll be down in ten minutes.'

ATTIRED IN HER full dress uniform, Larice strode into the ballroom, her heels clicking on the hardwood floor in time with the clashing timpani of Krone's music. The Apostles gathered around the fire, drinking, arguing and behaving like naval ratings on their first shore leave in a year. Saul Cirksen had his pistol drawn and was taking potshots at the busts of forgotten notables of Amedeo.

Leena Sharto smoked a huge cigar and burned holes in the armrest of her chair, while Owen Thule knocked back shot after shot of hard liquor. Seekan gave her the briefest nod of acknowledgement as she approached. Jeric Suhr and Quint continued their endless game of regicide. Ziner Krone pressed a heavy balloon of amber-coloured liquor into her hand.

His skin gleamed dark, dangerous and powerful, and

the scarring on the side of his face pulled tight in a grin as she downed the entire glass in one long swallow. It burned her, but it felt good. The heat and pain in her chest reminded her that she was alive. She looked at her fellow flyers and felt nothing for them. No emotions at all, not even contempt.

She threw the glass into the fire and it shattered with a brittle explosion.

Larice gripped Krone's jacket. She pulled his face to hers and kissed him hard on the mouth. He responded hungrily and pulled her to his wide chest.

'About time,' he said.

'Shut your mouth,' she snapped, turning and pulling him towards the stairs.

CRISP SUNLIGHT BEAT down on the hardstands of Coriana, heating the honeycombed landing mats, but leaving the day cold. Pilots, fitters and armourers milled back and forth between the planes, dodging speeding tow-rigs and flashing gurneys laden with missiles and ammo boxes. Peristaltic fuel lines snaked from juddering bowsers to feed the thirsty aircraft, and ground crew directed taxiing fighters and bombers to their designated runways.

Larice clambered over the upper fuselage of her cream Thunderbolt, checking the repair job the fitters had done and watching the controlled dance of military might as the Imperium took the fight to the Archenemy. With the defeat of the northern flanking thrust, all assets were being directed to aid the ground war in the west. Confidence was high that the newly established air superiority would soon result in victory.

She knelt beside an opened panel behind the canopy. The damaged armour plates had been replaced and a tangle of cables ran from the exposed mechanisms of the aircraft to a diagnostic calculus-logi servitor. One of the Martian priesthood studied the tickertape clattering from the brass-rimmed slate fitted to its chest, a soft burble of binary spilling from the shadows beneath its hood.

Larice slid over the wing to the crew ladder and swung her leg around to hook the top rung. She climbed down and dropped to the hardstand, slapping her palm on the warmed flank of her plane.

Seven Thunderbolts in the same pristine colour scheme as hers were parked in a neat row, just one of a dozen squadrons being prepped and made ready to fly. Three Lightnings surged from launch rails, powering skywards on blazing plumes of firelit smoke. She watched them go, shielding her eyes from the low sun as they rolled over their port wings to head west.

Her gaze lowered as she saw a young, good-looking pilot in a camo-green uniform approaching her. He cocked his head to one side as he drew near, like he wasn't sure he had the right person, but was going to ask anyway.

'Flight Lieutenant Asche?' he said. 'Larice Asche?'

'Yeah, who wants to know?' she said, walking down the line of her plane's fuselage.

The young man jogged after her and held out his hand.

'Flight Officer Layne Schaw,' he said with a beaming smile. 'It's an honour to meet you.'

Larice looked at the proffered hand and Schaw's earnest smile.

'Get the frig away from me,' she hissed. 'And don't tell me your name.'

I've been a fan of Matt's work since I first read it, and I think his Enforcer *trilogy featuring the Adeptus Arbites Shira Lucina Calpurnia is entirely made out of epic win with a splash of awesome sauce.*

For this story, Matt was interested in combining the activities of the Adeptus Mechanicus with the terrible instruments of warfare – the Woe Machines – used by Heritor Asphodel in several Gaunt stories, particularly Necropolis. *Forgotten and misapprehended nightmares lurk on one of the worlds the giant Crusade has already rolled past...*

Dan Abnett

THE HEADSTONE AND THE HAMMERSTONE KINGS

Matthew Farrer

'IT'S COMING FOR Him. It's carrying a Magos who'll examine Him.'

An instant after Jopell had said the words, Kovind Shek's long, wiry fingers gripped his suit-front and yanked him into a humiliating, stumbling fall into the dust between two slumped and broken engines. He lay there on one elbow, eyes closed, feeling the fine, tawny grit he'd stirred up as it drifted back down and coated his sweating skin with muck. The morning was chilly but having to double-time it into the graveyard in his heavy labourer's jumpsuit had begun it, and a growing brew of fears in his belly – being caught, being caught and his forged papers spotted, not finding Kovind, how Kovind would take the news when he did find him – had done the rest. Jopell was damp and he stank.

His master had already turned his back and was shouting orders again. Jopell didn't bother to open his eyes to look. It would be another labour-crew accident, one of the careful fatalities that Kovind didn't trust him enough to let him help organise. Over the clank of metal he could already hear the frightened groans of the men the accident was going to happen to. For some reason they all had to be men. Jopell had wondered aloud about that once and Kovind had kicked him in the gut hard enough to tumble him over backwards.

'A Magos who'll examine Him,' he muttered to himself again as he pushed himself up onto his arse. His legs jutted into a careless V in the dirt and his belly itched as it overhung them. He had delivered the message in the old Asheki dialect, and the pronoun form it used had a very precise set of connotations: the compound suffix showing respect due to a senior whose authority originated outside one's own lineage and manory, the vowel intonations carrying nuances of standing in the Customs, the Practices and the Traditions, and the accents denoting forge-work and engine-craft. Context did the rest. There was only one thing he could be talking about.

He leaned back, staring up between the crushed and tarnished steel hulls, and fixed on it: the little dark dot hanging high up above them, looking like a tiny splinter embedded in pallid skin. It had been there for two days; for two more before that it hadn't been visible at all, except at high magnification through the spyblock they'd stolen from the garrison post. It was taking its time, this 'Headstone'.

Jopell wondered if he should feel greater unease about it. 'Examine', after all. Or at least that would be the closest Low Gothic word for the Asheki *k'seoshe*, a term which referred to something more complex. It meant careful, competent disassembly by a knowing hand and study by a knowing mind, but with a thief's agenda – learning a device's lore outside the formal blessing of the Traditions, examining its naked secrets against its builder's will, an invasive hand and gaze devoid of respect or shame. It was what they were here to protect Him from. But they were weak now, in hiding since the hives had burned. Would they be able to do it?

He dropped his gaze at a shout from before him, in time to see a scrag-bearded victim duck under the reaching arms of one of Kovind's thugs and break clear. He was a clumsy runner, the loose-hanging suit flapping around his staggering legs and swinging arms. His mouth gaped with terror and exertion. One thug tried to break off after him, but they had the rest of the victims to restrain and a brawl broke out under the tilting hulk. Kovind cursed and shouted.

'Brother!' the man said as he homed in on Jopell. 'Brother, they're mad, get out of here! Get the soldiers, get the preachers, I don't know what they–' and then Jopell, who was good with distances and movement, came up off the ground and into him and broke his jaw with an elbow. The man's feet shot out in front of him as his head was knocked backward and his full-length landing sent up another puff of grit. A moment later meaty hands were dragging him back to the broken machine.

Jopell strolled after the kicking figure, some of his composure seeping back. The hulk was a Skybreaker train, the segments torn off one another and left in an ungainly pile by some ignorant Throne-licking hauler crew who'd have been acid-flayed for their disrespect in a righter world than this one. This segment, one of the rear ones as far as Jopell could tell, was badly balanced on the pile. Pict records and testimonies from the other crews would show that it had already looked liable to topple over. The gantry cranes had waddled into position on one side of it, where they could plausibly claim to have been trying to stabilise the pile for a cutting crew to start work.

These men weren't a cutting crew. Skilled cutters were valuable, and the most skilled ones knew about the Customs and even the Traditions and had the same loyalties as Kovind and himself. But they carried a cutter rig, an old one that could be spared, and Psinter was doing her thing in the Administratum compound. By the time the

bodies were found the records would show these men
had been a cutting crew indeed.

The muscle men had been bought with various combinations of favours, promises, stolen Adeptus scrip
and crude liquor. They thought they were working for
a slightly elevated version of themselves, someone with
rackets to protect and reputation to enforce. They didn't
know Kovind Shek's place in the Traditions. It worked
best that way. Now they shoved the victims into position, immobilised one pesky struggler with two heavy
heel-stomps to his knees, and backed away. They were
barely out of range when Kovind gave the signal and
the crane operator let the grip claw disengage. Two of
the men screamed, and then the pitted and blast-burned
side of the Skybreaker hulk came down on them like a
boot on a beetle.

The crane operator and Kovind exchanged thumbs-
up acknowledgements. The muscle men guffawed and
clouted each other on the shoulder to prove how
unmoved they were. Jopell heard a choking cry from
under the overturned hulk, but by the time he walked
over to join Kovind it had already faded and rattled out.

'Yes, I heard you,' Kovind snapped at him, although
Jopell hadn't spoken a word apart from that first message. But the man was talking to himself. 'Here for Him,'
he rasped again, more quietly now, staring up at the tiny
dark blemish in the sky just as Jopell had done. 'Less
time than we thought. We have to move.'

'A Rune Priest?' Demi-Lector Vosheni asked. 'Wait, no,
have I misheard?'

'I don't know, Master Demi-Lector, have you? Is there
a reason to suppose you have?' It was the first time in
hours that Sister Sarell had spoken, and several of the
Adeptus started at her voice. Vosheni spent a moment
gnawing the fold of leathery *ushpiil* leaf in his hand
before he answered.

'You're the one to explain it,' he said at length. 'Look,

does anyone else remember this? Emperor grant I'm recalling correctly, but I find myself thinking of that one as an Adeptus Astartes rank, not a Mechanicus. Anyone else? Or have I breathed in a gulp of hotstone and set my brain to decaying? An Adeptus Mechanicus Rune Priest – has anyone ever heard of one?'

'I've not even heard of an Adeptus Astartes Rune Priest,' put in Kinosa as she reached determinedly for the platter of seedmash before Vosheni could finish the lot. Like Vosheni, Kinosa was Administratum: the military liaison with the Guard garrison. Vosheni was from the reconstruction and tithing taskforce, and it had been his idea to convene a regular meal for the seniors of each Adeptus contingent at the Chillbreak fortress reconstruction site. Jers Adalbrect didn't mind the meals, but he wished that they didn't keep falling on his fast days. He politely sipped a cup of water and listened to the others bickering.

'Adeptus Astartes?' piped up Vocator Nember, and Sarell rolled her eyes. 'I don't recall seeing one, but then perhaps I did and didn't recognise him! Nearly a day I spent around them, when the Iron Snakes' emissaries attended upon–'

'You're remembering the *Pageant of Asaheim*, sir,' Adalbrect quickly put in before Nember could tell the story yet again. 'The play of the Apostate being crushed on Fenris. There's a song near the end of the first act that refers to Rune Priests among the Space Wolves.'

'Thank you,' said Vosheni through a mouthful of leaf. 'So this one's Mechanicus?'

'I don't believe the ranks are the same,' said Sarell, 'and it sounds more like a name coined outside the Mechanicus for someone whose actual function is rather harder to describe. Shall we ask this visitor's real title when he arrives?'

'If we even get the chance,' Nember snorted through his moustache, peering into his wine glass. 'What's the bet he stays hiding in their shrine in the middle of that

damned graveyard and we never see a scrap of him?
He arrived in one of those ships they use to lift Titans.
Titans! I don't care what reasons they dress this up in
in their communiques, he's not here to do any of that
ceremonial crap they said they needed this big damn
dignitary to do. I'll bet he's a junior enginseer who's
drawn the short straw and has to sit out in this sandhole
loading dead machinery onto that so-called Headstone
of his to keep it out of our hands.' After a pause just
long enough to be rude Nember added a little twitch of
his hand to demonstrate that 'our' meant the Adeptus
around the table, but none of them were fooled. 'Our'
meant the deeply mercenary consortium of trade houses
from Bardolphus who'd managed to get themselves
some sort of Administratum marque and were clawing
for a foothold in the Ashek reconstruction. When the
edict had gone out from the Mechanicus that the legions
of Woe Machines the Archenemy had left behind were
to be collected in a monstrous graveyard over the Chillbreak Delta, all that Nember's masters had seen was an
attempt to shut them out of something. It was an open
secret that Nember was there as a spy.

'I'm wondering if he's here to inspect the works,' said
Vosheni gloomily, looking at a stain on his cuff where
he'd let his tunic sleeve dip into the sauce dish. 'The
number of accidents, the violence...'

'Your job to fix,' Nember scolded him.

'And his!' Vosheni shot a finger out at Adalbrect. 'The
Missionaria Galaxia is here to make sure these people
are obedient servants to the Throne! What are you putting in your sermons about diligence? Temperance?'
Kinosa took advantage of his distraction to get the last
of the seedmash.

It's more complicated than that, Adalbrect started to
say, it always is. Why did people have this ridiculous
idea that the Missionaria just had to shout a sermon at
someone to throw some sort of switch in their heads
marked *instant obedience*?

'The work crews here are frail and mortal, Demi-Lector, as are we all.' Sarell got in before him. 'Most are war displacees, some are refugees from elsewhere on the world, some are refugees from other worlds repaying the cost of their transp–'

'I know about the blasted workforce, Sister, I administer it,' Vosheni cut her off, and then caught himself. 'Apologies, Sister Dialogus.'

'Accepted, Demi-Lector. But bear with my point. Spiritually these people have lain too long prostrate beneath grief and darkness. We are helping them back to their feet.' Adalbrect grinned. She was taking from his sermon of two mornings ago. He liked compliments. 'But until they get their strength back, sometimes they will stumble.'

'Y'know what we need to do?' Nember asked. His goblet was empty and his voice a little too loud. 'We need to get into that graveyard. See what it is they're doing in there. It's not right that these work crews get mark... marched in there and we don't get to follow them and see what they do with all that.'

'Inside the graveyard is acknowledged Mechanicus ground,' said Kinosa, 'same way as the temple compound belongs to the Ministorum,' and she tilted her head at Adalbrect and Sarell. 'And anyway, maybe you've forgotten that what they're collecting in that graveyard are unholy war machines that robbed many brave Throne soldiers of their lives. It was the Mechanicus that broke them so the aquila could return here. Show some respect.'

That shut Nember up, but Vosheni had taken one of his adept's braids in his fingers and was twirling it thoughtfully.

'Nevertheless.' They all looked at him. 'Nevertheless, let's not miss an opportunity. Our friends of the cog are reserved, but that doesn't make them our enemies. We're all Adeptus. Beyond a certain professional distance, I've found Enginseer Daprokk quite agreeable to work with.'

He smiled at Nember, who blinked at him. 'I think this great dignitary they've flown in, this great magos, is just as important as they've told us he is. And I think that a request... no. I think that an *announcement* that a delegation of the most senior Adeptus officials at the Chillbreak reconstruction site will be pleased to present their credentials and welcome such an important visitor to Ashek II is the least that such a position justifies.'

Nember scowled as he tried to get at the idea through the alcohol, but Kinosa grasped it straight away and toasted it with the last of her wine.

'It's a trip, then,' she said. 'I'll invite Tosk and Haffith, too. Let's add a military footing to this thing, make it harder for them to say no.'

'Where are they tonight, anyway?' Adalbrect asked.

'Snap purge in the east quarter of the labourer barracks,' said Kinosa, pouring more wine. 'Two new hauler crews came in yesterday with more dead machines. Seems one of 'em was trying to smuggle in a weapons cache on the side. That's still a military offence. They took it pretty seriously.'

'I'm not surprised,' said Vosheni. 'Or at least not at that. Who needs this rabble to decide they've inherited a job as the Archenemy's army? Joke, joke!' and he flapped an arm at Adalbrect, who'd half-risen with a slapped expression on his face. 'I know you do your job well, preacher, I joked. But honestly, why is some cheap hivestamp stub-gun so important to have out in a place like this? What are they going to do, rob the cooks at the refectory tent for another helping of starch broth? Who needs weapons in an empty desert?'

'THAT'S FOUR FULL crews fully armed. They only got one stash in the haulers, the others are safe. We'll get them to Orange Five crew at midmorning meal tomorrow. Then we're ready.' Psinter was trying to keep her voice quiet and level, but there was an unmistakable satisfaction in it. It had been a hard thing to organise in secret, and their sudden need for haste had made it harder.

Kovind Shek pursed his lips and stared at nothing in particular. His long fingers stretched out and plucked up a stylus from the clutter across his little desk, made the motions of writing the words *Orange Five* half a centimetre above his writing pad, and dropped it again. It was a habit he was training himself into, to help him remember things. Not a perfect substitute for his old stacks of bound waferbooks, but a much safer one. After the Guard had busted one of their weapon mules, there had been another random snap-search right the length of the southern avenue, and the Ministorum brute squad had torn down and burned three barrack shanties.

'All our people, then?' asked Jopell. 'All of them?' The other two resistance members gave no answer but a scowl, partly in response to Jopell's question and partly in response to him saying anything at all. Neither of them wanted him there. Kovind was the trusty, the crew chief who was allowed to supervise the native Ashek labourers. Psinter was his lieutenant in the Traditions and the Practices, and his peer in the Customs, but they had only been able to manoeuvre her into a junior forewoman's job on the haulers. Jopell's descent was recent offworld, only four generations on Ashek, with only tenuous ties to the forge-manories and none to the Inevitable Conclave. But in the turmoil after the hives had burned, he had ended up in the work crew draft, had played the compliant and grateful freed civilian so well he had been installed in a foreman's job straight away, and now if they were going to plausibly pass off these meetings as the quiet evening chats between a crew chief and his offsiders Kovind had to have him there. Jopell usually understood that well enough to keep his mouth shut.

'All our people,' said Psinter, glaring at him. 'The accident fatalities,' with a salutary nod to Kovind, 'have given us regular pretexts to reorganise the crews we started with. We're still under-armed compared to

the cog-lickers, though. Our edge over the Mechanicus
picket-guards is going to be numbers and surprise, not
hardware. And probably not discipline, either. Our
people are enthusiastic, but they're not soldiers. A lot of
them are going to die.'

The three of them looked at each other. None of them
valued the lives of their followers any more than their
own: the Traditions discounted such things and the
Customs exalted a very different set of priorities. But
it presented a challenge. Neither Kovind nor Psinter
needed to describe that challenge out loud. Jopell did
anyway.

'If we rush the pickets and only a couple of people
know what they need to do in there, odds are they'll die
and the crew won't know the next move. Tell everyone
on the crew and that's a real dangerous secret we've just
told a lot of people.'

Kovind couldn't quite restrain himself: a fist came
down on the little table hard enough to make the lan-
tern blink. The three of them fell silent for a moment as
the bootsteps of a camp patrol scuffed by outside.

'Want to try blabbing again, Jopell?' hissed Psinter.
'Just because, you know, you didn't do it properly the
first time and those...' She took a breath and lowered her
voice. 'They didn't hear you loud enough?'

I didn't say anything any more incriminating than
you, Jopell thought, but what he said was:

'Why don't we just use the delegation convoy?'

'AND SO, THE graveyard, murmured Jers Adalbrect as
they passed beneath the machine-icons swinging on
their leaded chains, and the red-shrouded heads of the
Mechanicus escorts turned to look at him. 'A casual
vocalisation,' he said to them before they could question him. 'Disregard, please.' They stayed studying him
a moment longer, and Adalbrect wondered if he were
going to be questioned. The 'casual vocalisation' trick
was something one of the Logisticae adepts had taught

him, back on... damn, was the Augnassis mission really
four deployments ago now? The Mechanicus don't talk
to themselves, Mamzel Rindon had told him, they don't
exclaim when they're surprised or mutter under their
breath when they're pissed off. But the ones who work
with the rest of us know we do this *casual vocalisation*
thing. Easier to just get into the habit of reporting to
them that that's what you were doing. He'd noticed a
couple of the other Missionaria staff had picked up the
habit too.

It took the guards a few moments more to decide
there was nothing to concern them, and their gaze
swung away again. They hadn't appeared to confer
about him: taped to Adalbrect's sternum was a small
metal plaque that vibrated when it detected silent cant-
casts, and there had been no telltale buzzing against his
breastbone.

The graveyard, he said again to himself, and this time
kept his lips together and the words in his throat. It
seemed more appropriate that way. The whole delegation had fallen into silence as they made their
salutations to the picket guards and reboarded their
carriers.

These were not just ruins that studded the cracked
ground in the thickening dusk. They all knew about
ruins. After months on Ashek it could hardly be otherwise. They knew about tragedy and death and the
horrifying, industrial scale on which an engine of war
dealt those things out. They knew the cost at which
the Archenemy's forces had been broken here, and the
legacy the diabolical engineer known as Asphodel had
left behind. They were not even strangers to the graveyard. They had watched it growing, filling and creeping
outward beneath the dust-haze, as the columns of haulers slogged across the hardpan and the cranes tirelessly
lifted and dragged. But now, here, in amongst them in
the day's last gore-coloured light...

The glint in the carrier's running lights was the spread

claw of one of the fat four-legged Murdernaut assault machines, the fingers curved, tapered, sleeker than the Imperial engines' weapon limbs. Even severed, the menace of the open claw was enough to make Adalbrect start back from the window as though the thing had actually tried to clutch at the carrier's balloon-tyres. There was no hint of where the claw's owner might be, and Adalbrect's imagination painted it out there in the darkness, somehow awake again, prowling pilotless after them, looking for warm meat on which to exact vengeance for its lost limb.

Adalbrect shivered and used his right hand to grip the steel aquila token that hung from his left cuff. The sharp points around its edges dug into his palm and he concentrated on the pain.

The engine shifted and growled as they rolled up a brief slope, skirting the wreck of a Coffin-Worm slumped as though exhausted and brooding, its head down, the canopy behind which its crew would have sat shattered, its legs buckled and splayed out on either side of it. Its armoured back hunched up above its main hull. Behind it another one lay on its side, the plates of its flank flaring outward from the explosion that must have gutted it. Adalbrect started again as the remains of the armourglass in its canopy flashed the light from the carrier's own windows back at him. For a moment it looked like eyes had come to life under the low metal brow. He twitched his gaze away, as if there really had been something in the hulk looking back at him, and looked to the skyline ahead. Two Flensing-Wheels leaned together in silhouette against the red smears of dusk like conspirators whispering plans. Half of a third lay in front of them, he saw as the carrier drew closer, and he imagined that what they were whispering about was revenge for it. He watched them draw nearer, took in the spikes that studded their surfaces and the hooks that reached out from their rims, saw the pocks of high-density stub-rounds that stippled one from edge to edge and the great crater in the centre of the other where the cockpit had been torn or blasted out, gimbals and all.

This didn't feel like a graveyard to Adalbrect. It felt like the game parks that had surrounded the Suzerain's spring palace on Engatto Minoris, full of feral beasts that had watched their all-too-fragile little carriage convoy go past with resentful, watchful stares.

They crested the rise, saw the graveyard plain in the ebbing light, and Adalbrect shuddered. The unease that had been seeping into him all trip had soaked through his tense muscles and twitching nerves, and reached his bones.

The dead Woe Machines swarmed the plain, shoulder to shoulder and flank to flank. The high-backed Coffin-Worms leaned this way and that, and the hooks studding the Flensing-Wheels seemed to claw at the sky as though they wanted some of Ashek's bloody sunset for themselves. Ahead of them towered a cairn of wrecked Blight-Balls, all caved in or ripped open or perforated with lascannon craters, sagging and spilling against the flank of a ruined Skybreaker gun-train whose torn-off tread mountings gave it a staggering lean. Jammed in between the greater machines were ungainly rows and piles of the lesser, whole or in fragments: bulbous Stalk-Tanks, thick-shouldered Murdernauts, batrachian Rackmouths. Adalbrect spent a moment puzzling out an incongruously neat stack of intermeshed girders until he realised he was looking at the severed scaffolds from one of the infamous Abattoir Trees. He remembered the name from the shuddering Guard sergeant who had begged to be allowed to throw himself off the roof from which three orderlies had just dragged him.

Once he'd made the association Adalbrect found his gaze riveted to the stained and dented metal meshes. He fancied that as the lights moved over them he could see the points of the harpoon-barbs, although he knew that that was impossible. The Guard had been meticulous about smashing every weapon mount on the Trees

before they had allowed the wrecks to be dragged away.
The tech-priests had been furious about it.

The meshes passed out of sight, behind the buckled
steel ruins of some building-sized engine now so utterly
crushed that Adalbrect couldn't identify it at all. He
closed his eyes for a moment, and realised that in the
back of his mind he could still hear that sergeant's voice,
hoarse and low and begging. His mind started to lay in
the other sounds of the depot hospital, the sounds the
men had made as they fought against their memories
of what the Ashek war had done to them, and then his
eyes were open again and his nails dug into his palms
as he looked around for something to distract him from
the memory.

But the burst of gunfire from the nose of the second
carrier-eight was not what he had had in mind.

It took a moment for him to realise what he'd heard and
jolt upright, and he could see the same reaction from the
others as they broke out of the reveries lulled upon them
by the rumble and rock of the vehicle and the parade of
dead metal grotesqueries past the windows. Then someone in the driving cabin woke up too, flicked the lights
from white to battle-stations red, and another flurry of
shooting burst out on their tail, a quick whicker of las-shot
and two coughing booms from a single-action stubber
over the top of a man's voice screaming in anger and pain.

Sister Sarell was already half out of her seat, her arm
across her body to where the lacquered bolt pistol hung
at her hip. Vosheni, Kinosa and their two clerks had
gone into a huddle in the front seats, and for a moment
Adalbrect wondered if they were closing up for protection
or trying to console each other. Then the huddle broke
and he realised that they had been reciting a prayer over
the mag-cells that they now snapped home into slender-
barrelled laspistols. Adalbrect looked around to see
Haffith, the Colonel's man, kneeling in the aisle between
the seats, his eye glasses shining animal red in the lights,
calmly readying a short Guard-issue stub carbine. Finally

goading himself into motion, Adalbrect jerked himself into the aisle and snatched his own laspistol out of its holster.

'Stay low and breathe easy, brother,' said Haffith behind him. 'Never any sense in charging out until we know... wait...' Haffith's voice trailed off and his head cocked: he was listening to something over his vox-bead. Adalbrect nodded, realising how hard he was slamming his breaths in and out, and made himself relax. After a few more moments of quiet he remembered his office, re-holstered his gun and reached for the aquila-headed rod of rank that rested at the window where he'd been sitting. If he was going to step out of here into a fight then his enemies would know they faced an ordained servant of the Imperial Cult. One fingertip stroked the collar beneath the aquila's claws where pressure would set the combat blade sliding up through the mount.

The stub gun boomed again, right outside the carrier's windows, but Adalbrect's head was clear now and he didn't jump. He was about to ask Haffith what he'd heard when the speaker link from the driver's cabin crackled.

'Tosk. Stowaways from the second carrier. Three have cover by our right side, giving support for another element following the convoy. Step on them, please. Tosk out.'

Haffith was already moving to the right-hand hatch, but Sarell was there before him and Adalbrect hastily fell in behind. With only a little hesitation Vosheni made to lead the other Administratum officers to join them but Haffith shook his head. He motioned Vosheni towards the hatch-handle, whipped two fingers across his lips when the Demi-Lector made to speak, then gave a thumb-up when the man nodded, stayed silent and took a grip.

Haffith jabbed out four fingers, then three, then two, then one, then Vosheni hauled on the handle, lurched back as the hatch slid towards him faster than he'd expected, collided with a seat and overbalanced.

There was a moment of pure anticlimax as a cool breeze spilled gently into the cabin, and then Sister Sarell swung out of the hatchway by one arm, bolt pistol held out in the other and shouting a battle-blessing from some feral world in a voice that had no business coming from such a small frame and narrow mouth.

'Thunder for Him, wings for Him, words for Him! Thunder for Him!' By the time Haffith had stepped through the hatch behind her, dropped and spun, Sarell's weapon had spoken twice and Adalbrect winced at the flat, echoless *whud* after each shot. Once heard, the sound of a bolt shell detonating inside a body was not forgotten.

Haffith had vanished until Adalbrect stepped through the hatch, dropped in his own turn, landed in a huff of breath and saw the Guardsman rolling in under the carrier, trying to get an angle where his rounds wouldn't punch through his target and pierce the tyre. Almost as an afterthought, Adalbrect turned to look at the enemy.

Normal. He didn't know what he'd expected to see, but not this. Two utterly unremarkable men, thick-built and shorn-headed, dressed in the yellow workers' coveralls he saw in ranks in front of his shrine every day. They were splashed and stained with something darker, and their eyes were stark and wide. Scattered between them were the ruins of what had been a third until Sarell's rounds had hit home.

He realised his own body was moving. One stride, and here came the slick metallic sound of the nanotempered adamantium blade extending from its mount in the carved aquila, triggering the movements driven deep into his muscle memories over hundreds of hours of drill. A deep low lunge put all the weight of body and weapon behind the blade as it went into one man's throat. There was a quick red snap of las-fire as his hands convulsed on his gun and then he jerked himself off the blade and crumpled amid the stink of blood and scorched gravel.

The second shuddered a moment, too paralysed to decide to shoot Håffith or Adalbrect, and then Haffith found an angle safe enough to shoot out the man's knee. He went down soundlessly from that, only just drawing breath to cry out when Adalbrect's blade came in again, another throat strike that silenced him for good.

Suddenly the world was full of sounds again. Shouts and footfalls from behind the carrier. The hatch of the driver's cab swinging open behind him. His own breathing.

Boots crunched into the stony dust behind him and a hand clapped Adalbrect on the shoulder.

'Valiant,' said Colonel Tosk. 'Might've wanted to shoot them, but valiant.'

Adalbrect turned and held up the rod. The blade was still out and the golden aquila was shiny with blood.

'The aquila doesn't shirk a fight, colonel.' He blinked. 'With respect.'

'Respect indeed,' Tosk answered him, his hand still heavy on Adalbrect's shoulder. 'Feel up to joining my man there to get the rest of them?'

'Uh,' said Adalbrect. He hadn't quite thought that there would be more of them. The colonel's hand was turning him to face Haffith, who was already tilting his head.

'They're scattering into the machines,' the adjutant said. 'Let's get some of us on their traces.' He stepped away and Sister Sarell fell in behind him.

'Lots of pairs of eyes, that's the way,' Colonel Tosk put in. 'Join in with the Mechanicus guards, look like you're helping, and tell us anything you notice about these stowaways. Same comes back to you, of course.'

Adalbrect nodded, shifted his grip so that the aquila was held high like a standard, drew his pistol with his other hand and followed Haffith and Sarell out into the graveyard.

* * *

THEY STILL SMELLED. Adalbrect hadn't expected that. They didn't stink, but they smelled. He could pick up a faint metallic tang to the air from the scorched hulls, and the more cloying smell of oils. The desert-scent was flat and barely noticeable, but something thicker had clotted under it and Adalbrect realised he was smelling blood. Not the fresh stuff on the head of his sceptre, but the stale blood and vitals of the Imperial Guard and who knew how many innocent Asheki, still coating the spikes and hooks of the Heritor's Woe Machines.

That thought hit him in the gut, and a moment later when a las-shot spat against the hull over his head and knocked the patina off the metal, he found himself thinking *I'm wearing blood* as he felt the powder settling on his face. He dropped into a crouch, unthinkingly leaned back against the hull behind him, and then yelled in pain.

Straight away another two shots skewered the hull, smoke puffing up from the impacts an arm's length from him. He answered with his pistol, shooting jerkily into the gloom with no clear idea of where the shots had even come from, until Haffith snapped 'Fire discipline!' over his shoulder and laid down one-two-three measured stub bursts at something Adalbrect couldn't see. He tried to drop further into a crouch but the bright and gleeful pain skewered further into his shoulder and he let out another yell. Something was holding him up. Gritting his teeth and growling over the sensation, he tried to shift, then to push himself up, and each time the barb twisted in his shoulder and held him still and wriggling like an angler's bait. Breathing hard, he muttered a verse of Tobisch's Fourth Psalm under his breath – *'with a mirror to His radiant Throne I burn away the night'* – and made himself hold still. Haffith was gone into the shadows, no telling where, but the evening around them had come alive. From somewhere off to Adalbrect's left came a string of metallic clangs and two voices cursing, one in the hoarse Ashek continental dialect and one in the rolling vowels of the Pragar lowhives. After a few moments they were drowned out by a snarling chainsword motor directly ahead, which revved and then dropped long enough for Adalbrect to hear Sarell's voice in the middle distance and the *screech-bang* of bolt shells.

Adalbrect became aware that a foul, greasy adrenaline sweat was oozing into his clothes and giving a chilly edge to the breeze. He shivered and then grunted again when the movement shifted whatever it was that was hooked into his back. He tried to find a way to stand that would take the pressure off it, tried to find a direction he could move that felt like it was lifting him free, and each time he ended up standing in his half-crouch, whispering prayers that increasingly sounded like gabble to ward off panic. He was afraid of what he might do to himself if he panicked even more than he was afraid of what would happen when his legs, already cramping, couldn't hold him in a half-squat any longer. Bracing himself for the pain, he tried shifting his weight and stretching each leg out in turn while he kept the pistol nosing at the shadows around him, but he couldn't stop a groan from leaking out between his teeth as the barb winkled back and forth in his flesh. With the groan, the burst of shots from deeper in the graveyard and the tightening of his senses from the pain, he didn't hear the approaching footsteps until they were next to him.

'He's one.'

'I know, I can see, hurry up.'

'Do what with him?'

'Do's you think, but hurry.' Curt vowels, consonants clicked against the teeth. Ashek talk, although he'd need Sarell's ear to identify the region. Adalbrect gulped air, closed his eyes for a moment and rummaged in his mind for the rhetorical tools he'd practised on his voyage here. He lifted up his rod of office, sweat bursting out of him again as the movement flexed the pierced muscles next to his shoulder blade.

'See the aquila,' he said. He'd woven the phrase into so many of his sermons that the words should be almost talismanic to anyone who'd heard him. 'See his gaze on you now? His wings spread wide and there's room for us all in their shade.'

One of the shapes had turned its back. A flogging, that would have meant at the Chillbreak mission square, turning the back on a raised aquila. Adalbrect could see it making small, panicky darts of its head. Then the other labourer pushed its masked face up to his own.

'Know you for the preaching-man, so quick now. What's your aquila want with the Kings? You understand these things.' The man's voice was quickening and lowering. 'What's the aquila want with the Kings? What's this Headstone? *What?*'

Adalbrect was paralysed. The urgency in the voice was as palpable as the gouging in his back, but the pain was disorienting him and he couldn't start to make the connections. Kings? Kings? Was that what the hive-lords had been called before the Archenemy had deposed them? The Missionaria Galaxia was accomplished at speed-briefing its agents, but its learning sessions weren't geared to situations like this. What was going on?

Then the man switched his little punch-cleaver to his left hand, reached out with his right and gripped the blood-painted golden aquila as Adalbrect's arm sagged.

'Eh,' he muttered, seemingly to himself. 'Dead thing. No use.' He was turning to his companion and never really got the chance to see that that had been the wrong thing to say.

Adalbrect swung his right arm up and jammed his hand in behind his head as though he were trying to scratch his back with the pistol barrel. Face contorted, he fired, fired again, and a third time, hearing the snap of the shots, and the gouging pain turned searing.

A moment later the barb that had held him came loose as he shot through its mounting and Adalbrect

stumbled forward, half-embracing the man who'd inter-
rogated him. Both of them shouted, Adalbrect in pain
and the Asheki in angry surprise, as Adalbrect's laspistol
went off straight into the ribs of his companion. The first
shot staggered him, spasming and choking with a smoking pockmark drilled into his torso, and the second and
third struck him in the chest and silenced him.

Adalbrect saw stars as the other man's forehead
cracked into his own, and felt his legs start to sag. He
tried to turn the movement to his advantage, gripping
the enemy's shade-shawl and pivoting, desperate to
avoid falling back against the barbed hull a second time.
But the shawl tore and the man kicked him hard in the
belly, sending him sprawling on the packed stones with
his shoulder shouting in pain.

'We listen to our Kings, not to you,' he heard through
the pain. 'This is the night they find their voices. Hear
that, eagle-licker?' The man was grabbing for his dead
companion's gun, barking out some syllables that Adalbrect didn't catch. A benediction for a comrade or an
appeasement to the weapon, he couldn't tell.

And it didn't matter, because he was rolling onto his
side with his teeth bared. Another insult to the aquila,
and this one would die for it. Two insults, two lives.
Not enough payment to extract, but the best a mortal
could do.

'Wings for Him!' he snarled and used the burning in
his back as fuel to drive the rod forward. It caught the
man in the sternum, the blade burying itself until the
aquila's heads were pushing into his skin, and he let
out a groan like a bending girder and fell to his knees
with the rod in front of him. As Adalbrect struggled up
onto his feet the man tilted forward, grounding the rod
and sinking onto it, until Adalbrect yanked it out and
away with his left hand. The man continued to hunch,
the back of his neck bare with the shade-shawl gone,
and Adalbrect whirled the impromptu weapon up
and over. His arm was strong and the head of the rod

heavy, and the man's neck parted in one stroke.

A moment later the strength dropped out of him. He went down on one knee, breath rasping and the gouge in his shoulder burning like hot cinders jammed under his skin. He worked the catch on the rod and with the blade retracted Adalbrect planted its pommel on the dirt and leaned his head against the blood-sticky gold, murmuring lines from the Militant Pilgrim's Prayer.

'*And another struck down, and another, and let each be dust beneath that righteous tread...*'

'Here he is!' came a voice he didn't recognise, swimming into his head through the dark and the pain. 'The young fellow, the bluecoat. Got him, he's back here!'

'What? He didn't even move!' That was Haffith's voice, somewhere behind the bobbing orange lanterns that were appearing through the gaps in the dead machines. The lieutenant's tone was bantering, only not. 'Brother Adalbrect? That you? I wondered where you'd run off to. Didn't occur to me you'd just decide to hole up and... wait... no. Wait. Are you injured? Throne's foot, yes, all right, you two! He's injured, let's get him moving. Brother, can you tell me where you're hit?'

Adalbrect shook his head. His mouth was suddenly very dry, wringing his words down to a croak, and he could feel his balance going. A vision danced by him of falling forward with a great flap of flesh ripping free from his back. He clenched his fists and concentrated on not falling. Not falling. The dark hulks around him tilted and the ground seemed to float up towards him and then away again. He groaned. *Not* falling.

'Agh, all right, I see what's happened.' Haffith was up by his side now, peering behind his shoulder in the lantern-light. 'Steady him, get his arms, don't let him fall. We have you, brother, stay with us. You're in shock. Say a prayer of fortitude with me.'

They went over the words together. Haffith knew a slightly different version to Adalbrect, but they finished on the same lines, and by that time each of Adalbrect's arms was being gripped by a burly convoy guard. His thoughts were sluggish and his head wanted to loll forward, but he finally realised what had seemed so odd about saying the prayer. His hands were empty.

'Mhhmmm...' he managed, then scraped his tongue along his teeth and worked his cheeks until he had enough moisture in his mouth to talk. 'My aquila. I dropped it. Can you take it... out of the dirt?' Haffith bent for a moment and then Adalbrect felt the familiar weight and grip in his hand. It settled him a little.

'Don't move too much, brother, and don't get any closer to that bastard's hull again. You can see there's plenty more of those shitsump barbs left on it. I'm not game to try and– wait. Sister! Sister!' At the edge of the lantern-light there came a pale glimmer of tunic and a glint of gold: Sister Sarell was coming back to them.

'The preacher's wounded. I'd like one of us to stay with him until we get an all-clear.'

'Do you think they'll double back?' Sarell asked.

'Who knows? At this point we barely know what they're even doing. Some of them hid on the delegation convoy and helped a second lot break in behind them. No telling what they want.'

'But I'm betting it's not to shake the magos's hand when he arrives,' Adalbrect managed to gasp out. Breathing deeply hurt his shoulder, but breathing shallowly made him dizzy.

'He'll have already had instructions to delay his landing,' said Haffith. 'He'd better have.' He stood for a moment longer, then stared up at the sky where the speck of the Headstone hung, high enough to still catch some yellow-red daylight. Haffith looked at it a moment, cursed to himself and turned to Sarell.

'Change of plans, sister and brother. Master Adalbrect, can you walk?'

THERE HAD NEVER been any question but that Kovind would carry the main key into the graveyard. He had fretted a little about the other two, knowing how short time would be once they were under way and that not even Psinter would be able to get to two Kings in time. So Jopell was luckier than he knew that he'd hit on the plan to infiltrate the Adeptus convoy: that had earned him the third key and the leadership of the third crew. Nobody else had even remotely the seniority in the Traditions, or even in the worldly hierarchy of the manories. The three of them it was.

He carried the key the way the rakes of the outer manory walks used to carry their knives: gripped loosely in his left hand, the length of it turned back against his arm under his sleeve, the metal cool against his skin. His autopistol was in his other hand and he kept it up and ready as they ran. It was further into nightfall than he had anticipated and as it had darkened he'd been afraid that it would be harder to keep direction through the maze of wrecked machines without the reassuring might of the Kings against the skyline to urge him on. But now he felt unstoppable, as though he were running on a high-speed pedway back in the High Hive, carried along unerringly. The higher mysteries were not for Kovind Shek. He was steeped in Asheki culture, the Customs of knowledge, the Traditions ordering its holders, the ancient Practices of engineering that the glorious Heritor had shown them how to bring to majestic and terrible perfection. But on a night like this he could almost feel the most sublime mysteries that the Heritor's preachers had sung and danced and screamed about, some power that was carrying him through the night on sombre wings.

The greater moon was beginning to show, and now he *could* see them, towering over the piled-up machines around them like hive-spires over manufactory blocks. The Heritor's four greatest children. The Hammerstone Kings.

The Mechanicus guarded the approaches to them, but only during the day when the labour crews were roaming the graveyard. His way to the feet of the Tread-ing King was clear, and he couldn't help himself: he fired a jubilant autopistol burst into the night sky and whooped for his crew to follow as he opened his stride.

The key seemed to prickle against his skin. Kovind Shek lifted it to his mouth and kissed it, vaulted the ram-prow of a Nadzybar's Fist assault engine, ducked reflexively at an exchange of stub-shots behind him, and ran on.

ADALBRECT'S LEGS HADN'T been injured, but that wasn't the problem. The problem was the iron barb sawing away in his shoulder and the waves of grey washing across his vision. His left arm was draped across Sarell's shoulders and he clung to his aquila rod with his right hand as though it were an anchor to consciousness.

'If we just try and wrench it out we'll rip your shoul-der to pieces,' Sarell said. 'You bumped up against a Flensing-Wheel hull. Those spikes are made to shred the flesh.'

'Thank you,' he managed. 'Think you... said that... already.'

'Well, you need to keep your mind occupied.'

'With something other than... what's in my shoulder, maybe? *Ahh!*'

'That was my fault. I moved my arm. Not on purpose. Those scriptures about the righteousness of pain in battle take on a new perspective at times like this, don't they?'

'Something *other* that what's in my shoulder.'

'We're almost at the carriers. And we haven't been shot at. And you threw two enemies of the Emperor out of this world and into the endless emptiness where they'll never stand in the way of the light again. What have we to complain about, really?'

'*Nngghn*. Don't! Hurts when I laugh.'

'Your fault. I'm not joking. The Sororitas never joke.'

'Never?'

'So far as you know. *Medic!*' Sarell shouted ahead to the face peering at them through the carrier cockpit window.

PSINTER DIDN'T LET herself look up at it, not yet. The route to the Blighting King led through an area where the new crews had dumped piles of Gallowspider wreckage from the fourth battle of High Defile. Weaving among them, she couldn't afford to stop and look up and she didn't dare take her eyes off her path while she was moving.

'Covering you!' shouted Gatter, the chief of the crew she'd been given to lead, over the crackle of the las-salvoes he was spraying back behind them with never a hope of hitting anything. 'Cover her!' he shouted again, this time by her ear, and what shooters they had left behind them obligingly sent a ragged little volley off into the dark. Over the end of it Psinter could hear the answering Imperial las-fire, slower and more deliberate. More accurate, too, because when Gatter yelled 'Two down! Three!' she realised she hadn't heard cries. Whoever was chasing them was firing killshots.

She jinked to her right and found a path through the middle of a torn-in-half 'spider chassis that would get her into the next aisle and able to spring towards the King in cover. She almost paralysed herself trying to stop and weigh it up – a dangerous few metres, but the thought of dying in an Imperial's gunsight with her mission incomplete was unbearable. Before she'd consciously made the decision she had swerved again, panting, running with exaggerated upward twitches of her knees as though she could already feel cuts on her legs.

'Throwing!' yelled Gatter and Psinter heard a clink of metal bouncing off metal, then the throaty explosion of one of the hand-bombs they'd cobbled together from cutter-fuel and scourcrystal. 'Covering!' he yelled again, and more las-fire. Stupid macho idiot. He had puffed up his chest when he saw his crew was escorting a woman to the King, and had been running and shouting the whole way, ignoring her orders. If they lived through this she was going to hang his balls from the King's...

Too late. He hadn't followed in her footsteps, had tried to clamber through the Gallowspider frame instead, and now he was shrieking and kicking in a tangle of wire he hadn't bothered to look at before he brushed at it. The 'spiders were decked with memory-cored razorwire – the casualty rates among their cutter crews was insane – and as Gatter thrashed it contracted and hoisted him upward. Blood started pattering down onto the dust under his boots.

'Pull yourself together,' she hissed at him. 'Stay still so you're not cut any more and keep shooting as long as you can!' There was no sign that he heard her. She pondered shooting him, but that would let their followers know there was at least one more left out there. She couldn't see any of the rest of her crew at all.

She only needed a few more minutes. Psinter flitted away into the moonshadows, the key to the Blighting King gripped in one hand.

'Graveyard Shrine, do you read me? Graveyard Shrine, please respond on any band. Graveyard Shrine! I am Sister Goha Sarell, travelling in a Munitorum carrier towards your location.' Adalbrect was kneeling in the passenger compartment of the carrier with Kinosa steadying him and Vosheni sponging blood from the iron stump sticking out of his shoulder. Even the attempt to pull away his jacket had been agony. A numbdrop from the carrier's medical kit had blurred the pain a little, but blurred his wits along with it.

'Tell me again what they said?' asked Kinosa, scowling with the effort of keeping him stable as the carrier rocked through a ninety-degree turn.

'Th–' Adalbrect's mouth clicked dry. He was dehydrating from shock, and nobody had brought a water-flask. 'This is the night the Kings find their voices. Don't know what it means.' He bowed his head again. He was shamefully glad of his dry mouth, of an excuse to stop talking. This had to have been planned under their noses. A whole plot, a whole belief system ticking away while he had happily gone on sermonising at them every six hours and writing sunny letters back to the Missionaria compound at the High Hive ruins. Participation in litanies and hymns is encouraging. Positive reaction displayed to the aquila and the parables selected by the head of mission. Congregants appear to be accepting the spiritual need for the confessional and the scourging rack.

Congregants have risen in arms and proclaimed four Archenemy war-engines to be their Kings. Adalbrect closed his eyes.

'Graveyard Shrine!' came Sarell's voice from the cab, tinny through the internal vox. 'This is Sarell, Adepta Sororitas Order of the Quill, to any Mechanicus personnel listening! We have reason to believe this insurgent raid is directed at the... Hammerstone Kings. R-Respond!'

'What is that?' asked Vosheni, and Kinosa made an uncertain little sound in her throat. Adalbrect, who had thought it was just another note in the ringing, rustling headache stealing up on him, opened his eyes and listened.

A moment later the carrier slammed to a halt. Vosheni and Kinosa cried out; Adalbrect pitched onto his face on the floor matting and howled in pain.

But they could all hear it now, over the vox. Even when Sarell wasn't speaking, it was getting louder. Some kind of machine-cant, some counter-transmission, but nothing that was intelligible to them.

Just chatter.

JOPELL KNELT IN the cockpit of the Poison King, wheezing softly with exhaustion, watching the flickering frost-blue light of the key and listening to the chatter. A fat-barrelled shotgun sat by his side. A crude thing, not a manufactorium job, it looked like it had been made on the sly by sympathisers in the reconstruction camps. Jopell liked that. It meant there were more survivors carrying on the old ways of Ashek than just the ones who'd followed the coded messages and come out to the graveyard. While the Traditions were kept alive and the Customs followed and the Practices taught, Ashek II was still her true self. The Inevitable Conclave would form again. And Asphodel would return to them. Jopell was sure of it.

He opened his eyes and half stood, grunting as his leg muscles cramped: too much running and climbing then a long cold stop. The Poison King had a poor view: it had done most of its work either right up against Hammerstone fortresses or Legio Tempesta Titans, where big windows were a target, or else at tens of kilometres away with its ugly crest of missile batteries, when all the fighting was over auspex or missile cameras and windows were a distraction. He peered through one of the little armoured slits, although this high up there was little to see.

Across from him, just over a kilometre away, was the slope-backed Blighting King, its collar of rocket-tubes casting the giant chassis into shadow, the smooth line of the launching-ramp up its back now jagged from Imperial bombing. Psinter should be in there by now, lugging her key and her power cell, getting ready to create the second link in the circle.

And the third... Ignoring the muffled sounds of stubfire that were starting to float up through the liftwell, Jopell walked stiffly to the second wall and bent to a vision-slit there. The Treading King struck a fierce silhouette against the horizon, the front of its body locked in its reared-back position, all four front limbs still posed like a pugilist's. He had heard that the Treading King had ripped the turret off a Shadowsword superheavy tank and dropped it onto the gatehouse at the Passage Stair fortifications to crush a void-shield link. He'd heard that it had simply torn both arms off a Reaver Titan that had allowed it to get too close. In the dark, Jopell's smile was rueful. It would have been wonderful to see the Kings reawakened, repaired, revenging themselves on the cog and the aquila alike, but he wouldn't see it. Even if he could sneak back down through the guts of the King and away, he had been given the Poison King to break into, and it had its name for a reason. Its broad treads had taken it out onto the hotstone flows, sucking up the radioactive silt and sifting out the precious rare elements, processing them in foundries in its belly whose complexity and compactness were testament that Asphodel's genius was not just in machines of destruction. Jopell had climbed up the King through those very foundries, crawling along mineral conveyors and squirming his bulk through the sifter shafts, and now he was coated in toxic metals and bathed in radiation. He already thought he could feel his fingertips and toes going numb. He doubted he'd live a week.

But how could he be unhappy? How could he resent not living to see the Kings ride again, when here, now, he had done the deed that made that awakening possible? Jopell's little smile grew, split his face, became a happy little laugh. The blue of his key was flickering green as Psinter's transmission came from the cockpit of the Blighting King, and as the shooting below got loud enough for Jopell to hear the ricochets and smell the smoke he saw the red flashes that were transmissions from the Treading King. The chatter was amplifying, ramifying as it raced around the circuit that the three Kings' brains had made. They had done it.

Jopell walked to the floor hatch and peered down the ladder in time to see the orange wash of a hand-bomb explosion, the concussion rocking him back a little with his ears now numb to the chatter. He nodded approvingly, grabbed the floor hatch and dragged it over and shut. It was a primitive fitting, but the Poison King was the first King the Heritor had built here, and the most functional. Kovind had saved the grandest one for himself, of course, but at a moment like this Jopell couldn't even bring himself to resent the bastard. They had done it, after all.

Jopell checked the load in the shotgun, then jammed the butt down through the locking wheel to hold it in place. He positioned himself over it so his corpse would fall onto the wheel and weigh the hatch down, then reached for the trigger. He was still smiling as the blast blew all the chatter out of his head.

THE ACT OF craning his head back made Adalbrect groan, but he had got some strength back into his legs and he lurched forward towards the Graveyard Shrine behind Sarell. Even to his blurred vision it was impressive: a grey, floodlit ziggurat topped with a heavy ironwork Machina Opus and sprouting a coronet of gridwork transmission masts. Those were what Sarell was frantically gesturing to as she closed with the two adepts who watched them from the top of the ceremonial steps.

'Daprokk! Which one of you is Enginseer Daprokk?' Adalbrect thought he was probably imagining the expressions of surprise as the two red cowls looked at one another, but a moment later one of them, the one whose gown and hood were the brighter scarlet, descended to meet them. The enginseer's face was in shadow but for four small violet eyelights.

'Enginseer? The one I spoke to on the vox? You didn't say whether or not you could hear what we could hear. Can you hear that?' Behind them the door to the carrier was open and they could plainly hear the odd transmission chattering beneath a layer of static. Sarell waved her hand towards the noise. 'Please confirm you can hear it.' For someone whose calling was studying communication and language, Sarell was being astonishingly blunt with the robed shape in front of her, but the enginseer's reply was perfectly calm.

'Our transmechanic is evaluating the signal according to the mysteries of her order, which I shall not discuss. The signal is not considered to pose a threat to our installation, and certainly not to yourselves. Its relation to the insurgent action here tonight shall be evaluated. That action is being brought under control. There is no cause for impatience, Sister.' Daprokk had apparently only just noticed that Sarell was literally hopping from foot to foot. 'We may proceed to treat your wounded as a token of hospitality, our Order to yours.'

'No!' she shouted into the enginseer's face, enough to make him recoil with a hand out. 'Jers, tell him!'

'The Kings are finding their voice,' Adalbrect croaked as the eyelights turned and regarded him. 'It's not just some... harmless thing. They're doing something with the Kings.'

'Initial source of the signal may correspond, under analysis, to–' Daprokk took another step back as Sarell interrupted him again.

'You don't need–' With an almost audible effort she got control of herself, and said, 'Magos, you don't need to analyse the signal. You need to block it. Now. Things are happening that we are not in control of. We must re-establish control. Adalbrect overheard the insurgents talking about the Kings finding their voices. Our forces have chased insurgents who were breaking into the Kings. They know about that ship of yours, the Head-stone.'

'The Headstone! They are directing a plan against it? Against Magos Tey?'

'Against the dignitary you are bringing to examine the graveyard, sir, and this is bigger than we thought they were capable of and they're in the Kings now and we don't know what they're going to do in there.' Daprokk's hands and the dendrite arching over his head were all making small, involuntary movements. The darker-robed adept at the top of the stairs stood unmoving. It – he? – had been joined by another figure, stocky and thick-legged with a strange metal hump standing up behind its head. Neither of them spoke a word. 'Can you guarantee that the Headstone is out of range of any weapon they might bring back online? Can you guarantee that this transmission is so harmless that we can just let them make it? We don't have the power or the skill to do this from the carrier, but you have these gantry antennae and a transmechanic.' Sarell took a deep breath and made a deeper bow. 'Enginseer, please. Will you consider what I have told you?'

The violet lights under the cowl seemed to stare at her for an age.

THE END DIDN'T come quite as Kovind Shek expected.

He had been alone by the time he reached the Treading King. The bulk of his men had spent themselves in staggered ambushes to slow down their pursuers, and the rest had holed up in a row of wrecked Blight-Balls and begun a ferocious firefight with a platoon of Mechanicus guards coming from the Graveyard Shrine to try and intercept them. Under cover of their last two hand-bombs, Kovind had swung up through the scaffolding around the King's rear legs, slipped in through a plasma breach and begun working his way up through the compartment levels by touch and memory.

The Treading King had been stormed, not abandoned or killed with firepower, and every hatch had been blasted open. There was no way for him to secure the route behind him and so, after he'd ridden out the heady rush of seeing the three colours of the transmission loop, Kovind had made ready to double back and fight. He had only allowed himself a short glance out of the command window at the night's final prize, and had fought back the urge to weep a little: Asphodel's greatest creation, the mighty Inheritor King, its magnificent train of spires and steeples surrounded by such junk and pawed over by cog-lickers and eagle-lickers and...

But he had remembered his dignity. He was a man of

rank, one of the few with a bloodline that had allowed
him to take part of his world's name as a badge. He
could not have asked for a death more fitting to that
rank, not if he really stopped to think about what he was
doing. He reloaded his autopistol and felt the weight of
the hand-bombs in his satchel.

The chatter sped up again, acquired a squeal and then
a bass note. Kovind had coded some of it himself, had
Psinter refine and recompile it, had drawn on mysteries he had had etched directly into deep memory and
could barely recall consciously. Now in the brains of the
Kings it was feeding into a matrix that Asphodel himself
had laid down. What concepts, what layers of logic and
unlogic, might that mind have wielded? Kovind glanced
back at the transmission deck. The three colours were
still there, the three Kings' brains all parallel-processing
the code as it grew. The telltales on the power-block
he had connected to the codecasters were still green, It
could run for an hour yet. Could he hold off any Imperial invaders that long? He could try.

And then the subtle song of the chatter matrix was
defaced. An ugly hoot of interference blared out of the
codecaster lectern, scraping through Kovind's transmission. He stood there for a moment, pistol dangling in
his hand, mouth open, as the lights on the great key
flickered, darkened for a moment and came up again,
struggling to find their old rhythm. Now in among the
chatter was a reedy discord, weaving around a crackling
syncopation that Kovind knew had no place in his code.
They were being jammed.

In a bound he was back at the console, but what could
he do? How could they have prepared for a countersig-
nal? Could they? Kovind growled aloud and looped a
fist around to strike himself in the mouth. Focus. Act
your rank. Self-recrimination was for lessers.

What could they do? Recoding on the fly was out of
the question. Modify the frequency? How could he get
a signal to Psinter or Jopell, if they were even still alive?

Override the code for a moment? Try to work an instruction into it? Kovind was unaware that he was making panicked little moans under his breath as he scanned the console, looking for the right controls.

This ended with glorious battle in the halls of the Treading King. This ended with his little work entering the greater work and the Hammerstone Kings walking again. It didn't end like this, not with the squalid little redcloaks and their filthy–

The hellgun shot cratered the top of Kovind Shek's spine and the back of his head, and the explosive vaporisation snapped him forward at the waist. His face bounced off the controls and his corpse slid slowly down the lectern. By the time it had sunk onto its knees the Guard were in the command bridge and a boot kicked Kovind's body aside. A moment later the chatter squealed to a stop as Haffith tore the great key out of the codecaster and broke it in half under his heel.

'HAS TRANSMECHANIC AJJI managed to confirm what the signal was?'

'No, magos,' Daprokk answered. The breeze plucked at his red cowl. The two of them were standing beneath the Machina Opus atop the shrine ziggurat, using vocal conversation that the wind would render hard for vox-thieves to overhear. 'We... selected a course of action that incidentally matched that which the other Adeptus had... happened to...'

'You took their advice, enginseer. No need to pretend you didn't. I was watching you, remember? I'm not holding it against you.' Daprokk's hands twitched for a moment.

'Without knowing what the signal was,' his interlocutor went on, 'we've no way of knowing whether we managed to defeat its purpose or not. Speaking as part of a priesthood that takes gaps in knowledge as an affront, still this is a particular concern.'

'The Sister seemed to believe that it was an attack

that was to use the three most functional Hammerstone Kings as weapons against the *Ramosh Incalculate*,'
Daprokk ventured. 'An attack on you, even, sir. The
initial purpose of the delegation was to meet you, but at
the time they set off they apparently believed you were
still on board the Headstone.'

'Even they're using that nickname now, then?'
Daprokk didn't know how to answer that. 'No matter. I don't believe this is any reason to alter my plans,
Enginseer Daprokk. Except in one respect. I think it is
time to speed them up. When the transmechanic has
completed her current analytical cycle ask her to create
an encrypted tightlink to Shipmaster Tobin, please.'

Daprokk made the sign of the cog, canted a formal, if
slightly rushed, salutation, and hurried to the lifthead,
noetic speech already radiating out from his personal
links and feeding into the shrine's manifold. The other
magos, in his dusty robe that was almost as much russet
as red, watched him go. The successful jamming of the
transmission had not eased his mind any.

He walked around the sculpture, adjusting his vision
for the floodlights, and stared up at the King the insurgents hadn't managed to breach. The Inheritor King's
colossal raked prow and spire-bridge loomed over the
shrine in the dark.

'Not the reception I'd wanted,' murmured Magos-
Parralact Galhoulin Tey. 'I wonder what will happen next?'

DEEP NIGHT IN the graveyard. Blackness and silence in
the bridge of the Inheritor King. The breeze-blown dust
against the windows could not be heard in here, and the
combat shutters were drawn, sealing the little wedge-
shaped chamber off from the gentle Asheki moonlight.
The great throne where Asphodel had sat, the coding pit
where he had crafted his chattercodes, the pulpits from
which his lieutenants had commanded this King and
passed his orders out to his armies, all now empty and
lost in the dark.

There were no lights on the control banks. No movement of instruments, no colour or sound in the readouts. No printout spools. No glowing runes. No power.

Almost none. Deep in a system core that the King's conquerors had dismissed as inactive, a warm little worm of electricity still flickered. At the call from the Blighting King it awoke, flexed and sparked for a split-second to accept the transmission instructions from the Poison King. Finally, in barely a blink, came the inload that the intelligences of the other three Kings had compiled between them. Only a blink before the suffocating fog of jamming squeal came frothing up from the machine-shrines' masts, but enough.

For the half-year since Asphodel had fled this chamber the secret nerve-matrices buried deep in the King's brain had been without function, empty. Blank paper, an unsown field.

Now the pen had been wielded. Now the seeds were here.

In the darkness of the Inheritor King's core, an intelligence began to wake.

In the comparatively short period of time since he unleashed his fiction upon the readers of the Black Library, the talented Mr Dembski-Bowden (that's 'bow' as in the front of a boat, not the thing that fires an arrow) has more than proved his chops with some frankly pant-damaging pieces of writing awesomeness. For the sake of balance, however, and for the entertainment of those who get the reference, I feel this introduction should also include the words HI DAN ABNETT.

Regicide is named after the chess-like game I feature a lot of people playing in 40K. The story's set on Balhaut, site of the great battle that started the whole Sabbat Worlds Crusade. In revisiting this ground zero origin point, Aaron is also delving into areas that are now increasingly occupying me in the Gaunt books: the Blood Pact, the nature of the enemy, and the nature of the Crusade itself. Although set twenty-five years before the 'present' in Gaunt continuity, this story provides a powerful addendum to both the story of Warmaster Slaydo, and the revelations made in the novel Blood Pact.

Dan Abnett

REGICIDE

Aaron Dembski-Bowden

I

SHE SPOKE THE words with a knife in her hand and a lie on her lips.

'Tell me what happened, and I'll let you live.'

Even if he had nothing else left, he still had his voice. She hadn't taken his tongue.

'You know what happened,' he said.

In the knife's reflection, he caught a glimpse of what was left of his face. The smile he couldn't seem to shake was a mess of split lips and bloody gums.

Her face was covered by a carnival mask. Only her eyes showed through, and they didn't look human.

She said, 'Do not struggle,' as if she expected him to actually obey.

Do not struggle. Now there was an amusing idea.

His shins and wrists were leashed together by pulley ropes. It looked like they came from an Imperial Guard tank. Probably *his* tank, he realised. Either way, there'd be no breaking free in a hurry. Even with her knife in his hands, it would take an age to saw through those ropes.

His head sagged back into the mud and the dust. While his eyes ached too much to see clearly, the sky met his sore gaze with bruises of its own. Choked and grey – heaven promised a storm – but the moon yet showed through cracks in the caul of clouds.

He lay in the rubble, knowing that before this place was a ruin, it was a battlefield, and before it was a battlefield, it was a public marketplace. Apparently something of a pilgrim trap, where relics and icons of dubious validity found their way from sweating hands into bandaged ones; a desperate industry based around hope, fuelled by deceit and copper coins.

He blinked sweat from his aching eyes and wondered where his weapons were.

'Tell me,' she came even closer, and the knife turned in the moonlight, 'what happened on the eighteenth hour of the tenth day.'

Already the words felt like a legend. *The eighteenth hour of the tenth day.* She whispered it like some sacred date from antiquity, when it was only hours before.

'You know what happened,' he said again.

'*Tell me,*' she repeated, feverish in her curiosity, betraying her need.

His smile cracked into something more, promoting itself to a laugh – a laugh that felt good even though it hurt like hell. The sound was made by a punctured lung, flawed by cracked ribs, and left his body through bleeding lips. But it was still a laugh.

She used her knife as she'd been using it for over an hour now: to scrawl letters of pain across his bare chest. 'Tell me,' she whispered, 'what happened.'

He could smell his own blood, rich over the scent of scorched stone. He could see it, trickling falls of red painting his torso below the jagged cuts.

'You know what happened, witch. You lost the war.'

* * *

II

HE WAS IN a different place when he next opened his eyes.

His neck gave protesting twinges as he looked this way and that. The arched doorways, the broken gargoyles littering the floor, the stains of ash marking the pyre-sites of holy books...

This was the Templum Imperialis.

Well. One of them.

Muffled thunder betrayed the presence of distant artillery. Whoever this witch was, she'd barely moved him from the front lines.

He swallowed, but it was too thick and tasted of blood. Fists tightened as he tested the bonds that leashed his wrists to the chair. Nothing. No yield, no slack, and the chair itself was fastened to the floor. He was going nowhere.

'Stop struggling,' her voice came from behind. Footsteps echoed in the small chamber as she moved to stand before him. 'There is no dignity in it.' Her words were coloured by an ugly, halting accent. She wasn't just from off-world – she'd barely spoken Gothic in her life.

'Who are you?' he asked, and punctuated the demand by spitting blood onto the tiled floor.

She stroked her fingertip along the hideous mask covering her face. 'I am Blood Pact.'

The words meant nothing to him. Unfortunately, what she did next meant a great deal. With a chuckle from behind the mask, she reached for a weapon sheathed at her hip.

'Your sword, yes?'

Instinct drove him to test his bonds again. He tried not to look at the blade in her hands – seeing her touch it with her seven-fingered hands made his heart beat faster. He'd preferred it when she'd been holding the knife.

'That's better,' she smiled. 'It is time to speak some truths.'

'You're not going to like anything I say.' He forced the words through a wall of tight teeth. 'Drop the sword.'

With her free hand, she stroked his jawline, the gesture gentle, grazing the unshaven skin without scratching it. Her fingernails had crescent-moon bloodstains beneath them, but they were old, from previous inflictions of pain.

'You want this sword,' she whispered, 'and you want to see the colour of my blood as I lie dead upon this floor.'

He didn't answer. With her free hand, she lowered the black mask that covered half of her face. It was a carnival mask, perversely featured and rendered in dull iron, with a witch's hook nose and curving chin. The face it revealed was both lovelier and uglier, all at once.

His captor took a deep breath, inhaling the scent of recent battle and burned books.

'You are one of the Argentum.' She licked a slow circuit of her black lips, as if tasting the word. Even her smile was tainted. Her face was a canvas of meticulous scars, inflicted by a madman's hand.

He laughed again, though thirst made the sound ragged and raw.

'What is amusing?' she asked, closer to sneering than speaking. 'You think we cannot recognise the difference between Imperial regiments?'

'What gave it away?' He inclined his head to his silver shoulder guard, where the Warmaster's laurel-wreathed skull was displayed in detailed engraving, and banged his silver vambraces against the back of the chair he was tied to. The same sigil was repeated on each of them, in echo of the Warmaster's own armour.

Had he been able, he'd have shot her through the eye with his hellgun, which was – assuming it was still in one piece – embossed with silver aquilas on both sides of the stock.

'Perhaps I dress like this because it's cold outside,' he said. 'All the silver keeps me warm.'

She smiled, as if indulging a spoiled child.

'You are one of the Argentum.' He didn't like how she mouthed the word, like she hungered for it. 'The Silver Kindred.' She swallowed, and something wet clicked in her throat. 'The Warmaster's Own. How proud you must be.'

He didn't dignify that with a response.

'You will tell me what I wish to know,' she insisted with stately politeness.

'Never in life.'

Fine words, but they came out badly, slowed by blood-thickened saliva. Throne, he wished she'd put the sword down. The hurt of seeing it in her hands went beyond a matter of personal pride – beyond even regimental honour.

'We know the customs of the Silver Kindred,' she said, and her voice was rendered gentler still by the whispering hiss of profane fingertips on sacred steel. 'To lose your weapon is to betray the Warmaster, isn't it? It carries the harshest penalty.'

She didn't wait for an answer, instead drawing the blade from its scabbard. Steel sang in the air as the blade scraped free. He winced, and hated himself for it.

'This pains you,' she told him, not quite asking because the answer was so clear. 'It hurts you to see your blade in enemy hands, doesn't it?'

Once more, his words were thickened by exhaustion and a bleeding mouth. 'You have no idea what you're talking about.'

As he spoke, she turned the sword over in her hands, seeking something. There, etched onto the grip: an Imperial eagle of white gold. She smiled at her captive, and spat on the God-Emperor's sacred symbol. Her saliva hung down in a string, dripping from the sword onto the filthy floor.

His eyes closed, and he imagined his hands slipping through her dark hair, fingers curling to cradle her skull while his thumbs plunged into her slitted eyes. Her screams would be music.

'Look at me,' she commanded. 'There. That's better.'

She stepped closer. He had one shot at this. One shot.

'I'm going to kill you,' he promised through the threat of tears. 'In my Warmaster's name, I am going to kill you, witch.'

'Your Warmaster.' She cast the sword aside without a care. It tumbled across the floor with a clash of abused metal. 'Your Warmaster is nothing more than crow shit by now. He is as dead as your Emperor, a feast for the carrion-eaters. Now tell me what happened.'

This again.

'You know what happened,' he said. 'Everyone knows.'

'Tell me what you saw.' She stepped even closer, the knife in her hand again. He hadn't seen her draw it. 'You are one of the Argentum. You were there, so tell me what you saw.'

One shot. Just one. She was close enough now.

The knife's tip kissed his jawline, stroking along, scratching patterns too soft to break the mud-marked skin. As the blade caressed his lips, she smiled again.

'Tell me what happened, or you die a piece at a time.'

'You don't want to know what happened. You just want to know how he died.'

She trembled. There was no disguising it. The knife pricked his cheek at her lapse of control, and tears drip-dropped – one from the left, one from the right – almost in unison from her fluttering eyelashes. She had to moisten her lips to speak, which she did with a black tongue.

'How did he die?'

In a traitorous moment, he realised that she was beautiful. Pale, poisonous and corrupt. But beautiful. The corpse of a goddess.

His breath misted on the polished knife blade. 'He died first. And we killed everyone who came for his body.' No need to lie when the truth was enough to hurt her. 'I saw your king die, and we shot every weeping bastard that came to claim his body.'

'He was not *my* king. My lord is Gaur, for I am Blood Pact. But Nadzybar was the best of us, nevertheless.'

'Now,' the captured Imperial grinned, 'he's crow shit.'

The knife lowered in a slackened grip. She didn't try to hide the spilling tears. 'Tell me what happened,' she said again. 'Tell me how the Archon died.'

Their eyes met. His were human, with irises of rich hazel. Hers hadn't been human in years: mutated, slitted the same way a snake's eyes are split by black pupil slices – just as disgusting, and just as captivating.

Just one shot at this. One chance.

With his shins leashed together, there was a chance he could hammer a two-booted kick up into her throat, crushing her trachea and damaging her larynx. At the very least, she'd be stunned and muted, preventing an immediate call for aid. At best, she'd die from the trauma of impact, asphyxiating soon after.

One shot. One chance.

He could see it, hear it, feel it. Perhaps he'd miss. Perhaps his boots would smack into her chin, meeting her jawbone with a sick, sharp *crack*. Her lovely face would snap back on a bent neck, and instead of rising to flee, she'd fall like a puppet with cut strings.

One chance.

Her guard was down, but... not enough. It wasn't worth the risk.

Not yet.

Bide your time.

III

HIS RANK WAS senior sergeant. His regiment was the Argentum: also known as the Silver Kindred, the Warmaster's Own, and – on the Munitorum rosters – the Khulan 2nd Huscarls, assigned as bodyguards to Slaydo himself.

He wore the same silver shoulder guards and ornate vambraces that the Warmaster wore, for his uniform was a lesser reflection of Slaydo's own finery. Carried in a scroll case strapped to his thigh was a parchment copy of the 755 Crusade Charter, issued by the High Lords of Terra, granting permission for Imperial forces to declare a crusade into retaking the Sabbat Worlds.

In his webbing, he carried a printed, leather-bound copy of *A Treatise on the Nature of Warfare* – required reading for command candidates, and the seminal work from the pen of Lord Militant Slaydo, written in the decades before his ascension to Warmaster.

Slaydo knew his first name, and addressed him by it. Familiarity had long begun to erode the boundary between the officer and the soldiers that served him.

'Commodus,' the Warmaster would always say in his gruff tones. 'Still dogging my footsteps, boy? Still keeping up with this old war hound?'

Commodus Ryland, senior sergeant, was not with the Warmaster now, but he was still breathing. He intended to keep it that way.

Bide your time, he thought.

So he said: 'I'll tell you.'

And did just that.

IV

'I have dreamed of this many times, but in my worst nightmares, I did not witness this.'

– Slaydo, Warmaster of the Sabbat Worlds Crusade

HISTORY WOULD SAY all of Balhaut burned that month. For once, these words could be spoken without a poetic simile or a mind to dramatise an event into the pages of Imperial archives.

Day and night, earth and sky, Balhaut burned.

Bal Prime and Boruna Hive, Zaebes City and the Western Plains, the Tark Islands and Ascension Valley. Every critical site on Balhaut endured punishing orbital bombardment, the skies above them alight with the Warmaster's anger.

Balopolis, the capital city, died in the heart of those flames.

Through sulphur skies, great whale ships breached the ashen cloud cover, gliding groundwards. Each one was fat with armour plating and swollen with legions of troops – Guard carriers, each eager to be the first on the surface and disgorge its soldiers into the Last Battle.

In the years to come, when Balopolis was a shrine-city – a monument to the trillions slain over the Crusade's course – the memorials for this invasion would paint a glorious picture. Ten days of victory after victory; ten days of unstoppable Imperial advance into Archenemy territory. Wreckage from the Archon's annihilated fleet rained onto the world below, each hunk of ship's hull raising cheers in the Imperials that beheld it.

With no capacity to flee the planet's surface, the enemy leaders barricaded themselves inside their strongholds, legions of loyal followers between them and Slaydo's landing forces.

By nightfall on the ninth day, Slaydo had driven his bleeding forces into the heart of Balopolis with a crusader's zeal. His army besieged the High Palace itself, regiment after regiment marching into the wasteland that Balopolis had become. Every record of the Great Victory would describe this in excruciating – and verbose – detail, for Slaydo's death was only hours away.

Comparatively few records would recall the Warmaster's face on the morning he met his fate.

V

'YOU LOOK TIRED, sir.'

In the wake of this observation, the old man scratched at his beard with soot-blackened fingers. His fingernails were darkened by dirt crescents beneath them, and his beard – once a feral red – was now stone grey, dashed with flecks of colour like fading fire.

The old man forced his scarred lips into what passed

for a smile. It looked like a gash of mirth slitting his beard.

'I am tired, boy. It's what happens when you get old.' He returned his gaze to the burning skyline, at the ruined cityscape of once-grand Balopolis. Through the devastation rolled a horde of iron beetles – Leman Russ tanks and Basilisk gun platforms of every class. The walls of the High Palace stood cracked and crumbling under the onslaught of entire siege tank companies. Even the air tasted of ash and engine fumes.

'Not long now,' he said, and closed his eyes, unsure if he was hearing his heartbeat or the pounding of distant guns.

'You should rest while you can, Warmaster.'

Slaydo snorted. 'I'm not ready to call off the hunt yet. What about you, Commodus? Still keeping up with this old war hound?'

The sergeant answered with a grin.

VI

WHEN THE PALACE walls came down, Imperial cheering shook the city.

From his vantage point at the western edge, the Warmaster exhaled a shivering breath. Around him, the Argentum stood proud, hellguns primed and officers exchanging last words with the men.

'Do you see that?' the old man asked. The question was to none of them and all of them, and it made the old man smile to say it. 'Watch how the verminous tide claws its way through the breakages.'

Commodus looked on, squinting through his visor. Battered armoured personnel carriers, scorched tanks, broken squads of men in mismatching armour... all fled through the rents that Imperial guns had hammered through the palace walls. Those Archenemy troopers still outside were falling back for the last time, to stand and fight with their Archon.

'I've heard that rats always flee a sinking ship.' The old man's smile was like a bad scar. 'But these vermin flee into one.'

His hand rested on the pommel of his sheathed sword as he watched the cracked, burning palace ahead – its battlements of white stone tumbling, falling, breathing out clouds of dust as they died.

Around those immense walls, the dead slept in their thousands, a carpet of split flesh and stinking blood punctuated by the graveyards of slain tanks. Slaydo turned away at last, blinking eyes that suddenly stung.

'What is it, sir?' asked one of his men.

'Such bravery,' the old man almost laughed. 'Such sacrifice. Hear me well and mark my words. No accounting, no retelling, will ever do these days justice. Balhaut will become a memorial after the victory we've bled for here.' Slaydo brought his gaze back to the razed city streets, and the bodies that blanketed them. There was nowhere else to look. The skies burned. The city was rubble. The dead were everywhere.

'And what else could it become? We've made a tomb of this world.' Every one of the Argentum that heard those words also heard the crack in their master's voice, audible despite the mumble of distant artillery, and the rumbling of engines as the regiment's silver-painted troop transports idled nearby.

Carron, the squad's vox-officer, approached with the receiver in hand. The bulky vox-caster backpack strapped over his shoulders hummed in the light rain.

'Warmaster,' Carron offered the receiver to the old man. 'It's Colonel Helmud of the Pragar.'

Slaydo took the speech-horn. The men smiled at his terrible habit: he cleared his throat loudly while his mouth was next to the vox-mic.

'Slaydo,' he said, once he'd spat sooty phlegm onto the ground.

'It's Helmud.' The voice was rasped by bad frequencies. 'The walls are going down like pieces on a regicide board. We're ready, Warmaster. This is it. We win Balhaut this day.'

Slaydo didn't answer. His calloused fingers stroked the grip of the blade still sheathed at his hip, and he stared at the urban ruin acting as a mass grave for the loyal dead.

'Warmaster?'

'I'm here, colonel.'

'The Palace will be ours, sir, but for a few thousand lives.'

Slaydo drew his sword for the first time in four hours. Gold flashed as it caught what little light broke through the smoke-choked sky.

'Start with mine,' the Warmaster said, and hung up the receiver without waiting for a reply.

His blade fell in a chop, the order to advance. After a brief respite, the Argentum went back to war.

VII

COMMODUS WASN'T A bad driver, but nor was he a particularly good one.

Vellici, the squad's previous driver, had got it in the neck the day before – a sniper with a truly evil aim had tagged him through the Chimera's front vision slit. Commodus and three of the others had buried the body, while the rest of the squad did what they could to clean up the tank's interior. Vellici seemed to have a lot of blood, not uncommon in a man as big as he was. Sadly, at the end, it had all been on the wrong side of his skin.

Behind the driver's seat, a ladder let up to the gun turret. The old man stood up there, peering from the open hatch with tired eyes. The men had commented on this many times before, citing that he was making himself an easy target.

The old man always replied the same way. *This tank is festooned with flags, beribboned with honour markings, and*

as silver as Luna's smiling face. If the enemy want me dead,
they already know where to shoot.

Hard to argue with that.

Commodus drove the Chimera up an incline of
rubble. Something – metal on metal – passed under the
tank's hull with a sickening grind.

'Don't ask,' Commodus called back to the others,
'because I don't know.'

The old man leaned back down into the dim, sweat-
smelling interior. 'It was wreckage,' he said. 'Leman
Russ. One of theirs.'

Commodus trundled on through the palace grounds,
tank treads crunching over rubble. What was once an
immense botanical garden stretched out in all directions, blackened and starved. The palace's cracked
battlements rose ahead, while around them was nothing
but a sea of advancing Imperial troop carriers.

A shot clanked against the hull, making every man
tense.

'We're in range,' said Yael, in the back.

'Thanks, genius,' said one of the others.

The shot was the first of many. Hailstone-loud, the
others started arriving moments later.

The turret hatch slammed closed, and the old man
descended the ladder with a cackle.

'First in, my boys,' he grinned as he primed his
laspistol. 'And last out. Let's win this war.'

Commodus laughed, even under fire. 'Good to see
you back, sir.'

The old man's eyes gleamed. 'He's close now, my boy.
I can smell him.'

VIII

THE CHIMERAS SKIDDED to halts, churning the garden's soil
beneath their tracks.

Ramps crashed down. Men ran from the scorched and
battered hulls of their transports, seeking cover in the

statuary and rockeries of the botanical garden. Getting through the outer walls had been simple enough. Now came the true test: fighting chamber to chamber, hallway to hallway, into the palace's heart.

Time to abandon the tanks, then.

Commodus hunched into cover behind the statue of an angel with its face shot off. Thirty metres away, his Chimera leapt into the air, performing a tortured half-spin, before its left track exploded along with half the hull. Steel rained down around him, clanging off already-broken angels and breaking several more.

More rockets streaked down from balconies and windows above, inflicting similar punishment on the Imperial Guard tanks clustered in the garden. One of the Warmaster's flags, emblazoned with the laurel-wreathed skull he wore as a personal emblem, fluttered down to drape itself over the head of a nearby angel, hiding its face like a funeral shroud.

Commodus didn't exactly find the comparison touching.

Next to him, breathing in something between a laugh and a wheeze, Yael clutched his hellgun tight to his chest.

'I'll miss our tank,' he said.

Commodus ignored the weak attempt at humour. 'I counted seven emplacements on balconies. The Emperor only knows how many of the bastards are squatted at windows up there. I got to twenty before it was too dangerous to keep looking.'

'Should've counted faster, sarge.'

'Funny.' Commodus tightened his vambrace. 'Voxing for Vulture support is going to be like pissing into the wind, isn't it?'

'Into a storm, more like.' Yael raised his head, and his rifle, between the angel's stone wings. 'No saviours from the sky are coming to blast us out of this one for a while yet.'

Commodus hunched lower as a solid shot cracked

off the angel's shoulder. He blinked stone dust from his eyes. This was going nowhere.

'Where's Carron?' he asked.

Yael snapped off a shot. His hellgun whined for the half-second it took to power up, and spat a spear of hissing energy skywards. Both men heard the scream as one of the red-clad enemy soldiers toppled from the window above. The panicked shout ended with a wet smack. Something that had once been human was smeared across the stone tiles.

Yael sniggered. 'He won't be going home to his mother's farm.'

Commodus was still scanning the view from ground-level. 'I said *where's Carron?*'

'Not a clue, sarge. No, wait – there he is. Pinned down behind the primarch.'

'The primarch' was a statue of a robed figure, towering above all others around it, depicting one of the Emperor's blessed sons. In better days, it had doubtless been a beautiful piece. The weeks it had suffered under the tender mercies of the Archenemy invaders had not been kind. It now stood deprived of one arm, its face annihilated by hammers, and fresh bullet-scars appearing on its stone flesh with each moment.

With several of the Argentum using it as cover, it was drawing a withering hail of fire from above.

Carron crouched beneath the statue's plinth, firing up at the walls with his pistol.

'I see him,' said Commodus. 'Not a good place to hide.'

'Not at all,' Yael agreed.

Carron rose up to take another shot. He was immediately lanced by three separate snipers. The first shot was enough to kill him outright, blowing mess from the back of his head before it even snapped his neck back. Carron collapsed in a heap that didn't even twitch.

'Dead at Rogal Dorn's feet,' Yael remarked. 'Now there's an honour not many can claim.'

Commodus added his fire to Yael's, shooting up at the windows. 'That's Guilliman,' he said. Another body turned end-over-end as it fell from above.

'How do you know it's Guilliman?'

Apparently, their return fire was drawing notice. A spray of solid slugs cracked around them, defacing their angelic protector all the more. Both Yael and Commodus ducked, using the respite to recharge their weapons.

'Are you blind? It's holding a book in its hand.'

Yael recharged first. He cracked off a shot in the direction their most recent attackers were firing from. 'So? I'm sure Rogal Dorn could read, sarge.'

'It's the Adeptus Astartes holy book.' *Throne, what an idiot.* 'The one with all their laws.'

'If you say so.' Yael didn't stop firing. 'Always hated mythology classes.'

Another of their squad hunkered down into hiding with them, breathless from the sprint into cover.

'Grunner,' both of them greeted him. He looked as tired as Commodus felt, all sickly and hollow-eyed. When he reloaded, it was with clumsy hands.

'Shit, why are you two so happy?'

'Born this way,' Yael replied, still shooting up at the balconies.

Commodus answered with a question of his own. 'You tired, Grunner?'

'Been a long week, sarge.' Grunner forced a smile onto a face lined by middle-age, too many close calls, and one hell of a sleep debt. 'All over soon, though. Even the old man says so.'

Commodus nodded. The old man knew best.

Vulture air support arrived almost two hours later, and annihilated the western face of the Golcir Battlement with strafing runs and rocket barrages. The Argentum had been pinned the entire time, taking casualties from the Archenemy's last-ditch efforts – with no way to advance, and suicide to retreat. Such was the price paid by the Slaydo's Own for '*first in, last out*'.

Each man and woman in the uniform was a veteran storm-trooper, hand-chosen by the Warmaster himself. With grenade and hellgun, every soldier accounted for themselves, raking the windows and walls with unrelenting firepower. Bodies tumbled and toppled from their gun-nests, though more of the ragged enemy took the places of the fallen. Resistance was forever fed from the garrison within.

On beast-loud engines with turbines sucking in air, the Vulture gunships banked over the battlements to unleash their payloads. The horrendous fire being spat down at the Argentum ceased, hurling itself into the skies to repel this newest threat. Seven gunships died, hulls burning and spinning, only to hammer into the same walls and rooftops they were already attacking. Even in death, they still served.

When the wall came down in an avalanche of dead soldiers, gunship wreckage and powdered rubble, Yael was one of the first to make a break for the opening.

Commodus remained where he was for long enough to close Grunner's lifeless eyes. Only then did he scramble up from cover, picking his way through the ravaged botanical garden, stepping over the bodies of his brothers and sisters – and the twisted remains of those they'd killed.

One of the dust-covered Argentum corpses grasped at his boot with a bleeding hand.

Commodus went to his knees, rolling the body over. Not only was it not dead, it also wasn't one of the Argentum.

'Commodus...' the old man said, 'don't leave me here.'

A voice that had bellowed orders on hundreds of battlefields now left Slaydo's cracked lips as a strained whisper.

With the walls down, it was difficult to see through the dust. Commodus cleaned the Warmaster's face with trickles of lukewarm water from his canteen. Little blood showed through the filth on his uniform, but the whistling rasp in Slaydo's breathing told enough of a tale.

The sergeant lifted Slaydo's silver breastplate, and there it was. A knife-sliver of sharp rock, stabbed into the old man's stomach. A chance thing; no doubt ricocheted from the ground as the walls tumbled down.

Commodus was already drawing breath to shout for a medic when a fierce claw latched onto his wrist with a talon's grip.

'*Don't you dare,*' hissed the old man. 'Think of morale, you fool. We're inside now. *It's almost over.* Now shut your mouth and bind that wound, or... or I'll find a new senior sergeant.'

Commodus spoke as he obeyed. As soon as the rock shard came free, blood followed in an eager flow. 'This is straining your heart,' the sergeant said. 'The trauma first, and the blood loss will–'

Warmaster Slaydo spat dust onto the grass, his lined face the very picture of impatience. 'I like you, my boy, but you've always talked too much. Now tighten it up, and get me to my feet.'

'Sir, you need to–'

Defiance gave the blow strength, and the sergeant flinched back as Slaydo's backhand crashed against the side of his helmet.

'I need to finish the hunt, Commodus. And so do you. *Now get me to my feet.*'

IX

THE WARMASTER'S WEARY stagger soon became a lurching walk, then a subtle limp, and then nothing more than clenched teeth and a shine in his eyes. Spite and defiance drove him on where the pain should have driven him to his knees. Better than any of the memorials to come when this day was done, these hours exemplified Slaydo's life in the eyes of the men and women serving him.

In his hand was Liberatus, the silver-wrought sabre granted to him by the High Lords of Terra at the Crusade's commencement. With it, he carved down the enemy when he could reach them, and pointed the blade to aim the Argentum's weapons when he couldn't.

The palace's corridors, once the halls of the reverent and decadent alike, had fallen into disgusting disrepair during the Archon's occupation. The Imperials battled through ruined halls that reeked of piss, great corridors once home to works of religious art, used as latrines by the Archenemy's forces and populated by wreckage where statues once stood.

Slaydo's voice grew stronger with every step he took. Blood ran from the curved blade at his side and his eyes glittered, as though he stared at sights unseen by any of his men.

'Clear,' Commodus called to the seven Argentum troopers with him. At the other end of the corridor, which had once housed masterpiece landscape paintings from twelve other worlds, the last enemy soldier fell dead.

'Good shot, sarge,' said Yael. Commodus had nailed the bastard in the throat from at least seventy metres away. 'If you'd been doing that the whole time, we'd be done by now.'

The sergeant just nodded, his usual banter nowhere in evidence.

'The stairs ahead lead up to the Western Palisade battlements,' Commodus said to the Warmaster. 'Or we can move around to the Central Cloister, cutting left through the servants' passages.'

'The Palisade,' Slaydo ordered. 'He will be seeking us, just as we seek him. No retreat now. No flight off-world. He knows this is the end.'

'Are you s–'

'The Palisade.' The Warmaster raised his sabre high, as

if declaring a cavalry charge from antiquity. 'It happens under the open sky. She told me herself. It's time to end this.'

X

THE EIGHTEENTH HOUR of the tenth day, and the Western Palisade reached out for a kilometre – a wide rampart of gun emplacements, dead bodies and annihilated walkways along the palace walls. The bombing had taken its toll here, as had long-range shelling from Imperial artillery.

Rain slashed down in a torrent, the kind of cold downpour that so easily penetrated clothing to leave skin feeling greasy. Slaydo advanced along the stone battlements, Liberatus in an ungloved hand, the elegant gold etching along the silver blade turned to flickering amber as it reflected the burning city below. The coiled engravings shimmered in the caught firelight, weaving like serpents along the steel.

'I was so certain,' the old man whispered. 'So very sure.'

The Argentum storm troopers fanned out around him, powered backpacks buzzing in the rainfall, hellguns thrumming in ready hands. Several squads had linked together in the last advance. Commodus stayed at the Warmaster's side.

'They're all dead up here, sir.' He kept his voice neutral, masking both disappointment and concern.

'I was so very certain,' the old man repeated. Slaydo looked out over the razed city, then down the long rampart with its population of broken weapons batteries and slaughtered enemy soldiers. 'She told me it would end like this, you know. In the rain.'

Commodus cast a worried glance at the others. The Warmaster leaned against an unbroken section of wall and took a shuddering breath. 'I'm tired now,' he said. 'And I ache like you wouldn't believe.'

The sergeant had seen the wound now eating at the old man's life, so he could indeed believe it. Gut wounds killed slowly, but they killed with a vengeance. The Warmaster would never leave Balhaut unless he fell back to proper medicae facilities soon.

'What are your orders, my Warmaster?' asked Trejus, a sergeant from another Argentum squad. Commodus waved him away.

Slaydo wasn't listening, anyway. The fight had bled from him. In a palsied hand, he clutched a small bronze relic formed into the shape of a young woman. The figurine was no larger than a finger, and the old man's knuckles whitened around it in his fervency.

'Not like this.' He hissed the words as he stared at Balopolis in flames. The fires raged through the parts of the city still standing, savage enough to resist the rainfall.

He closed his eyes and listened to the rain. Liberatus steamed as water hissed against the live blade.

'Gunfire,' said Commodus behind him.

'*Contact, contact,*' Argentum troopers were calling to each other. '*There, contact, dead ahead.*'

Slaydo turned in time to see his most loyal bodyguards raise their weapons and stream beams of energy down the ramparts. A raw, roughshod pack of robed figures was emerging from an arched tower doorway, moving onto the battlements, returning the welcome with lasguns and solid-slug rifles of their own.

Three of the Argentum were punched from their feet by the first barrage, where they died with faces upturned to the oily rain. The others scrambled for cover, laying down a curtain of fire that ripped through the mob's ranks.

Slaydo saw none of this. He saw only that the mob of enemy warriors – clad as priests and worshippers rather than soldiers – were led by a creature that may once, perhaps, have been human.

A toothless, howling maw opened far too wide in a

face flayed down to bare muscle and bone. It saw the old man and screamed, birthing a hundred voices from its rippling throat.

How it saw him, he didn't know. The creature had no eyes in its empty sockets – no eyes in any of its three faces, all of them howling, bellowing wordless bile through their cavernous jaws. Fingers with too many joints grasped at the air in twitching need, and the thing broke into a disgusting run on legs that seemed too scarecrow-frail to support it.

All three faces kept shrieking as it sprinted through the rain.

Slaydo surprised his men by bursting out into raucous, genuine laughter. He shouted an oath to the Emperor and His beloved Saint Sabbat, and ran towards the daemon that seemed to breathe by howling.

'Sir!' Commodus cried out. '*Sir!*' The old man didn't even look back.

After a decade of crusading across conquered worlds and billions of lost lives, the Warmaster and the Archon met at last on Balhaut, in the eighteenth hour of the tenth day.

XI

EVERYONE HELD THEIR fire.

The old man and the robed creature met between the warring sides, their blades clashing and sparking as they cut against each other. There was no hesitation, no careful assessment of the opponent's fighting style; the human and the once-man hurled themselves at one another with no thought beyond seeing a nemesis finally dead.

Several Argentum soldiers, Commodus among them, tracked the battle through their gunsights. Each one ached for the chance to take one clear shot, while the mob of enemy soldiers bayed and whined like frightened dogs – some chanting, some weeping, some merely panicking. None raised their weapons, as if even risking to aim in their master's direction was some great sin.

'I can hit the son of a bitch,' Yael murmured, staring through his targeter. 'I swear I can.'

Commodus was certain he could, too. But he still ordered 'Don't,' in a quiet voice. 'Don't risk it.'

'Is that *him*?' one of the others asked. 'That thing is the Archon?'

The Imperials watched the skinless creature lashing at the old man with a sword that moved too fast to betray any detail. Its robes were a beggar's rags, streaming from its skeletal body in the wind and rain. Exposed veins formed webways of tension along its flayed limbs and three skinned faces. Worst of all was the way it moved – with something insectile in its jerking grace, limbs with too many joints lashing out like a praying mantis.

The old man had never looked more alive. Age forced him to block blows rather than duck them or weave aside, and sweat beaded his flushed face, while mist left his panting mouth. And yet, he exuded vitality in a way none of them had seen since before Balhaut began. Throne, he was even laughing.

The creature that called itself Nadzybar snapped its seven-fingered hand at Slaydo's throat, gripping for long enough to hurl the old man off-balance. Its serrated blade sliced out below Liberatus, tearing across Slaydo's thigh and ripping silvered armour plating clear, scattering it over the stones.

The old man sagged and struck back, favouring his injured leg. As he doubled his efforts, his blood wasted no time, escaping from his body in a flooding stain down his thigh. 'Femoral artery,' said Yael softly. 'Shit, this'll be over fast.'

'Stand your ground!' Slaydo called back to them. He couldn't spare them a moment's glance, such was the Archon's ferocity. 'I am the Emperor's will! I am the sword of His Blessed Saint!'

Sparks lit up their faces as both man and monster

duelled in the midst of their men. Both blades glowed
a dull orange as they heated up, their crackling power
fields abused almost to breaking point.

'Fix bayonets,' Commodus ordered. 'To hell with this,
I'm not going to stand here and watch him die.'

XII

BEFORE THE ARGENTUM could even draw close, Nadzybar
let fall the blow that would end the Warmaster's life.

With a three-mouthed howl, the creature hacked its
serrated sword into Slaydo's side. The old man breathed
blood through his slack lips, almost vomiting redness
onto his uniform.

'Kill it!' Commodus screamed, and broke into a run,
his hellgun lowered like a lance, tipped by his silver
bayonet. Nadzybar was stroking Slaydo's features with
its long fingers, nail-less fingertips running over the old
man's lips and unshaven jawline. As it stroked the dying
man, a breathless, wheezing purr rumbled from its open
maws.

It turned to regard the Argentum as they charged, staring sightlessly with its three faces. It still didn't release
the old man from its possessive, gentle grip.

Worshippers streamed past the Archon, flooding
either side of the creature, screaming and stabbing with
spears made from furniture, shooting at close range with
stolen rifles. The Archenemy's forces were down to the
very dregs.

Yael swore as a spear-tip gashed open his cheek and
ripped his helmet free. He killed his attacker with a
hell-round to the face, and followed up by ramming his
bayonet into the next cultist's throat. Commodus, simi-
larly engaged, spat blood and lost a tooth, hewing left
and right with his rifle, clubbing the scum from their feet
and letting his squadmates stab them as they lay prone.

He managed a single glance through the melee, seeking out the Warmaster.

The momentary glance tore laughter from his lips, and he screamed something that was almost a cheer.

XIII

SLAYDO ENDED THE embrace when he pulled his sword from the monster's stomach. The creature's fingers left his rain-wet face, twitching in the air before Slaydo's eyes.

Organs, blackened by cancer, slipped through the tear in Nadzybar's belly, flopping to the stone floor in puddles of bloody juice. Ropes of intestinal tract looped out in sloppy pursuit.

Nadzybar licked at its lipless maws, trembling, sinking to its knees.

The old man's blood-scented breath washed over the Archon's faces as Slaydo rested Liberatus on the creature's skinny neck. Consecrated steel kissed pale, quivering flesh.

It was a trial just to speak, but the old man managed three words.

'For.

The.

Emperor.'

The holy blade chopped once. Flesh parted with vicious ease, releasing a torrent of stinking black blood.

Nadzybar, the great Archon – fell to the ground. Its head rolled the other way, tumbling under the boots of its worshippers.

Before the body was even still, the old man let his sword fall from strengthless fingers, and roared up at the raining sky.

His triumphant cry was answered, but not by his men.

XIV

THE ARCHON FELL, and the ragged worshippers lost their minds.

Many collapsed where they were, weeping and

screaming, tearing at their hair and beating at their scabrous flesh. These were easy prey for Argentum guns, and they died on their knees, joining their master in whatever hell was reserved for the blackest of heresies. Others abandoned their melee with the Imperials, shrieking in secret languages as they ran for the staggering figure of the Warmaster. With knives and fists they fell upon him, dragging him down, and their bloodied daggers rose and fell for those precious, fevered moments before the Argentum could butcher every living being not wearing their colours.

Commodus was the one to drag the last cultist clear. He kicked her against the battlement wall, broke her jaw with the butt of his rifle, and ploughed three shots into her head.

Nothing remained above her shoulders. Lacking a face to spit into, he spat onto the medallion she wore: an emblem of the Archon's three faces in crude brass.

'Clear,' he shouted.

Commodus turned as the Warmaster called his name.

Slaydo lay where he'd fallen, his uniform dyed with blood, most of which was his own.

'It's done,' he said. The smile curving his lips was sincere, and his voice remained strong.

'It's done, my Warmaster,' said Commodus. He could still hear gunfire across the palace, some of it drawing closer, and he looked away long enough to wipe his eyes. 'We have to get you out of here.'

'Yes, yes,' he huffed. 'Come on, then. Stop standing there crying like schoolchildren, and help an old man to his feet.'

'Make a stretcher,' the sergeant ordered Yael. 'Out of whatever you can.'

'Don't you dare obey that order, Yael.' The Warmaster rose on shaking legs, aided by those nearest to him. 'I may be dying, but I'm not lazy. I'll march out of here on two feet, like the Saint herself intended for me.'

Yael and Tiri supported the old man, keeping him

between them as they walked. True enough, he walked
with them, rather than letting them carry him.

'Carry my sword, Commodus. There's a useful fellow.'

'Yes, my Warmaster.'

XV

THE BUILDING TREMBLED in sympathy with the distant
artillery.

The masked woman was unashamed of her tears – or
at least felt no shame in silently crying before one such
as him. She remained before him for the entire retelling, never interrupting; not to offer him water when
his voiced cracked, nor to ask for any clarification. She
stood above him the whole time with the knife in her
hand.

'That's what happened,' said Commodus. 'That's how
your king died.'

The hook-nosed carnival mask leered in exaggerated
mirth. 'He was not my king. I am Blood Pact. I serve
Gaur. But Nadzybar was the finest of us all, and I will
mourn him for the rest of my nights.'

'He looked far from fine when I saw him last.'

She didn't seem insulted. 'It grieves me that anyone
witnessed him at his panicked, hopeless end. But the
Powers willed it, else it would never have come to pass.'

Commodus swallowed, trying to moisten his sore
throat. 'You know the rest. The battles in the palace. The
Argentum rearguard. The Warmaster escaping.'

'Yes.' She came lower now, back to the half-crouching
position when, last time, she'd cut into him with the
dagger. 'I expect you believed yourself valiant, didn't
you? To delay us, so a decrepit and dying man could
escape with your brothers and sisters.'

Commodus was not a vain man, but if that wasn't
something he could be proud of, he didn't know what
else could be.

'I have one question,' she asked, and he knew she

was smiling behind the mask. 'What happened to your friend? Yael?'

'He was in the rearguard, next to me. I know he was hit, but I don't know how badly. All I know is that he killed four of you.'

She leaned closer, pressing the knife blade to his throat. *Here it is,* he thought. *Here we go.*

But she didn't kill him. She blinked, her eyes flicking to the dagger in her own hand. 'Wait,' the masked woman whispered. 'You carried the Warmaster's sword. You mean... your sword...'

Commodus grinned into her face. 'Throne, you are one *slow* bitch.'

She turned to glance at the ornate sword she'd cast aside before. The sword she'd believed was his.

It was all the distraction he needed.

His boots thudded up between her legs, striking with the strength he'd been saving for half an hour, then powered into her lower stomach, sending her sprawling backwards into the table. He rose to his feet, still tied to the wooden chair, and launched after her in the most frantic hop – surely ludicrous to see, if anyone had been looking.

He drop-kicked her as she was picking herself up, both boots smacking into her face, breaking her cheek, her nose, and her freak-show witch-face mask. The chair crumbled beneath him as he crashed down, various jagged wooden limbs wrenching into his spine and shoulders. His wrists were still leashed behind his back, but that didn't matter. He was free enough now.

Commodus was on her as she moaned on the floor, his knee slamming down into her throat, crushing any hope of breath. The woman's slitted eyes were wide in her purpling face as she clawed at his thighs and chest, raking at the exposed wounds. Commodus breathed in agonised hisses, not letting up the pressure for a moment.

'Should've called for help when you had the chance,' he said.

She kicked ineffectually at his back, and hammered increasingly weak punches at his front. Her face was blue now. Commodus grunted and pushed harder. Vertebrae in her neck gave muted, snapping clicks as the pressure increased.

At last, she fell limp.

The sergeant stayed where he was for another thirty heartbeats, making certain she was never getting up again.

Several minutes later, after an ungainly performance of freeing himself from the tank cable bindings, Commodus picked up *Liberatus* from the floor and pulled the exquisite sabre from its plain leather sheath.

Lightning ran the length of the curved blade as he thumbed the activation rune.

'Pleasure talking to you,' he said to the woman's corpse, and took one look at the chamber's only door, before promptly leaving through the broken window.

XVI

As ESCAPES WENT, it was hardly graceful. She'd cut him up good, and his injuries put paid to any attempt to bolt with decent speed.

Commodus leaned into a staggering run, spit running from his clenched teeth, swallowing the pain with each breath. Below the chest, his uniform was dyed red in the places it wasn't completely shredded. Dozens of cuts ran down his legs. The insides of his boots were hot and squelching, and it wasn't with sweat.

Blood loss would take him down soon; so the witch would kill him with her knife, after all.

More than once, Commodus went down on all fours, scrambling over rubble in a bid to keep moving no matter how often he lost his balance. The city around him was in absolute ruin – a levelled wreckage of shattered buildings and broken roadways. The palace, ostensibly retaken by the Imperials hours before, loomed to the

south. Half of it still burned behind fallen walls. The
witch and her friends really hadn't dragged him far.

He'd made it almost five minutes away before las-
rounds started dogging at his heels and slashing past his
shoulders.

The sergeant hurled himself behind the closest rise
of rubble, the Warmaster's sword gripped in the hand
without half its fingers broken, and stole a look to see
who his pursuers were.

Two of them, running over the wasteland, firing from
the hip. They wore the same grotesques as the witch had
worn – those hook-nosed carnival face masks leered
in metallic delight – and came clad in the same scarlet
uniforms.

Blood Pact.

He hoped there weren't many more of these mali-
cious bastards out there. Were they some newly founded
cult? An enemy regiment they'd not crossed paths with
before?

Whatever they were, he certainly couldn't survive
another one of their knifey-knifey interrogation sessions.

Commodus sank down into the dusty rocks and
started crawling. If he couldn't run, it was time to hide.

XVII

THE FIRST RED-CLAD soldier passed through the ruins of
what had been a museum only three days before. He
entered with his rifle up to his cheek, aiming into corners and at chunks of rubble each time he heard a noise.
Perfect movement, keen senses. Head high, ready to fire.

And completely missing the faint trail of blood on
the floor.

When he passed another slab of fallen masonry, a
sabre lashed out from beneath and cleaved through
both his shins. He went down firing, hitting nothing,
and died a moment later when the sword of Warmaster

Slaydo chopped through his neck in one clean blow.

Blood sizzled and turned crispy black as it burned on the energised blade.

One down. One to go.

Commodus pulled himself clear, cursing at the cramp taking over his left leg. It made a bad limp even worse, and even availing himself of the dead Blood Pact's lasgun didn't bring a smile to his face.

In a game of cat and mouse, when one side was reduced to dragging himself through the dust, the evidence started to rack up for just who would be playing the rodent. Commodus hauled himself over to a pillar, leaning his back against what was left of it. His assets were a stolen lasrifle – half-empty – that smelled a little like an open coffin, and one of the finest, most potent power weapons in the Imperium of Man.

Working against him was the fact that the other Blood Pact soldier almost definitely knew where he was – even if his slain fellow hadn't had the chance to scream, he'd still fired a fair few shots as he went down – and the equally troubling fact that Commodus was slowly but surely bleeding to death.

Good odds, Yael would've joked. But Yael was probably dead, too.

The sergeant blinked to clear his blurring vision. It worked on the third try.

Stand up, he thought. Just stand up first.

Commodus buckled the old man's weapon belt around his waist, used the pillar for support to lift himself to his feet, and gripped his new rifle.

Now get the hell out of here.

He made it another two minutes before his pursuer tracked him down.

By this point, Commodus could barely breathe with his mouth and throat so dry, and blinking did nothing to stop his vision from swimming.

Something clattered to the ground. He could still feel the lasgun's weight in his sore arms, so it must've been the sword. Or a piece of his armour, perhaps. It didn't really matter.

'Eshek gai tragir,' barked the Blood Pact, from behind him. 'Eshek gai tragir kal-kasakh!'

Commodus turned, seeing a red smear against a grey haze background.

'I don't speak...'

Wait, what language is that?

'Eshek gai tragir!' the Blood Pact yelled again.

'I don't speak... Evil,' Commodus said, and started laughing.

He raised his weapon, but his hands moved like he was underwater. He heard the Blood Pact's rifle crack once, and the red smear moved in a blur.

He felt himself falling a moment later. There was no change in the pain, no amplifying of the agony he already felt. They'd carved him to pieces already. Shooting him wouldn't change a damn thing.

More gunfire rang out. More voices bleated. Commodus wiped his eyes, but couldn't see a thing through them. Not that there was much to see, anyway. They'd levelled this beautiful city. Life at the Warmaster's side, that was. Life in the Guard. Kill a whole world to break one viper's back.

By the Saint's sacred arse, he was tired. Dimly, he wondered where he'd been shot. Everywhere hurt as much as everywhere else.

This is what dying feels like. This is what the old man had fought through, right to the end.

Tough old bastard.

He was on all fours when the Blood Pact descended upon him. Their hands grabbed at his ripped clothes, taking his weight, lifting him to his feet, asking if he could hold on a little longer, and saying his name.

'I don't speak Evil,' he murmured again, and collapsed into Yael's arms.

* * *

XVIII

'SENIOR SERGEANT COMMODUS Ryland,' called the voice.

'You can go in,' said the immaculately clad body-guard. Commodus did just that, though his limp made it slow going.

When he'd first woken up that morning, the sawbones had threatened to have away with his leg.

'Take the leg,' Commodus had said, still flying high and grinning hard from the pain-inhibitors, 'and I'll shoot your balls off.'

He limped through the open doorway now, hoping his leg really would start to bend again soon.

Inside the Warmaster's tent, twenty officers in a variety of uniforms stood around a central table that seemed to be drowning in print-papers. Commodus made no eye contact with any of the brass, and stole a glance at one of the paper scrolls that'd fallen onto the floor.

A casualty list, from the Hyrkan 8th.

He glanced at the table again. Throne, these were the casualties of the last two weeks. A forest must've been slain to make that much paper.

'Commodus Ryland?' asked the same nasal voice that had called him in. 'I believe you have something to present to me.'

'Yes, my Warmaster.'

In a smooth motion, he offered the beautiful, fresh-cleaned sword out, hilt-first. Even leaning forwards like this made the healing muscles in his back catch fire. He trembled as he offered the blade, feeling his leg begin to go.

A hand gloved in white lifted Slaydo's sword from his grip. It was all he could do not to reach for it and steal it back.

'Yes, yes,' the sword's new owner trilled. 'Lovely weapon. Served the old man well. My thanks, sergeant. You did gloriously.'

Commodus stood straight and saluted. He still

avoided the Warmaster's eyes, instead fixing his gaze on the man's silver-white breastplate that encased a physique edging into portly.

'Thank you, my Warmaster.'

'I may have something for you in the future, to recognise your valour in the field. You're dismissed for now, sergeant.'

He saluted again, and turned to limp out.

'Ryland?' The Warmaster seemed to voice his name through a nasal sneer. 'I've not seen your report yet. Those traitors in the ruins, sergeant – what did they call themselves?'

'Blood Pact, my Warmaster.'

'Ah, yes, that's it. Thank you.' Macaroth, heir to Slaydo, Warmaster of the Sabbat Worlds Crusade, turned back to his command staff.

'Blood Pact,' he said to them. 'I do not like the sound of that at all.'

This one's by me, and it's the only story in the book that's appeared somewhere before.

It's a Gaunt's Ghosts story that was commissioned as the convention-only exclusive for the 2008 UK Games Day. As with all such chapbooks, it was always intended that the story would be anthologised eventually to make it available to a wider audience, and this seemed like the right place.

The Iron Star fits directly into Gaunt's Ghosts continuity, falling precisely between Only In Death and Blood Pact (ie, between arc three, The Lost, and arc four, The Victory). It's the story of the aftermath of the battle of Hinzerhaus, during which Gaunt was severely wounded...

Dan Abnett

THE IRON STAR

Dan Abnett

I

UNDER AN IRON star set in a sky the colour of raw meat, the Ghosts of Tanith made their loyal but weary advance towards...

Dammit. What was the place called? He thought about it for a moment. The *somewhere-or-other* bridge. He was sure the name would come back to him. He looked around for his map, but his eyes were hurting again, and he couldn't find it.

It was a bridge, anyway. Another bridge. Another fething objective. This particular bridge lay at the western tip of... of... the *some such* plateau, on a world called... called *who the feth cares any more*.

Truth be told, he certainly didn't. It was just another world and another battle.

The Ghosts didn't care either. They simply advanced, loyal but weary, weary but loyal, neither quality first, neither quality last.

They were tired, there was no mistaking that. They toiled through the mud, under the raw-meat sky, heads

147

low, hearts lower, their banners as limp as their spirits, lonely in life, and lonely in death.

In the distance, across the mire, the black figures gathered to watch them.

During long crusades, Guard regiments could stay on the frontline without rotation for years at a time. Such was the size of the Imperium, whole seasons could be lost simply making shift aboard carrier transports from one zone world to the next.

The Ghosts of Tanith had been on frontline deployment for decades, without rotation, since the day their home world had blinked out in a hot puff of scatterlight.

He had been petitioning of late for his regiment to be rotated out of the line. He had become increasingly insistent on the subject. The phrase 'loyal but weary' appeared in almost every one of his dispatches to High Command. Late at night, under canvas or in the mudstink of a dugout, or in the noon heat at a roadside during a rest stop, he worked hard to get the tone of his petitions right. *If it pleases you, sirs... begging your accommodation on this small matter, my masters...* The Ghosts were not cowards, but they had been pushed hard for too long. They yearned for respite and rotation. They were tired.

He knew he was.

His face was more drawn and lean than ever. These days, he walked with a bone-sore limp. When he washed, on those few, precious occasions when water actually pumped through a trench camp's shower block, he stood under the pitiful rusty trickle, scrubbing lice and dirt from his limbs, and found himself looking down at a body scored and welted by the traces of so many old wounds that he had lost track of their origins. This? Where had he got this? Fortis Binary? And this, this old puckered gouge? Where had he come by that? Monthax? Aexe Cardinal? Vervunhive?

It no longer seemed to matter. These days, it was often

a struggle just to remember where he was.

'Are we still on... on *thingumajig*?' he had asked his adjutant that morning while shaving.

His adjutant, whose name he was sure he knew well, had frowned, thinking the question over.

'*Thingumajig*? Uh... yes. I believe so, sir,' the adjutant had replied.

The names really weren't of any consequence any more, the names of cities or continents or worlds. Each one was just a new place to get into, and then get out of again, once the job was done. He'd stopped worrying about the names. He just concentrated on the jobs, loyal but weary, weary but loyal.

Sometimes, he was so tired he even forgot his own name.

He dipped his old cut-throat razor into the chipped bowl, washing off the foam and the residue of shorn bristles. He looked at his reflection in the cracked shaving mirror. Though the reflection didn't seem to have a face at all, he recognised it anyway.

Ibram Gaunt. That was it. Ibram Gaunt.

Of course it was.

II

HIS EYES HURT. They hurt at night, when he was working at his latest pleading dispatch by the glow of a lamp, and they hurt by day, under the radioactive glimmer of the iron star. They hurt when he stared out across the mire to look at the black figures gathering to watch them.

The iron star was an ugly thing. It throbbed in the sky like an ingot cooling from the furnace. The sky was marbled black and red, like hung meat. The throb of the star made his head ache and his eyes run. Sometimes, when he dabbed the tears off his face, his fingertips came away red.

* * *

III

A SCOUT CAME running back along the muddy track. The track was so muddy that it was impassable to wheeled vehicles. The Tanith were up to their shins in the slime. The strange part was, there had been no rain, not a drop of rain since they had made planetfall on who the feth cares anymore. Well, none he could remember, anyway.

Things lurked in the mud. If you scraped it back, or dug it away to commence trench work, you risked striking the turret tops of tank regiments that had been sucked down under the ooze, or exposing the bodies of dead men, pale and sightless.

'There's so much mud,' he said, watching the scout as he approached. 'So much mud, but no rain. Why is that?'

'Don't you know where you are, Ibram?' asked Medic Curth.

'I don't,' he smiled. 'That's a terrible confession for a commanding officer to make, isn't it?'

She grinned back. Curth was thin, but very pretty. 'Under the circumstances, I'll forgive the lapse, Ibram.'

'Good,' he said, nodding.

'So, where are we?' he added. 'Remind me?'

She leaned down and whispered into his ear.

IV

A SCOUT CAME running back along the muddy track. It was Leyr. No, Bonin. No, it *was* Leyr. 'Ten units,' Leyr reported. 'They're dug down behind that stand of trees to the left of the bridge.'

'Well, we've got to get across the bridge,' Gaunt said.

'Of course we have,' said Medic Curth.

'This really isn't the time for a medical opinion,' Gaunt told her.

'Sorry,' she said, with a deferential nod of her head. She stood back to let some of the senior officers close in around Gaunt.

'The bridge is vital,' Major Baskevyl said.

'Agreed,' said Captain Daur.

'No question about it,' nodded Captains Arcuda and Obel.

'Absolutely vital,' Commissar Hark concurred. 'We have to get across it, or–'

'Or what?' asked Cadet-Commissar Nahum Ludd. The young man looked nervous. He glanced sidelong at Hark. Commissar Viktor Hark looked daggers at the youngster. 'Try to keep up, Ludd,' he hissed. 'We have to get across the bridge before someone dies.'

'Oh,' said Ludd. 'Oh, right.'

'Another ten units,' said Curth.

'Another ten?' Gaunt asked. 'I thought there were just ten. Just ten, wasn't it, Leyr?'

'Uhm, yes, sir. Ten units,' said Leyr.

'Just enough to hold us here,' said Curth.

'We really have to bring this operation to a successful close,' said the old doctor, Dorden.

Gaunt nodded.

'Of course we do,' he said. 'I want this operation finished by nightfall. Ten, then. Ten. What are we looking at? Regular Gaurist forces or what? Ten units of what?'

'Blood, sir,' replied Leyr.

'Blood Pact?'

'Yes, sir.'

'Well, that's a tough dance on anybody's card,' Gaunt said. 'May I take a look?'

He hurried up through the mud behind Leyr. The mud was deep, and it kept slowing him down, sucking at his boots, so that he advanced like a man wading through a dream. His heels, deep in the mire, kept knocking against skulls and helmets and the turrets of long-lost armour pieces.

Bonin, Mkoll and Maggs were waiting for them at the turn of the track. They hunkered down together behind a swirl of razor wire.

'How are you holding up, sir?' Maggs asked him.

'Don't ask him questions, Maggs,' Mkoll hissed. 'We're not here to ask him questions.'

'Sorry,' said Maggs.

'I'm fine, since you asked, Maggs,' said Gaunt. 'Why did you ask?'

Maggs looked awkward.

'It's been a long tour,' Bonin said. 'You look tired, sir.'

'Do I?' Gaunt responded.

'Just... Just want to make sure you're all right,' nodded Maggs.

'Don't I look all right?' Gaunt asked.

'You have tears,' Maggs began. He pointed to his own cheek. 'Tears that look like blood,' he added.

'Oh, that keeps happening,' Gaunt tutted, wiping his face. 'It's this iron star. Don't you feel it too?'

The scouts nodded.

'So, come on,' Gaunt said. 'I've come all the way up here to see. Show me.'

V

'TEN UNITS OF blood,' said Mkoll, passing the scope to Gaunt. 'There, in the trees, to the left of the bridge.'

Gaunt peered through the scope. His eyes hurt. The trees weren't trees at all. They were angular stalks of chrome metal with thin, rod-like branches. The branches supported luminous white blossom, flower heads that glowed like lamp-packs. The trees were standing in a long thicket on a bank of mud that wallowed down into the river below the bridge. There were bloated bodies drifting in the stagnant water of the river. For a moment, Gaunt was afraid that he might be able to name every single one of the dead.

'To the left,' Mkoll advised.

Gaunt adjusted his sight. He saw the Blood Pact. Ten units, all right. He could make out crimson spiked helmets, black-iron grotesk masks, and infantry uniforms dyed maroon with blood. They were clambering up the

riverbanks, milling like fire-ants, constructing siege platforms along the stinking river to support mortars. He
could hear the scrape and hum of their tools.

'Ten units, all right,' said Gaunt. 'Mkoll?'

'Yes, sir?'

'What's this bridge called again? I forget.'

Mkoll hesitated. 'It's the... the... *somewhere-or-other*-
bridge, sir.'

Gaunt laughed. 'You don't know either, do you, chief?'

Mkoll laughed back. 'So many worlds, so many objectives, sir. What can I tell you? Let me check my maps.'

'You do that,' said Gaunt. 'My eyes hurt.'

'That'll be the iron star,' said Leyr.

'We have to seal this artery right now,' said Curth.

'Seal it?' asked Gaunt.

'Yes,' she said. 'This artery here.'

'You mean the river?' asked Gaunt.

'Uhm... what?'

'You mean the river?' asked Gaunt.

'Of course,' she said. 'It's vital we tie it off and seal it.'

Gaunt nodded. 'Well, we've got ten units to handle,
but I agree. Mkoll?'

'Oh, we can manage it, sir,' Mkoll assured him.

Gaunt nodded. He looked at Curth and frowned.

'I thought I left you with the command team, medic,'
he said.

She pulled down her surgical mask and smiled at him.
'You did, Ibram, but you know me,' she said. 'If we're
about to get casualties, I need to be up front.'

'Good. Good thinking,' he murmured.

VI

THE BRIDGE, THE *something-or-other*-bridge, was a dirty,
iron monster. It looked as if it had been wrought from
metal extracted from the iron star's heart, and left to
cool. It stretched out across the stagnant river on its pil-
ings, ominous and forbidding. The bridge was so long,

and the dead river so broad, they couldn't see the far side. Gaunt wondered if he'd ever get across. It seemed like such a long way, and he was very tired. It felt as if time was running out.

'Is it true, sir? Is time against us?'

Gaunt turned. Kolea, Varl, Domor and Criid had advanced to join him. He was pleased to see them, four of his best officers, four of his best Ghosts.

'What was your question?' he asked.

'Time, sir,' said Gol Kolea. 'They say time is against us.'

'Ten units of Blood Pact, right on the river here,' Gaunt replied. 'We've got to get this artery secure and get across the bridge by nightfall.'

Kolea nodded. Varl and Criid exchanged uneasy looks.

'How are your eyes, sir?' asked Domor.

Gaunt looked at him. 'Sore. They hurt. Thanks for asking.'

'Shoggy' Domor gestured to the bulbous augmetic eyes that had earned him his nickname and smiled.

'I know how it is with eyes,' he said.

'Of course you do, Shoggy,' Gaunt replied. 'It's just this iron star. It hurts my head.'

'Nobody likes it,' said Varl.

'Sorry to say, we just have to get on and make the best of this,' said Gaunt. 'So, this artery? This river? How do we seal it? Suggestions?'

'We could burn it,' said Kolea. 'Cauterise it.'

Gaunt nodded. 'Bring up the flamers. Hurry back to your companies and prepare to lead them forwards.'

The four of them hesitated.

'What are you waiting for?' Gaunt asked.

'We wanted to stay with you,' said Domor.

'We wanted to stay by your side,' said Varl.

'That's very loyal,' Gaunt replied. 'Get your Ghosts ready, and I'll join you on the bridge. Come on, look lively! Do you want to live forever?'

Reluctantly, they backed away. Criid stared at him.

'We don't want you to die,' she said.

'That's enough of that, Criid,' Curth called out.

VII

GAUNT STOOD ON the rise above the dead river. The iron star throbbed. His eyes hurt.

He looked at the chrome trees and their luminous blossom. He heard the scrape and hum of the Blood Pact work teams, finishing their defences.

He turned.

The black figures were still gathering out across the mire. There were half a dozen of them now, silent, faceless, watching.

'You've gone quiet,' said Curth.

'What?' he asked.

'You've gone quiet,' she repeated. 'Ibram? Say something.'

He sighed.

'It's those fething figures,' he said. 'Those black figures. They've been watching us for a while.'

'What figures?' Dorden asked.

'Can't you see them?' he asked. 'There. Out there. Watching us. There was only one to begin with, but there are more now.'

'Ibram?' said Curth softly. 'There's no one there.'

'Yes, there is. I can see them. Stay here.'

'Ibram?' Curth said. 'Ibram, where are you going?'

'Stay here, Ibram,' Dorden urged.

'Stay with us,' said Curth.

'Just a moment,' he replied. 'I'll be right back. Just give me a moment.'

'Ibram, you can't go wandering off on your own,' said Curth. 'It's not safe.'

'Just give me a moment.'

He started to walk, sliding, slipping in the mire, his boots digging deep. He tried to keep sight of the black figures. Behind him, the voices calling out to him faded away.

It was further than he thought. Twice, he tripped over buried helmets and tank hatches, and fell. On both occasions, he lay in the mud for a while, not entirely sure he ever wanted to get up again. He was tired. His eyes hurt.

He staggered on, knee-deep in the wet, red mud. It smelled of rot and death. No surprise there. Battlefield mire often reeked of the blood and viscera that had soaked into it. Over the years, he'd become accustomed to the smell, but this was particularly strong, like an open gut wound or fresh arterial spill.

The black figures didn't seem to be coming any closer, no matter how hard he toiled towards them. They remained distant, watching.

'Who are you?' he yelled, but his voice was hoarse and the black figures declined to answer.

VIII

'WHERE HAS HE gone?' Curth asked. 'Ibram? Ibram, come back!'

'He's not responding,' said Dorden. 'We've got to bring him back.'

'Ten units!' Curth yelled. 'Now!'

'I don't think he can hear us,' said Dorden. 'He's too far away.'

'Someone's got to bring him back,' said Curth. 'Someone's got to reach him and bring him back!' She pulled down her mask and looked around. 'Larkin? Over here! On the double!'

IX

HE COULDN'T SEE the black figures any more. They'd somehow vanished into the mist. He had gone too far and lost his bearings. No-man's-land stretched away in all directions.

Well, that was stupid, he told himself. I have no idea where I am any more. I'm lost out here.

The iron star was the only constant. He looked up at it, ignoring the pain in his eyes. Perhaps he could take a bearing off it and find his way back. He couldn't even hear Curth and Dorden any more.

He was so tired. He sat down in the mud, and wiped his eyes. His hands became wet with blood. So stupid to have wandered so far.

He thought about lying down and taking a nap. His head would be clearer after a nap. Just a quick nap. Just a moment to rest his eyes.

He looked up. The black figures stood around him, silent and grim. Mist fumed around them, battlefield vapour. The figures gazed down at him from under their hoods.

He rose to his feet, aching, unsteady.

'Who are you?' he asked.

None of them replied.

'Who the feth are you and why are you watching me?' he demanded.

The figures remained silent.

He lunged forwards and pulled at the nearest figure's cowl, trying to see its face.

'Who are you?' he yelled.

There was a loud crack, and the figure's head exploded in a clap of light.

Gaunt turned.

'What are you doing all the way out here, sir?' Larkin asked, lowering his long-las.

'I...' Gaunt began.

He turned back. The figures had vanished again.

'Did you see them?' he asked Larkin.

Larkin was quietly reloading his piece.

'Ominous black figures, gathering around a battlefield and waiting for slaughter to begin, you mean, sir?' he asked.

'Yes. Yes!'

'I see 'em all the time,' said Larkin, slapping his next

hot-shot load in place, 'but I'm not the most reliable witness, am I?'

'You've got the best eye I've ever known, Larks,' replied Gaunt.

'Maybe. Through a scope, maybe. But my brain, it's wired funny. I see all sorts of feth. I'm surprised at you, though.'

'What do you mean?' asked Gaunt.

'You? Jumping at shadows? Going off by yourself into feth knows where?' Larkin grinned. 'You were always the level-headed one. More even than Mkoll or Daur or Rawne. You always kept it together.'

'I still am, Larks,' said Gaunt. 'But I saw them. The black figures. You saw them too. You put a round through one of their skulls!'

Larkin shook his head. 'I fired a warning shot to get your attention. You were floundering around out here in the mud, yelling at no one like a total idiot.'

'Was I?'

Larkin nodded. 'It wasn't a good look. It didn't inspire much confidence. Pardon me for saying so, sir.'

Gaunt sat down in the mud again, heavily.

'I'm just so tired, Larks,' he said. 'You know? So tired. We've been on the line too long. I don't know how much longer I can do this.'

'Longer than the rest of us, I trust,' smiled Larkin, 'or we're all fethed.'

Gaunt looked up at his loyal master marksman. 'Larkin,' he said. 'I see things. I keep seeing things. Worse than that, there are things I don't see. I know they're there, but I don't see them.'

'Your eyes, is it?' asked Larkin.

'Yes. They hurt.'

'That's no surprise, seeing as what they did to you.'

'What? What does that mean?' asked Gaunt.

'Nothing. Forget I said it,' said Larkin.

'Who did what to me?' Gaunt asked.

Larkin shook his head. 'You've seen a lot, that's all I'm

saying, sir. In your career, you've seen a lot of stuff, more than many men could stand seeing in a lifetime. You've seen destruction. You've seen death. You've seen friends and comrades perish right in front of you.'

'I have. I really have,' said Gaunt.

'Let's get you back to the line, shall we?' Larkin asked, offering Gaunt his hand.

'You can see the way?' asked Gaunt.

'Of course, I'm Tanith. I may not be a scout, but I've got the Tanith instinct. Follow me. Let's get you out of here before the black figures come back.'

Gaunt frowned. 'I thought you said there weren't any black figures?'

Larkin shrugged. 'Just because I see 'em all the time, doesn't mean they're real. Come on.'

X

THEY TRUDGED BACK towards the Ghost lines under the iron star.

'I'm tired, Larks,' Gaunt said, after a while. 'Let me rest for a moment.'

'Not here,' Larkin replied, 'it's not safe. Keep going. You can rest when we reach the lines.'

'I've got to stop,' said Gaunt, 'just for a moment. Let me stop for a moment and close my eyes.'

XI

'I BROUGHT HIM back as far as I could,' said Larkin sadly. 'He doesn't want to come any further.'

'He's got to,' replied Curth. 'He's just got to.'

'He's not listening to me any more,' said Larkin. 'He's just stopped.'

XII

SOMETIMES, WHEN HE was able to steal an hour to sleep, stretched out in a habitent, or curled up on a rotting bunk in a dugout, he dreamed of a world called Jago.

The dreams were powerful, and full of miserable and lingering pain.

Given that he had stopped remembering, or even caring to remember, the names of the places he and the Ghosts had toiled through, loyal and weary, weary and loyal, he wondered why Jago in particular had remained in his memory and his dreams.

It had been a dry, dusty, wind-blown place. The dust had seeped into everything, and the wind had made a sound like air singing through the openings of skulls whose tops had been sawn off. Dry and dead, that was Jago. Dry and dead, and not oozing with mud and humid like... like *who the feth cares anymore*.

He had other dreams, sometimes. An old man called Boniface sometimes quizzed him about theology and philosophy in an old library. The old man, scarred and mutilated beyond belief, sat in a brass chair. In the dream, Gaunt would ask Boniface about his father, and the old man would refuse to reply.

Another dream involved someone called Uncle Dercius. Uncle Dercius would arrive unexpectedly. Gaunt would be playing with a carved wooden frigate on the sundecks, and would look up in glee as Uncle Dercius walked in. Uncle Dercius had a strange look on his face. He had a gift for Ibram. It was a signet ring.

In a different dream, someone called Colm Corbec was waiting for him in a woodland glade. Tall, bulky, bearded, Corbec was dressed in Tanith black, and smiled when Gaunt approached. Gaunt could smell the resin sap of nalwood. He knew Corbec was the greatest friend he'd ever had, and the greatest friend he'd ever lost.

Another dream, ebbing from some memory of a hive city, was filled by Merity Chass, of the noble House Chass. She was young and beautiful, and became even more beautiful when her dress slid away. Her voice was as soft as her skin. She said...

* * *

XIII

'FOR THRONE'S SAKE, wake up!'

Gaunt started. Astonishingly, he had actually been dozing off. That had never happened before, not in three decades of soldiering. *I must be getting weary. Loyal but weary.*

'Don't fret, Rawne,' Gaunt told his number two. 'I'm right here. Just resting my eyes.'

'It's Curth, Ibram.'

'Oh. Yes, of course.'

'You were a long way away from me then.'

'I'm just tired, Curth. Just napping for a moment.'

'Try to stay with us. We've got to close this artery and cross the bridge.'

'Before nightfall.'

'Exactly,' she replied.

'Let's get this done, then,' he said. 'I want to talk to the flamers.'

XIV

THE FLAME TROOPERS gathered around him. Brostin, Dremmond, Lubba, Lyse, Nitorri and the rest. They stank of promethium fuel, their stock in trade.

'Where the Throne are your flamers?' Gaunt asked.

'Well, we left them outside,' said Lubba.

'Outside?' Gaunt asked.

'Lubba meant back on the track over there, sir,' Dremmond said quickly. He nudged Lubba with a heavy, grubby arm. 'Idiot.'

'Our tanks are being topped up just now,' said Brostin, with a broad grin. 'We're all ready to go. You give the word.'

'You understand the objectives?' asked Gaunt.

'Why don't you run through them, just for us?' Dremmond suggested.

'Haven't the company leaders briefed you?' asked Gaunt.

'Well, of course they have,' said Brostin.

'Immaculately,' said Lyse.

'We just, uhm, like to hear it from you in person, sir,' said Brostin.

Gaunt chuckled. 'Very well. We have to get across this bridge by nightfall. Ten units of blood. Blood Pact. You've got to cauterise this artery right now.'

'Artery?' asked Lubba.

'This river.'

Lubba nodded.

'Not a problem,' said Brostin. He took out a lho-stick.

'Not here!' Curth called out.

'I'm not going to light it, doc,' Brostin protested.

'They'd see the spark,' said Gaunt.

'Who's that, sir?' asked Brostin, sucking on his unlit lho-stick.

'The Blood Pact down on the river.'

'Oh, absolutely,' Brostin replied. 'That's why I'm being careful. We're ready to go as soon as you want.'

'Then get to it,' said Gaunt. 'And Brostin?'

'Sir?'

'Say hello to Mister Yellow for me.'

XV

THE IRON STAR throbbed. The bridge waited. It seemed all too close to nightfall.

Gaunt adjusted his cap, brim first, checked the load of his bolt pistol, and drew out his power sword, the famous blade of Hieronymo Sondar. It purred as he switched it on.

He rose up, the mud squelching around his boots.

'First and Only!' he yelled.

Whistles blew, and line officers called out orders for readiness.

'Straight silver!' Gaunt instructed. Clicks and clatters sounded down the Ghost formation as the Tanith fixed their warknives to their bayonet lugs.

'Flamers advance!' Gaunt called.

The flame-troopers climbed up out of the forward dugouts they'd crawled to. As they rose, their tanks thumped, and spears of liquid flame spat down across the river's edge. On their hastily constructed siege platforms, the Blood Pact troopers screamed as inferno engulfed them.

Mortar charges, carried over the dead river on pontoons, began to catch off and explode. Bodies and fragments of splintered wood were hurled up into the air on ferocious spurts of fire.

'Advance!' Gaunt ordered, and the line officers repeated the call. He began running. Sword raised, he slipped and slithered in the mire. He heard the Ghosts behind him, the crack and fizzle of lasrifles, the roar of voices.

Enemy fire began to whip his way. It was so bright and quick, it hurt his eyes.

'Keep on them!' he yelled.

'Steady, Ibram,' Curth warned.

'Get into cover, medicae!' he shouted at her.

'I'm staying right with you,' Curth whispered.

He ploughed on into the billowing smoke. The air smelled of fyceline, blood and slime. Stray shells *whumped* in and kicked up mud that spattered across him. Blast concussions made the smoke eddy and swirl in curious patterns, like ripples on water. The noise was overwhelming.

He saw shapes moving towards him in the smoke ahead. Blood Pact troopers loomed into view, charging up from the river to meet them. Feral sounds and inhuman heresies issued from the screaming mouth-slits of their iron masks. Grim human trophies, like finger-bones and ears, jangled from their webbing and their munition belts.

Some of the Blood Pact carried lasrifles, with bayonets fixed. Others brandished spears or billhooks, or spiked hammers made for trench fighting. Their howls rose in intensity as they caught their first glimpse of the Imperial troops.

'Into them! Break their backs!' Gaunt shouted. 'The Emperor Protects!'

He didn't falter in his stride. If anything, he ran faster, raising his bolt pistol to shoot, swinging his sword back. For a beautiful moment, the weariness left him. It just lifted off him. He felt as if he could take on the Archenemy single-handed. He felt the way he had done as a young man, with the whole galaxy before him.

He fired two shots and knocked down a pair of charging Blood Pact troopers, who went over as if they had been demolished by wrecking balls.

Then he was in amongst the rest. He swung the power sword, and the blade went clean through a throat. A billhook sang towards his face, and he chopped it away and then drove the sword, point-first, through the billhook-owner's torso. Shapes whirled around him. This was the killing time, close combat, face-to-face, without quarter or compunction. Gaunt had tangled with the Archon's Blood Pact often enough to know that they fought like wolves, and seldom relented. Many were hard-bred Imperial Guardsmen, who had defected, or who had been seduced away from the power of the Throne by the perversions of Chaos. The Blood Pact was one of the few forces in the Archenemy's host with proper military training and discipline.

Ghosts slammed into the brawl around him, black shapes stabbing with glittering silver bayonets. Lasweapons went off point-blank, thumping bodies off their feet into the mire. Figures wrestled and grappled.

Gaunt shot another Blood Pact trooper who was charging at him with a spear, and then ducked as a trench-mace came down to crush his skull. He kicked out the legs of the trooper with the mace and, as the man fell, Gaunt cleaved his sword through his shoulderblades and spine. Another came close, at Gaunt's elbow, and Gaunt made a quick back-turn and rammed the pommel and grip of his sword into the man's throat. The Blood Pact trooper stumbled backwards, choking, and Gaunt finished his work with a fencing master's thrust. Two more hurled themselves at him. A rusty bayonet grazed Gaunt's arm, ripping the sleeve of his storm coat. He fired wildly, instinctively and, though wild, the bolt-round blew a leg off at the hip. The other enemy trooper swung his billhook down, but Gaunt blocked it with his sword. The powered blade cut the billhook in half. Gaunt sliced his sword-arm backwards, and ran the blade in a slash across the man's chest. Blood exploded from the massive wound. The trooper dropped to his knees, masked face tilted up at the sky, and Gaunt took his head off.

'Tell your heathen masters the Ghosts have come for them!' he yelled into the darkness.

Las-bolts rained down through the smoke cover like incandescent drizzle, and made sucking, sizzling punctures in the mire. Gaunt heard the rasp and belch of flamers from nearby. Further off, mortars were grunting like bullfrogs at the river's edge, and autocannons were rattling like infernal mill engines.

Gaunt looked around, trying to assess the fight, but the smoke was shrouding everything. All he could see was blurred figures mobbing in the half-light. Someone lobbed a star-shell into the sky, where it wobbled and bobbed like a second, brighter iron star, but it did nothing to improve visibility.

His blood was up. As he faced down and killed three more Archenemy troopers, Gaunt recognised the fury in his heart. It was the old fury, a courage and a determination he had begun to fear he'd lost. These last few years, it had started to feel as though its fire had died out, leaving nothing in his soul but dull embers.

Some gust of passion had breathed upon those coals, and rekindled the flames. With a measure of sadness, Gaunt realised that he only ever felt decently human when he was locked in the madhouse of battle. His dead soul blazed, and his dull limbs cast off their aches and pains. His mind became clear. His life, the very essence of his life as an Imperial soldier, was here, vital and vibrant in the insanity of combat.

Only on the razor-edge of life and death could he feel alive. Only in death could he live.

A Blood Pact officer, an etogaur, lunged out of the cinder-smog. He was a massive beast, with corded muscle bulging under his bloodstained coat. His grotesk was dirty gold. His huge greatsword was running with Imperial gore.

The etogaur growled as he looked around for another Guardsman to butcher.

'Over here, you son of a gak,' Gaunt roared.

XVI

ANA CURTH BENT over her patient. Battlefield medicine was not a precise art. Her scrubs were smeared with blood.

'I don't understand,' she said. 'His vitals are bright and strong, but he seems to be slipping away.'

Dorden put his hand on her shoulder. 'We've done all we can.'

'No.'

'Ana, we have hundreds of casualties to treat. Per-haps–'

'No,' she said, emphatically. 'I'm not going to give up.'

'Look at his wounds,' Dorden said, nodding down at the stricken patient. 'The Blood Pact has done its work as brutally as ever.'

'There's still a chance,' she said, reaching for a clean scalpel. 'There's always a chance.'

XVII

THE ETOGAUR UTTERED some abominable battle-cry, and expertly whirled his greatsword around his head and shoulders in a display of strength. It was a powered blade, and its gleaming length crackled with indigo sparks, like thread veins of electricity.

Gaunt's bolt pistol was spent. There was no time to reload. That suited him fine. He wanted this to be sword work.

The etogaur rushed him. Gaunt raised the sword of Hieronymo Sondar to parry the first swing, and managed to do so, but the sheer power of the heavy blade's impact jarred his wrist and forced him to brace his stance. The etogaur was fast. He evidently knew swordplay, and he revealed a master's finesse, even though he was wielding a monstrous, heavy blade designed for wholesale slaughter rather than duelling.

Gaunt blocked three more quick blows, turning his sword with a dextrous touch. The etogaur was using the sheer weight of his blade for momentum, swinging each blow into the next, changing his grip on the double-handed pommel to swoop and turn the greatsword around his body for maximum kill power.

The etogaur brought the greatsword around in a body-line cut. Gaunt stopped it dead with a flat-blade parry, and then drove back, robbing the etogaur of swing momentum. With brute force, the etogaur hefted up his blade, and tried to swing again. His sword was twice as long as Gaunt's. He had reach. He had power.

His boots sloshing in the mire, Gaunt outpaced him, and turned around his left flank. The etogaur tried to turn, but Gaunt drove in a slice that the etogaur barely parried away. He was wrong-footed, unbalanced.

As the etogaur tried to regain his poise and bring his greatsword up, Gaunt ripped his sword in. The weight of the blade cut through the greatsword's grip. It cut through the etogaur's right wrist, and severed all the digits of his left hand.

The etogaur uttered a bark of disbelief. He took a step backwards, blood squirting from his wrist stump and his dismembered hand. He stared at Gaunt through the eye-slits of his dirty gold mask, awaiting the finishing stroke.

Gaunt aimed his sword at the etogaur, tip first. 'Run,' he said. 'Run and tell them. The Ghosts of Tanith have come, and they will kill you all.'

The etogaur began to howl. He turned, and stumbled away into the smoke, bleating out his distress and his terror.

Gaunt allowed himself a smile. He could feel tears of blood on his face.

Turning, he saw a Ghost nearby, beset by two Blood Pact troopers. He hurled himself into the brawl, and severed the spine of one of the Archenemy warriors with his sword. The beleaguered Ghost used the advantage to lance the other Blood Pact marauder with his bayonet.

'Are you in one piece?' Gaunt asked as the Ghost yanked his blade out of the corpse.

'I'm all right, sir,' the Ghost replied. Gaunt realised that it was Beltayn, his adjutant.

'Good to see you, Bel. How're you holding up?'

'This is a pretty bad fix, sir, isn't it?' said Beltayn. His face was ash-white.

'We'll be fine, Bel.'

'I think, sir...'

'What?'

'Something's awry.'

Gaunt laughed and gestured at the smoke, flames and corpses around them. 'You figured that out all by yourself, did you?'

Beltayn shook his head.

'I mean, I've heard things on the vox,' he said. 'We've broken their spirit here, but it sounds like they've got reinforcements moving in on our flank.'

'More Blood Pact?'

'No, sir. From the vox-bursts, it sounds like the Sons of Sek.'

Gaunt felt a chill. The Blood Pact were daemons enough. Their cohorts had been raised by the Archon with the specific intention of matching the Imperial Guard in the Sabbat Worlds theatre. Anakwanar Sek was the Archon's most fearsome lieutenant commander. Inspired by the example of the Blood Pact, Sek had developed his own elite force. Gaunt had seen the Sons at work on... where was it... Gereon, that was it, Gereon. The Sons of Sek had appeared to be even more formidable than the Blood Pact. The Sons had an appetite for atrocity. The Ghosts had yet to enjoy the dubious pleasure of meeting them in full combat.

'Where's Rawne?' asked Gaunt.

'I don't know, sir,' Beltayn replied.

'Baskevyl, then? Daur? Kolea?'

'I can't get them on the vox.'

'Get me Corbec, at least!'

Beltayn looked at him oddly.

'What?' asked Gaunt.

'Colonel Corbec, sir... he's been dead these last five years.'

Gaunt paused. 'Of course he has. Of course he has...'

'Sir?'

'Bel, we have to get this bridge secured before nightfall.'

Beltayn looked up at the smoke cover overhead. 'And when will that be, do you think?'

'I don't know. We just have to get the bridge secured.'

'I don't even know where the bridge is any more,' said Beltayn.

'It's over that way,' Gaunt replied, gesturing over his left shoulder. 'It's close. Bel, I need you to run back and rally the main force. I need you to find Rawne or Kolea and get them ready. Let them know we're about to be flanked by the Sons. Tell them I'm gathering up the forward elements and heading for the bridge.'

'Is that wise, sir?' asked Beltayn.

'The bridge is our objective, Beltayn. We need to secure it. Tell Rawne I'm forming up every Ghost I can find and leading them towards the bridge approach. He's got to cover our arses from a flank attack. Come on, Bel. It's not rocket science!'

Beltayn nodded. He took up his las and turned to go. Then he paused, and offered Gaunt his hand.

'Bel?'

'In case we don't meet again, sir,' said Beltayn. 'I want you to know that it's been an honour to serve.'

Gaunt took Beltayn's hand. 'It's been an honour to serve *with* you, Dughan. But we *will* meet again.'

'We'd better,' said Beltayn, and ran off. Gaunt watched until his adjutant had vanished into the shrouding smoke.

He turned, and continued to advance.

Blood Pact bodies littered the mud, some already sinking into its fathomless embrace. Gaunt thought he'd find Ghost platoons ahead, but there was no sign of them. They'd pushed in beside him. Where the feth had they vanished to?

He reloaded his bolt pistol as he trudged forwards. He could smell the river. The spinning, twisting smoke was eclipsing the sky. All sounds and signs of fighting had abated.

His eyes started to hurt again. He couldn't see far in the damned smoke.

Then he saw Nessa.

XVIII

NESSA BOURAH WAS one of his finest snipers. She'd served through the Vervunhive siege as part of the people's resistance, and joined the Ghosts at liberation.

Nessa had taken up a shooting pitch in a muddy foxhole on the river bank, and was scoping for a target. Saturation bombing during the battle of Vervunhive had rendered her profoundly deaf. Without a spotter, she was entirely unaware of the Blood Pact trooper closing in behind her, machete raised.

Gaunt raised his bolt pistol, sighted it, and blew the Blood Pacter's head off. Nessa jumped in surprise as the body crashed down beside her. She turned and raised her long-las.

It's me, Gaunt signed.

Nessa lowered her rifle.

'You took me by surprise,' she said, in her delicious, slightly nasal accent.

'Not as much as he would have,' Gaunt suggested.

She touched his chin, and turned his face towards her.

'So I can see!' she demanded. 'So I can see your mouth!'

Sorry, he signed.

He got down in the foxhole beside her, making sure she could see his face.

'Where are the others? The others?' he asked.

Nessa shook her head. 'I haven't seen anyone. It's quiet.'

'Something's wrong,' he said.

'What?'

Something's wrong, he signed. He'd made a point of learning the art after Vervunhive. Nessa wasn't the only deaf trooper in his regiment. Many of them, like Nessa, had eschewed augmetics, favouring the strength of silence in war.

'We should be very quiet,' she agreed.

If we should be quiet, why aren't you signing to me? he signed.

'I'm deaf. I can read your signing,' she said. 'How would you read mine?'

'I don't understand,' he said.

Nessa reached out a hand and ran her finger along his cheek, circling his right eye.

'I did like your eyes so very much,' she said. 'They were so strong. I suppose they can be replaced.'

'Replaced? What are you talking about?'

'They took your eyes, sir. Out in the wastelands of Jago, they took your eyes.'

'What the feth are you talking about?'

She shrank back. 'I'm sorry,' she said. 'I thought you knew.'

'Knew what? No one's taken my eyes. I can see you. Nessa, I can see you!'

'Just like I can hear you,' she replied. 'It's funny, that, isn't it?'

'Nessa—'

'I'm sorry. I'm glad you can see me. I really am.'

'I don't understand,' he said. His eyes had started to hurt again. The iron star was burning down through the smoke.

You're blind and I'm deaf, she signed. *What a great partnership. I just wish I could stay here with you.*

'Nessa?' he cried. 'Nessa?'

Gaunt was alone in the foxhole. Nessa had gone. Her long-las and ammo belt lay beside him, as if she'd just been there. He could still smell her.

'I'm not blind,' he told nobody. 'I'm not blind. I can see this. I can see the river. I can see the bridge.'

XIX

THE BRIDGE SEEMED as far away as ever. As the smoke slowly cleared and dusk settled, Gaunt watched the bridge from the foxhole cover. He studied it through Nessa's scope. Where had she gone? She'd been right there.

She'd been right—

He saw movement down by the bridge. He adjusted the scope and, by the evil light of the iron star, saw the black figures gathering at the mouth of the bridge. There were a dozen of them. They were watching him.

He took up the long-las, checked its load, and wondered about his aim. Could he hit one of them at this range? Nessa could, Larks too, but Gaunt was not a trained marksman. Maybe he could place a shot amongst them and scare them off.

They were beginning to annoy him. What did they want? Did they want him? Had they come for him? He wasn't having that.

He lowered the rifle. There was no point wasting ammo. He was going to need it. He could hear drums,

drums beating the skewed, alien tempos of the Sons of Sek.

There was going to be a great deal more bloodshed before the night was out.

He wondered if he had the strength to face it. He was so tired. His eyes hurt.

What had Nessa meant? Who took my eyes?

His body ached. Sleep seemed like such a perfect release. Just for a minute, perhaps? A few minutes sleep.

He closed his eyes.

XX

There was a long, squealing tone, a warning note.

'Flatline!' Dorden cried.

'Paddles!' Curth yelled, tears in her eyes.

'It's no good–'

'Paddles! Seventy mil adrenolec shunt! Another ten units!'

The note whined on.

'Ana, it's a flatline. There's no purpose in prolonging–'

'Give me the fething paddles now!' she demanded.

XXI

HE DID NOT dream. There was only darkness. It was a lonely place. He couldn't even sense the iron star any more. There was just a sound, a persistent whining note. It cut through his empty, dreamless darkness, droning, squealing, monotonous.

He woke with a start, slammed awake as if by some vast shock. The whining note quit, and was replaced by the thump of the enemy drums.

He was still in the foxhole. The world was cast in twilight. *Who the feth cares anymore* was just minutes away from nightfall.

Something had woken him. Some kind of contact had brought him back from the darkness of his sleep.

'This'll never do,' a voice said.

He sat up. 'Who's there?'

'Going to sleep on the job? You'd have given us double RIP duties if you'd caught us doing that,' another voice chuckled.

'Who's there?' Gaunt demanded, reaching for his bolt pistol. 'I can't see you! Who's there?'

'Of course you can't see us,' said a third voice. It was very flat and artificial, and carried no emphasis or emotion. It sounded sarcastic. 'You can't see anything.'

'But it's all right, sir,' said a fourth voice, a young voice. 'We can see *you*.'

'So you're safe,' said the first voice. It was a rich, genial, reassuring voice. 'For now, anyway.'

'Gotta get moving, mind,' said the flat sarcastic voice. 'Can't stay here forever.'

'And we can only look after you for a little while,' said the second, chuckling voice.

Gaunt rose to his feet, swinging the bolt pistol around blindly. 'Show yourselves!'

'Well, if it makes it easier for you,' sighed the first voice.

Gaunt blinked. Four men were suddenly visible, crouching around the foxhole, staring in at him. They were Ghosts, in black Ghost kit, their weapons loose but ready in their hands.

'Better?' asked their bearded leader.

'Corbec?' Gaunt whispered.

'Hello, 'bram,' said Colm Corbec with a grin. 'Been a while. Looks like you've been through the fething wars.'

'Colm, it's good to see you,' said Gaunt, lowering his pistol. 'I thought I was alone out here. What are our strengths? How many other Ghost platoons made it this far?'

Corbec smiled and shook his head. He glanced at his companions. 'Just the five of us. We'll have to make do, won't we, lads?'

The other three nodded.

'It's good to see you,' Gaunt repeated.

'You're not seeing us,' said the owner of the monotone voice. 'You're not seeing anything. They took out your eyes.'

'Hush your drone, Feygor,' said Corbec. 'He doesn't understand.'

Feygor shrugged.

'But it *is* good to see you again, sir,' said the biggest of the four Ghosts with a chuckle. 'Maybe we should toast to old times with a sip of sacra?'

'We need clear heads just now, Bragg,' said Corbec. 'We've got to get to the bridge.'

'Well, it was just a thought,' said Try Again Bragg.

'There's no point us trying to get to the bridge,' said Gaunt. 'There are only five of us. What good would that do?'

'It's what matters,' said the youngest Ghost. 'It's why we're here.'

'I don't understand, Caff,' said Gaunt.

'Let's just get over the bridge, sir,' said Caffran. 'Then you'll understand everything.'

XXII

THEY LEFT THE safety of the foxhole and began to track their way down towards the bridge. The river was a dead thing, full of corpses. The ruins of the Blood Pact platforms smouldered in the evening haze. Gaunt could still hear the drums of the Sons of Sek, pounding like an irregular heartbeat.

Caffran took point, sweeping ahead with his lasrifle. The boy was good, sharp, a potential scout. Gaunt tried to remember why he hadn't promoted Caffran to Mkoll's unit. It was a clear oversight. Gaunt must have had a good reason not to send the boy on.

Corbec and Feygor flanked Gaunt, weapons ready. Corbec was humming an old Tanith wood-song. The sound of it made Gaunt feel much more comfortable. Just like the old days. Corbec would hum along to

Milo's pipes. Why didn't that happen any more? Where had Corbec been, these last few combat tours?

Gaunt remembered Beltayn saying something about Corbec. He couldn't quite recall what it was.

Feygor was quiet. Everything he said sounded like a petulant sarcastic jibe thanks to his artificial larynx. He kept his comments to himself.

Try brought up the rear, lugging his twin autocannons. 'Just like old times, huh?' he said.

'Noise discipline!' Corbec hissed.

'Yeah, just like old times,' said Bragg.

Caffran held up a hand for full stop. They halted. Gaunt readied his pistol and his sword. He'd wanted to bring Nessa's long-las, but Corbec had told him Nessa might want it back and he should leave it be.

'Caff?' Gaunt called.

Movement, Caffran signed.

'Great,' said Feygor. This time, his sarcasm was intentional.

The drumming had got louder and faster, like a racing heart.

'What have we got, Caff?' asked Corbec softly, crawling forwards.

'Sons of Sek between us and the bridge,' Caffran reported. 'Dozens of them.'

'What about the watchers?' asked Gaunt.

'The what?' asked Feygor.

'The watchers in black,' said Gaunt.

'Oh, them,' said Bragg. 'They're just your imagination, they are.'

'What?' asked Gaunt.

'Everyone shut up,' said Corbec. 'We're about to wade into the deep and stinky. Everyone locked? Everyone loaded?'

'Yes, sir,' the three Ghosts replied.

''Bram?'

Gaunt nodded. 'I'm ready, Colm. Who wants to live forever?'

'Well, *you*, I hope,' said Corbec. 'For a while, at least. That's the whole point of this.'

Gaunt looked at him.

'You've got to live, Ibram,' said Corbec. 'You've just got to. That's the way of it. You're important, more important than you can imagine. You and the Ghosts, it's going to be down to you. The whole Crusade depends on you. Win or lose, it's going to be down to you in the end.'

'I don't know what you're talking about, Colm,' Gaunt said.

'I know you don't,' said Corbec, 'but you will.'

'You said "me and the Ghosts",' said Gaunt. 'You're Ghosts too.'

'Yes, we are,' said Bragg. 'We *really* are.'

'Let's do this, shall we, gents?' Corbec suggested. 'On three. One, two...'

XXIII

THE SONS OF Sek were the hardest bastards Gaunt had ever encountered on the field of war. Chasing for the bridge, the five Ghosts ploughed into them. The fight turned to hell. It wasn't exhilarating. The old fury didn't relight.

It was a bloody, butchering slog. It was war at its darkest and most tenacious.

The Sons came at them from all sides in the twilight. Drumming was the only sound Gaunt could hear. Feygor, Caffran and Corbec slammed off shots as they came in, and Bragg followed on, blasting with his cannons. He mowed them down. The Sons of Sek were so many, he didn't have to try again. Gaunt's sword swung and struck. He emptied his bolt pistol four times.

He thought they would be overwhelmed. He thought they weren't going to make it, but they were fast, and they were good, and they had surprise on their side, despite the incredible ferocity of the Sons of Sek.

They were Ghosts. They were five of the best Guardsmen the Imperium had ever produced.

They covered one another. They checked and turned with expertise. They watched the flanks, they plastered the angles, they fired in turns to stagger reloading. At any given point in the action at least three of them were shooting.

They cut through the Sons like an elite strike force, because they *were* an elite strike force. They were immortals. They were gods of war.

They reached the bridge.

XXIV

'ON YOU GO, then,' said Corbec.

'We all go across,' said Gaunt. He turned to look at the four Ghosts. They were standing, weapons ready, in a semi-circle behind him, facing the bridge.

'That's not how it works,' said Feygor.

'We can't cross the bridge,' said Caffran.

'But *you've* got to,' said Bragg.

'I'm not about to leave you here,' said Gaunt.

'That's just how it goes,' said Corbec. 'You go on alone from here. You cross the bridge. We stay on this side.'

'Why?'

'Because we have to,' said Corbec. 'We can't cross over, but you can. Now go on with you. Don't make us wish we hadn't made this effort. Cross the fething bridge, 'bram. Cross it.'

'But–'

'Cross it!' snapped Bragg.

'You'll see us again soon enough, sir,' said Caffran.

'Unless you do end up living for ever,' said Feygor.

Gaunt turned and looked at the bridge. It was vast and empty and iron, and it seemed to stretch away as far as he could see.

'I don't know,' he said. 'I'm tired. My eyes hurt. I don't know if I can make it all that way.'

'You have to,' said Caffran. 'They're waiting for you on the other side.'

'I'm so tired, Caff,' Gaunt said. 'Can't I stay here with you?'

'Get on with you!' Corbec growled.

'I don't think I can make it all the way,' said Gaunt.

'We can't come with you,' said Corbec. 'We can't carry you over there. Someone else will have to help you.'

'Colm?' Gaunt said, sinking to the ground.

'See you in another life, all right?' said Corbec.

Gaunt was alone.

XXV

'Get up,' said Rawne.

Gaunt looked up. 'Eli?'

'Get up, you fether. Get up.'

'Eli?'

Rawne peered down at him. 'Don't you dare do this to me, Gaunt. If anyone's going to finish you, it's going to be me. Don't you dare do this.'

Gaunt clambered to his feet. 'I don't like your tone, Major Rawne.'

'Oh, bite me,' said Rawne. 'Come on, you bastard. You're coming back with us.'

'Us?' murmured Gaunt.

'Seyadhe true, soule,' said Eszrah ap Niht. Eszrah and Rawne scooped Gaunt up between them and began to walk him across the bridge.

'It's so fething far,' muttered Gaunt. 'And the Sons of Sek... the Sons of Sek are right behind us.'

'The Sons of Sek can eat my arse,' said Rawne. 'You're coming home with us. Throne, you weigh a ton. Try using your legs! Help a fether out!'

'I'm trying, Rawne. My eyes hurt so much.'

'They put your eyes out in the wastelands of Jago,' said Rawne. 'The Blood Pact torturers virtually hacked you to pieces. Curth and Dorden, they've been fighting to patch you together again. You'll get new eyes. Augmetics. You'll get grafts and organ bionics. Just keep walking.'

'Jago?' Gaunt whispered. He began to remember.

'Oh, don't be such a pussy, Gaunt! I've come all this way for you!' Rawne tried to check his temper. 'Me. Me, for Throne's sake. Don't you dare die on me now!'

'I...' Gaunt said, feeling himself almost dragged along by Rawne and the Nihtgane. 'I remember. The iron star.'

'The what?' asked Rawne.

'The iron star,' Gaunt replied. 'A heated poker, a branding iron, stabbing into my eyes, burning them out, taking them. Oh Throne.'

'Stay with me, Ibram! We're almost there!'

'Histye, Soule,' whispered Eszrah ap Niht. 'Life, it bekkons.'

XXVI

THE WATCHERS IN black were waiting for them at the far end of the bridge.

'Give him over to us,' one said.

'Yeah, feth you,' Rawne replied, struggling to hold Gaunt upright. 'Feth you very much!'

'He's gone too far,' said the leader of the black figures. 'The poor, poor boy. He's seen enough. Let him sleep now. Let him rest. We'll take care of him. Don't eke out his agony. Don't force him to come back into a world that he hates.'

'Get out of our way,' said Rawne.

'Ibram's at his end. It would be a mercy,' said the leader of the black figures. 'We'll take good care of him, Eli. Trust us. We'll nurse him into the darkness. It's what we do.'

He lowered his cowl. It was Zweil. Around him, the other ayatani priests pulled back their hoods.

'Come on, Eli,' Zweil said. 'He's done enough. Let him rest. Let us sing him to sleep. Let us anoint his body and send him off to the final rest. He deserves it. He *deserves* it. His war is done.'

Slumped between Eszrah and Rawne, Gaunt slowly looked up.

'Father,' he said, blood dribbling from his gutted eye sockets, 'I thank you for your compassion. I really do. Rest is so tempting. It's so very, very tempting. But I don't think I'm done yet.'

Zweil sighed. 'I was only trying to help.'

'Then don't help me die, father,' Gaunt said. 'Help me live.'

XXVII

The ayatani priests carried Gaunt's body off the bridge onto the far side of the river. Wet with Gaunt's blood, Rawne and Eszrah followed them.

'I've got a pulse!' Curth cried.

'Thready but solid,' Dorden noted.

'Ten units of blood!' Curth ordered.

'Will he live?' asked Rawne, pulling down his surgical mask.

'You've all been through here,' Curth replied, 'all the Ghosts. You've tried to reassure him, and keep him stable. Yes, Eli, despite everything, I think he might live yet.'

'He deserves the peace of death,' said Zweil, sitting at the end of the cot. 'I could still give him the last rites.'

'I don't think that's going to be necessary, father,' said Dorden.

Gaunt stirred.

'Colm...' he murmured.

'He's dreaming again,' said Rawne.

XXVIII

From: Curth, medicae functionary, Tanith First.
To: Acting Commander, Elikon HQ, Jago.

It pleases me to be able to inform you, sir, that Colonel-Commissar Ibram Gaunt has roused from his coma. The injuries Colonel-Commissar Gaunt suffered at the hands of the Blood Pact torturers were severe (please see my request for augmetic optical implants). He suffered three systemic organ failures on the table, and the loss of his eyes is a terrible mutilation. Skin grafting will continue for several months.

I am, however, delighted to report that Ibram Gaunt is alive.

Your honoured servant
Ana Curth (medicae).

XXIX

'ARE WE STILL on... on Jago?' he had asked his adjutant that morning while shaving.

His adjutant, Beltayn, had frowned, thinking the question over.

'Jago? Uh... yes. I believe so, sir,' he had replied.

The names really weren't of any consequence any more, the names of cities or continents or worlds. Each one was just a new place to get into, and then get out of again, once the job was done. He'd stopped worrying about the names. He just concentrated on the jobs, loyal but weary, weary but loyal.

Sometimes, he was so tired he even forgot his own name.

He dipped his old cut-throat razor into the chipped bowl, washing off the foam and the residue of shorn bristles. He looked at his reflection in the cracked shaving mirror. Though the reflection didn't seem to have eyes, he recognised it anyway.

Ibram Gaunt. That was it. Ibram Gaunt.

Of course it was.

Nik and I have collaborated on a number of things, most particularly raising a family, but from a Black Library perspective, it's probably our co-writing of two Warhammer novels – Gilead's Blood and Hammers of Ulric – that are most significant.

Over the last few years, Nik's spent more of her time invisibly deployed as a proofreader and editor, and she remains my first reader and primary editorial filter. But in the last year she's written two novels as the yen for writing has returned. It's nice to see her writing again, and we were lucky to get this story before other glamorous commissions whisked her away.

In the third Gaunt arc, The Lost, and especially in the novel Traitor General, I explored themes of resistance fighting and enemy occupation, classic wartime motifs that seldom get an outing in 40K terms because they're hard to make workable. This isn't a return to occupied Gereon, but it's a visit to a planet very much like it, held in the sway of the Archenemy of mankind...

Dan Abnett

CELL

Nik Vincent

It wasn't safe to pray anywhere on Reredos.

The room was dark and cramped, and the floor beneath Ayatani Perdu's feet was earthy and sodden, and smelt of things he preferred not to think about. His boots leaked, and his feet were trying hard to shrink from the organic dankness that penetrated through the old hide. He was trying almost too hard to concentrate on the prayer, to imbue his voice with the conviction that he did not always feel, but his discomfort was getting the better of him.

Perdu's congregation never seemed to grow or diminish. There was room for half a dozen, and half a dozen always showed up for his services. The faces varied, depending on who was sent to do what jobs, and on who lived and who died. War changed things, and when the war was over and the occupation established, that changed things too. The resisters were the most devout and the biggest risk-takers; they needed priests, and they needed safe places where they could exchange

185

information or pool resources. The two coincided here.

He was surrounded by men, taller and thinner than dusk shadows. They stank too. They had come off the agri-galleries, tired and hungry, but at least they didn't have to worry about their feet. He did not envy the aching in their bones from arching their backs and stooping their shoulders to fit into the rooms that he could stand erect in, but he did envy their prosthetics, their elongated, telescopic shins and tapered spade-like feet that meant they were never ankle-deep in anything.

'The Emperor protects,' he said. He wondered if he believed it.

'The Emperor protects.'

The words were barely out of his mouth the second time when Perdu heard the wet thud of someone going down. The man had been standing behind Perdu. He didn't know his name. There were no names any more, nor conversations, nor even rumours. Three years was a long time to learn that lesson, but now, no one talked, no one shared, no one speculated. The work that was done was done quietly. His work was done only in these places, these rooms that were assigned to him, with these people, who came to him for strength and solace, who came to him because they believed, against all reason, that the Emperor would protect.

He was an agent of the God-Emperor and of the beloved Beati, and he was an enabler of the resistance movement on Reredos.

He dropped the prayer book and turned, in time to see the foetid air swirl around the collapsed figure. He bent over the body, his prayer book banging against his chest as it hung from the chain around his neck. It swung out, almost catching the dying man on his brow. He rasped a breath and reached up a hand. Perdu placed the book in the agri-worker's hands, and reached out his own clean palm to crack the man's chest filter.

Perdu had to bang hard on the filter, twice, before he could twist it and draw it out of the man's chest. It was caked with a gritty purple mass of spores mixed with the mucus that the agri-workers now produced in such vast quantities that ceramite tar-buckets were used as spittoons in the drinking holes that surrounded the galleries where the men lived and worked. Perdu had seen what this crap could do to rockcrete floors, pitting and scarring, and eating away at all but the most impenetrable materials.

The congregation dispersed as Perdu tried to save one man in a world that was being eaten away and gobbed out in mucus chunks by relentless occupation forces.

The ayatani priest pushed two fingers into the hole in the man's chest, like a kid with a jar of ploin-kernel butter, turning them around the circumference of the filter and digging out the unholy shit that had taken the victim's breath away.

How many times had he done it before? Dozens, certainly, scores, maybe even hundreds. And how many men had he saved?

There was too much of it. Why hadn't this damned pute cleaned his filter? He must have left it for days. Did he have some sort of death wish?

Perdu eased the man flat onto his back. He hated laying him on the cold wet filth, but had no choice. He straddled the body, placing one knee on either side of the filter, and pushed his fingers back into the cavity. The pressure of his knees pushed more of the filth out onto his fingers, and he scooped it up and flicked it out onto the floor before going back for more. The body seemed to be breathing, but it was the action of Perdu pumping his legs against the chest that was causing the rasping gulps that he could hear only too clearly in the corpse's throat. He was a corpse. His face was grey and his lips blue. His eyes stared blankly out of his head, bulging slightly as though he'd been strangled. This creeping asphyxia was worse than being throttled; it was worse than anything.

'The Lady's...' Perdu began as he pushed his knees

once more into the corpse's chest. He felt a rib give way, and took off the tension, dropping his knees onto the cold dank floor to either side of the body, horrified by his attempts to resurrect the man.

He drew the back of his hand across his forehead, and dropped his head down onto his chest.

He could feel the gritty mucus spreading beneath the knees of his trousers, and started to rise to his feet. There was nothing more for him to do. His congregation had left him; he was alone. Time stood still as he hovered over the body for several more minutes. His eyes shifted to the floor, to the oil-slick of purple sputum that was spreading and leaching into the ground around the corpse, around where his knees had been, bubbling, and corroding the trampled surface. The fabric of his trousers was smouldering slightly, and he tore away the ragged scraps, knowing that there was no mending the cloth.

He noticed edges in the purple mess, hard lines that shouldn't have been there. Tentatively, he ran his fingers through the spreading mucus and began to retrieve tiny tablets of ceramite, chips that had been shaved away from Emperor-only-knew what. They were small and irregular in shape; they had been improvised.

Perdu had not seen their like before, but he knew what they were. This was not the usual useless waste of life. This death had a purpose. This man had sacrificed himself, given his life in the service of the God-Emperor to deliver the information on the ceramite chips to one of the many anonymous resistance cells in the hive.

Perdu took a flat, narrow flask from his webbing, and gently poured some of the contents into the pool of mucus, but the water had no effect. He tipped the flask between his lips, and proceeded to wash his mouth out with the remaining liquid, moving the quantity of water around and over his tongue and teeth before gargling with it, and then sending it around again. When he was satisfied, he spat the mixture of water and saliva onto the mucus, and worked the frothing mess with his fingers, fingers that no longer bore surface skin, let alone prints. He had only one pair of gloves, and he would rather risk his skin than their destruction.

After several minutes, Perdu gave up the search, and looked down at the half a dozen mismatched shards lined up on his finger.

His time was up. Suddenly, he knew that the room was no longer safe. He'd stayed too long, and he wouldn't be able to use the site again. He scraped the chips off his finger into the still-open water flask, and pulled his gloves on. The right one would be useless by the time he took it off again, but there was no time to clean himself up. He could feel the burning in his fingers as the mucus set to work to destroy his flesh.

Perdu pushed the dead man's filter cap back into his chest, and rolled the corpse onto its side to cover evidence of the mucus; the idiot enemy wouldn't look under the body. He did not wait for the enemy excubitors to appear with their narrow frames, distended bellies and grotesque masks. They were grey-skinned monsters with plugs and hoses embedded in their pallid flesh, harsh voices translated through grilles that produced guttural combinations of grunts and too much purple spittle.

Out on the street, the quality of the light told Perdu everything. He did not need to look up to know that a glyf was hovering nearby, six or eight metres above his position, its bright runes swirling and pulsing through the air, ready to penetrate the minds of any pute fool enough to look at it. They wafted over populated areas of the planet, checking for those who were not consented, who didn't carry imagoes in their arms, or whose imagoes limited their free passage. They altered the quality of the air with their ethereal light, and with the buzzing insect noise they made, rising to a pitch when they homed in on some poor transgressor. Perdu smelt the hot acrid bloom of battery acid that the glyfs emitted, judged that the incessant purring noise was stable, and walked in the opposite direction.

He didn't see the boy, his one connection to an active cell; he didn't look for him. The lessons were slow to learn, but anything or anyone watching him would see something pass between them, and then they'd both be in trouble. He knew the boy was there; a boy was always there, waiting for the next piece of the puzzle, the next message, the next order. No one knew who was giving the orders. Perdu didn't know any of the boys' names, and so far as he was aware, they didn't know his. He didn't even know if they were all boys. He didn't know how many other ayatani priests were involved in resisting, either. He didn't know how many cells there were in this hive, this agri-works, on this continent, or on the planet. Singular individuals had known these details once, but they were all gone, and those left behind had learned their lessons.

Perdu retreated. He was permanently in retreat. Virtually the entire planet was in retreat. There were rumours of fighting forces in one or two of the larger hives, guerilla stuff, mostly, but very little reliable information was available from one place to another; all comms-channels were under the control of the occupying forces, albeit their security wasn't impenetrable, and leaks were exploited at every opportunity.

Communications were necessary to the smooth running of the agri-galleries out on the great plains of Reredos, where the land had been given over to food production for the occupying forces and for export off-world. They were feeding the enemy with the foetid purple slop, the fast-growing fleshy pods that putrefied almost before they ripened, spilling out the spores that were killing the stilt-men who tended the plants. They had once provided the finest cereal crops in the galaxy. There had been no compromising the product by hybridisation, no dwarfing, no genetic modifying for higher yields, and virtually no disease-resistance. Eighty per cent of production used to go to slab for the Emperor's armies, but the rest, the glorious twenty per cent, had provided the raw materials for the foremost hop and barley brews in the Imperium for a thousand years.

The chest filters kept out the worst of the dust from the papery old-gene-stock hops that used to be grown in the galleries, and prevented the workforce breathing on the priceless crops. The best of the stilt-men were rewarded with augmetics that increased their agility and pushed up their quotas. Not only could they tend the tallest, most fragile reaches of the plants, but their telescopic shins could be extended so far that they could also cover vast acreages of the tunnels furthest from the habs and sinks without the need for polluting vehicles.

The great, arched galleries used to spread across the plains, clean and white and gleaming; now two-thirds of them were grey and carbonised, allowing little light in through their purple-stained covers, and the canker was spreading. The hops were long-gone, torn or burned out by the guards who patrolled the agri-works, the work-force toiling around and above them, elegant, fragile by comparison to the pale, angular, barely human beasts that were their keepers.

'IT'S OUT?' ASKED the old man, slouching over a beaker of something that might once have seen the inside of a barrel that might once have held hop-brew, but not recently. The woman standing on the other side of the counter didn't look at him; she turned the cloth once more around the cloudy glass in her hand and placed it on a shelf.

'No,' she said.

'The chips?' he asked, shielding the words between his mouth and the beaker he was lifting to it.

'Passed,' said the woman.

'The boy?' asked the old man as he lowered the beaker back to the counter.

'No,' said the woman, moving along the counter to another customer.

They had to get the damned things out of the galleries. More of the tunnels were being cleared for replanting, and the Emperor only knew what the new crop would do to them. The carbonisation would petrify them, or the spores would corrode them, and if not that, the by-products of so many deaths among the agri-workers and the mucus that the survivors scooped out of their filters every day could do just as much harm. They were the most important resource the resisters had, the key to bringing the Imperium to the planet's rescue.

They couldn't stay where they were, but getting them out was proving a slow and complex business. Just getting through the first part of the process, making the chips and getting them to the priest, had cost dearly, and time and resources were short.

He couldn't ask why the priest hadn't handed the chips to the boy, or what the priest planned to do with them. He was at two removed, so he didn't even know the priest's name, or anything about him. He'd return to the cell with nothing. He often did. Nothing had ever been quite so critical; no single thing had ever signified the salvation of the entire planet.

THE LASRIFLE BANGED and bucked in Bedlo's hands when it should have made a satisfying krak and held steady. He and his cell-mates had been inside the building for two days, out of sight of the excubitors and the glyfs, trying to turn themselves into an effective resisting force. Practice made perfect.

He issued instructions and advice, his voice sounding too loud between shots. Hand signals were better if the new recruits could learn them, but weapons familiarity was the real priority.

His gakking gun was defective. It was going to take him out as readily as it'd kill the enemy. He lifted the rifle away from his body, pulling the strap over his head, and threw it away in disgust.

'That's it,' he shouted. 'Debrief.'

Wescoe shouldered her long-las and left Bedlo to it. She'd been doing this for long enough to know what the debrief would involve, and she and Mallet took it in turns to patrol the perimeter of their practice area, to keep the kids safe while they learned how to resist. It was her turn.

Mallet picked up Bedlo's offending lasrifle and began to strip it down. He said little or nothing, ever, but he knew arms, was obsessed with them. The war had been good to him, and the occupation better.

Bedlo had come to the cell almost by accident when his own, his third, had been destroyed in a skirmish: a stupid mistake caused by one of his cell-mates butting up against the enemy during a routine sweep of their hive quarter. The resulting firefight had taken out several of the enemy guard under a senior excubitor's command, and, looking for retribution, the enemy had deployed a grenade launcher with great effect. The whole decrepit mess of the quarter had come crashing down, and when the excubitor had counted the bodies, and realised that Bedlo and one or two others had escaped, he set a hound loose.

Whoever the enemy butcher had been, and it was rumoured that he had direct links to the Archon, he'd been thorough. There was still no effective way to take out a wirewolf, and not much chance of avoiding one, either. So this was Bedlo's fourth resistance cell, his first as leader; he'd only been with them a matter of weeks when they were almost wiped out. He'd jumped two places to take the lead, and began recruiting immediately. He had no idea how long Mallet had been with the cell, but the man was indestructible. He was a born fighter, but lacked the communication skills to lead effectively. Wescoe was effective, too, and clearly a veteran, but she shrank from command, and seemed happy enough for Bedlo to take the lead.

As the cell-mates squatted or stood together in one corner of the room with their backs to the remains of the pitted, charred plasboard walls, facing the imaginary enemy should he infiltrate, Mallet tossed Bedlo the lasrifle end-over-end. The boss caught it in his right hand, and then dropped it vertically through his grip to check the balance. It was better, and there were no dodgy sounds when he caught the housing in his fist. He turned and shot a round. The bang sounded closer to a krak, but not close enough.

Bedlo tossed the weapon back to Mallet.

'If that's the best you can do, we need a more reliable weapons supply,' he said.

Mallet started to strip the las down, again, squatting on his haunches. The boy closest to him, Tilson, shuffled sideways, widening the gap between them. The movement wasn't lost on Bedlo. Trust wasn't at a premium, it was non-existent.

Mallet didn't listen as Bedlo went through the motions.

'Command,' he said, raising his index finger as the two new boys watched. 'Disperse,' two fingers together, the way a child might make a finger-pistol. 'Attack,' a flat hand thrust forwards. The instructions weren't complicated, but new recruits were always a liability, whether they were young and keen or young and scared, and they were always young.

The perimeter check only took Wescoe a matter of a couple of minutes. There was only one entrance/exit point a couple of hundred metres from the room where the boys were being put through their paces, and a couple of blind corridors to the left and right of the practice room. She was good in the dark, used to it, and didn't resort to using the lamp-pack that she carried in her webbing. She very soon wished that she had.

Wescoe checked the entrance, ducking to left and right, her long-las raised at her shoulder. There was nothing. She turned, hugging the left-hand wall to her back, the first blind corridor coming up twenty metres away on the right. Then she saw it, a narrow, intermittent beam of grey light. Her hands tensed slightly around the las, and her pupils dilated a fraction as the corridor darkened again. There was just a chance that a glow globe had flickered spontaneously, but the building had been disused and derelict since it had come under heavy fire during the war, years ago, and it seemed unlikely to Wescoe.

'Voi shet–' she heard, cut off, and followed by a scuffling sound and a series of thuds. Someone else was in the building. Her cell was not alone.

Wescoe let out the breath that she realised she had been holding, and switched to the right-hand side of the corridor, as the light seemed to have come from the dead-end on the left. She knew that the passage was barely ten metres long before it was cut off by an impenetrable barrier made of the rubble that was all that remained of that wing of the old building. If she had to engage, she had better be fast and efficient. The enemy was right on top of the cell; only a few metres and a bad plascrete wall separated them. A split second later, she was aiming her las into the dark mouth of the blind corridor.

Mallet lifted Bedlo's lasrifle to check its heft, and thumbed the sight.

They all heard the noise on the other side of the wall. Tilson winced at the sound of the alien tongue as the enemy shouted out, and they heard the scuffling thuds of clumsy bodies. Mallet knew that the enemy was no longer imaginary. He didn't speak, but he was off his arse and onto one knee, braced in the entrance to the room, almost before they heard the shots fired, and well ahead of the boys properly registering that they were under attack.

He had Bedlo's weapon in his hand, so he fired it.

Brak!

Even after stripping it down several times, Mallet didn't trust the las-rifle, so he kept firing it, wild in his right hand while his left went straight to a pistol at his hip. Before Bedlo had turned to shout an order or find a weapon, Mallet was already letting loose an uneven volley of mismatched shots.

Bedlo dropped, flat to the floor, stalling for time he didn't have.

Tilson, squatting next to him, was staring at him, eyes wide, a hole in his throat. Bedlo listened for a split second to the odd *brak* of his second-hand, twenty-second-hand, lasrifle. Mallet was doing a job covering them. Then he looked up to see the other boy, Shuey. The little pute had found a gap behind Mallet and was bracing himself against the rock-hard mercenary, using the older man's shoulder to steady his aim. They half-stood like some bottom-heavy, two-headed creature, three weapons between them, firing at an enemy that Bedlo still hadn't seen.

Bedlo rolled onto his back and took hold of the improvised flamer that had been assigned to Tilson. He rotated and flipped, and, still flat on his belly, opened up with a splutter of fuel that had begun as promethium, but which had been spent and then filtered, cooled, refined back to low-grade, secondary-use liquid fuel, before being spent again, filtered, mixed with the bio-pute that came off the old hops and rehashed as semi-demi domestic fuel-oil. He didn't hold out much hope.

The flamer spat a spray of greenish, cloudy liquid, but didn't catch. Bedlo triggered the igniter, but it was out of synch with the fuel delivery system, such as it was, and clicked uselessly.

Bedlo took a moment, and listened to the weapons discharging. He could hear Mallet's side arm and the distinctive sound of the old lasrifle, and he could make out the slower, but steady report from Shuey's weapon, an old Guard-issue las that had belonged to some uncle or other; contraband from a long-lost war that they all still seemed to be fighting, and his passport into the cell. There was no other sound.

In the moment that Bedlo was taking to assess their

situation and gauge the danger they were in, Mallet shifted his aim by precisely sixty-two degrees, and ignited the semi-demi with a round from the gakked las.

Bedlo stood, faster than he thought was possible, and then felt like a fool when the ignited fuel produced only a dull yellowish flame and a slow trickle of blackening smoke. It'd leave a scorch-mark on the floor if it was allowed to burn for long enough, but not much else. In any case, it was too little, too late. The battle was already over, and the flamer had played no part in it.

Bedlo held his closed fist in front of him: the signal for cease-fire.

Mallet and Shuey held their weapons, but did not fire again, and the dingy space was quiet. Whoever, whatever, had started the firefight had stopped almost before Mallet had engaged.

Mallet looked at Bedlo.

'Boss?' he asked.

'Where's Wescoe?' asked Bedlo.

'The broad?' asked Shuey.

'The broad,' said Bedlo, crossing to the threshold to check out the results of the attack.

He returned a moment later, carrying the long-las that had belonged to Wescoe, arguably the most useful member of the cell. He'd never called her 'the broad' to her face, but that's what she was, a dangerously efficient killer old broad with more experience than they'd ever live long enough to rack up between them, except perhaps for Mallet. In his other hand was the autopistol belonging to the excubitor that Wescoe had taken out right after he'd shot Tilson in the throat.

Bedlo and Mallet examined the scene. She had died defending them, but had taken at least one of the three enemy guard with her. Their bodies lay beyond the entrance to the practice room and scattered in the mouth of the blind corridor. All the bodies were riddled with shots, and it wasn't clear who was responsible for the kills, but it didn't matter. A trail of blood led out towards the exit point, and it was clear that at least one guard had retreated, wounded. Bedlo gestured at the dark stains.

'She dealt with the immediate threat,' he said, 'but he must've had a buddy.'

'Why didn't she just–?' began Shuey.

'Just what?' asked Bedlo. 'What would you do stuck with a psychopath and a couple of boys?'

'And you... Boss,' said Shuey defiant behind his blushes.

THEY ALL HEARD heavy footfalls approaching, maybe a couple of hundred metres away. Bedlo gestured behind him and they retreated back into the practice room. Bedlo turned and scooped up a tarpaulin that was bunched up against the foot of the wall behind them. He took his boot to the plasboard and, once Shuey realised what he was doing, he joined in. Two hefty kicks each, and the false wall collapsed, allowing the resisters access through the derelict building and into the sinks. Wherever they trained, they always established a way out. It was one thing planning a skirmish or an attack, having a goal in mind, but no one wanted to get caught on manoeuvres with their trousers down and no back door.

'Haul arse, you stupid pute!' yelled Bedlo, not bothering with hand signals.

Mallet, guarding the entrance, fired a series of shots into the dark corridor, and then turned swiftly and followed Shuey and Bedlo out through the hole in the wall.

Two occupation guards in mismatched, incomplete fatigues and body-armour elbowed each other and tripped over the excubitors' bodies as they struggled to get to the resisters, but they were too late. They looked down at Tilson's body propped against the wall, dead, but upright, and then turned and walked away, apparently satisfied, the expressions on their masks unchanging.

Bedlo, Mallet and Shuey split up to regroup another day, two men down, and two weapons up, and the odds still stacked against them.

'LOGIER,' SAID THE old man, acknowledging the stilt-man as he sat facing the other way and began to dismantle one of his prosthetics, obsessive about maintaining them in pristine condition.

'Ozias,' said Logier.

The two men had known each other for Logier's entire life and for half of Ozias's. Logier was the son of a friend and colleague, long dead. They understood one another beyond being comrades, friends or allies, and they trusted one another, at least enough to use their names. Ozias had been running the agri-cell since the first threat of attack by the Archenemy eight years before; he had field-control of the low drinking hole, and had recruited the woman who ran the place to keep tabs on the traffic of information for him. The agri-workers would not fight the war; that job was left to the PDF and to a couple of regiments of Imperial Guard caught in the crossfire when they should have been on R&R. Ozias knew that reinforcements would come; that when the Warmaster became aware of the connection, of the precious resources, when he knew why Reredos must be defended, he would send more troops.

'The chips?' asked Logier.

'The priest has them,' said Ozias. 'He didn't pass them.'

Logier turned, and the two men looked at each other for a moment before Logier turned away again.

'We don't know why,' said Ozias. 'He was slow to evacuate after Calvit gave up the chips, probably trying to resuscitate him.'

'The Emperor protects,' said Logier, returning to the task of maintaining the hydraulics in his shins. 'I'll go to him,' he offered, after a moment. 'I'll make sure the chips get to the hive-cell.'

Ozias slumped a little lower in his seat.

'I wouldn't ask,' he said.

'I'll go,' said Logier.

'Yes,' said Ozias.

Ozias caught the eye of the woman at the counter, drained his beaker slowly, picked it up, and returned it, without looking at her again, or turning to check on Logier.

It was done.

AYATANI PERDU WAS not comfortable in the no-man's-land between the hive and the agri-galleries, but he always found himself there when they were most at risk. He'd been assigned this room two years ago, and used it whenever things got tough in the hive. It was bigger than the other rooms he used, and was part of an old warehouse complex. He knew how the rooms and corridors of the building connected, and how they'd been modified as the building had fallen into disrepair. It had only one storey, and no windows, but the ceiling was high and his voice echoed slightly in the space. The room was closer to the galleries than the hive, but patrols and glyfs were fewer and further between, here, and the boys that transported information were safer, for the most part. It didn't matter; he used the safest rooms available, and preached his sermons just the same.

There were half a dozen of them in his congregation, again, no more, no less. The vacancy had been filled, and the most active resisters, or those most in need of his ministrations, had taken their places. They had collected in a small group at the far end of the room, not attempting to fill the space.

Perdu felt the chips in the palm of his left hand inside his glove. The right glove was a ragged mess with two fingers missing and was good for very little; it didn't keep him warm or dry and it wasn't safe for concealment. The skin that had been so quickly eroded from his fingers by the purple mucus was growing back warm and too pink, and he covered it as best he could with old bandages – washed and reused a hundred times, yellow and fraying, but better than the alternative – and with the half-eaten glove.

'The Emperor protects,' he said, low and breathless. He did not want the prayer to end, not knowing what would come after it.

A man at the back of the group coughed, a new man. No one looked at him, but the congregation melted away without a word to their priest, without a murmur or a question, without a suggestion that they were aware of the recent death or of the replacement congregant. They had done what they needed to do, had set up contacts and passed on information, all without fanfare and with absolute discretion. Perdu bowed his head, unwilling to meet the gazes that did not rest on him. He looked down at the stilt-man's shins, at the gleaming hydraulics, obsessively cleaned, pristine, as if new. No new augmetics had been issued since the invasion, but these didn't look eight years old.

'You still have the chips?' asked Logier.

'I...' began Perdu. 'A man died,' he said.

'You know the drill,' said Logier. 'We pass information to you, and you pass it to the boy–'

'So that he can get killed, too,' said Perdu. 'That isn't good enough, any more.'

Logier turned from the priest, and crouched, drawing a stiletto from a sheath concealed in his shin. He made a casual hand signal, hoping the priest would understand. The stilt-man had heard something. The enemy was close.

Perdu dropped to Logier's left and behind him, and felt his way along the wall into the darkest crevice of the long room, careful not to turn his back. He was crouching in the corner, low on his haunches, but strong in his stance, when he felt something touching his arm. He put out his hand and took hold of the small, cold grip of a weapon that Logier handed to him. His eyes had adjusted to the low light levels and he could see Logier, who appeared to have a lasrifle raised at his shoulder, the stiletto, a bayonet, affixed.

He looked down at the firearm in his hand. It was small and neat, and well cleaned, a defensive weapon, useful at close quarters.

There was a thud, and the *thwoom* of burning fuel as the room lit up orange and red from the light of a flamer. Still, Perdu couldn't see the enemy. He watched Logier as the stilt-man darted towards the entrance and fired into the narrow gap between battered wall panels where no door had ever stood. The cacophony from beyond suddenly separated into various sounds in Perdu's mind, each one crisp and complete, and read-able: the weight of a boot hitting an earth floor, the click of a thumb against a trigger, the slow exhale of a sniper taking his shot, the feed mechanism of a misshaped autogun as it struck home, the odd grunt of the enemy.

The enemy, thought Perdu. One enemy. He took sev-eral awkward steps, long, but close to the ground, his centre of gravity slightly lower than it would have been had he been standing, and placed a hand on Logier's back.

Krak! Krak! Logier fired two more shots into the breach, sending ancient plascrete dust cascading from the makeshift walls with a sound like pouring sand.

Perdu thrust an arm over Logier's shoulder so that the stilt-man could read his signals without moving. The priest pointed at the breach with a single finger and then held that finger upright in front of Logier's chest. There was no direct line of sight between their position and the enemy's. There were two of them, and only one opponent.

Thwoom! and the room was lit up anew. The flame hit nothing. It scorched the earth floor of the room a little, crystallising particles and making them glow red, but Perdu and Logier were out of the line of fire, and there was nothing else to burn.

Krak! Krak! Logier returned fire.

Perdu counted to three, rose to his full height and, in one motion, crossed to the right of the breach, Logier's side arm raised in two hands in front of him. Logier followed Perdu's lead, stepping forwards as Perdu fired his pistol across the breach, not attempting to engage the enemy.

When Logier stepped into the gap and turned, he was face-to-face with his assailant, less than a metre away, looking the startled foe squarely in his gummed, blood-shot eyes. This one wasn't wearing a mask. He carried a flamer high on his long back, cradling the business end under his arm while he brought the autogun up to firing position. His torso was naked, the grey skin slick with sweat, and spreading sores clustered around the plugs that sat high up on either side of his chest. Logier took in the entire scene in a split second. He didn't shoot.

Perdu heard the stiletto bayonet entering enemy flesh once, and then again. He heard the wet sounds of evis-ceration, and heard the thud of a hard body falling.

'Let's get out of here,' said Logier, stepping back through the breach, and Perdu followed without think-ing.

'CAN I TRUST you?' asked Perdu when they had cleared the area and he was sitting in a room in a hab some-where; he didn't know where.

Logier laughed.

'We're long past trust, priest,' he said. 'You don't know my name, and I don't know yours, but we have business together.'

'I won't pass the chips to a boy and risk getting him killed,' said Perdu.

'Then you'd better be up to delivering them,' said Logier. 'I'll be damned if I'm going to take them from you after that little fiasco.'

'Occupation forces are everywhere,' said Perdu.

'Everywhere you are,' said Logier. 'You didn't pass the

chips because of them, and they knew where you were again tonight. I'll pull the plug on this if I have to. I'll abort. How do I know they're not onto you? How do I know you're not a collaborator?'

'I'll do it,' Perdu insisted between gritted teeth.

'This isn't a game,' said Logier, standing to take a dish from a small neat woman who was working at an ancient stove at the far end of the room, too close not to hear what passed between them.

'Can I trust her?' asked Perdu, gesturing towards the woman.

Logier laughed again.

'We knew you'd try to resuscitate him,' said Logier.

'What an Emperor-forsaken mess–' Perdu began.

'Like I said, it's not a game,' said Logier, weary. 'You took too gakking long. You were being watched, and now the boy's out of the mix.'

'I'll deliver the chips,' said Perdu.

'It's complicated,' said Logier. 'It's crucial. What happens next could change everything. I was told that I could talk to you on a need-to-know.'

'I don't want to know,' said Perdu, 'I just want to do my part.'

'Yeah, but you need to know,' said Logier. 'We're organised, effective, and we don't lose men. The boss sent me because he had no other choice. We need allies in the hive, armed and ready, and we need a safe place to transport...'

'Transport what?' asked Perdu.

'You must've heard the stories... We can still win this war, we just need to be ready when–' Logier said.

'The Warmaster–' Perdu began, but Logier interrupted him.

'The less you know the better for you,' he said, 'but you have to know that this is critical. We know there's a leak, a collaborator. We don't know who.'

'And the chips?' asked Perdu.

'Directions,' said Logier, 'to a cache. We need to get

weapons to the outside, to another cell. They need to prove themselves before we can transport out... We can only get the weapons so far.'

'One of the hive-cells? That's where the boys run the information to.'

'The chips contain the coordinates of the cache site, but they need all six. We planned to send them out in batches, but we couldn't–'

'You couldn't sacrifice a second man,' Perdu finished for him. 'How do I find the hive-cell? The boy?'

'He won't go back to the cell unless you pass him the chips, and that's impossible, now. I've got a name... One of yours.'

'Mine?' asked Perdu.

'A priest called Revere.'

The little woman at the other end of the room had been quiet throughout their conversation, but now she began to move pans and dishes around, making too much noise.

'You must go,' said Logier, picking up the woman's signal. Perdu didn't answer, he simply rose and turned to go back the way he had come. Logier pointed towards the little woman, who was holding aside a rug that hung on the wall adjacent to the stove, covering a second exit point. Perdu looked from the woman to Logier.

'Follow your nose for a couple of hundred metres, and then take the north corridor for half a kilometre; you'll find a landmark.'

Perdu ducked out of the room without another word.

AYATANI REVERE STOOD before Bedlo, Mallet and Shuey, his prayer book clutched between his hands as if he were wringing the life out of it. The fervour in his voice was making Shuey's eyes shine.

'The Emperor saves His grace for those who follow Him unto death. Shy not from duty, shy not from ill nor pain, nor suffering. Glory be to our lieutenant, to the Emperor's lieutenant in all things, to Wescoe for the gift of her life to her comrades, to Reredos and to the Imperium.'

There was silence for a moment, and then Shuey's hands came together in one resounding clap before he realised that, as stirring as the priest's speech was, this was no time for applause.

'With more weapons, with better weapons, Wescoe might not have died,' said Bedlo.

'She died to save the rest of us,' said Shuey.

'Indeed she did,' said the priest.

Mallet was sitting on his haunches, his back to the wall, as always, stripping down Bedlo's las, again. Bedlo looked down at him. The mercenary had continued with his work right through the ayatani's service to Wescoe. He had not looked up from his task nor joined in the rite. It was as though Wescoe had never existed, as though she didn't matter to Mallet. In that moment, she mattered very much to Bedlo. His relationship with Mallet had always been strained, but now it reached a tipping point.

Bedlo swung his fist, batting the weapon out of Mallet's hand. Mallet had a knife to his boss's throat before anyone had registered what had happened.

'Steady,' said the ayatani. There were several moments of tension as the priest appraised the situation; a wrong move now and the cell could be destroyed, and some of its members with it. Revere knew that Mallet was a difficult man and Bedlo was highly strung. The moments stretched on, and Shuey looked pointedly at the priest for an answer to the stand-off. Eventually, the ayatani looked from Mallet to Bedlo, winked, and let out a sustained laugh, loud and low, and long, his mouth wide open.

Mallet withdrew the knife, picked up the discarded las, and returned to his position and his job. Shuey looked from Mallet to the priest, and then to Bedlo for his reaction. Bedlo straightened his jacket and regained a little of his dignity.

'The information should've come through by now,' he said. 'Where's the boy?'

'He'll come to me when it's time,' said Revere. 'The agri-cell is strong and able, but they need us. They'll give you what you want. They'll share the power, but you'll have to prove yourselves. There will be more recruits, and more weapons, you can count on that.'

Mallet looked up from adjusting the sights on the las. 'And more dying,' he said.

'If the legends are true,' said Revere, 'if they can be proved, the Emperor will save Reredos, and all the dying will be done by the foe.'

PERDU STOOD AT the narrow cross-street beneath the overhang of a disused manufactory, a small, domestic place for making clothes, and looked across at a hole-in-the-wall drinking place run by one of the many widows trying to scrape a living at the arse-end of the hive. A blue light shone for a moment at the basement window, barely visible at ground level but for the soft sheen it gave to the wet walkway. This was the address he'd been given for Ayatani Revere, but he didn't feel comfortable. He wasn't sure.

Perdu felt like he'd been dodging excubitors and glyfs far more than usual, and wondered whether Logier was right, whether he was being followed. He took a deep breath and tried to find the courage to cross the street to his destination.

While he was bracing himself, a shutter above Perdu opened a crack and then closed, and moments later someone took hold of the crook of his arm, and began to steer him in the direction he'd been facing.

Perdu didn't look at his diminutive companion, but knew that it must be a woman or perhaps a boy. He didn't like the thought of either; he was doing this to save a boy. He rubbed the fingers of his left glove against the palm to make sure that the chips were still there. They were.

Only a couple of metres away from the door to the hovel, Perdu's companion feigned a fall and thrust a leg out under the ayatani's feet, sending him crashing to the damp pavement.

Perdu tensed to spring back to his feet and defend himself.

'Stay down,' whispered his companion, leaning over him and faking a quick body-search. Perdu shoved his left hand behind his back, and looked into the face of a boy of about fourteen. The kid kicked him hard, once in the gut, and shrieked before making a dash for it.

A little more light spread onto the pavement from behind Perdu as the low door to the hole-in-the-wall opened, and a tall, solid man with a serious expression stepped to his aid. Perdu went along with the conceit, allowing himself to be helped, when no help was needed, leaning on the larger, older man as they both ducked into the drinking-hole. This had to be his contact.

'You have the information?' asked Revere as he leaned over Perdu, ostensibly to check his wounds, although there was no one in the room to see them other than the widow.

'Revere?' asked Perdu. 'Aya–'

'Emperor save us, man,' said Revere, glaring intently at the younger priest. 'No names here, and no titles, either.'

Perdu looked into Revere's eyes for a moment or two, not sure what he was reading there, but fearful nonetheless. Slowly, still looking at the ayatani, he removed his gloves and placed them on a stool close to a small open fire. He put out his hands to feel the warmth of the yellow flames.

'I'll warm myself a little,' said Perdu, 'and be on my way. There's no harm done.'

He didn't look at Revere again, and, after a few minutes, he gathered himself together and left the room as he had found it, except that his gloves still sat on the stool. Revere scooped them up and pocketed them. He rolled an oilcloth rug away from the floor and reached for the handle to the cellar door, set in the planks beneath.

'THE PRIEST?' OZIAS asked the barmaid, his beaker to his lips.

'Two of 'em,' said the barmaid.

Ozias had got his confirmation that the chips had finally reached their destination. He put his beaker down on the counter for the widow to clear away, and left.

REVERE DIDN'T LOOK at the chips, he simply gave them to Bedlo, pressing them firmly into his hand.

'Do what you must, with the blessings of the Emperor,' said the ayatani.

'The Emperor protects,' said Bedlo, looking the priest in the eye.

He waited until the old man had blessed them all and said a prayer over their weapons before leaving them to their plans. Then, leaving Mallet to strip down the las-rifles and autopistol while the others kept watch, Bedlo examined the ceramite chips. He had to take a glass to them, but he was soon able to make out the markings, compass directions inscribed on the obverse of the chips and digits denoting degrees and minutes on the reverse. Working methodically around the compass points from north, Bedlo lined up the chips in order, and then turned them over and read the directions.

He turned to Mallet and said, 'Give me that map. This can't be one location.' Mallet took a wand from his belt, a little longer than a pencil, cylindrical, about half a centimetre in diameter. There was no apparent join in the rod, but Mallet quickly had it in two pieces and was soon extracting something from inside. He shook out a piece of silk about forty-five centimetres square, covered in a morass of fine lines and tiny handwritten labels, all squared off on a grid with an arrow pointing north and coordinates running along two sides.

The map was a rare resource, hand-drawn and redrawn at every opportunity over several years by a former cell-mate, now dead. Mallet blew on the floor between him and Bedlo, throwing up a small cloud of pale dust, and laid the map down, facing his boss.

Bedlo cast his eye methodically over the map, bringing a finger to rest at their current position. He took the empty rod in his other hand until he had rechecked the coordinates, and then tapped the map in two other places, forming an irregular triangle of three points on the map. Then he tapped the first place again, pointing at their initial destination.

'It's less than a kilometre from here,' said Shuey, looking over Mallet's shoulder. Mallet snatched up the map and began to fold and roll it up again.

'That must be the site of the cache,' said Bedlo. 'The second coordinates are something else.'

'Nothin's for nothin',' said Mallet. Bedlo looked up and eyed him, suspiciously.

'The second set of coordinates signify the site of a raid,' said Bedlo. 'They want us to do a job, earn our stripes.'

'And?' asked Shuey.

Bedlo stretched his hand out at arm's length in Mallet's direction.

'Gimme that,' he said.

Mallet tossed Bedlo the ancient lasrifle that still didn't sound right when he fired it. Bedlo weighed it in his hands for a moment. Then he wrapped both his fists around the business end of the barrel, and pulled his arms back and his shoulders around. When he swung, he swung hard, levelling the butt of the rifle squarely at the lumpy, rockcrete cellar wall. The weapon made exactly the sort of *krak* when it exploded against the wall that it should have been making when he pulled the trigger. He'd hit the wall so hard with the las that the remnant of barrel in his hand was badly bent and virtually unrecognisable. Bedlo dropped it on the floor, but Mallet was already sorting through the debris for salvage.

'I never want to see that piece of shit again,' said Bedlo. 'Get some fuel for the flamer, and I'll show them how to burn.'

PERDU LOOKED UP at the five bowed heads before him. His faithful five stood hunched in an arc around him. All of the faces were familiar, even though their heads were bent and cast in deep shadows. He hadn't thought to see Logier again, but there he was, looking right at him, his sixth man. He did not bow his head to the Emperor. Perdu held his gaze while he continued to recite the final prayer, and Logier slowly lowered his head, and finally closed his eyes.

'You came back,' Perdu said to Logier once the rest had dispersed.

'A man must find comfort and strength where he can,' said Logier, without blinking.

Perdu wanted to say something, but couldn't think what.

'You want to know that I delivered the chips?' asked Perdu.

'No,' said Logier. 'Good evening, ayatani.'

'The Emperor protects,' said Perdu, reflexively, as Logier ducked through the low doorway into the dark alley beyond. Perdu tucked his prayer book hurriedly under his cloak, ready to follow the stilt-man. He wanted to confront the agri-worker, but didn't know why. It didn't matter; he was too late. There was no one in the alley when Perdu entered it, not even the boy.

MEN SELDOM MOVED around in groups anywhere on Reredos. Groups made the occupation guards suspicious and the glyfs twitchy. They tolerated twos, but only women and children could move around in groups of three or more, and then not always unmolested.

There was no way that Bedlo's cell could travel together to the cache, so he split them up and sent them on different routes.

Bedlo would have liked to have the old ayatani on his side, but he didn't know whether Revere would show up or not. Bedlo wasn't his boss, and he knew that Revere answered to the Emperor, if he answered to anyone at all, so Bedlo could only give him the time and place of the raid, and wait and see. He was Shuey's boss, though, and he paired him up with a new recruit called Ailly. Bedlo knew that Shuey was keen and sharp, and would've made it into the Guard, no problem, if the war hadn't cut Reredos off from the Imperium; but he didn't yet trust Ailly, who had only just joined them and could still prove a liability.

Bedlo had to trust Mallet, despite the tensions between them. He had no choice; the man was virtually a law unto himself. He wasn't predictable, but he could always be relied upon to turn up for a fight. Bedlo sometimes wondered if he'd switch allegiance, if he ever found his position untenable. It would not surprise him.

Bedlo spotted Mallet halfway along the arterial road out to the galleries, walking south, almost at a right angle to his position, tacking towards their destination. Bedlo was travelling almost directly east–west, and he'd given the boys the long route, circling the lower west quarter of the hive and traveling north to their location.

The cell members would meet at the cache and travel together from there, albeit not in a group that could be picked out by the sentry guards that patrolled close to the skirts of the galleries.

Bedlo wished he had augmetics. He was beginning to feel conspicuous among the stilt-men that lived, ate and slept in this quarter. Still, his pack looked convincing enough, and he'd rigged up an old filter cap to look like it was fitted to his chest. He could be mistaken for an agri-worker at a glance, even if he wouldn't pass a more thorough inspection. The pack, which was standard-issue for the agri-workers, neatly contained the flamer, which he'd taken from Mallet who had cleaned and prepped it ready for use. Bedlo only hoped that the fuel Mallet had managed to half-fill the reservoir with was actually flammable.

Boys were the same the planet over, and Shuey and Ailly were no exception. It had been so long since augmetics had been issued that the boys working the galleries were indistinguishable from the hivers, and from those that lived in the no-man's-land between the galleries and the hive proper. The foe sometimes used them for sport, but even as easy pickings they were noisy irritating little putes, and were mostly left alone.

Mallet preferred to zigzag his way along the edge of the hive rather than spend too much time too close to the galleries. He didn't trust the open land or the regular rows of tunnels extending into the distance. He didn't like the way they regularised the perspective of the place. He was comfortable in the hive where he could see no further than the next corner or intersection, and no one could see him from any distance, especially the damned glyfs. He wove his way back and forth, along alleys and side-lanes, along the backs of windowless buildings and through endless covered ways. Above was never a good place.

THE CACHE WAS hidden in an old hop-drying silo in no-man's-land, one of half a dozen squeezed together onto a shred of land too small to contain them. The round buildings, only four storeys high, stood cheek by jowl with each other. They seemed to bulge outwards, casting heavy shadows against the surrounding manu-factories, which had once operated as brew-houses and mash-vats but which now contained the fleshy purple pods and roots that the foe relied on for sustenance. The narrow, dark, round buildings with steep roofs and venting cowls in their chimneys were totally unusable by the Archenemy. They'd tried to store their produce in them with disastrous results. The hot dry air that was good for the papery hops putrefied the enemy crop almost before it had been stowed, and no new use could be found for the frothing black liquid that resulted. The mess had been left, and the buildings with it.

Logier entered the kiln at the south corner of the site. He was able to move around freely, his augmetics his passport to virtually all agri-areas. He would spot the hive-cell, but they would not recognise him, and enemy guards were thin on the ground. Most of the glyfs hovered over the galleries further out that were too distant for the excubitors to patrol effectively. The local population had no interest in the crops, and only those used to working with the foetid vegetation could stand to be anywhere near large quantities of it. There were enough guards to keep an eye on the workforce, but they had become fat and complacent over the three years of occupation, and unfettered access to the crop had made them bloated and slow.

The hop silo was warm and dry, and no longer smelt of anything. The putrid pods had quickly liquefied and then solidified to form a glassy black surface perhaps thirty centimetres deep on the floor. There was a tide-mark a metre high on the walls where the original crop had been loaded to, but other than that, there was no sign that the silos had been used for anything other than their intended purpose.

Neither friend nor foe had been near the silos for the better part of three years, so they had become a useful exchange point for goods crossing no-man's-land, and were a convenient link between hive- and agri-cells.

Logier had added rubberised slips to the spade-like feet of his augmetics, in order to gain some purchase on the glassy floor surface, and he walked across the silo to examine the cache, arranged on pallets and in makeshift containers on the far side of the room alongside a size-able hand-barrow. Ozias had put together a fine hoard of weapons since the inception of the agri-resistance-cell, and they had plenty to spare for the right cause.

Logier stripped a las out of its canvas cover and held it to his shoulder. Then he pulled out the sight and offered it up to the rifle. He hefted the thing in his hand for a moment, and then separated the pieces and put them back in their cover. He did the same for an autopistol, and then checked a row of flamer-tanks sitting neatly side-by-side on the top of a stack of pallets. None of the weapons were complete, all were broken into their component parts, and fuel and ammunition were stored separately, as per Ozias's instructions.

If the enemy got hold of the cache they couldn't use the weapons against the local workforce immediately and, by the time they'd organised themselves, and assembled and loaded the weapons, their tiny minds would, very probably, be on something else, something more immediate.

However, the weapons were not ready for use by the cells, either, so, if they were caught by the enemy guards, they'd better be armed.

MALLET WAS SITTING on his haunches, shoes and socks removed and placed neatly next to him; he always recce'd his surroundings, and he'd taken one look at the shiny black floor and decided bare feet were his best chance of staying upright on it. His back was against the curved far wall of the silo, and he was half-hidden by the pile of pallets that held the flamer tanks. He was assembling, checking and stripping weapons, one by one, working his way, methodically, from the lasguns to the autopistols and then on to the flamers, before checking out the camouflage and the skins full of stink-mash that only the enemy would see fit to drink.

As Bedlo entered by the single door in the silo, Mallet instinctively lifted the autopistol he had just finished checking, and aimed it squarely at his boss. Bedlo didn't see Mallet for several seconds, and Mallet didn't make himself known, enjoying the feeling of power and control. Bedlo only knew he was there when Shuey and Ailly poured through the entrance, tripping over each other and skidding on the surface that offered no grip for their boots. The boys couldn't help laughing as they travelled several metres on their arses, totally out of control. Mallet took aim and shot a round into the glassy floor between them. It was like hitting crystal taffy with a sugar-hammer. Shards of the petrified plant-life spun through the air, collecting light, like black diamonds, on their way to falling with a tinkle back to the glass surface and into the boys' hair and clothes.

Shuey gagged and doubled over, falling to the hard surface as the shot released the stench of the pods in their live state. Ailly, trying to evade the shot, slid across the floor, landing in a heap against the pallets, knocking several of the empty flamer-tanks onto the smooth, black floor, and beginning the process all over again.

Mallet looked up at Bedlo, the only man still standing, glaring down on him, and said, 'What?'

Logier had seen all of the cell members entering the silo, only four, and had stayed for a moment or two in case there were others, but could see no likely candidates in the environs. He began to walk away when the shot was fired, and was not tempted to stay to witness whatever madness was going on within. The hive-cell had a reputation, born of a catalogue of misadventure, madness and catastrophe, often with a glamorous, devil-may-care attitude thrown in for good measure. That was why Ozias had chosen them, and that was why Logier could never see them as a threat.

Shuey was torn between laughing at Ailly trying to regain his feet, and retching at the stink that was coming off the floor shards. Then he caught sight of the stand-off between Mallet and Bedlo. He thought for a moment, and then winked and let out a resounding guffaw, copying the low belly-rumble that Ayatani Revere seemed able to muster up from nowhere at a moment's notice. The boy stopped struggling, Bedlo turned to look in Shuey's direction and Mallet went back to checking weapons. The spell was broken.

'Let's load the barrow,' said Bedlo. 'I want us out of here.'

LOGIER WATCHED AS the barrow wove through the narrow alleys of the under-slum. The hive had always had rents and wastes at the lower reaches, but, since the war and during the occupation, this place had become darker, sadder and more sinister. The people were incomplete specimens, veterans of the agri-galleries or the occupation, men without limbs or senses: the crippled, blind, deaf and damaged, who would never experience the augmetics that were available throughout the rest of the Imperium. They lived out their pitiful existences in this backwater, trading between themselves and collaborating with whomever, whenever the need arose. There was no honour among thieves or vagabonds, only survival, which, three years deep into the occupation, meant that everyone was life-limited, and everyone knew it.

The under-slum was also the favourite haunt and hunting ground of the basic-grade enemy troops, the mindless animals that did the bidding of the Archenemy. They were tough, cruel beings, without hearts or minds, any moral compasses they might once have had stripped out and trampled long ago. They were, by turns, brutal and lazy, and they took pleasure in the most vicious side of life. The deaf, blind and legless were easier to kill than the hivers or agri-workers, and no one counted the bodies.

The under-slum was where the bestial element of the enemy forces took their R&R and exercised their pleasures: hunting, torturing, brutalising, raping and taking revenge for the horrors meted out to them by their superiors. The locals didn't fight back, but only begged for a faster death; no one was naive enough to beg to live.

Fresh enemy troops had been brought into Reredos

in the usual rotation, and the outgoing guards were filling their boots in the under-slum before being shipped
out. The place was teeming with hundreds of bodies,
hungry and thirsty for food, drink and violent sport of
all kinds, and the hive-cell was moving in to supply a
share of that.

BEDLO HAD INSTRUCTED the boys in loading the hand-
barrow while Mallet checked weapons. They all
discarded the arms they were carrying, except for
Mallet, who trusted nothing more than the autopistol
that had served him so well for so long; it didn't stop
him bagging a Guard-issue long-las, though, just for
good measure. Shuey gave up his uncle's rifle without
a second glance when he saw what was on offer from
the cache, and soon both of the boys were carrying their
weight in arms. Mallet didn't like it. He didn't like any
of it. He wanted to carry the arms they could use and
stash ammunition.

He wasn't the boss, but when he looked hard at the
boys, they both cowered a little. He gestured at the
weapons.

'Put them back,' he said.

The boys turned from Mallet and looked to Bedlo for
a decision.

'Take one good weapon each,' he said. 'The rest aren't
going anywhere.' Shuey took a lascarbine and Ailly a
rifle, and they all began to fill their pockets and webbing
with ammo. Mallet didn't want to bother with flamers, either, given that it was virtually impossible to get
decent fuel for them, but Bedlo had become obsessed
with the weapon since he'd destroyed his brakking las,
and Mallet didn't want to go up against the boss.

Bedlo and Mallet lay flat on their bellies on the hand-
barrow. It was too risky for anyone to be seen carrying a
weapon, so they were all stowed on the barrow with the
two men, and the whole lot was covered in skins con-
taining the stink-mash brewed by the agri-cell for enemy

consumption. The unarmed boys yoked themselves to the handles and rolled the barrow out of the silo and into no-man's-land. The occupation forces didn't waste glyfs on the under-slum, and, if anybody asked, they were doing the work of the Archenemy, delivering contraband mash to the troops. No one would prevent them; these things were understood and tolerated. The enemy troops were expected to blow off steam in the under-slums, making them more reliable in their dull duties, and downing huge quantities of stink-mash was one of the ways they accomplished that. They would drive straight into the midst of drunken enemy troops at their most vulnerable and take them out, wholesale.

Dozens of the enemy animals would be packed into 'The Drum', the old playhouse in the east quarter of the under-slums. It had once listed up-and-comers and has-beens on its cheap hoarding, but now it was a kind of freak-show. Anyone could tread the worn, battered boards of the raised platform stage while the baying crowd took potshots at them, with coin or curses, often with the food in their paws, but rarely with live ammo. A beast might saunter onto the stage to strike or strangle an act that didn't satisfy; two or three might rush the platform to tear some hapless dancing cripple limb from limb for looking at them the wrong way. The risks were high and the rewards scant, but people still came to try their luck. Troops on R&R were generally discouraged from carrying weapons as mortality rates among the basic grade had been very high in the early days of the occupation. Without enemies to fight, they made enemies of each other.

Shuey and Ailly hauled the barrow into the kitchens at the rear of The Drum, and waited. The streets had been buzzing with the enemy, two, maybe three times as many of them as usual, but The Drum was quiet. Perhaps it was too early for it to fill up.

Bedlo looked towards Mallet, under the weight of their camouflage. Mallet's eyes were only centimetres from his, but Bedlo could read no expression in them.

'Boss?' asked Shuey, trying to see through the skins and canvas-covers to get instructions from Bedlo.

Bedlo didn't answer, not yet, but kept looking into Mallet's eyes, trying to appraise the situation, trying to work out why it was so quiet.

'I'll see if I can find someone,' said Shuey to the other boy. 'Keep guard.'

Keep guard, Bedlo thought, lying on his belly with his lasgun poised. He's not armed, and he's never done this before, and Shuey tells him to 'keep guard'.

'Yo!' shouted Shuey as he disappeared through a swing door.

Then nothing.

Several minutes passed. Then there was an odd, bestial roar.

SHUEY PUSHED THROUGH the swing door that he felt sure would lead him further into The Drum. He'd expected to be stopped on the way through the under-slum. He hadn't been with the cell for long, no one lasted long in an active cell that took risks, but he knew that nothing ever went to plan, that something always went wrong. The barrow wasn't stopped and the four men travelled all the way to the playhouse without drawing any attention. Odd.

Shuey began to whistle, low in his throat, in an attempt to make his breathing even. He was nervous. Why was he nervous? Why was it so quiet?

Shuey found himself in a large, dark space with a low flight of steps to his left. He wanted to get a view of the room and assess where the enemy would enter from, how easy it would be to hide in the space and pick the animals off, one at a time, or mow them down with the flamers.

It was good that they were early. They'd have time to recce, to set up. They'd be in and out, safe and sound, in no time.

'Yo!' shouted Shuey, again.

He stepped out onto the boards, his knees soft, his body bent over slightly in a classic sneaking-about pose. He didn't have a gun. He should've armed himself before coming through that door.

Shuey's eyes adjusted to the light and he turned to look out into the room. He thought he spotted something, maybe ten metres away at the back of the room. Then he thought he heard something, a shuffling, grunting sound.

Shuey blinked as they came into view, five metres away, walking towards him. There were a couple of dozen of them at least. They weren't drunk, and they weren't partying. They hadn't left their weapons at home to keep their hands free for slapping men, feeling up women, and grabbing at any food that passed within a metre of them.

They were tall, hard, dirty creatures with distended bellies and arched backs, wearing stained, mismatched fatigues; many of them also wore the masks. They carried blades and cudgels, and lasguns and flamers. The angular excubitor in the middle had a flamer strapped to his back that was leaking a clear, pinkish drip of promethium from the hose that was pointing at him, and a heavy brass collar around his neck, pierced for plug-ins.

Shuey tried to make himself smaller, caving his chest in and pushing his knees together as the fresh smell of his own urine assaulted his nostrils.

The creature with the flamer spat a gob of lumpy phlegm onto the floor in front of him. Shuey's eyes moved involuntarily to inspect it; it was frothing and purple and smelled of infected lungs, bad breath and stink-pods.

'Voi leng atraga,' said the creature, and thumbed the trigger on his flamer. The brute next to him elbowed him in the side, indicating that he shouldn't set fire to the little pute, and stepped forward, bouncing a flattened, club-shaped cudgel off his high, narrow shoulder.

Shuey saw the first swing come as if in slow motion. He wanted to duck, but didn't, because the blow was coming at his waist height, not around his head. If he'd had his wits about him, he might have stepped back, out of range, but his wits were currently evacuating his body via his backside, so there wasn't a hope of relying on them for anything.

The first blow winded Shuey with a faint *boof*! And he thought he heard a couple of his ribs breaking. His eyes were very large and his feet were still planted on the boards. Why hadn't he fallen over?

The thought struck him that he was on the stage in The Drum. He knew what happened here. All the world crossed that stage, and plenty of it never made it to the other side.

He looked hopelessly out at the enemy troops gathered around the skirts of the stage. It didn't matter what he did, Shuey was dead. He tried to purse his lips and blow, but no sound came out. He tried to dance, but his feet wouldn't move. His eyes grew huge as he saw the lasgun aimed at him. The aim lowered and a shot was fired.

Shuey's knee buckled, and he clutched at it as he went down.

'Ut dreh!' said one of the guards.

Shuey placed his hands flat on the floor of the stage and tried to take his weight, but his left hand had landed in the pool of blood and slid out from under him.

'W-what... magir?' gasped Shuey.

'Get up,' said the trooper again.

Shuey stood on his one good leg for long enough to have that shot out from under him.

He didn't live for long once the enemy beasts were on the stage with him. No one on Reredos had died with dignity for three years, but few had perished with less than Shuey could muster on that stage.

Finally, Shuey's broken body was tossed off the stage, and a whoop went up. Their appetites whetted, the foe wanted more, and they wanted it now.

They started to stamp their feet and jeer, and a fight or two broke out among the couple of dozen blood-hungry beasts.

AILLY STOOD NEXT to the hand-barrow not at all sure of what he should do next. His face was white and his eyes huge as the whoop went up. The last thing he had heard was Shuey calling out 'Yo!' as he left the kitchens, but that was minutes ago, and this was bestial, aggressive and frightening. The boy had never heard the like before. He was still standing, aghast, when Mallet handed him a weapon.

The boss had a flamer on his back and a long-las in his hand, and appeared to have stuffed several grenades into the front of his jacket as hard-looking lumps bulged there. Mallet carried his faithful autogun and the long-las was slung over his shoulder.

'What about...' Ailly began, finding his voice for a moment.

'They're through there,' said Bedlo. 'It's time.'

'But...' the boy began again. He was trembling, and he didn't think that he could move his feet.

Mallet slapped Ailly once, hard on his back, almost propelling him forwards with the force of what was supposed to be a comradely, reassuring gesture, and handed him his rifle.

Bedlo moved to the door into The Drum proper, and held up the forefinger of his left hand: command. Then he held his flat palm out in front of him. Mallet stood beside Bedlo, ready, as always. The boy wondered if he would ever be ready.

The next moment, they were through the doors and into the darkness of the playhouse. Bedlo fired up his flamer and orange light spread before them, picking out the enemy, one at a time, lined up in front of them, in formation. They were ready, too, and there were a lot of them.

Ailly heard an odd rattling sound right next to him

that made him jump. He lifted his hand slowly towards his face, the hand that should have been holding his weapon. He realised that the sound was his rifle falling to the floor. He had lost his grip on it. He had lost his grip on everything.

He could see the strange, angry men facing him, walking towards him as if through water, slowly and deliberately. He could not see their mouths moving behind the strange impassive expressions on their masks, but he could hear a long, slow moan that didn't sound like words at all. He couldn't hear the krak of Mallet's las, but he could see the blast residue of individual shots issuing from its barrel.

What was happening? In the Emperor's name... What was happening?

Mallet was the first to fire. He had fought his entire life. He had skirmished and ambushed; he had stood on the front line and been the last to retreat; he had fought at any distance, fired any weapon and indulged in hand-to-hand combat when there was no other option. He had never faced down so many of the enemy at close quarters, without hope.

He fired his las almost continuously, picking off any target he could home in on instinctively. Death held no fear for him; it didn't even make him angry. He had been killing for eight years, legitimately. He'd been killing for twenty years. He'd lived killing, and he would die killing, given the chance.

Bedlo triggered his flamer and watched as the scene was revealed. It was not what he had been led to expect.

This was not how it was supposed to be. How had this happened? Why had this happened? Who had betrayed them? Where was Shuey? Why hadn't he come back to warn them? How many of the enemy were standing in front of him? Was there any way to retreat? Could they escape? How many could he kill before it was over? How had this happened? Who was to blame?

Three minutes later, Mallet was astounded to realise

that he was still alive, and still shooting.

The boss had given up on the flamer, and was shooting his las into a crowd of enemy soldiers that he could barely make out in the gloom.

Ailly had not managed to fire a single shot. His feet were planted heavily and his arms were limp at his sides. Everything was happening very slowly, and he thought it had been hours since they'd left the kitchens.

Somehow, the animals had managed to separate the boy from Mallet and Bedlo. The more experienced resisters had moved slowly to the right, away from the stage and the worst of the fire that was being returned by the enemy.

Bedlo didn't know what he was hitting, if he was hitting anything, but he knew that he wasn't being hit. It was as if they were missing him on purpose. Bedlo and Mallet wove to the right. The boy didn't move.

The enemy formed around Ailly, almost ignoring the two older men. They started to laugh and point. They got very close to him. The boy thought that he was going to stop breathing. They wanted him to move; he wanted to oblige, but he couldn't.

Someone took a potshot at the floor. At least, Ailly thought the foe was shooting at the floor, but then he felt something in his foot. It was wet and hot. He didn't dare look down, and he couldn't fall down. What were they saying? Why couldn't he see their mouths move, but could hear their strange grunts? Nothing would come into focus.

Then one of the foe picked Ailly up, over his shoulder, and took him up the steps onto the platform. He stood the boy back on his feet, and jumped off the stage, back into a pack of his comrades.

Ailly was mute and incapable. His eyes were blurry and he still couldn't hear properly. He wasn't terrified any more, though. He couldn't possibly stay so terrified for so long.

He wanted to do what they wanted him to do, but he

didn't know what that was. He didn't know that Shuey had danced and convulsed for them. He didn't know they'd had their sport before they'd killed him. He should be dead already.

There was a square of light, suddenly, in front of him. Two dozen enemy beasts were silhouetted, back-lit by the door that opened out into the daylight. Everything came back to Ailly in a rush. He could hear the howls and jeers of the crowd, and see the enemy as they turned to face the intruder. He could smell the blood that Shuey had left on the stage. He could feel the pain in his wounded foot. He could feel the muscles in his gut clenching around his stomach, and the heave in his oesophagus as his body reacted to the situation.

His movement still wasn't voluntary, but whatever was compelling Ailly's body to react forced him to lean over before he emptied the contents of his stomach onto the stage. He could not stand after that.

Whether bored or exasperated, or simply reactive, someone shot the man that had opened the external door to the playhouse, more than one someone. The tall, grizzled old man went down under a hail of fire. He died, instantly, from one of the seventeen shots that found ways into his torso before he fell.

Ailly didn't recognise the man who had come to their aid; he only saw his dark outline jolting against the light with the impact of las-fire. He was conscious now, more conscious than he had been since entering the kitchens, and it was his conscious state that killed him. The boy dropped slowly, silently to the floor, without a single shot being fired in his direction, and without any fanfare or any sign that he was about to die. It didn't matter what had killed him. It didn't matter whether it was a stroke or a heart attack. It didn't matter whether an aneurysm had erupted in his fragile body.

Ailly died without a fight, without firing a shot, and with only a flesh wound in his foot to show that he had been in any danger. There was no dignity. There was never any dignity.

Bedlo and Mallet turned as the playhouse door was thrown open to the scene. For a split-second, Bedlo thought that someone was coming to the rescue, perhaps the cell that had armed them. For a moment, he had hope. Mallet felt nothing, but simply kept on shooting at the enemy, glad of the extra light, once he had squinted the suddenness of it out of his eyes.

He did not wonder why the enemy was not shooting at them. He knew why.

After killing the last man in, the enemy returned to taunting Mallet and Bedlo. The boy had pissed them off by dying before he'd done anything to entertain them, and they wanted their revenge. They wanted something so badly that several of them had embarked on pitched battles between themselves, and three had died at the hands of their comrades. Bedlo and Mallet had injured several others between them, but both of their kill-rates increased dramatically with the extra light that was coming in through the door that no one had bothered to close.

Mallet kept shooting all the time that no one was shooting back to kill. He wanted to give them a dose of their own medicine, and started to aim at legs and arms instead of heads and chests.

The beasts started to work on separating Mallet and Bedlo. It didn't matter any more. They were very close. Mallet watched one of the animals swing at the boss's head, making him stagger. Then, another swung at his knees, and Bedlo was having trouble standing. Then two more started shooting at the floor, close to Bedlo's feet, and Mallet saw the boss's head bobbing up and down to his left. It looked for all the world as if Bedlo was dancing.

Mallet kept aiming and kept shooting, all the time keeping one eye on Bedlo's progress. Soon Mallet was looking up at his boss as he stood on the wooden stage, beaten and bloodied. Mallet swung his las over his shoulder and took the three paces required to pick up the flamer that Bedlo had shrugged off several minutes earlier.

He'd never done what he was about to do. He'd seen it done, once, by some psycho fool in the Guard who'd known what he was doing, and whose actions had made them all cheer and whoop. He didn't know if he could do it. He knew that doing it inside was suicide, so, he'd be dead, either way.

Most of the enemy beasts were facing the stage, watching their macabre little show. Mallet took hold of the flamer's strap, and felt the weapon's weight in his hand. The tank wasn't full, by any means, but there ought to be enough.

Mallet took his autopistol in his right hand, and started to swing the flamer in his left. Once he'd got the momentum up a little, he turned to face the stage, and, using the weight of the flamer's tank, he swung the weapon through the air, letting go of it at the top of its arc. He didn't have time to aim the autopistol in the confined space, and fired it almost as soon as he'd loosed his missile. The flamer had gone almost straight up, and bounced off one of the tie-beams that held the building together. It plummeted back down, exploding a very little above head height, spraying great gouts of flames out over the heads of the enemy. Above was never a good place.

The flamer had gone up almost vertically, and come down the same way. Mallet was standing directly beneath the explosion, the autopistol still pointing roughly in the direction of the fuel tank. He was the first to die, but he took half a dozen of the enemy with him. The beasts' attention was torn away from the unfortunate man limping around in circles on the stage in front of them, most of it.

Those still involved in skirmishes furthest from the stage heard the explosion and felt the building shake, but they were close to the door left open by the intruder, and tumbled out laughing and hooting, forgetting what they'd been squabbling over.

Several more of the enemy managed to pick themselves up in the first moments after the explosion began to subside, and made their way out of the building, staggering, limping and complaining.

One of the last survivors looked around for a minute or two, dazed by the explosion. He finally found what he was looking for. He bent over a tall body with bulbous joints in the mismatched fatigues and body-armour that the foe wore, and hefted the thing over to look at its face. He took the dead head in his hands and gently knocked foreheads with it. Then he looked up at the man still staggering around on the stage. He aimed his laspistol at the wretch a total of seven times. Six of the bullets maimed. When the last came, Bedlo was going insane, wondering if his end would ever come. The final round detonated one of the grenades in his chest, and then another, making his corpse jolt and squirm on the stage, too late to entertain the troops.

The fire did not burn for long. There was no one to make repairs on The Drum, and no supplies with which to make them. Some of the under-slum dwellers made a crust or two cleaning out the blood, shit and bodies. It was a good day, and the show went on again the day after, despite charring to the stage and a few new stains to the ceiling.

When Logier paid off the cleaners, he took evidence of all the dead cell members, including the old ayatani priest, Revere, who'd come through the front door, bold as brass. The Archon wouldn't be too impressed by the number of his troops that had gone down at The Drum, but it had to be worth it to take out a cell, and break the morale of resistance fighters everywhere. He'd proven his worth as a collaborator, and made a fool of the old man.

* * *

OZIAS STOOD IN the entrance to the alley at the rear of
The Drum, watching Logier complete his transactions
with the low-lifes that had done his bidding. He pressed
his back against the wall of the alley as Logier passed
him, tossing something up into the air and catching it.
Ozias tucked in behind him where he couldn't be seen.
He would move fast, before they'd left the under-slum.

Two or three minutes later, Ozias got his chance.
Logier turned down a narrow alley between overhanging buildings, little more than a dim corridor, the light
at the end several hundred metres away.

Before Logier had a chance to turn and see who had
followed him into the alley, Ozias moved up quickly
behind him and put his bolt-pistol to the back of the
traitor's head, taking it off with one shot. He caught
the body as it fell, and laid it down close to the wall
of the alley. He preferred to be face to face with the
enemy, but saw no advantage in taking that chance
with Logier.

Ozias had learned a long time ago never to trust
anyone, but, in a pinch, he might have trusted Logier.
He would have been wrong. It was impossible to know
whether the remaining members of his cell were faithful, but he sincerely hoped so. This clean-up operation
had cost him weapons, and men had died; however
reckless the men of the hive-cell had been, however
much of a liability, resistance fighters had died.

Ozias emptied Logier's pockets, taking the evidence
collected from Bedlo's, Mallet's, Shuey's, Ailly's and
Ayatani Revere's bodies. He would give them to the
priest, Perdu, to inter.

AYATANI PERDU COULD feel the damp sod of the floor
beneath his feet. These little rooms with floors that never
dried out were havens to the half a dozen worshippers
that came to his services. Sometimes he wondered how
that could be.

They had died. They had all died. The two men, the

two boys and the tough old ayatani had all perished, and for what?

They were supposed to be fighting for the same thing, for the preservation of some form of the Imperium on Reredos. They were supposed to be fighting against the enemy, for the people. The factions had been exposed. Their lives had proven to be as disposable as they had ever been to the foe. Perdu looked from one face to another. He did not recognise any of the congregation. He thought about feeling fear, but he couldn't. The only emotion available to him now was resignation.

Perdu let his eyes fall to the prayer book that he held open in his hands. He did not need to look on the words, they were engraved indelibly in his mind, but he looked at them anyway. He looked for comfort in them, but found that he felt only that the inevitable would happen, and that maybe it was better in the end.

Perdu finished his prayer, but remained standing with his head bowed over his book. As he looked at the words, a button appeared in the spine-fold of the open pages. It was domed and heavily engraved, with a thick ring shank on it. He could read a single word encircled by the shank. It read, 'pray'.

He did not look up, and was not surprised when a second button dropped onto the pages of the book, a pair to the first. The shank encircled the word, 'mercy'.

Within moments a third button had been dropped onto the book, and then a fourth, a fifth and a sixth. The room was empty.

Ozias and the five remaining members of his cell left the young ayatani priest to his musings. It was the first and last time that they ever attended a service together with someone other than their own priest, but these were unusual times. This was the beginning of something; this was the beginning of a plan to rescue the entire planet.

Perdu looked down at the buttons scattered on the pages before him, their shanks gleaming bright gold in the dim light, casting highlights and shadows on the pages; the shanks circling some words, and the domes of the buttons covering or overshadowing others.

Perdu read the six words in their golden rings. 'Pray to the lady for mercy'.

He took up one of the buttons between the thumb and forefinger of his right hand and realised that the light wasn't shining off it, but was emanating from it. He looked at the domed surface of the ring, and saw, among the deep engraving and the glistening gems, not only a thing of great beauty and value, but something of worth beyond anything that he could comprehend. The button bore the sigil, crest and arms of the Lady, the Beati, Saint Sabbat.

She had worn the buttons on her breast, had blessed them with her association. The Lady had found a following on Reredos because she had been part of its history, and must now represent the better part of the planet's importance to the Emperor. How could the God-Emperor forsake His daughter? How could He forsake them?

Nick Kyme's gripping novels, including his dwarf-filled War-hammer adventures and his forays with the saturnine Salamanders for 40K, have won him armies of fans. Given the subterranean and volcanic themes present in both of the above, it's no wonder there's a whiff of the combustible and petrochemical to this muscular, take-no-prisoners tale, which reacquaints us with an Imperial Guard regiment, high-born and imperious, who have often been a thorn in the side of Gaunt and his Ghosts. I'm sure you'll agree it's nice to see them again, especially as they're moving up from their supporting role and stepping out into the limelight.

Or should that be the firing line?

Dan Abnett

BLUEBLOOD

Nick Kyme

'We were there. We were there on Vigo's Hill. It was to be our end. Our final hour. Our last stand. Until She came and everything changed.'

– 'Last Stand of the Longstriders', a transcribed account of the Vigo's Hill Massacre, M41. (Circa 774. M41, in the nineteenth year of the Sabbat Worlds campaign.)

THE PILLAR OF fire exploding from the desert forced the gunship to bank sharply. A series of warning runes flashed in the cramped cockpit alongside the Valkyrie's steering column. While the pilot fought to control the vessel, the rest of the crew felt the sudden thrust of motion in the tightening of their grav harnesses. Somewhere, a muffled emergency klaxon droned. In the troop hold men were scattered like debris, amidst vocal curses and angry shouts of pain.

Major Regara stood defiantly in the open hatchway of the Valkyrie, *Warbird*, with one hand on the guard rail, the other snapped to behind his back. Framed by the hold's exit hatch he cut a stern, precise figure, the epitome of Volpone starch and sturm.

'Have you ever seen the Euclidian Squalor-Pits, lieutenant?' he declared to the burning air outside. The fire-flare tinged his grey-gold armour a ruddy orange and the squalls from the explosion seared his tanned features with a prickling heat.

Regara didn't flinch. The role of imperious officer, master of war was one he played to military perfection.

The plume of fire died away to a trickling smoke that carpeted the landing zone in a grey fog. They were coming in hard – ninety birds touching down in minutes, scorching the sand to glass with the roar of descent jets.

'No sir, I haven't.' Lieutenant Culcis clung to the guard rail opposite the major and stood just behind him.

Regara looked down into the dispersing smoke, through the growing dust cloud created from the Valkyrie squadrons' downthrust.

'It's like a Volponian bathhouse compared to this hole.' He scowled and the gesture pulled at a scar running from his smooth-shaven chin to the edge of his collar.

There were troops below, a few kilometres from the landing zone, getting closer by the second. It was an encampment, several encampments in fact. Together they were more like a city, hundreds of disparate regiments, all part of the Crusade reserve, billeted in tents, prefabs, re-appropriated local structures or simply gathered in the open with only a few windbreakers to impede the sandstorms. Like borer-ants at this distance. Millions of them.

'Tell me again, lieutenant,' said Regara as they approached their final landing vector. By now the chatter over the inter-company vox, comprising, in the main, barks of dissatisfaction from the other Volpone officers at the explosive welcome they'd received, had ceased. Nine companies. Nine hundred men. A full battalion of the Volpone 50th awaited landfall in silence.

All except Regara. 'What do we know about this hole, other than it's at the arse-end of nowhere?'

A tremor of mild turbulence shook the ship's hold, forcing the major to shift his footing. The bionic leg he wore in place of the organic one he lost on Nacedon whirred and groaned. Compared to most Guard prosthetics, it was a work of art.

'Sagorrah,' Culcis began, regaining his footing after he'd stumbled with the sudden bucking of the gunship. 'A collection world. Approximately one hundred and fifty-two separate regiments are in residence, of varying strengths and fighting viability. A depot, sir – Sagorrah has over three hundred promethium wells, a reserve of several million tonnes, vital fuel for the conquest of the Sabbat Worlds.'

Regara discerned the depot's central hub, a vast factorum structure attended by a multitude of vast sunken silos.

Another explosion, farther out this time from a distant well, thrust a lance of fire into the hot sky.

Regara turned, uninterested. His eyes were like flint as he regarded the young Culcis.

'I blame Nacedon,' he said candidly.

'Sir?'

Culcis had been on that world, too. They'd fought side-by-side with a ragged bunch of barbarians from Tanith, a backward planet that had long since been atomised from existence. The Colonel, Gilbear, had an especial loathing for the 'Ghosts', as they were known. Regara, one of the wounded left behind by Volpone command and subsequently saved by the bravura of the Tanith and their medic, had had the audacity to recommend the Ghosts for commendations. It hadn't translated well.

Regara turned his gaze back to Sagorrah. A landing party was mustering a few hundred metres below. Though they were little more than slowly resolving specks, he was able to make out the crisp uniform of a Munitorum officer. Clerks, associated ground staff and servitors surrounded him. Regara was reminded of flies buzzing around a carcass. This entire sinkhole was a foetid carcass.

'Only reason I can think of that Gilbear shipped us here. Must've pissed the colonel off royally.' Since Monthax, relations between the Volpone and the Tanith had improved but between two such polar opposites, there would always be needle. Grudging respect was one thing; outright commendation was quite another. In retrospect, Regara thought he must have sustained a head wound in addition to his lost leg during the Nacedon action. How else could he explain his recommendations?

'Defending a promethium well,' he muttered ruefully, the screech of stabiliser jets smothering his voice to a thought. 'Where is the glory in that? It's no task for a Volpone.' No, Gilbear didn't like Regara. The feeling was mutual. Being left to die by your commanding officers will have that effect on a man.

As the desert basin closed, Regara's gaze was drawn to a vast brawl erupting deeper in camp in the distance. He discerned several bulky troopers in commissarial black breaking up the fight and breaking heads.

The major's expression grew disdainful as the last few metres to the ground fell away.

'They're animals, sir,' remarked Culcis, the down-draughts from the engines forcing him to clamp a hand down on his officer's cap. Their raucous din turned his comment to a shout.

'Chain a dog in the sun long enough, lieutenant, and it'll eat its own tail,' replied the major, dragging a rebreather over his nose and mouth to keep out the worst of the dust. 'Gilbear must really hate us,' he said to himself, as the Valkyrie touched down and the eighth through seventeenth companies of the Volpone 50th arrived at Sagorrah.

It was to be a most unpleasant stay.

REGARA LOOKED AT the Munitorum officer's proffered hand with something approaching disgust.

'Welcome to Sagorrah Depot,' said the officer, fighting to be heard above the slowly cooling engines.

Despite himself, Regara shook the odious man's hand. He learned his name was Ossika, a stoop-backed, sun-burnt wretch of a creature. Ossika had the look of a man who'd spent too long inside a Departmento-appointed office-hub, logging and charting, turning the slow logistical wheels that fed the great war engine of the Crusade. Idly, the major wondered who Ossika had annoyed to be 'rewarded' with this duty.

Introductions were made crisply and efficiently from both parties. They were walking from the landing strip when Ossika spoke next.

'Quite a few birds you've got in tow,' he said, wiping a dirty kerchief across the strands of hair threading his bald patch.

Culcis sneered but kept the gesture hidden beneath the brow of his officer's cap. It was a gesture of ostentation and strength, making it clear to all and sundry that the Volpone were at the summit of the hierarchical chain.

Behind the lieutenant strode the rest of the cadre: Speers and Drado, both corporals, both aides to Regara and Culcis respectively. Sergeant Vengo followed. He'd been quiet since embarkation. A head wound sustained in a recent combat action meant he'd only just returned to service from the medicae. After him were the seven remaining Volpone troopers from Regara's command squad. The other eight company captains and their associated officer cohorts would join them later. Operatives from Ossika's staff were already liaising with them in a holding station just outside the landing zone to assign billets.

'Almost stretched our landing field to capacity,' Ossika concluded – Regara did not deign to respond – leading them towards a Salamander-class command vehicle. There was only room enough for Ossika, the two Volpone officers and their aides.

Culcis nodded to Vengo as he climbed aboard, to which the grim-faced sergeant nodded back and then turned on the rest of the troopers.

'March formation, crisp and straight!' he bellowed. 'Show this rabble the quality of the Volpone 50th!'

The Salamander was already rumbling away, its engines stuttering with the repellent sand that seemed to clog up everything – Culcis brushed at the rust-coloured rime it left on his buttons and lapels, the raised plates of his carapace armour – before Vengo had the men assembled. They'd rejoin the rest of the battalion and prepare the major's command station for his return.

As the command vehicle picked up speed, the camp grew slowly around them. Lieutenant Culcis found his eye drawn to the various regiments, cooling their heels and awaiting reassignment to the Crusade frontline.

No soldier liked being away from battle. After a while, fighting and survival became ingrained behaviour. Anything else was anathema, a foreign way of existing. Most couldn't take the silence of ordinary life. It ground at the nerves and made men who were sane and balanced in a trench war react insanely and violently when at peace – judging by the sheer levels of disorder and discontent apparent on Sagorrah, that fact was evidently true.

Culcis recognised some regiments. Vitrians, Roane Deepers, Castellian Rangers – he'd fought alongside them all at one point or another. On the field of battle, they'd spilled blood together; out here in the desert, they reacted with hard stares and aggressive postures. Sagorrah was a powder keg, Culcis realised. All it needed was someone to light the fuse.

'This place is a wretched dump,' said Speers. The aide was a wiry-looking man, but tall and brawny like most of the Volpone. You couldn't tell by looking, but his head was completely shaved under his grey bowl helmet.

'The phrase is shit-hole,' offered Drado. The pug-faced corporal smacked his lips and scowled. 'You can even taste it on the air.'

Culcis had to agree with him. As well as the reddish patina slowly crusting his uniform, there was a disagreeable tang on the breeze. Like metal.

Major Regara didn't comment. He'd taken a position

at the front of the vehicle, hands braced across the flat-bed's holding rail as he glared imperiously at the other officers in the camp. But Culcis knew he echoed Speer's and Drado's displeasure.

'We'll need to make the best of it,' the lieutenant said. He noticed fetishes and other icons hanging from the guide poles of several tents. Since the Saint had emerged on Herodor and with her victories elsewhere on the Sabbat Worlds, there'd been an upsurge in religious affectation amongst some quarters of the Guard.

Culcis needed no gewgaws or false reliquaries. He touched the indigo aquila that fastened together the armaplas of his collar – that was all the symbol he needed.

'No, lieutenant,' said Major Regara from the front of the command car. 'I have no intention of us staying long enough to warrant such a concession.'

If Ossika, standing to the major's left at the front of the car, thought anything about that he kept it to himself.

The Salamander had started to gain a steep rise. As it crested the hill, a large bastion-like structure loomed. Its grey-black walls, buttressed flanks and soaring watch-tower screamed operational command station. It was the seat of Ossika's power. Beyond it, the horizon line hinted at hills and other structures. Only their vague outlines were visible, the rest was lost to the distant heat haze.

A line of troopers was filing towards them as the Sala-mander began to slow. They were a ragged group with tattered uniforms, sleeves and fatigues cut back with knives to expose tanned, muscled limbs to the sun. They carried tribal tattoos on their slab-like faces, jagged and harsh like painted blades on skin. They also wore their hair long, bound up in topknots and ponytails. Several wore feathers or spikes of bone in their ears, noses and hair. They'd been issued with lasguns, but carried spears and blades in abundance. Culcis counted at least four snipers. It looked like they'd been hunting.

The lieutenant knew enough to recognise a feral regiment when he saw one. Such men were barely human. They had more in common with beasts. Truly, this was a pit of filth the Volpone found themselves in.

'Hail, brothers,' said their leader, his guttural accent so thick as to make the words near incomprehensible, as the ragged troopers went by in column.

Regara studiously ignored them.

Culcis conceded a nod as they drove past them. Alongside their officer was a trooper holding a scrap of cloth that might once have been a banner. It was wrecked, riddled with bullet scars and burn damage. Inwardly, the lieutenant despaired at such a lack in decorum and self-respect.

The gate to the bastion shadowed the Volpone as they approached it, smothering Culcis's thoughts. As it ground open on slow, noisy hinges, Regara looked over his shoulder. The ragged regiment, some thirty or so men, had already disappeared behind them.

'Dogs in the sun, lieutenant. Dogs in the sun.'

Culcis kept his eyes on the gate, grateful when they could finally drive inside to the cool, recycled air of the bastion.

REGARA GLARED THROUGH a viewport in the bastion's upper tier at the grounds below.

'A heavy presence of guns,' he said, noting the frequency and concentration of armed patrols as they overlapped at the bastion's fenced-off perimeter. 'There are over a million Guardsmen stationed at this facility.'

The troops Regara saw pacing the grounds wore Departmento Munitorum grey. Their kit and posture suggested storm-troopers. It seemed a little excessive.

Ossika looked up from his desk where he'd begun compiling reports and logs concerning the depot's current logistical situation. He was currently occupied with filling out the Volpone's billet papers. 'That's the issue,

I'm afraid – too many troops with too much time on their hands. We had a string of break-in attempts before I had to increase the guard rotations.'

Regara turned on his heel, a deep and unimpressed frown marring his face.

An open tiled floor led to Ossika. The Munitorum officer's desk and series of wall-mounted file cabinets were the only furnishing in an otherwise austere and spartan room.

It wasn't to Culcis's tastes. He and the two aides waited silently, halfway between Regara and Ossika in the middle of the tiled floor. The room's only other occupant was a slack-faced lex-savant, lurking in the penumbral gloom like a ghoul. Culcis hadn't seen it move since they entered. The Volpone had removed caps and helmets, and enjoyed the cool air from the recyc-units. Culcis wanted to run a hand through his fair, close-cropped hair but officer doctrine forbade it.

'How many break-in attempts?' Regara asked, stalking up to where Ossika was hiding behind his desk.

'In the last month?' Ossika leafed through a raft of data-slates. It took him a few seconds to find the report he wanted. 'Sixteen.'

Regara's expression hardened to rock. 'And the brawling, the discontent I observed as we entered camp?'

More leafing. This time it took Ossika a little longer. When he'd unearthed what he wanted, he answered, 'Again, in the last month...' He trailed off, deciding to show the Volpone major instead.

Regara scowled as he read the data-slate. 'Unacceptable,' he whispered. 'This is unacceptable,' louder this time, with a barb in his tone directed at Ossika. 'Who is in charge of discipline at this facility?'

'I am.' The quiet *hiss-clunk* of a closing door made them all turn to see the commissar who had just entered the room.

He wore a long black storm coat, buttoned to the collar. His peak cap carried the Commissariat iron skull icon and a thin film of the ruddy mixture currently dirtying the Volpone's uniforms. He was thin, and looked like a sliver of darkness. Glare-goggles fastened over his eyes only added to the mystique.

Culcis noted, despite the dingy confines of the chamber, the commissar didn't take them off.

'Arbettan,' he said, saluting the major. '*Lord Commissar* and sworn prosecutor of the Emperor's will.'

'Your charges are in disarray, commissar,' answered Regara, dispensing with protocol.

'Men off the line will occupy themselves as they will, major,' Arbettan replied. Behind him, almost lost to the shadows, lurked two bulky-looking cadets. Culcis could tell by the bulges in their frock coats that they carried side arms. Probably bolt pistols. 'Disorder and discontent are inevitable,' he went on. 'But rest assured, my men and I have the situation in hand.'

'Commissar Arbettan has been at Sagorrah for several months, major, and done an exemplary job,' offered Ossika unhelpfully.

'And the explosions,' Regara countered, ignoring the toadying Munitorum clerk, 'are they "in hand" also?'

Ossika started to answer, 'We believe there are insurgents–'

Arbettan cut him off. 'The outlying townships are riddled with cultists. Sanguinary tribes, most likely. We theorise that some are infiltrating Sagorrah and committing acts of sabotage against some of the smaller, less well-guarded wells.'

'Blood Pact?' Culcis ventured.

The commissar turned his fathomless black gaze on the lieutenant. 'Intelligence suggests no. A minor offshoot is the insurgents' probable orientation. It is under control.'

'The pillars of incendiary that almost downed some of my gunships suggest otherwise, commissar,' said Regara.

Like a lamp-house but with its light extinguished, Arbettan swung back to face the major. 'Like I said, just minor wells. I suspect the Archenemy is trying to sabotage the fuel reserves and impede the Imperial war effort. So far, their attacks have been negligible. Patrols are tasked daily with the rousting of the outer slums beyond our borders. We'll find the head of the insurgents...' Arbettan's slow smile made Culcis think of a death-adder, '...and cut it off.'

Regara's expression suggested he didn't entirely believe the commissar.

'Now,' Arbettan continued, 'if you gentlemen will excuse us, I have private business to discuss with Mr Ossika here.' He looked to the Munitorum officer. 'I assume all is in order?'

It was obvious to Culcis that Arbettan was throwing them out. He saw the tic of consternation in Regara's cheek and the tightening of his jaw as Ossika pushed the Munitorum facsimile of the billet papers towards the Volpone major.

'Signature, if you please, major.'

Regara eschewed Ossika's neuro-quill, instead accepting his own pen from Speers. He signed quickly, his script flat and functional.

'I'll need a ratified list of men and materiel also,' Ossika added as the Volpone were leaving.

Regara didn't turn around. He made sure to glare at Arbettan before he left, though. Culcis stayed behind a moment after the others to hand the list to Ossika then he too departed.

As he exited, he noticed the two cadets behind Arbettan relax. Though it was hard to tell for sure in the half-dark, Culcis swore their hands had been resting on their side arms.

THE VOLPONE OFFICERS returned to their billet a short while later. The Salamander command vehicle, this time bereft of Ossika, took them back down the approach road to the bastion and, after a few kilometres, to what appeared to be a disused stockyard.

Regara's headquarters were located in a deserted gatehouse. The other Volpone officers occupied similar structures radiating out from that central one. There wasn't enough room in the actual buildings for all the troops, but Ossika had supplied the 50th with a sizeable pitch. Most of the men and their sergeants bunked in tents just beyond the stockyard's footprint.

'Even the wine is off,' moaned Drado, sipping at his fluted glass with a disdainful sneer. He tipped it onto the sand – such waste was equal to a week's pay for most Guardsmen – and dabbed at his mouth with a napkin.

Culcis had long lost his appetite for alcohol. Like Drado, he sat in a well-appointed officer's chair at the threshold of the billet. And also like his aide, he agreed the wine tasted bad. For such a rare vintage, it was like sipping copper-filtrate. Instead, he was occupied with watching Sergeant Pillier putting Eighth Platoon through its paces on the makeshift drill-yard.

Every man was wearing full combat regalia, packs and helmets despite the heat. They moved fluidly to Pillier's orders, precise and efficient. Culcis swelled with pride. Truly, the Volpone were the finest body of men in all the segmentum, perhaps the galaxy. And yet... they had not earned the glory they desired or believed they deserved. It was the nature of war, especially a war like that raging across the Sabbat Worlds, to chew up men of honour, to spit on glory and grind it to paste in the great machine. The Volpone were just one of many. For some in the regiment, it had been a hard lesson to learn.

'And my boots are scummed to all hell and back,' a narked Drado continued. He gestured to his footwear, which was gummed with clods of ruddy sand. 'Have you ever experienced such a foul desert as this one? It's uncivilised.'

'I'm more concerned by the failing discipline in camp,' Culcis admitted as Pillier's men conducted an expert bayonet drill. He had several disciplinary reports sitting on a small table between them. Drado had purloined them on their exit from the Munitorum bastion. Culcis doubted they'd be missed. The reports made for grim reading. Summary executions and all classifications of violent misconduct as laid out in the Primer were at alarmingly high levels. Suicide and desertion rates were also climbing. Lassitude could have detrimental effects on fighting men, the lieutenant knew that as well as any-one, but the level of disorder hinted at in the parchment papers he was half-reading seemed abnormal.

'Arbettan doesn't strike me as soft. So why is there so much disorder in the ranks?' Culcis recalled Nacedon, the feeling in his gut as the Blood Pact had closed on them, the sense of something... *wrong*. These were men but they were also something more and less than that. It was hard to define but he felt it at Sagorrah, too.

The sudden crack of a firing squad rang out, punctuat-ing the lieutenant's thought. Fourth in the last hour and those were the ones they could hear from their billet.

Before Drado could answer, the shadow of Sergeant Vengo falling across the two men interrupted them. Vengo still had that thousand-yard stare as he waited for Culcis to give him permission to speak.

'What is it, sergeant?' the lieutenant asked.

'Orders from the major, sir,' he said in a neutral tone.

Faced with the hollow shell that was Vengo, Culcis was reminded of the meat grinder again and the fact that the Volpone, like so many, had been sacrificed upon it for Macaroth's glory.

Vengo pulled a piece of folded parchment from his jacket pocket and handed it to the lieutenant.

Breaking the wax seal, Culcis read first to himself and then aloud so Drado could hear him.

'We're assembling a force to go into the slum-zones at the Sagorrah perimeter,' he said. 'Fifty men ready for 18.00 hours in the muster yard.'

Drado checked his chrono. 'Just under an hour, sir.'

Lieutenant Culcis nodded. 'Get Sergeant Pillier to draft in the rest. Seems Major Regara wants to get his boots a little dirtier. Can't blame him.'

Drado was on his feet and heading for the drill sergeant when Culcis stopped him.

'And pack this up. We're done drinking.'

Drado couldn't suppress a disappointed frown but continued about his duties without pause.

'Very good. Sergeant Vengo,' said Culcis. 'You're dismissed.'

Vengo saluted and marched away.

When he was gone and Culcis was alone, the lieutenant looked to the distant hills. Beyond, he imagined the slum towns. City fighting was brutal. Under the right conditions, it could turn a poorly-armed force into a deadly one. Few Guardsmen relished it over pitched battle. Even trench warfare was preferable.

Culcis brushed the rust-coloured rime from his sleeve. It was tacky and reeked of metal. He was just glad to be getting out of camp.

THE THUD OF automatic weapons fire sounded above Culcis's head as he crouched behind the wall. The brick was baked white and chipped with bullet holes. Though it was approaching evening, the sun set late on the collection world. The street was swathed in shadow, though. The tight confines of its ruined buildings, the tattered tarps and half-demolished awnings created a sort of urban canopy overhead that promoted claustrophobia and paranoia.

'Scopes,' said Culcis.

Drado, squatting next to him, passed them over.

Poking the magnoculars through a gap in the shattered wall, Culcis could see all the way to the end of the street. His squad were pinned in a narrow defile, too much open ground between them and their targets to make a bayonet charge a viable tactic.

Still, they didn't need to.

Grainy thermal imaging showed Culcis what he needed to see – six insurgents, three with autoguns, another carrying a makeshift burner and a team with a heavy stubber. The cultists were wily enough to hold the cannon in reserve. The autogun fire was desultory, intended to draw the Volpone out.

Culcis's men were split, half and half, across the street. While he took refuge behind the wall, the others hunkered down behind a broken down trans-loader. The heavy Cargo-X was thick enough to take automatic fire. His squad was in no immediate danger.

'I have eyes on,' the lieutenant said into his microbead. He was no longer wearing his cap and had on the same type of low-brimmed bowl helmet as his men. He related coordinates to the other side of the street where a blind target marker waited.

'Light them up, Trooper Korde, if you please.'

The marker aimed the laser sight of his hellgun according to his lieutenant's direction. A beam flashed into the street darkness. Culcis followed it through the magnoculars and saw one of the cultists look down to the glow against his chest.

A few seconds later and the dense *thwump* of artillery filled the air. The view through the magnoculars was swarmed with white as the explosions from the mortar barrage overwhelmed its thermal imaging.

Culcis put them down and turned his back as a dust plume billowed down the street towards them. When the roar of explosives had died down and the dust settled, he looked back again. The end of the street was a ruin. A smoking, fire-wreathed crater remained where the cultists had been a few seconds earlier.

'Way is clear. Squad advance.' Culcis got to his feet and led them out.

LAS-BURSTS BURNED THROUGH the air between the Volpone and their enemies. Bright beams crisscrossed a space of about fifty metres in a deadly lattice of fire. Hunkered down in doorways and behind clumps of broken rockcrete from the remnants of destroyed buildings, Regara and his squad were holding and returning fire.

The cultists were occupying a fortified position at the end of a T-junction, an upturned hauler-truck and an improvised wall of sandbagging. Their shooting was inaccurate and lazy. The major despised them for it. His Volpone were outnumbered three to one, or so he'd judged, but by little more than a disorganised rabble.

'Steady fire!' bellowed Vengo, part of the major's squad. The men responded with short, sustained bursts, forcing the cultists down. Two even fell, shot through with hellgun beams.

Regara tapped his micro-bead. 'Corporal, we're wasting ammunition.'

'Almost there, sir,' a breathless Speers replied a few seconds later.

'See that you are.'

For another thirty seconds the fire exchange continued, both sides at an impasse. Then a line of explosions ripped into the cultists from behind and Vengo screamed the order to charge.

The Volpone ate the metres up the street to the enemy position in seconds, a pall of smoke spilling from behind the makeshift defences which they vaulted with assault-course efficiency. Vengo was at the front and killed a man by thrusting a blade into his neck. A second he smashed with the butt of his hellgun, ramming the man's nose into his brain and killing the cultist instantly.

Regara wasn't to be denied. Despatching a fire-blackened enemy survivor with a nonchalant burst from his hellpistol, he went on to kick an onrushing cultist with his bionic leg. The effect was dramatic as the wretch was sent screaming ten metres backwards, crumpling in a heap with his insides a mulched mess.

It was all over in a few seconds. The combination of smoke and frag grenades unleashed by Speers, who then went on to scrag several cultists from behind, had created destruction and a diversion for Vengo to launch the assault.

'You have a talent, Speers, I'll give you that,' Regara conceded as he was reunited with his aide.

'Thank you, sir,' the corporal replied, nodding before wiping his knife on the tunic of a dead cultist and sheathing it.

'Disgusting creatures,' said Regara, levering one of the dead over with his boot. The cultist was emaciated and filthy. He wore a stitched-together amalgam of flak armour, reused several times judging by the wear, and his footwear was little more than rags. The lascarbine he carried was old and poorly maintained. The sighter was ruined. Regara doubted he could have hit anything unless it was point-blank. Perhaps the grenade diversion had been unnecessary after all.

'How by Throne have these scum given Arbettan so much trouble?' he muttered. 'What say you, Sergeant Vengo?'

Vengo replied with a muted shake of the head. His eyes were distant and glassy.

Regara didn't get a chance to question him about it.

'Sir...' It was Speers. He had his hellgun trained on one of the fallen cultists and was waving the major over.

One of the enemy lived. He was half-buried under a chunk of hauler-truck. The broken engine block had crushed his feeble body but he was breathing. He was also talking.

'What's he saying?' Regara fought the urge to shoot the creature through the skull. Some enemy intelligence might prove useful and unlock some of the mystery around Sagorrah.

Leaning down to listen, Speers frowned and then looked up. '*Tongues of Tcharesh*, he just keeps repeating it over and over.'

'What's that in his eye?'

Speers took a closer look. 'Some kind of cataract, maybe?'

The cultist's right eye was shot through with purple veins. There was also a dark crust on his lips.

'Does that look like blood to you, sir?' Speers continued.

Regara noticed Sergeant Vengo was drawn to a marking on the wall, daubed in the same matter coating the dying cultist's lips. He was staring at it. The major found he couldn't focus on the precise image. It kept changing.

'Destroy it,' he said.

A moment's indecision by his men increased Regara's urgency. 'Do it now.'

Trooper Basker came forwards with his flamer and doused the patch of wall until the image was scoured away. All the while, Vengo didn't retreat. He only backed off once it was gone.

The stricken cultist's mantra grew louder, rising to an agitated shriek. Speers killed him with a shot between the eyes.

'Making my head hurt, sir.'

Regara looked back to the scorched section of wall where the strange icon had been. 'Yes, it was,' he said, noting that Vengo had returned to squad position and was organising the men.

'Corporal, situation report,' the major added to his aide. He had no desire to linger any longer than was necessary but felt it pertinent to check on their progress.

Speers pulled a data-slate from his pack and put it in front of the major. It showed a litho-pict mapping out a section of the slums. Regara's five fire teams, supported by elements of the Castellian Rangers and Harpine Fusiliers, had penetrated and cleared the outer markers of the eastern approach into the sector.

It was a moderate offensive, more of a fact-finding mission in truth. Regara wanted to gauge the level of insurgent presence in the slums, fathom its strength and likely dispositions. Once he had those details in hand, he could organise a widespread purging operation that would wipe out the traitors utterly. As it stood, he had operational command and just shy of two hundred men at his disposal, spread over an area of several square kilometres. This was just the first approach. There'd be more, and judging by the feeble resistance they'd met so far, such forays wouldn't be long in coming either. The glyphs were... *bothersome*, however.

'How are we faring, corporal?'

Speers regarded the data-slate, navigated through a few screens to get a wider geographical view of the area. 'So far we've mapped thirty-two per cent of this quadrant, sir.'

'And Captains Siegfrien and Trador?'

'Reporting steady progress. Resistance minimal.'

'I expected more,' he admitted to Speers.

'Sir?'

'The insurgents are dogs, by all that the Emperor is holy, but I thought they'd at least be organised.'

'You think Commissar Arbettan isn't taking his job seriously?'

'I'm not sure what I think at this juncture.'

The vox crackling to life interrupted Regara's train of thought.

Trooper Crimmens handed him the receiver cup without needing to be asked.

'This is Major Regara.'

Captain Trador of the Harpine responded. 'We encountered some glyphs, major, daubed on the brick-work. One of my scouts, Jedion, has just voxed it in. Please advise.'

Regara went back to the scorched wall for a third time. His voice was full of conviction. 'Destroy it, captain. Destroy any and all glyphs you come across.' He cut the vox link, handing the cup back to Crimmens.

Regara's face was grim. 'Pack it away, Speers, and have Sergeant Vengo move the men out. We've lingered here long enough.'

Less than a half-hour later the major's squad was moving low through the north-east quadrant of the slums.

They passed an open alleyway. It was long, and at the other end, Regara saw some of the Harpine tracking past in their green armour-mesh, stubby lascarbines held low in a grip suited to a crouched-running advance. Since they'd entered the slums, the major hadn't seen any of Siegfrien's men. Most of the Castellians formed the rearguard, anyway, their mortars and autocannons providing vital long-range support to take out particularly entrenched insurgents.

Regara battle-signed for his squad to continue forwards at pace.

The narrow streets that fed like corrupted arteries through the slums gave way to an open plaza. It was huge, some kind of provincial square, and bore recent signs of battle. Several dusty craters gouged clay flagstones and exposed the sandy earth beneath. Toppled columns created barricades of debris that broke the expanse into several discrete sections.

Across the carnage, Regara spotted Lieutenant Culcis and his squad moving into position. At the far end of the plaza, some three hundred metres or so distant, were a pair of tall towers. They looked empty, but then nothing was ever as it appeared to be in an urban engagement. Just arriving were a second squad of Volpone, led by Sergeant Pillier, and two squads of Harpine Fusiliers. A third entered through a side street just ahead of Regara. It was the group he'd seen down the alleyway a few minutes earlier. They took up an advanced position, dropping a tube-launcher into a particularly deep crater and aiming it at one of the towers.

SILENCE ROLLED ACROSS the shattered esplanade. A hot breeze kicked up grit and created coiling dust eddies. The creak of hinges, the shriek of bending wood and the hollow echo of the low wind passing through the carcass of the city provided a haunting chorus.

For the first time since they'd entered the slum zone, Culcis felt unease. He'd already noticed the major and

Sergeant Pillier. All told, there were sixty men occupying the massive plaza, almost half the strength of the Imperial insertion force.

Culcis brought up the map of the eastern approach to the slums to his mind. All of its streets and conduits led to this point like tributaries to a river. All other ways had been blocked by toppled buildings or stacked trucks and the wreckage of other vehicles. That alone should have tipped the lieutenant off.

He surveyed their surroundings through the magnoculars, waiting for the order to advance. Regara had brought them to a halt. Wisely, given the environs. Culcis noticed an altercation brewing between one of the Harpine and his sergeant. The lieutenant couldn't tell what they were arguing over, only that it was getting heated. Such insubordination was to be expected of lesser regiments.

Lower breeding, he told himself but was then put in mind of the appalling discipline at Sagorrah in general. Something niggled at Culcis at the back of his mind and he called for the vox. When he managed to raise the Harpine, all he got was a fairly breathless and crazed reply from their comms-officer.

'He's lost it, sir. Jedion. He's raving at the sergeant. He's–'

The sound of a gunshot interrupted him.

To his horror, Culcis watched the Harpine sergeant slump to the ground. It took the Volpone lieutenant a few seconds to realise that Jedion had taken his pistol from him and shot his sergeant dead.

The vox was still going in his ear.

'...Throne above! He's killed him. Scav me, he's only scavving shot the sarge...' The Harpine comms-officer wasn't talking to Culcis any more. The return was muffled and distant. He'd dropped the receiver cup and was pulling out his lasgun.

Through the magnoculars, a ball of something cold and unpleasant growing in his gut, Culcis watched

Jedion waste the comms-officer too. The man bucked, a ragged hole opened up in his chest and the lasgun went off. A stray shot capped one of the missile tube team across the plaza. In an audacious display of bad luck, the gunner fell and triggered the weapon.

Culcis's eyes widened as he followed the erratic trajectory of the missile, spilling contrails of smoke in a spiralling arc as it left the tube's housing. It was headed straight for them.

'Down!'

Fire and thunder engulfed them as the missile struck rockcrete and pulverised it.

For a moment, all Culcis could hear was a whining refrain in his ears like tinnitus. His vision blurred, his eyes watering with the smoke. Coughing up wads of black phlegm, he fought for his bearings.

Korde was dead, half of his torso a blackened ruin from where the blast had taken him. Varper's eye was streaming blood and he'd lost his helmet somewhere in the explosion. Other than that, just cuts and bruises. When Culcis emerged from the clearing fog, he was still a little dazed. Drado's voice came through loud and clear, his strong grip supporting his commanding officer and helping him back to his feet.

'Those bastards! How dare they open fire on the Royal 50th!'

He had murder in his eyes. Drado wanted to retaliate, but a choked command from Culcis stayed his hand. Something was wrong. The Harpine were struggling. More fights had broken out in the aftermath of the sergeant's slaying. Jedion was down, but others were turning their guns on one another too.

It was anarchy.

REGARA TURNED AWAY to shield himself as Culcis was engulfed by the explosion.

'Corporal, report! What by the Eye just happened?' he bellowed against the roar of the missile's detonation.

Speers was nonplussed. 'Don't know, sir. The Harpine...' his gaze tracked across the plaza to their allies, '...they just started shooting one another.'

Captain Trador was moving out of cover to try and restore order. His bolt pistol was in hand and his command squad were in tow. The Harpines with the missile tube waited uneasily, unsure what they should do. Meanwhile, Jedion's former regiment were tearing themselves apart.

'This is unconscionable!' spat Regara, reaching for the vox cup offered by Crimmens. He was about to try and raise Trador when he noticed the glint of metal in one of the towers. There was no time to shout a warning before the Harpine captain and his men were chewed up by heavy bolter fire.

In a few seconds the Harpine command was reduced to a visceral mist by the chugging cannon. Regara ordered retaliatory fire into the tower but it was too late and largely ineffective. The cultists were too heavily defended.

From the left flank, just north-west of the beleaguered squad of Harpine, twenty cultists armed with autoguns and mesh-carapace filtered from their hiding places. These men were not the rabble the Volpone had encountered earlier, they were military-trained and well-equipped. They advanced in a staggered formation, the front ranks firing snapshot while the rear ranks stopped to kneel and aim. Three of the Harpine went down before they could even muster a counter.

Bellowing orders to hose the tower with las-fire, while repelling the fresh wave of attackers, Regara got a closer look at the enemy.

As well as the military-grade kit and training, the cultist-elite wore half masks that divided their faces down the bridge of the nose. The left side was open, showing off the purple cataract and their scar-ravaged flesh; the right was covered by a dirty powder-blue mask split by a savage klown-like grin.

Despite the efforts of the Volpone, the Harpine were swept away under a furious assault of blades and close-range automatic fire. As the cultists continued their assault, some laying back to occupy the dead Guardsmen's defensive position, several were cut down by salvoes from Pillier's squad.

'All Volpone, pull back to my position,' Regara shouted into the vox as the heavy bolter in the tower started up, chugging overhead.

More cultists were spilling from the opposite side of the plaza, another twenty advancing in five-man kill-teams, heads low and hugging cover.

'WE WERE DRAWN in,' said Culcis. Whickering las-fire from the cultists split the air around him, making him duck behind the chunk of broken column.

Varper took a bolt to the throat, slumped back and never moved again.

Regara wasn't listening. He was bawling at Siegfrien down the vox, demanding he bring in his troops as a matter of urgency. As the major slammed down the receiver cup, drawing a wince from Crimmens, he sighed. 'They'll never make it in time. We're too far advanced.'

The las-fire was intensifying. The cultists had got into an enfilading position and seemed content to hold it. Meanwhile the heavy bolter continued to disintegrate the scant cover the twenty-something Volpone had left to hide behind.

'This was an ambush, sir,' Culcis persisted. 'And what about the Harpine? There is something seriously wrong here.'

Regara didn't answer, he was thinking. Hard. Trying to find a way out of the crap-storm the Volpone were embroiled in. Their return fire was admirable. Every man jack of the 50th shot in disciplined bursts, never giving in to panic, conserving ammunition. In a few minutes, it would matter for nothing.

'Sir!'

'I know, lieutenant,' snapped the major, 'but what use is it to us, now?'

'We need to warn Captain Siegfrien, tell him to turn back.'

'We are unaffected,' Regara countered, but his gaze straying to the vox showed he was listening.

'For now.'

Regara gritted his teeth, eyed the tower where the muzzle flash of the cannon flared like an angry star. 'If we could just take out that gun...'

As if the Emperor was listening and had answered his prayer, another flash lit up the tower, silencing the heavy bolter. A few seconds later, a cultist slumped forwards against the firing lip. Even from distance, Culcis could tell half the man's head was missing.

More shots streaked from the shadows, their firers unseen and unknown. Six more cultists fell dead with burn holes through their heads and necks. Not to turn up his nose at an opportunity, Regara ordered his squads to redouble their fire, picking off the cultists as they were thrown into sudden confusion. Without the heavy bolter pinning them down, the Volpone could move.

They advanced in small teams, four and five men strong, flanking left and right across the plaza. As one team came forwards, another held back providing covering fire until they were in position. Then the forward team took over fire support and so they crept outwards until they were pincering the cultists.

'Where's that fire coming from? Did Siegfrien have advanced units already in position?' asked Regara, snapping off tight, accurate bursts with his hellpistol. He spun a cultist on his ankle, burning a shot through his abdomen and shoulder.

'Negative, sir,' said Speers, advancing alongside the major. 'The Castellians are still inbound.'

The las-bolts from the shadows continued, both

behind, in front and to the flanks of the rapidly crumbling enemy force.

'Douse that tower!' Culcis pointed to where the dead heavy bolter gunner was still slumped. Drado and two others filled it with las-beams, shredding the fresh team of cultists who'd sneaked in to retake the gun. 'Take it out. Permanently.'

Trooper Henkermann was brought up, flanked either side by Drado and Lekke. Two incendiary rounds from his grenade launcher burned the tower completely and collapsed in the roof. The heavy bolter would no longer be a threat.

'Forward the 50th!' roared Regara, as the Volpone stormed the slowly retreating cultists. Gone was the enemy's military discipline, eroded in the face of a superior foe that now had the tactical advantage.

The major was first in, parrying a bayonet blow with his sabre. He kicked, breaking the cultist's shin with his bionic leg, and rammed the blade through the traitor's face when his defences crumpled in pain.

Culcis shot another enemy in the chest, almost pointblank, before shouldering the wretch over to engage a second.

Speers lobbed a pair of frag grenades into the midst of a fleeing group, who disappeared in a storm of fire and shrapnel a few seconds later.

And it was done.

The cultists were slain to a man. Upon investigation, each was revealed to have a purple cataract blighting their left eye like the others the Volpone had seen. And they wore the same sigil upon their armour as had been daubed on the brickwork.

Regara ordered Basker and his flamer up to burn them. The Volpone were dragging the bodies into a pyre to be immolated when their mysterious allies showed themselves.

'I don't believe it,' Drado articulated what they were all thinking.

Major Regara kept his reaction behind a mask of aristocratic arrogance.

With little choice, Lieutenant Culcis came forwards to receive the Guardsmen that had saved the Volpone's collective arses. The taste in his mouth was bitter when he acknowledged the leader of the ragged regiment they'd met on the road. Just over thirty men emerged from the shadows, all told. They moved in pairs and teams of three and four, from all across the plaza.

'Hauke,' said the leader, slapping his chest. Like his kinsmen, the ragged officer was dressed in dark tan fatigues, cut off at the knees and elbows to reveal even darker skin. Blue and grey whorls, jagged teeth and concentric circle tattoos daubed his body. A feather earring hung from his left lobe – some of the others had bones or necklaces of teeth and bird feet.

Hauke had a lasgun looped on a strap across his back. In his belt he carried two long knives and a bandolier with spare ammunition. He grinned, showing perfect teeth and warm eyes ringed with a sort of kohl. An aquiline face framed thin, reddish-brown lips and an angular nose not unlike a beak. His captain's rank pins were bright and well-polished but the rest of his uniform was dishevelled.

'Lieutenant Culcis, Volpone 50th.' Culcis saluted but didn't shake Hauke's hand when it was offered.

Hauke let it fall. He tapped his chest again. 'We are Kauth, last of the Longstriders.' He thumbed over his shoulder at the trooper carrying the scrap of banner Culcis had seen them with earlier. A small cadre of men had fallen in next to Captain Hauke, whilst the rest fanned out amongst the enemy dead that Basker and the rest had yet to collect for the pyre.

To Culcis's repugnance, he realised the Kauth were cutting trophies off the dead: fingers, ears, teeth – anything they could carry and thread on a piece of twine.

Regara saw it too. The major wasn't best pleased.

'Desist at once!' he raged. 'We're men of the Imperial

Guard, not savages!' He looked quickly to Vengo who was loitering nearby, his gaze lost in the middle distance. 'Sergeant, impede those men.'

Like a switch had been flicked in his head, Vengo moved in to intercept the Kauth with a small combat squad from the Volpone nearest to him.

There was arguing immediately. Not all of the Kauth could speak Gothic and ranted back in a feral tongue.

A clipped command from Hauke, more like a squawk, halted the Longstriders in their tracks. He frowned.

Before he had a chance to speak, the major was on him.

'I am appalled, sir,' he said. 'Butchery is the province of the Archenemy, not good Emperor-fearing men of the Imperium. This is not the jungle or some arse-end backwater bereft of order'– Culcis raised an eyebrow at that remark, that's exactly what it was – 'it is the sovereign soil of the Imperium.' Regara was incensed and working himself up. The near miss with the cultists had affected him, maybe something else too. He wasn't done and looked Hauke up and down with an aggressive sneer. 'And you call those uniforms? You are a disgrace to the Imperial Guard. I do not recognise you, sir. No, I *refuse* to recognise you.'

Hauke was nonplussed, even a little amused, though he kept it veiled in case of more reprisals. 'We saved your life, brother.'

'You did not. And I have the sworn testimony of over twenty men that will attest to that. The record will show the Volpone's courage in this combat action.'

'Sir?' Culcis felt he should intervene. The Kauth *did* save their lives, whether Regara cared to acknowledge it or not.

The major turned on him, crimson with rage. He hissed through gritted teeth. 'They are a rabble, lieutenant. Less than that, they are tantamount to animals. I will not recognise them.'

'Seems you'd be better with an eye rather than a new

leg, eh, brother?' said Hauke, genuinely. 'Man who can't see truth at end of nose is poor indeed.'

Regara didn't even look at him, instead spitting his words candidly at Culcis. 'Get them out of my sight, lieutenant. Do it now, or I shall order Sergeant Vengo to open fire.'

Culcis bit his tongue. These men were savages, yes, but they *had* saved the Volpone. He also didn't trust Vengo not to turn this altercation into a bloodbath. 'At once, sir,' he said at length. Regara stalked away to let his second-in-command get on with it.

'You need to get your men to stop doing that, captain,' Culcis addressed Hauke.

'It is right of Kauth to trophy-take from slain.'

'Not when you're fighting alongside the Volpone, not when you're fighting for the Guard. Do it now, sir.'

A shrilling cry issued from Hauke's lips, a sign to his men to desist and gather. Some frowned, wanting to resume cutting, but they obeyed and converged on the banner bearer.

'Very good,' said Culcis. 'Is that your regimental standard?' he asked, noting the scrap of cloth the Kauth had flocked to.

'Blessed by the beati,' Hauke replied. 'On Vigo's Hill where Longstriders stood their last, or so we thought until *She* came.'

'Saint Sabbat?' Culcis couldn't keep from scoffing. He regained his composure quickly. 'You were blessed by Saint Sabbat.'

'Aye.' Hauke was solemn as a priest. He believed it. Judging by the stern expressions of his men, they all did.

Culcis shook his head, his incredulity obvious to all but the unassuming Longstriders.

'Here, brother.' Hauke offered Culcis a pair of cigars. The leaf was dark and thick, and redolent of liquorice. No doubt Hauke had won, stolen or been gifted them by another regiment in the reserve.

Culcis hesitated.

'Good,' said Hauke, pushing the cigars onto the lieutenant. 'Take them.'

Grudgingly, Culcis accepted the offering, swiftly pocketing the smokes before Regara could see, and politely asked the Kauth to return to camp.

Hauke nodded. He gave another shrill cry, almost avian, to his men and they departed the plaza quickly. In a few minutes they'd blended back into the slums and it was like they were never there.

Culcis rejoined the major who was conversing with Corporal Speers.

Siegfrien had just raised them on the vox and Crimmens was handing over the receiver cup.

'Give me that,' Regara snapped at the vox officer, his ire obvious and enflamed. 'Negative,' he barked down the cup at the Castellian captain. 'Pull back, we're returning to camp for an immediate debrief and mission post-mortem.' He thrust the vox at Crimmens, punching it into his chest, and stalked off.

Regara never made eye contact with Culcis once.

It was going to be a long walk back to the deployment zone and an even longer drive back to Sagorrah.

GRIM. THAT WAS how Regara had described the situation on their return to camp. Culcis was forced to agree with him. The major had requested a private audience with Commissar Arbettan to discuss what went wrong during the mission and his concerns regards 'warp taint' evident in the slums. Culcis wasn't so sure it was only confined to that area. At least they hadn't seen the Kauth again. Either the Longstriders were keeping a low profile and they'd just missed them in the throng or they'd never gone back to Sagorrah. In any event, it was a small mercy as far as Culcis was concerned.

Sitting at one of Refectorum B-62's benches, idly fingering his Guard-issue mess tin and knife, Culcis was lost to his thoughts.

Drado snapped him out of it. 'Mind if I sit, sir?' he

said, setting down opposite the lieutenant.

'Looks like you already have,' Culcis answered dryly. 'What's the word in the camp?' he added, watching Drado attack the Guard chef's slop with too much gusto. Sometimes Culcis wondered whether the corporal was Volpone at all, that perhaps he'd been switched with another regiment for some Munitorum clerk's amusement. Not so. Drado's blood was as blue as any of them.

The Royal 50th had their own chef, of course, their own small army of retainers and staffers in fact. Culcis had chosen to slum it in the ranks. Something wasn't right and he wasn't about to discover the source by staying in the regiment. Most of the men were disgruntled at having to lower their standards. Drado, despite his fierce aristocratism, was actually coping rather well.

There was a low hubbub of aggression pervading throughout the mess hall, several disparate regiments jammed together in its hot, sweaty confines. The men were on edge, the Harpine especially. Losing one of their captains, though the circumstances had been covered up, was chaffing at what little fortitude they had left.

'If I might be so bold,' ventured Drado. 'What do you think happened out there?'

Culcis shook his head slowly. 'Fegged if I know, corporal.'

'That Harpine – what was his name again? Jedion, that was it – he just seemed to lose his mind. And then there were the glyphs...' Drado let his theory trail off, as if fearful that voicing it out loud would give it power.

'I've heard of combat stress taking men to the brink, but I've never seen a trooper shoot his own regimental sergeant over a petty squabble.'

'Undisciplined dogs,' Drado muttered, shooting daggers at a belligerent group of Harpine who'd just bustled their way inside. 'Sir...'

Culcis had seen them too. His gaze was weary. The atmosphere was on a knife-edge. When the Harpine had settled into line, the lieutenant relaxed the grip on his hellpistol, snug in his belt and concealed beneath the mess table.

'No sign of that feral mob?' he asked Drado.

'None at all. Speers reckons they never came back to camp. How would we find them if they did, anyway?'

'Why would we want to?' asked Culcis, though he still had the cigars given to him by Captain Hauke. Didn't feel right to discard them. Perhaps he was the one who'd swapped regiments when he wasn't looking. They were all different since Nacedon. Even Regara, though the major fought it with every aristocratic fibre.

Drado leaned in close. 'I did hear about another sixteen scheduled executions this morning. And the number of violent acts of misconduct has doubled since yesterday.'

After their disastrous foray into the slums, the Volpone had returned through the night. By the time they'd made reports, broken down kit and secured it in the armoury at their billets, it was approaching another arid Sagorrah morning.

'Only sixteen?' Culcis remarked dryly.

'Apparently, Arbettan has a long list of offenders he's working through,' Drado replied. 'Hold on...' he added.

Culcis followed his anxious gaze to the mess line where Corporal Speers had just cut in.

'Stinkin' glory boys, what gives you the right?'

Evidently, the Harpine weren't pleased. One, a big fellow as broad as the Volpone's Colonel Gilbear, advanced on the corporal.

'Step back, dreg,' Speers replied, with an arrogant side-glance at the disgruntled Harpine trooper. His tags read: Maggon.

'I say again, what gives you the right?' This time the Harpine trooper got in the Volpone's face, determined to make his point. He prodded the corporal's arm with his finger.

Speers first looked down at the finger then up at the Harpine. The Volpone were big, strong men, of fine stock, but this Maggon was a giant. The top of Speers's shaven head only came up to the Harpine's chin. It didn't seem to faze him. 'You want to lose that, keep talking. Otherwise, get back in line and know your place.'

'You arrogant bastard...' The Harpine was about to seize the Volpone's arm when a shot rang out, hard and heavy like a bell chime. Blood and tiny chunks of brain matter spattered Speers's face as Maggon's head exploded like a crushed egg.

Vengo was on his feet, a smoking bolt pistol in his outstretched hand.

'Oh shit...' Culcis was up too, pulling out his hellpistol with frantic fingers. 'Put the weapon down, sergeant.'

The refectorum was plunged into shocked silence. The Harpine lolled against the mess counter as his legs gave way before slumping into a heap at Speers's feet. The corporal turned on Vengo.

'What in the hells are you doing, sergeant?'

Vengo's eyes were blank of expression. His face was utterly devoid of emotion.

'Gun down. Now,' insisted Culcis, his tone level.

Maggon's blood was spilling across the refectorum floor, wetting the boots of the men in line next to him, including Speers.

'Put it down, sergeant,' the corporal pleaded, hands up in a plaintive gesture for calm.

'Throne above, Vengo,' said Drado. 'Just do it.'

Culcis had moved up alongside and saw Vengo's left eye twitch. He shifted the bolt pistol, aiming for the next Harpine in line.

'Dogs in the sun...' he chuckled. 'Need putting down,' and tensed the trigger.

Culcis shot him in the side of the head.

Vengo fell, the bolt pistol skittering out of his grasp for Speers to stoop, retrieve and disarm.

The room breathed a collective sigh of relief.

'Everyone stay where they are,' Culcis ordered. The

other troops in the hall were too shocked to disobey. It wouldn't last. The lieutenant crouched next to Vengo's cooling corpse. 'You see this?' he asked Drado, who squatted down next to him.

The left eye had a purple tinge, just like the cultists.

'Holy Throne...' breathed the corporal.

Culcis flashed a glance at the rest of the Harpine in the refectorum. It didn't look good. Only Regara and Arbettan entering the room stopped things from getting really ugly.

Relief had turned to anger. There was shouting, accusation. Some of the men were pulling side arms – the ones who carried them, anyway. Others were seizing mess knives for improvised weaponry. Blood was in the air, that same metallic stink that laced the breeze around Sagorrah and the slums.

'Hold!' bellowed Arbettan. 'By the order of the Commissariat, hold or I shall summarily execute anyone who does not.'

Regara's eyes widened in surprise when he saw Vengo. 'You did this, lieutenant?'

'He was mad, major. Something snapped.' He added, beneath his breath, 'Look at his eye.'

The major stooped to regard the corpse. Surreptitiously he made the sign of the aquila. 'Throne of Earth...'

He stood and swiftly about-faced. Commissar Arbettan stared at him through the blank, soulless lenses of his glare-goggles. Three of his shadows had moved in behind him, exuding menace.

'This is Volpone business,' said Regara, quickly. 'I'll deal with it.'

'Captain Trador dead, thirty of his men also,' – he looked down disdainfully at poor Maggon – 'make that thirty-one. I'd say this is beyond the remit of the Royal 50th, major, wouldn't you?'

Regara never moved. 'That said, *I* will deal with this. I'd say you've enough to contend with in this camp at the moment, commissar, wouldn't you?'

Arbettan didn't looked impressed, or about to let it go. Two more cadets came out of the shadows.

'Your goons are outnumbered,' Regara told him. 'We've dealt with commissars before. Are you really going to push this?'

A few tense seconds passed by, the air as thick as glue, before Arbettan scowled and left the refectorum, his shadows slinking after him.

'Thank you, major,' said Culcis once the commissar had gone.

Regara was livid. 'Get them out,' he said, eyes wide with anger, 'all of them. Right now. Including Sergeant Vengo. Report to my billet when it's done. As soon as it's done, lieutenant.'

Culcis nodded, 'Yes, sir.'

'Speers,' Regara paused by the corporal on his way out of the mess hall, 'a word.'

THE MAJOR HAD done what he could to smooth things over with the Harpine. By the time Lieutenant Culcis had finished up at the mess hall, securing Vengo for transport and sending the men back to their billets, Regara had had several conversations with the Harpine officer cadre. Speers had left without word, on some errand for the major, so just Drado and Culcis were left to tramp from the refectorum to Regara's billet.

They attracted scathing glances from the Guardsmen they passed on the way. Some of the regiments they hadn't even seen before, yet they seemed to hold the Volpone, any outsiders in fact, in suspicion and belligerence.

Walking the densely populated avenues of Sagorrah, Culcis felt strangely exposed.

'Quicken your pace, corporal.'

'Beg your pardon, sir?' asked Drado with an incredulous expression.

'You heard me. We are in hostile territory,' said Culcis.

'Quicken your pace and keep your side arm ready.'

Drado noticed the looks they were getting too, now. He brushed at the rust rime on his jacket nervously. The ruddy scum on his boots was making them feel leaden; so too was his anxiety.

'My heart is pounding,' he admitted.

'Just combat tension,' Culcis replied. Drado's body knew it was about to get into a fight before his mind did and was preparing for it.

A group of tankers, brawny-looking men with oil-smeared features and olive drab fatigues bearing a split-skull motif, jumped off their armour rigs where they'd been loitering. They looked like engineers, carrying wrenches, cutting torches and other tools. A boxy Chimera lay open with the guts of its engine strewn across a blanket. The machine parts were gummed with the ruddy substance marring the Volpone's boots and uniforms.

The tankers didn't seem to care.

'This way,' said Culcis, taking them down an empty side street, between two unoccupied billet houses.

Drado followed, even though it wasn't the direct route to the Volpone camp.

'Wait,' the lieutenant hissed, ducking them into an alcove. The area was thick with native structures, mostly disused warehouses and stockyards.

'Sir, what are you–'

Culcis silenced him, crept deeper into the shadows of the alcove, eyes on the street. 'Wait,' he insisted.

A few minutes later, the tankers swaggered past, still tooled up and looking for the Volpone.

After they were gone, headed further down the street and bypassing Culcis and Drado completely, the lieutenant pulled them out of hiding.

'Come on,' he whispered, breaking into a jog and doubling back.

'They were going to kill us, weren't they?' said Drado.

'I don't honestly know, corporal. Whatever they had in mind, it wasn't good.'

Culcis and Drado made for the Volpone billet with all haste. They took an oblique route, keeping away from crowds and sticking to the side streets, hugging the shadows when they could. It took a while.

Sagorrah was headed for meltdown. Over a million Guardsmen, armed and armoured for war, approached the brink, and Culcis had no idea why.

THOUGH REGARA GLOWERED from behind his desk, Culcis was relieved to have finally reached the major's billet.

His retainers had appointed the Volpone headquarters at Sagorrah well. The gatehouse had been gutted of debris. Thus cleared, the major's men had added luxuriant carpeting, portraiture and the fine blackoak desk Regara was currently leaning on. There were charts and data-slates strewn upon it. A plump-looking leather chair, with a blackoak frame to match the desk, sat idly behind him. A pair of cooling units lost somewhere in the shadows of the room's periphery hummed dulcetly and kept the ambient temperature pleasant.

In one corner, a chaise longue with a small table sat next to it. There was a decanter on the table, the crystal vial stoppered to prevent the wine within becoming exposed to the air. Against the opposite wall, a steel rack where the major stowed his hellpistol on a holster and his uniform jacket and storm coat.

Anterooms were hinted at beyond but right now the focus was on the scowling major and the slew of intel on the desk before him.

They were late, much later than Culcis had intended. Explanations would have to wait. Regara wasn't about to heed them.

'We can be agreed, I think,' said the major, 'that this is no ordinary spate of insubordination afflicting Sagorrah. Something is at work here that goes beyond boredom and disaffection. Sergeant Vengo's death was proof enough of that.'

'He hadn't been the same since Monthax,' offered

Pillier, filling in for the deceased officer. They all remembered Monthax, and the eldritch storm. No one could
truly say they'd been unaffected by it. Vengo, it seemed,
had suffered worse than most. It had unhinged him,
somehow left him vulnerable to whatever malady was
plaguing the depot.

The four other men present – Regara, Culcis and their
aides – all acknowledged it but no one spoke further.
Some battles, glorious or not, were best left unremem-
bered.

The major spread his hands over the data-slates and
parchment reports in front of him. 'We have here the
bulk of Arbettan's incident reports concerning the
appalling lack of Sagorrah discipline. Corporal Speers,'
he added, gesturing to his aide, who was sporting several cuts and bruises, largely lost to the half-dark of the
room, 'was kind enough to procure them for me.'

'Does Arbettan know?' asked Culcis. If the commissar had knowledge of this transgression it might make
whatever the Volpone had to do next difficult, if not
impossible.

Speers grinned, revealing a bloody tooth. 'Not unless
he can find where I stashed two of his enforcers,' he said.
'Which he won't.'

'While we were waiting,' Regara gave Culcis a dark
look, 'I had Sergeant Pillier draw some conclusions.'

Pillier came forwards into the light from a glass-
shaded desk lamp and pulled a map of the Sagorrah
depot from under the morass of files.

There were small red dots littering the map, denoting
areas where incidents of violence and discord had been
reported according to severity and frequency. Pillier had
been busy. Culcis didn't realise they were quite so late,
but swallowed his shame and concentrated on the map.

'Can you see something in it, lieutenant?' asked the
major. 'A pattern, perhaps?'

'I see a void,' he said, not looking up. He pressed his
finger against a section of map which had an absence of

dots. 'Who resides in this part of the camp?'

Regara had a list of where the billets had been assigned and to whom. He was smiling, a smug grin affecting his noble countenance.

'It's the Kauth.'

The rest of the room stayed silent, awaiting Culcis's reaction.

'The Longstriders? But they aided us out in the slums, saved our collective arses, major.'

Regara dropped the list on top of the map and leaned in. 'Facts are, there's no way insurgents could get so close to the promethium wells without help. What we saw with the Harpine, the way they were turned, and Vengo...' Regara let that one float a little before he went on, 'Someone in this camp is opening the door for these attacks.'

'And the Kauth are suspects because they're *not* affected?'

'It is because they are not affected that suggests they can operate even in the same conditions that are debilitating every other man jack in this stinking cesspit! How else do you do that unless you are the ones propagating the taint?'

Culcis frowned. 'But we are also still ourselves, sir.'

Regara straightened and pushed out his chest. 'We are Volpone, lieutenant. We are not like the dogs shackled to this gnarled stick of an outpost. Our breeding and superior training keeps us immune.'

'Tell that to Vengo, sir.'

The major flushed with anger but mastered it quickly. He seized his lapel and pulled on it, exposing the rust rime to the light. 'It is *this*, and *this*,' he added, showing the scum on his boot. 'The air is filled with it, the entire camp polluted by something as pervasive as the sand in the desert. We have been here for a matter of days, lieutenant. The Kauth have been in the reserve for much longer than that. They should be as crazed as the rest of the Guard.'

The smile returned. It was as if all of Regara's private theories and suspicions about the feral regiment had been suddenly and conclusively confirmed.

'It has to be them,' he said.

Culcis wasn't so sure but kept it to himself. Instead he said, 'The mood in the camp is reaching fever pitch. Drado and I were almost attacked walking from the mess hall to the billet. It was why we were so late.'

Regara's eyes narrowed and his smile thinned to a mirthless flat line. 'I'm sending thirty men to the Kauth billet. We'll apprehend these traitors ourselves since Arbettan is evidently incapable.'

'Only thirty?' asked Culcis. 'The Longstriders are scum but they are skilled in the art of killing. Thirty men would put us at roughly equal strength.'

'Have some backbone, lieutenant!' snapped the major. 'You are Volpone, more than the equal of any man in the Guard, especially a ragged band of savages like the Kauth. Besides,' he added, calming down, 'we can't risk a show of greater strength. If the camp is as volatile as you say it might spark a reaction we can't control easily.'

Culcis nodded his acceptance.

'Lieutenant,' said Regara, 'I want you and Sergeant Pillier to take three squads to the Kauth billet and bring them all back here – under force of arms if necessary – for interrogation. Take Speers with you, too.' The corporal smiled. It put Culcis in mind of a gore-shark. 'His ruthless streak is bound to come in useful.'

'Ever since we met, I've wanted to scrag a few of those savages, sir,' he said, blissfully ignorant of the irony in his words.

'Right here, lieutenant,' said Regara, ignoring the bloodthirsty corporal, and prodding the area of the map where the Kauth were located. 'Take all necessary steps to apprehend them,' he warned. '*All* necessary steps.'

Speers tossed Culcis a lasgun from the armoury, and the lieutenant caught it deftly, checked the power gauge and shouldered it before taking his leave.

Sergeant Pillier and Corporal Drado followed close behind.

Speers lingered a little at a glance from his commanding officer.

'Make sure he follows through on this,' whispered the major. 'Bloody the dogs if you have to, but bring them here to me.'

Nodding, the corporal then turned on his heel and went after Culcis and the others.

THE LONGSTRIDER BILLET was deserted. It sat at the edge of Sagorrah Depot in a pitch that was little more than a scrap of barren earth. It was a contrast in styles to the opulence of the Volpone's billet, particularly Major Regara's accommodations. Scattered tents and doused cook fires defined the space. It was untidy and ragged, just like the men stationed there. The emptiness, its isolation from the rest of the camp only added to the eeriness of the place.

Once he was certain there was no one around, Culcis investigated further. He saw totems, fetishes, trophy racks and other disturbing evidence of the Kauth's feral nature, littered throughout the billet. And there was blood too, dark streaks like pronounced veins webbing the sand having dried in the sun. The metallic stink was as pervasive here as it was anywhere in Sagorrah.

'Doesn't look like anyone's home,' said Drado as he and Culcis were exiting their third empty tent. Speers, from another part of the billet, came jogging over to them. The Volpone had fanned out, tackling the area in teams of two and three, checking each and every one of the thirty or so tents pegged around the billet.

'Something isn't right,' the corporal hissed.

'What do you mean?' asked Culcis. 'What is it?'

'We're being watched. I can feel it.'

Sociopathic as he probably was, Culcis had also learned to trust Speers's instincts over their years of service together. The man had a knack for sniffing out trouble, as well as finding and creating it.

'All right,' he said, scanning the shadows at the edge of the billet, seeking enemies but finding none. 'Tell Sergeant Pillier and have him alert the men. We'll turn this sorry hole inside out if needed.' Culcis was reminded of the feeling he'd had walking past the tankers, the sense of impending violence.

Speers nodded and got about halfway to Pillier when a shout came from one of the other troopers. The Longstriders had returned and were making their way back to the billet in force.

'GREETINGS, VOLPONE,' SAID Hauke, extending a hand and giving Culcis a warm smile.

The lieutenant refused it and kept his arms by his sides.

'You never returned from the slums that first time we saw you, did you?'

Hauke shrugged, affecting a placid, easy mood. His men, now fully arrived in the billet and squaring off against the Bluebloods in packs, were entirely more restive. 'It seemed a shame to leave so soon. Much more to find, Volpone.'

'Your insolence is reason enough for your being apprehended,' Culcis told him, 'but Major Regara has some questions for you concerning another matter.'

'Oh yes? Tell me Volpone, what questions are these?' A flicker of annoyance marred Hauke's feigned bonhomie. Both the Kauth and the Volpone tensed, anticipating trouble.

'That's for the major to tell you, sir. You need to come with us. Right now.'

'And if we don't?'

'Then this camp is about to get a sight bloodier than it already is.'

Hauke's eyes narrowed as he considered what he regarded as a request and not an order. 'I like you, Volpone. We will come.'

Culcis tried to mask his sudden fluster but failed. 'Very good then.'

As the Kauth relaxed, Hauke looked to a pair of nearby hills, overlooking the billet. He made a noise like a shrieking prey-bird and two sentries emerged from their hiding place, each shouldering a long-las.

Culcis hadn't noticed, but Speers had taken up a position by one of the tents, his lasgun aimed at the very selfsame spot in the hills.

'I had 'em, sir,' he said, lowering his gunsights now the Longstriders had revealed themselves.

Culcis wasn't sure about that. He was only glad Hauke had been so gracious about being taken into Volpone custody. The spilling of more blood was the last thing Sagorrah needed. But he suspected it wasn't done with it, not yet. They made for the Volpone billet and only disarmed their prisoners once they'd arrived.

MAJOR REGARA WAS poised at the threshold of the make-shift holding room where they'd put Hauke and his three officers. He looked nonplussed at Culcis.

'They submitted without a fight?'

'Yes, sir. The Kauth captain stated he would be pleased to converse with you.'

Regara made the equivalent facial expression of a shrug and moved into the holding room where Speers and Drado were already waiting. Culcis followed the major, leaving Sergeant Pillier at the door on guard.

Drado was looking nervous as he cradled his lasgun. Seemed as if the near miss in camp had spooked him. The entire room felt tense, in fact. No stranger to conducting interrogations, Speers had already removed his carapace breastplate and was rolling up his sleeves when the two officers entered. Culcis leaned in to have a word in the corporal's ear.

'Let's just ask some questions first, eh?'

Speers sought Regara's nod of approval before he backed off.

The lieutenant took his place and addressed Hauke.

'What we all saw out in the slums with the Harpine is starting to happen here, in the Sagorrah camp.'

The Longstrider captain said nothing but stared intently, his eyes like burning sapphires.

'It's been slow at first but now the effects are starting to tell. The discord, the lack of discipline, the murders, executions and brawling are all a product of whatever is afflicting the camp. Likely some outside force, in league with the Ruinous Powers.'

Culcis caught Drado out of the corner of his eye making the sign of the aquila.

Hauke smiled without mirth, without warmth. 'And you think we Kauth responsible, eh, Volpone?'

'You are the only regiment unaffected by the taint.'

Now the warmth returned. 'We are *blessed*.' Hauke slapped his hand on the shoulder of the warrior next to him, his banner bearer. The pole with the ragged strip of cloth was held firmly but reverently by the Longstrider. It was the only item they'd refused to be parted from and Culcis had seen no harm in that.

'Touched by Saint Sabbat,' Hauke added, touching the fabric, 'for our fight on Vigo's Hill.'

'Explain.'

'After Herodor, we fought many battles. The world I don't remember,' Hauke confessed, 'there were many. Vigo's Hill stays in mind. We fought last stand. It was to be end of Longstriders. Until *She* came.'

Regara made a grunting sound and came forwards. 'You cannot expect us to believe this. The Saint rescued your sorry hides and touched your banner, thereby blessing you and your savage brethren? Likely you were cowering in the dirt or hacking trophies from your enemies, tantamount to beasts. Saint Sabbat would not bless *beasts*.'

'It is so,' said Hauke, without anger, without aggression. It was an irrefutable truth to him, as pointless to argue against as it was to protest for.

Leaning in to Hauke, the major scowled. 'Where are the others, the rest of the insurgents? Are there more glyphs around the camp? Is that how you're affecting the men?'

Hauke frowned as if hearing the answer to a puzzle he didn't quite understand.

'But you are not affected, Volpone–'

'Address me as major, you dog!' Regara looked to Speers, giving the corporal's brutalisation tactics sanction.

Speers grinned. Culcis was about to intervene, still unconvinced by the major's argument, when a new voice filled the holding room.

'I shall take it from here, major.'

It was Commissar Arbettan with Ossika loitering in the background.

They weren't alone. Arbettan had brought five of his goons with him. The meatheaded cadets bristled with violent intent behind the commissar. All wore the familiar pistol bulges just under their frock coats. The commissar had his side holster exposed. The pearl grip of an ornate bolt pistol was in full view. Ossika looked indignant but also slightly terrified.

'I told you back in the mess, commissar,' said Regara, straightening his back and thrusting out his chin, 'this is Volpone business. *I* shall deal with it.'

The tension had just racked up a few notches. Drado was sweating, fingers itching on the stock and trigger of his lasgun. Culcis flashed him a stern but reassuring glance to steady him. Speers was already sneaking his hand to the laspistol attached to his belt. As for Pillier, he'd been muscled out of the way by a sixth cadet and waited calmly outside. His eyes were on the major, as he waited to back up any decision Regara was about to make.

'Hand over the prisoners, Regara,' ordered Arbettan. 'Do so immediately and you'll be free of further repercussion, including the theft of Commissariat property and the assault of one of my men.'

'Thought you said he wouldn't find him,' hissed Culcis into Speers's ear.

The corporal gave a near imperceptible shrug.

Speers received a bladed look from behind Arbettan's glare-goggles. His jaw hardened in response and his hand crept a little closer to his pistol.

'Get ready...' said Culcis. Only one way this was going to go now.

'Yes, sir.'

Arbettan looked at Regara and smiled.

'In the Emperor's name, I condemn thee to death!' he cried. Ripping out his bolt pistol, he fired.

THE HEAVY BOOM of the bolt pistol filled the chamber, reverberating around its rockcrete bulkheads and columns like thunder.

Regara flinched, already tearing his hellpistol free, when one of the Kauth officers behind him bucked and exploded as the mass-reactive rounds destroyed him.

For Culcis, everything went into slow motion. He felt the warmth of sudden blood spatter against his neck and face, the percussive force of the expelled bolter round upon his back. He was moving. Head low, he made for the nearest column. Six in total, supported the makeshift holding room's puckered ceiling. Three stone bulkheads jutted from one flanking wall, dividing it into three discrete sections. It was huge, but was wide and long enough for a medium fire exchange. After the first shot fired that's exactly what happened.

Slipping out his pistol, Culcis snapped off a few shots and caught a cadet in the leg. A hot blue beam from Drado's direction pierced the same cadet's sternum and he fell.

Arbettan was moving too and returning fire.

In the space of a few brutal, muzzle-flaring seconds, every man in the tight chamber had gone for cover, hunkering behind the bulkheads and columns. Both forces retreated to opposite ends of the room and the space inbetween was littered with shells and las-tracer.

The air became charged with heat. The sound of dis-charged weapons fire was deafening.

Speers was hugging the wall. He leaned out to take a cadet through the throat with a finely aimed shot but spun as return fire glanced his shoulder. He went down, blood streaming along his arm before Culcis lost him from sight.

'Where are the Kauth?' he asked Sergeant Pillier, who'd just scurried alongside him.

Pillier shook his head, stooping low and tagging a cadet in the knee with his hellpistol. A muffled cry of pain rewarded his efforts before one of the cadet's allies dragged him clear. The chairs where they'd had the Kauth were tipped over and empty. Only the dead officer remained, face down in a pool of oozing blood.

'They have us pinned, sir,' said the sergeant, taking cover from the inevitable return fire.

Culcis leaned out of hiding to get a better idea of the situation. Exploding shrapnel forced him back quickly.

'They've spread out across the back end of the room, four cadets plus Arbettan.'

For their part, the Volpone had Culcis and Pillier crouched behind one bulkhead with Regara and Drado a metre away opposite them taking advantage of one of the columns.

Pillier was right – they were pinned. Arbettan had more men and probably the means to contact them. The nearest vox-bead for the Volpone and possible rein-forcements wasn't near enough.

Regara knew it, too. Culcis could see the realisation of it manifest on his face as livid anger. His hellpistol blazed in the half-dark, lighting up his visage. His shots were largely ineffectual – the commissar and his men were well hunkered down by now. Arbettan saw that as well.

'Give it up, Regara,' he shouted over the din. 'You are all dead men, anyway. The punishment for treason against the Emperor is death. Death! Death!'

'He's lost his mind,' Culcis muttered, unable to get a bead on any of them.

Something was moving out of the corner of his eye, ahead by the next most advanced bulkhead. It was Hauke and his banner bearer. They were crouched, like predators stalking prey. Each carried a small hatchet blade in his right hand.

Culcis bristled with self-directed anger. He'd thought the Longstriders were completely disarmed.

As if reading the lieutenant's thoughts, Hauke turned and smiled. He pointed two fingers at the loitering silhouettes that were Arbettan and his men.

'Pillier,' said Culcis, 'on my mark, direct suppressing fire against the right column.' Without waiting for a response, the lieutenant caught Drado's attention. Regara was too busy emptying his power pack in a frustrated rage.

'Corporal...' Culcis had to shout.

Drado noticed the lieutenant and nodded to his gesture as he caught on to the plan.

Culcis slashed his hand down at the same time shouting, 'Mark!'

The Volpone fired as one, lacing the columns at the far end of the room with las-fire and pressing the cadets back.

The Longstriders advanced, skirting around the bulkhead at speed and slipping up to a pair of cadets. When the first stuck his head out, Hauke slammed a hatchet into it. The cadet's nose and face caved. The second took a blade to the stomach – the grim handiwork of the Kauth banner bearer.

Arbettan saw what was happening too late and screamed in incoherent rage. He overextended himself, ducking a flung hatchet that pitched the man behind him off his feet, and Regara shot him in the chest. The commissar's pistol burst went wild, raining rockcrete on the Longstriders but otherwise doing no damage.

The Volpone were already moving, screaming at the last cadet to surrender.

'It's over!' yelled Culcis. 'Put up your arms.'

Momentarily shocked by the felling of his commissar, the remaining cadet found his wits but not his common sense – Speers, groggy but braced against a column, shot him through the heart before he could fire.

Dust motes and the strong scent of cordite laced the air with an unhealthy pall.

Regara strode though it like a smoke-wreathed avenger. Arbettan was stirring as the major reached him, still scrabbling for his fallen pistol.

Regara shot him through the head without ceremony, shattering his glare-goggles and displacing his cap.

In the far corner of the room, bunched in a foetal position, was Ossika.

'I di-di-didn't know,' he stammered, looking up through tear-rimmed eyes at Culcis. The lieutenant seized the Munitorum officer's chin and stared.

'He's clean,' he said to the major. 'Must be all the time he's spent in the bastion. The recyced air would've been purified of the blood taint.'

Regara was glaring down at the purple cataract webbing Arbettan's left eye. How long had it been there behind his goggles? How long had he been enslaved to the so-called 'Tongues of Tcharesh'?

'The cadets are the same,' he snarled, as Drado turned one of the dead over. 'All traitors.'

'We know where they are,' said Hauke, simply.

The major gave the Longstrider a disdainful look.

'We found caves, out in hills. We found source.'

Culcis remembered. They'd apprehended the Kauth returning from some scouting mission. Evidently they'd been busy after ignoring direct orders to return to camp.

'Sir?' he ventured, standing next to Regara.

'Sagorrah is going to explode when this gets out,' said the major, referring to the dead commissar. His eyes never left Hauke. 'You'll lead us there, to these caves,' he said. 'All of your men.'

Hauke nodded, leaving to gather his men. Sergeant Pillier went with him at Regara's order to release the Longstriders' weapons from the armoury.

'And us, sir?' asked Culcis.

The grim mask of Regara's face broke into a dagger smile. 'You, I and thirty men are heading into the hills, lieutenant.'

REGARA HAD LEFT Captain Stathan in charge. His instructions: protect the sovereign territory of the Royal Volpone 50th. Pillier stayed behind to deal with Ossika. The sergeant was to return him to the bastion with a full-squad bodyguard and await the major's return. Regara had wanted to decamp the entire billet to the Departmento fortress but that desire was outweighed by the practicality of moving almost nine hundred troopers over potentially hostile ground. For now, they needed to keep things as quiet as they could.

A red dawn was bathing the desert as Lieutenant Culcis arrived at the reconnoitre point with his squad. Major Regara was already there, panning a pair of magnoculars across the hills where the morning heat was shimmering the air.

The only other officer, Sergeant Brutt, nodded as Culcis hunkered down beside them.

'Thought we'd lost you again, lieutenant,' remarked Regara without looking up from his magnoculars.

Following on the heels of the Longstriders, the three squads had taken different routes through Sagorrah Depot. The infighting was getting worse. Culcis recalled a large, but thankfully distant, explosion lighting up one quarter. Gunshots and belligerent shouting were ever-present on the copper-tanged breeze. Deciding stealth was preferable over strength, the Volpone had crossed the camps in small groups, keeping clear of the worst of it and avoiding undue attention.

'My apologies, major,' Culcis replied. 'We had to detour several times.'

Regara grunted in what might have been acknowledgement, and gave the scopes back to Speers. The corporal's shoulder had been hastily bandaged. It was just a flesh wound and, as his aide, he had no intention of leaving the major in the lurch.

After a few moments, Hauke appeared in the distance.

'Here they are, the savage bastards,' Regara muttered.

Despite everything, he still didn't trust them. He was just pragmatic enough to realise he had to work with them.

Hauke waved them on. His men were nowhere in sight. Privately, Culcis marvelled at their stealth. Brushing the ruddy sand off his knees and elbows, the lieutenant followed the rest of the Volpone out.

DESPITE THE FACT they were in shade, the caves offered no respite from the heat. If anything, it was even hotter in their dusky confines.

'Hear that, sir?' asked Drado, leaning with his ear towards the darkness. With the Longstriders moving cautiously a few metres in front, they'd breached the threshold of the caves and were advancing slowly.

'Machinery of some kind?' It was a low thrumming sound, like the action of an engine constantly turning over.

'That's what I thought,' Drado replied. 'Could be the reason it's so hot. A generator perhaps?'

Culcis nodded. The air was growing thicker by the minute. Heat and the scent of metal cloyed it.

They moved on.

A PALPABLE SENSE of menace hung in the air like a bad tranq of combat drugs. Culcis felt his senses go instantly on edge. The Longstriders had felt it too. Hauke brought them all to a stop.

They were deep now, far into the subterranean. It was

stifling, the Volpone's uniforms dark with sweat. Even Hauke was dappled with beads of perspiration like tiny, transparent pearls on his tanned skin.

The Longstrider captain held up four fingers, utilising Guard battle-sign so the Volpone could understand.

Four hostiles.

Most likely sentries.

Four of the Longstriders hurried off into the darkness at Hauke's command. After a few minutes they returned with hatchets bloodied.

'Scratch four bad guys,' grinned Speers.

Something about his bloodlust unnerved Culcis. Worse still, he'd felt it too. They were closing on the source. The lieutenant only hoped they'd find it soon, otherwise the Volpone's guns might do the traitors' work for them.

THE FIRST THING they knew of the ambush was a grunt from Sergeant Brutt. The man crumpled, clutching ineffectually at the arterial bleed in his neck.

Caught in a narrow defile, concealed ridges above the Longstriders and the Volpone offered murderously advantageous firing positions to the enemy. Another Volpone and one of the Kauth were killed before both groups pressed to the walls, cutting down the angle of exposure, and returned fire.

Ahead of them, the machine thrum had built to a cacophony. The air was so redolent of metal it was like Culcis's mouth was filled with blood. He spat out a gobbet of saliva but it didn't help.

The source, the thing the Kauth had found and knew was in these caves, was just beyond, through a natural archway in the rock.

First, though, they had to break the ambush.

'I think this is the bulk of them, sir,' said the lieutenant, hunkering down alongside Regara.

'I agree,' the major replied between shots. 'We need only get a kill-team beyond that archway and take out whatever is causing this madness.'

Hauke was close by and had overheard them.

'Your men hold,' he said, indicating their gloom-shrouded opponents above them. 'Mine draw out,' he added, pointing first towards the archway and then to Regara, Culcis and his own banner bearer, 'We run.'

'That's suicide for your men, captain,' Culcis informed him needlessly.

'Sacrifice is part of Kauth way, Volpone. Hold, draw out, run,' he repeated.

Even Regara nodded this time.

'Very well,' he said, 'Corporals Speers and Drado too.'

'Yes, sir.' Culcis beckoned the two aides over as Hauke was relaying orders to his men. The fight had reached an impasse for now, both sides unable to lay any meaningful fire into the other. It at least allowed the Volpone/Kauth coalition to formulate their plan.

In a few minutes it was done and the kill-team was gathered together to make a dash for the archway.

'Just because the savages are offering themselves up on a plate to these bastards, doesn't mean they won't shoot at us,' said Regara.

Culcis nodded.

'Quick and quiet,' the major added. 'No delays, even if someone falls, even if *I* fall. Understand, lieutenant? Whatever's beyond that archway, we must be ready for it.'

Culcis nodded again, slower this time.

Regara gave the signal to Hauke that they were ready.

An ear-piercing shriek scythed out of Hauke's mouth and the order was given.

Suppressing fire lanced from the Volpone as they expended what was left of their hellguns to keep the ambushers at bay. At the same time, the Longstriders exploded into the open, moving back down the defile as if in retreat, guns blazing. Meanwhile, the kill-team led by Regara was running.

Culcis felt the patter of solid shot glancing off his

bowl helm but kept moving. Shots tore up the earth around them, *pranged* off jutting stones and ricocheted from the walls. The incoming fire was light. The Kauth had done their work well. Culcis was only glad he didn't have to turn and see them slain.

The kill-team breached the archway intact and found themselves in an expansive chamber.

It was like descending into some visceral hell-realm.

Walls like incarnadine flesh shone slick with blood. They were ribbed, too, like meat. The stink of it was strong. It was emanating from a deep reservoir in the centre of the room. Squatting over it was a vast and tortured machine. Twisted and spiked, it was a thing utterly unlike any engine Culcis had ever seen. The machine was some kind of drilling platform, part metal, part organic. It had four pseudo-fangs plunged deep into the earth, pumping and siphoning a clear liquid into the bloody morass.

It took Culcis a few seconds to realise the Tongues of Tcharesh had tapped into the promethium wells that veined the region in tributaries of vital fuel. Except now, the fuel was vital in the most literal way. It was alive, sentient and tainted by blood sacrifice.

Further machines were visible in silhouette beyond this first infernal engine, dormant but foreshadows of the insurgents' plan yet to come.

The very thing the Crusade reserve was meant to be protecting was the very thing driving them insane. The red rime of their jackets, the ruddy sand underfoot – the entire Sagorrah camp was tainted by the promethium-blood. Bad enough if an encampment of nearly a million Guardsmen was turned – Culcis paled at the consequences if the fuel was allowed to infect the rest of the Crusade forces. And the architect of that depravity was close by.

Crouched by the edge of the pool, a slain Guardsman in her talon-like clutches, was what used to be a woman. She was hideous. Even her presence felt anathema to

Culcis, as if she shouldn't even *be*. A dirty, blood-flecked smock covered her frail, bony limbs. She was withered and wretched like a corpse. Her lank hair was grey and matted with dark stains. Ranks of teeth stood in blackened nubs as she grinned at him.

Something hard and cold clutched at the lieutenant's chest and he forced it down through sheer effort of will.

'Stay close!' warned Hauke, indicating the banner.

Culcis, even the other Volpone, obeyed. As he neared the scrap of cloth, the lieutenant felt the discomfort from the witch's presence ebb.

'Emperor have mercy...' he heard Drado mutter.

Speers made the sign of the aquila. The corporal's hands were shaking.

Regara's mouth was drawn in a taut line.

The witch was not alone. A beast of a soldier, too broad and tall not to have been genhanced, was standing a few metres from the witch at the edge of the machine. His hard armour was dark and he wore a grotesk to hide his graven features.

Culcis knew Blood Pact when he saw it.

Drawing a serrated sabre, the soldier waved his retinue forwards – four men, all Tongues of Tcharesh elite like the Volpone had fought in the slum town square.

'Kill that witch,' Regara told him. 'Speers and I will deal with the Blood Pact.'

The kill-team split into two, Regara and Speers going for the Blood Pact officer whilst the others, led by Culcis, tackled the witch. Percussive las-fire echoed behind them, the rest of the Volpone keeping the traitor forces at bay.

Two narrow pathways fed off from a platform immediately in front of the archway and led around the edges of the chamber towards the hideous lagoon. It was here that the two groups diverged.

Whickering las-fire, the beams an unwholesome red compared to the purity of Guard blue, snapped at the earth around the advancing Volpone and their allies.

Racing down the right-hand channel, Culcis returned fire and lanced one of the Tongues of Tcharesh across the torso. The wretch staggered, grasping at the wound, and fell from the pathway into the bloody mess. He sank immediately, as if weighted down, as if something had... *dragged* him. The witch shrieked in delight. Another offering to the Ruinous Powers.

Drado caught a las-bolt to the knee before they'd reached the end of the pathway. He went on for a couple more steps before slamming against the wall, his face awash with agonised sweat.

No delays, the words of the major came back to Culcis, *even if someone falls.*

The lieutenant carried on. A lasgun shot, fired from the hip by Hauke, took a traitor in the throat, avenging Drado's wounding.

Both her guardians down, the witch was left vulnerable. Or so Culcis believed.

Nothing could have been further from the truth.

He glanced across at Regara. He and Speers had dispatched the lackeys and were engaging the Blood Pact officer. Though Culcis only caught a snapshot, the fight was brutal and close-quarter. Speers had gone to his bayonet, whilst Regara drew his sword. Adamantine steel flashed against Chaos-infused iron. Only the fact it was two against one kept both the corporal and major alive for more than a few seconds. They were holding their own, but only just.

Culcis focussed on the witch. He was flanked by Hauke and his banner bearer. The two Longstriders had pulled ahead. The banner bearer took aim with his lasgun but never fired. The witch extended an emaciated claw in his direction as a fountain of blood erupted from the Kauth warrior's mouth. The lasgun slipped from his nerveless fingers, falling uselessly to the ground. The banner bearer followed, tipping off the edge and plunging to his doom in the blood pool. Hauke reached for the banner itself before it joined him, snatching the weathered shaft like a lifeline, and dropping his weapon to do it.

Smiling, the witch advanced upon them both. She was preceded by an invisible veil of cold. Culcis felt daggers of ice puncturing his chest over and over. Needles of pain speared his forehead, and he clutched at it. Somewhere during this torture, he lost his pistol and fell to one knee.

'Emp–' he began, seeking benediction, when a froth of blood bubbled up from his throat. He choked then gagged. It was filling up his mouth and nose, a reservoir of vitae fattening his lungs with hot fluid.

Hauke was still moving, the banner clenched in his whitened fist giving him resolve. Culcis watched him draw his hatchet and close on the blood-soaked harridan. He swept the blade towards her head but incredibly she moved, far faster than any living thing should. Culcis couldn't be sure it wasn't just the fact he was dying and had started to hallucinate, but she... *blurred*, as if sliding from one plane of existence into another and back again. A needle-like punch-blade had also materialised in her grimy claw. She thrust it gleefully into Hauke's exposed neck. It went all the way through. The Longstrider captain lost his grip on the hatchet, before even realising what had happened and that he was dead, and crumpled into a heap. He shuddered once, the banner falling from his grasp, and was still.

She was near to him. Culcis could hear the witch's ragged breathing. He caught an impression of her withered form through his blood-filmed eyes. He felt the needle-blade closing rather than saw it. But as the witch threw back her foul head in exultation, something rolled against the lieutenant's clenched fist. As it touched him, his vision cleared, like a cloth wiped over glass, and some of his strength returned. Acting purely on instinct, Culcis seized the banner pole that had rolled down to him from Hauke's dead hand and shoved it upwards into the witch.

Her cackling turned to screaming horror when she saw

the banner pole jutting from her torso. Culcis roared, as much to banish his fear as to focus his anger, and thrust deeper.

'Hell-bitch, die!'

Convulsing once, the witch was done, her power extinguished.

Culcis braced the pole and snapped it off halfway, leaving the harridan impaled. He salvaged the end with the blessed cloth before kicking the witch into the promethium morass with his boot.

'Major!' he cried, aiming his recovered hellpistol across the hideous blood-filled chasm where the machine was pumping like a grotesque heart.

Culcis fired, and Regara ducked, opening himself to attack. Speers was already down and not moving.

The shot took the Blood Pact in the shoulder. It wasn't fatal but the sudden change in position, the attempted death blow when Regara had opened himself up, put him off balance. The major thrust upwards with his power sword. The Blood Pact officer's riposte and parry were a fraction too late and the humming blade sank into his chest. Regara wrenched it free, forcing the traitor to stagger and pitch backwards. The major didn't give him time to recover. He cut the bastard's head off with one swipe.

'Nearly done,' bellowed a weary Regara across the crimson gulf. He went into his webbing to retrieve a pair of krak grenades. The entire kill-team was carrying them. Culcis had made it as far as the machine already and was mag-locking his explosives to the engine's superstructure.

'Prime them for a ninety-second delay,' Regara told him when they met up where the two pathways converged.

Culcis nodded, working at the detonation stud to give them the ninety seconds to effect an escape. He'd ripped the scrap of cloth off the pole completely now and stuffed it in one of his combat pouches.

Both men bolted from the chamber. Regara had Speers slung over his shoulder like a meat sack; Drado clung to Culcis as the two of them hobbled out urgently.

Back into the narrow defile and the Volpone were finishing off the ambushers. At the witch's death, most of the traitors had fled or cast themselves over the edge. Her hold upon the insurgents had been strong, so her demise sent psychological shockwaves through her puppets.

The Volpone had reached halfway down when an explosion shook the caves. An incendiary flare erupted behind them in a bright orange bloom as the promethium lagoon went up in conflagration. The rest of the way upwards was frantic. In his panic to escape the sundered caves, Culcis caught their flight in flashes only. Smoke wreathed his world, together with the stink of burning. Darkness smothered his thoughts and senses.

Then there was light and the oppressive heat of the desert sun.

'Vox,' snapped Regara when they were out. Several of the men were rolling onto the sand, their minds and bodies near exhaustion.

The major took the receiver cup as it was offered and raised the Munitorum bastion.

A flustered, anxious Ossika answered.

'It's done,' Regara told him. 'The insurgents are finished.'

'Emperor's mercy,' breathed Ossika. Culcis was standing close and could overhear the conversation clearly. It sounded like the Munitorum clerk was crying.

'The fuel, Ossika,' said Regara. 'It's in the fuel. That's what's turning the men. It has to be destroyed.'

Ossika didn't sound so sure. 'What? All of it?'

'Every damned drop.'

'No, no, no, no. That fuel is for the Crusade. It's the war effort. Do you know how much–?'

Regara cut him off. 'It's tainted, man. A million Guard turned to Chaos, it doesn't bear thinking about.'

'But we can't... we... I need authority. Can't just destroy it.'

'Do it,' Regara told him in no uncertain terms. 'Do it, or I will come over there and do it myself, orders be damned.'

'I can't, major. I simply can't. It's not protocol, it's not–'

Regara severed the link, slamming the receiver cup back in its holder. 'We need the gunships,' he muttered, partly to Culcis, partly to himself. Then louder, 'Get them up. We march for Sagorrah.'

THE VOLPONE HAD to run through the encampments. They were just under thirty men but at least the presence of the Kauth's banner seemed to keep the belligerence felt towards them by the other regiments to a minimum. Widespread fighting had broken out. There were even firing exchanges. Sagorrah had descended into hell.

It was with some relief that they reached the Munitorum bastion alive and unscathed.

Regara and Culcis muscled their way past the few troops that Ossika had left that weren't suffering the effects of the blood-fuel and found the Munitorum clerk at his desk.

'Major,' he warned, shuffling through paperwork, trying to find the correct documentation to sanction such a measure as destroying the fuel. 'Major, you cannot do this.'

Sensing its master's distress, the lexicanum-servitor came forwards from its shadowy perch to intercede. Culcis shot it with his hellpistol.

'Step aside,' he told Ossika, training the weapon on him.

'You cannot,' he repeated, eyeing the twitching lex-savant on the ground, but he was moving. 'It's not protocol.'

'Hang protocol,' snarled Regara, pushing the clerk out of the way so he could get to a long-range voxsponder set in a brass casing behind the desk.

He raised the commander of the Valkyrie fleet swiftly. A terse explanation followed, the conversation riddled by static.

'Burn it, burn it all,' the major concluded. His face was grim when he set the receiver down again and he turned it on Ossika. 'Too late, now. Fire is coming to Sagorrah, and with it the salvation of thousands.'

FROM THE HILLSIDE, below the ridge, a flame storm rippled the horizon line like a bright orange ocean. In the distance, the fifty-strong fleet of gunships were pulling away and making for higher orbit, the smoke of their missile contrails lingering in the air like a threat. The incendiary payloads had done their work, igniting the promethium wells and vanquishing the tainted fuel in a series of glorious explosions.

There would be ramifications, Culcis knew. Major Regara would shoulder them, despite the fact he had undoubtedly saved almost a million Guard soldiers in a single, decisive act. Only a man with Regara's self-belief and arrogance could have even countenanced such a move. But it wasn't bravura; it was necessity that drove him.

It had once been called Sagorrah Depot, but now the vast plain that burned below was simply a sea of fire. The flames rose high, caught by the wind, their edges blackening as the fuel cooked off and so too the poison that had afflicted so many.

In a valley behind where Culcis and Regara stood, the regiments who had survived gathered. Orders had been received from Macaroth himself; the Crusade reserve was mobilising for war and that included the Volpone 50th. Some would not return to glory, some had fallen. Culcis was determined they'd be remembered. He took the scrap of cloth from his equipment and tied it around the barrel of the lasgun he was carrying. Planting the stock in the ground, he smiled as the ragged banner snapped on the breeze.

'What is that, lieutenant?' asked Regara, raising an eyebrow.

'Honour,' said Culcis simply. 'Honour for the dead.'

The major, for his part, didn't respond or object. He merely took in the view. The flames stretched for kilometres. It was as if the entire horizon burned.

Culcis joined him, feeling something jabbing him in the chest. He reached into his pocket and found the pair of cigars Hauke had given him in the slums. He'd completely forgotten about them. He offered one to Regara.

'Sir?'

The major took it after a short pause, nodding his thanks discreetly.

An errant pool of burning promethium thrown out in the initial explosion provided Culcis with a light. He then used his own cigar to light the major's and the two men smoked a toast. The fire, rising all the while, threw a lambent glow over them both. It was warming.

Culcis supped and raised his cigar, blowing out a smoky plume.

'To dogs in the sun, sir,' he said, his eyes filled with reflected flame.

'Dogs in the sun, lieutenant,' Regara replied.

Behind them, the first of the drop-ships were landing. The troops of Sagorrah were being re-appropriated across the planet to fresh fronts. War was calling.

Sandy Mitchell's Ciaphas Cain novels are a source of constant pleasure for me, and proof that you can always find a new approach in a shared setting like 40K. They're understated, subversive and very funny, and it delights me that the universe of Warhammer 40,000 can happily support a series that has humour at its heart.

A Good Man is also understated, and perhaps a little untrustworthy. It takes us back to Verghast, setting of the third Gaunt novel Necropolis, and we arrive just after the last of the fighting, in time to be lured into the shadows of the ruins of the wartorn hives, and inveigled by unscrupulous and unreliable individuals...

Dan Abnett

A GOOD MAN

Sandy Mitchell

As the tide of war swept across the Sabbat Worlds, most of us could be forgiven for taking more notice of its rise than of its ebb. But after the battlefronts moved on, leaving rockpools of conflict and its aftermath beached by their withdrawal, the vital task of restoring the Pax Imperialis was only just beginning. On world after shattered world, a veritable second crusade of those with the necessary expertise to manage the reconstruction followed hard on the heels of the first.

Which was how Zale Linder came to Verghast, around the middle of 771, among a swarm of Administratum functionaries charged with the restoration of good order there. He wasn't much to look at, so typical of his brethren that he might have escaped notice altogether, had he not worked so assiduously at coming to my attention; but that was to be later, and to really appreciate his story, I suppose we'd better start at the beginning.

We can only imagine Linder's reaction to his surroundings when he first set foot on the shuttle apron at

299

Kannack. Armed men were everywhere, in the uniforms of PDF regiments, or the Imperial Guard units left to garrison the planet, and the scars of the recent fighting were more than evident on the port facilities surrounding him. Come to that, as most of the shuttles approaching the Northern Collective overflew the glass-walled crater where Vannick had once stood, he'd probably seen some of the worst devastation even before his arrival.

For a man more used to the musty recesses of a scriptorium, the noise, bustle, and constant tang of combustibles from the surrounding manufactoria must have been disconcerting in the extreme. Nevertheless, by all accounts, he rallied at once, chivvying the small knot of brown-robed Scribes towards the rail terminal, though few of them were quite so quick to adjust to their new surroundings as he was.

The echoing hall with its multitude of platforms, from which services departed to destinations throughout the North Col and beyond, probably seemed as alien to the Administratum adepts as the landing field had been, but they found a local service into Kannack itself without much trouble. The Verghastites had become used to off-worlders by this time, particularly bewildered-looking ones speaking strangely-accented Gothic, and the booking clerk who wrote out their tickets in a flowing copperplate hand directed them to the correct platform with all the polite deference due to customers he'd overcharged by about five per cent.

The train rattled its way to Kannack Hub in little more than an hour, affording Linder a few brief glimpses of the spoil heaps and outlying reclamation zones, before burrowing into the side of the Western Spine like a worm into an apple. The last couple of kilometres of track ran within the lower hab levels, through tunnels and caverns of steel and brick, some spaces large and open enough to seem like small towns in their own right, while in other places the enclosing walls whipped by disorientatingly just the other side of the window.

The Hub terminal was more crowded than anywhere they'd seen so far, and the little knot of off-world adepts navigated it in an apprehensive huddle, following the directions they'd been given as punctiliously as the curlicues of an ancient text being restored to legibility by a fresh layer of ink. Once again, Linder took the lead, although he was by no means the most senior member of the party; but he had more local knowledge than any of the others, furnished to him by a friend and colleague who'd arrived in an earlier wave a year or so before, and who had corresponded diligently in the interim. He already knew how to flag down one of the municipal charabancs thronging the outer concourse, and how to distinguish the combination of numeric and colour coding which marked one heading in the right direction. How grateful his colleagues were for being saved a five-kilometre walk, mostly in an upwards direction, isn't clear, but I presume the majority were relieved to find what seats they could among the shift-change crowds.

What really matters is that Linder eventually ended up where he belonged, at the Administratum Cloister; but the details of his journey are important to someone like me, to whom details are everything. In that relatively brief trip from the landing field, he demonstrated the single-mindedness and adaptability which set him apart from his colleagues, and which were to lead him down darker paths than he could ever have dreamed he would walk.

The first intimation that something was wrong would have been when he registered his arrival at the Codicium Municipalis, where he had been assigned to work, and enquired about the friend who had preceded him to Verghast.

'No record of that individual exists,' the junior Archivist on the other side of the polished wooden counter informed him, with the neutral inflection peculiar to lowly functionaries trying to appear not to relish the chance of making the lives of their superiors more difficult.

'Please check again,' Linder said calmly. He'd been navigating his way around the labyrinthine ways of the datastacks for most of his life, and was well aware that information could be lost or mislaid in a myriad of ways. 'Allow for misspellings, and cross-reference with the arrival records of the landing field.'

'The results are the same, honoured Scribe,' the Archivist told him, after a wait no longer than Linder had expected. 'There is no reference to a Harl Sitrus in any of the informational repositories accessible from this cogitation node.'

'Then I suggest you commence an immediate archival audit,' Linder said, 'since the data I require has clearly been misfiled.'

'As you instruct, honoured Scribe,' the Archivist said, suppressing any trace of irritation which might have entered his voice; there were worse ways of wasting his time, which Linder could easily impose if sufficiently irked. 'Would you like a summary of the results forwarded to your cubicle?'

'I would,' Linder said, and returned to his assigned task of tabulating the adjusted output of the Kannack manufactoria, which had altered appreciably in both volume and substance in response to the recent upheavals. The task was a painstaking one, consuming a good deal of time and the greater part of his attention, so he was faintly surprised to find the report he'd requested dropping from the pneumatic tube over the angled surface of his writing desk less than a week later.

Setting aside the work he was supposed to be doing, Linder began working his way through the thick wad of paper, annotating it as he went with an inkstick. The anonymous Archivist had been thorough, within the limits of his competence, but Linder's greater experience and expertise soon began to pay dividends, and by the time he was making excuses to the senior Lexicographer for failing to finish his assigned task by the compline bell, he'd discovered a number of discrepancies in the archive records, each accompanied by marginalia in his elegantly cursive hand.

The majority of the anomalies he identified were in the files administered by the Bureau of Population Management, the department responsible for collating records of birth, death, and off-world migration, which it would then use to allocate resources where they were most urgently required. The devastation wrought on Verghast had rendered much of this material unreliable, so Linder was hardly surprised by this discovery, but one discrepancy perturbed him greatly. There was still no official record of Harl Sitrus's arrival on Verghast, even though the date was known to him; turning to his data-slate, he invoked Sitrus's first missive after landing.

We touched down at Kannack on 439 770, he read, frowning in perplexity. *That's a fair-sized hive, one of the largest left standing after the razing of Vervun and the scouring of Ferrozoica. Klath got us to the scriptorium eventually, after a few wrong turnings...* Linder read on, skimming through the familiar words. Nothing else struck him as significant, but the date was unequivocal. The frown deepening, he turned back to the hardprint on his lectern, and paged through the summary of transits from orbit that day.

Shuttle Damsel's Delight, *grounded pad seventeen, Administratum charter. Twelve passengers, personal effects, cargo amounting to 497 tonnes (stationery sundries).* That must have been the one.

To confirm the fact, he invoked the cogitator link, and examined the manifest in detail. Galen Klath, Lexicographer, and eleven other names. Sitrus's was not among them.

Troubled, Linder spent a further few minutes in search of Klath's whereabouts. His personal quarters were listed as within the bounds of the Administratum Cloister, but Linder lacked the seniority to access their precise location. That didn't matter, though; the department the Lexicographer was attached to was a mere thirty levels away, and a chance meeting would be easy enough to contrive. Perhaps he would be able to shed some light on the anomaly.

'SITRUS?' KLATH ASKED, his face crumpling in perplexity. He was much as Linder remembered him, short and rotund, which, together with his hairless pate, made him look uncannily like an oversized toddler dressed for masquerade in adult clothes. 'Why do you ask?'

'I've been looking for him,' Linder said evenly. Having to explain the obvious was another thing he remembered about the plump Lexicographer, which was one of the reasons he'd been so pleased to be transferred to his present duties, away from Klath's supervision. 'In his letters, he mentioned you were still colleagues.'

'I see.' Klath glanced round the crowded buttery, as though afraid of eavesdroppers. There were none Linder could see, just the usual crowd of men and women in inkstained robes, chattering idly as they grabbed some pottage or a mid-shift mug of caffeine before returning to their data-slates and hardprints. 'But I'm afraid I haven't seen him since the transfer.'

'He's transferred?' Linder asked.

Caught unawares by the brevity of the question, Klath nodded, chewed and swallowed, and replied with a stifled hiccup. 'To another department. He didn't say which.'

Linder echoed the nod, more slowly. There were over seven thousand separate bureaux within the cloister, dealing with everything from the disposition of tithing revenue to the certification of left-handed writing implements, and with nothing further to go on, his friend might just as well be on a different planet. 'Did he ever mention where he was living?' he asked, and Klath shook his head.

'He had a flat somewhere up on the Spine. Lots of people live outside the Cloister, if they can afford it. You young ones, anyway. Too much bustle if you ask me.'

Linder nodded again. He was still in the rooms assigned to him on his arrival, having little inclination to expose himself to the ceaseless activity of the wider hive, but Sitrus would have relished the proximity of taverns and bars, theatres and brawling pits. Ever since their first meeting, as callow Archivists, Sitrus had been hungry for experience, eager to meet life head-on, instead of vicariously through text and picts. It was an attitude uncommon within the sheltered precincts of the Cloister. Perhaps that was why Linder was so determined to see his friend again, instead of accepting that their paths had diverged forever when Sitrus boarded the first transport to Verghast over a year before.

'It must have taken everything he had,' he said. Rents on the Spine were high, the few adepts he'd met living outside the Cloister barely being able to afford a couple of rooms in a worker's hab.

Klath leaned closer, assuming a confidential air. 'Between you and me,' he said, 'I don't think he paid in cash. *Cherchez la femme*, and all that.'

'Really?' Linder considered this unexpected information. Sitrus had always enjoyed feminine company, he knew, but the only women he'd had any contact with before had been other Administratum adepts; which, given the circumscribed nature of the lives they led, had hardly been surprising. None of them could have afforded lodgings in the hive's most salubrious quarter, any more than Sitrus could. 'You mean he'd taken up with a local woman?'

Which would have been impossible, of course. Nothing in any of the letters he'd received had so much as hinted at such a liaison. But Klath was nodding slowly. 'I believe so,' he confirmed, with the self-satisfied air of someone passing on a juicy bit of scandal. 'For the last six months, at least.'

Six months in which Linder had received three missives from his friend. The first had dwelt at length on some interesting cross-referencing practices the Verghastite

Archivists were continuing to cling to in the face of the filing protocols imposed by the new arrivals, and the compromise eventually arrived at to general satisfaction, before rambling off into a description of a few of the local festivals; the second had consisted mainly of enthusiastic comments about the local cuisine, which Sitrus appeared to be finding very much to his taste; and the third contained little apart from an account of an inspection of one of the protein reclamation plants, to which Sitrus had been attached to take notes, and which he'd enlivened with caustic pen portraits of the rest of the delegation. None had so much as hinted at a romantic liaison.

Klath had to be mistaken. Nevertheless, Linder supposed, he might as well follow it up, if only to eliminate the possibility. *In that regard, the mind of a diligent bureaucrat isn't so far removed from the dispassionate pursuit of hidden truths peculiar to my own profession. Which meant that, from the moment Linder uttered his next remark, our paths would inevitably cross.*

'Do you happen to remember her name?' he asked.

AS IT TURNED out, Klath wasn't sure, but a little more patient probing on Linder's part elicited the vague recollection that Sitrus had mentioned meeting someone called Milena once. That was little enough to go on, but for a fellow of Linder's skills and resources, it was sufficient; there were only so many women of that name living in the Spine, and not all of them were of the right age to be of romantic interest to Sitrus; and not all those remaining on the list were single. That didn't discount them entirely, of course, but Klath had implied that Sitrus was living with his inamorata, and a husband about the place would have put paid to so cosy an arrangement. Knowing his friend as he did, I'm sure Linder was able to eliminate a few more potential candidates without too much difficulty, but whatever other criteria he chose to apply, he didn't bother to share with me during our subsequent conversation on the subject.

Once he'd got the list down to an irreducible minimum, the streak of determination which had first surfaced during his eventful journey from the landing field displayed itself again. Undaunted by the scale of the task he'd set himself, he began using the limited amount of free time at his disposal to contact the remaining candidates, eliminating them one by one.

Most were polite, if puzzled, simply assuring him they weren't acquainted with his friend; an assurance he generally believed, as a lifetime spent in the service of the Administratum had left him able to detect evasion or unease in the harmonics of the voice. A few were clearly suspicious of his motives, and a handful decidedly hostile; these he annotated for possible further enquiry, if he reached the end of his list without any useful result. Whatever his reception, he plodded on, until one of the voices on the vox reacted in a fashion he'd not experienced before.

'Good shift-change,' he began, for the fifty-seventh time. 'Is that Milena Dravere?'

'Speaking.' The voice was brisk, brittle behind a sabre-rattle of confidence. 'And you would be...?'

'Zale Linder. We've never met, but we might have a friend in common. Do you know a Scribe named Harl Sitrus?'

'You're a friend of Harl's?' The woman's voice cracked a little. 'Where is he? Is he all right?'

'I was hoping you could tell me,' Linder said, a fresh wave of bewilderment dousing the sudden flare of hope at her first words. 'I arrived on Verghast a few weeks ago, and I've been looking for him ever since.'

'Arrived?' The vox circuit hummed with speculative silence for a second or two. 'From off-world?'

'Khulan. I'm with the Reconstruction Administration.' Linder hesitated, wondering if this would be too much to take in. But it seemed to be the right thing to say.

'Oh, you're *that* Zale. Harl talked about you.'

'Did he?' Linder asked, conscious that the conversation seemed to be slipping away from him. 'What did he say?'

'That I could trust you.' The admission seemed a reluctant one. 'We should meet. Compare notes. Maybe we can find him together.'

'I could visit you,' Linder suggested, wondering if perhaps that was the wrong thing to say. The woman was clearly nervous, and might not feel comfortable about inviting him into her home. But she took the suggestion in her stride.

'Sixty-four Via Zoologica,' she said, barely hesitating. 'Can you find it?'

'I can,' Linder told her with confidence. He had a plan of the hive in his data-slate, newly updated with the latest alterations to roads and transit routes, where fresh construction was scabbing over the scars of Ferrozoican bombardment. 'But I won't be off shift until after compline.'

'An hour after compline, then,' Milena agreed, and broke the connection.

CHEERED BY THE unexpected acquisition of an ally, Linder returned to work with his usual diligence, and had apparently made considerable progress in disentangling the cat's cradle of information on his desk when he was unexpectedly interrupted by a diffident knock on the door.

'What is it?' he asked, with some asperity, resenting the disruption of his concentration.

'There's someone here to see you, honoured Scribe,' a pale-looking Archivist informed him, inserting just enough of his body across the cubicle's threshold to become visible.

'I'm busy. Tell them to wait.' Linder returned to his collection of slates and hardprints, already dismissing the matter from his mind.

'That won't be convenient,' I said, pushing past the Archivist, who promptly fled, his duty done. Linder turned back to the door, to find it clicking to, while I leaned casually against its inner surface. I extended a hand. 'Wil Feris, Adeptus Arbites.'

'Of course,' Linder said, as though my uniform hadn't already told him precisely what I was. Surprise was smeared across his face like a harlot's lipstick, but his handshake was firm, and once he'd registered that I was real and wasn't going away until I was good and ready, his expression became curious rather than alarmed. 'What can I do for you?'

'You've been looking for Harl Sitrus,' I said, resigning myself to leaning against the door for as long as the interview took. There was only one place to sit in the narrow room, and Linder showed no inclination to vacate it. 'So have I.'

'Do you know where he is?' Linder asked, and I shook my head.

'No,' I admitted, 'and that irks me. I'm not used to being hidden from. Not for this long, anyway.'

'Why would he be hiding?' Linder asked, an unmistakable frown appearing on his face. 'Surely you can't suspect him of anything?'

'Everyone's guilty of something,' I said. That was the first thing I'd learned on joining the Arbites, and before you ask, of course I include myself in that. But there are degrees of guilt, and culpability, and sometimes things aren't as clear cut as they seem.

'Not Harl,' Linder said, which surprised me; people usually react to that kind of insinuation by asserting their own innocence. 'Not of anything that would justify your interest, anyway.'

'I'm interested in a great deal,' I told him. Which was true; law enforcement on Verghast was in as big a mess as any of its other institutions, and the Arbitrators brought in to sort it out had been forced to take on cases which would have been handed to the locals on more smoothly functioning worlds. 'Including the falsification of records.'

'Harl would never do something like that,' Linder said, sounding genuinely angry. Most Administratum adepts would as soon profane the name of the Emperor as knowingly tamper with the data they were charged to protect.

'Don't you think it a little odd that so many records relating to him have disappeared?'' I asked, refusing to raise my voice in return.

Linder looked thoughtful. 'That might be the result of tampering,' he conceded. 'But you've got no proof that Harl's responsible.'

'Nothing definite,' I agreed. 'But innocent men seldom disappear into thin air. Unless foul play's involved.'

Linder paled; clearly this possibility hadn't occurred to him. 'You think he's been murdered?' he asked at last.

'It's possible,' I said evenly, 'but I doubt it. I think he wiped his own records to cover his tracks, and hide whatever else he tampered with.'

'Harl wouldn't do a thing like that,' Linder said again, glaring at me with unmistakable dislike. 'And I'll prove it.'

'I'll be delighted if you can,' I told him. He clearly knew nothing of any use to me. 'In the meantime, if he should get in touch, or you find some trace of him, be sure to let me know.'

'You can count on it,' Linder said, in tones which made it clear he regarded the interview as over.

HOW MUCH OF his interrupted chain of thought Linder was able to pick up after my departure I can only guess, but given his stubborn streak, I imagine he'd pretty much completed his task for the day by the time he left the scriptorium and headed uphive to meet Milena Dravere. He found his way with little trouble, consulting his data-slate from time to time, but generally moving through the shift-change bustle with a resolute determination which left the local operatives I'd assigned to watch him scurrying to keep up; no mean feat, given that most of them were Kannack born and bred. True to the picture I was beginning to form of him, he took little notice of the barrage of noise and spectacle most men would have found distracting, but remained obdurately fixed on his goal.

The only time he showed any visible sign of surprise was when he reached the Via Zoologica itself, and realised that the road broke through into the open air. He paused for a moment, looking down the long, sloping flank of the hive shining like a beached galaxy below, then strode on, his shadow flickering in and out of existence as it merged momentarily with the patches of deeper darkness between the waylights. As he neared his destination, skirting a crowded tavern from which jaunty zither music floated incongruously on the night air, he slowed his pace, paying greater attention to the address plates screwed to the smog-eaten bricks of the overhanging housefronts.

At length he came to his destination, and knocked, a little hesitantly. After a few moments a woman opened the carved wooden door a wary crack.

'Milena?' he asked, unsure of his reception. 'It's me, Zale.'

'Then you'd better come in.' The door opened wider, and he stepped inside, finding himself in an airy, well-lit entrance hall. His hostess was petite, dark-haired, and carried a small-calibre autopistol in her left hand. Linder had never seen a genuine weapon before, and was taken aback; but before he could protest, Milena had closed and bolted the door, and deposited the gun on a nearby occasional table. From the number of faint scratches in the marquetry surface, Linder surmised that the gun generally rested there, where it could be picked up easily whenever the woman answered the door.

She motioned him through one of the arches leading off the hall, and he found himself in a comfortably appointed living room roughly the size of his entire lodgings. He looked around curiously, noting the opulent decor, the artful scattering of antiques and *objets d'art*, utterly unlike the contents of any room he'd ever been in before.

'You have a very elegant home,' he said, hoping to break the awkward silence.

'Thank you.' Milena perched on the edge of a sofa, opposite the armchair Linder had selected as seeming least likely to swallow him whole. He was astonished at how comfortable it was; the furniture he was used to was generally selected for its utility, rather than comfort. Milena glanced round, as though lost in her own house. 'Harl found it for me.'

'He did?' Linder prompted, hoping for more detail. He couldn't imagine Sitrus combing the property vendors, even on a friend's behalf. Perhaps his new department had something to do with accommodation allocation, and he'd found out about it that way.

'He's helped a lot of people,' Milena said. Her face was drawn and tense. 'He's a good man. Whatever some people say about him.'

'People like Feris?' Linder asked, and the woman nodded, suddenly tense again.

'How do you know Feris?' she asked, her left hand clenching as though closing on the butt of her gun. Her eyes fixed on Linder's, disturbing in their intensity. She shifted, almost imperceptibly, a few millimetres further away from where he sat.

'I don't,' Linder assured her, 'and I don't want to. He came to the scriptorium, not long after I voxed you, and threw his weight around.'

Milena nodded. 'I thought he was monitoring my vox calls. He's probably hoping Harl gets in touch with me.' A flash of panic illuminated her eyes. 'If he does, they'll be bound to catch him!'

'He's too clever for that,' Linder assured her. 'But why would the Arbites think he's been doing anything wrong? The idea's absurd.'

'Of course it is,' Milena said, her voice blazing with

indignation. 'But Feris needs someone to blame, even if he can't prove anything. When Harl disappeared, he just jumped to the conclusion that he must be guilty.'

'More or less what he told me,' Linder agreed. He hesitated a little before going on. 'He did have another idea about what might have happened. But I'm afraid it's rather unpleasant.'

'Let me guess,' Milena said. 'He suggested Harl's been murdered, and someone's trying to cover it up.' She smiled, registering Linder's shocked expression. 'He tried the same trick on me. He doesn't believe that any more than we do.'

'Then why suggest it?' Linder asked.

Milena's posture became a little less hunched. 'To see if you'd let anything slip, of course. In case you were in on it.'

'In on what?' Linder began to feel completely out of his depth.

'Whatever he imagines Harl was involved in,' Milena said, as though explaining things to a child. I suppose it was at that point Linder first began to realise quite how out of his depth he was.

'Have you any idea what that might be?' he asked.

The woman regarded him steadily. 'Data falsification's about the worst thing an Administratum adept could be accused of, isn't it?'

Linder nodded. 'Short of heresy. I'm sure Harl told you that.'

'He did.' Milena's voice was low, as if, even here, they might be overheard. 'It wasn't a decision he took lightly.'

Linder felt the breath gush from his body, as though her words had been a physical blow. Slowly, he stood.

'I shouldn't have come here,' he said, biting back the angry words seething behind his tongue. 'I'm sorry to have intruded on you.'

'Sit down and listen, damn it!' Milena jumped up too, her fists clenched. 'I told you, he did nothing wrong!'

'You also just told me he falsified records,' Linder

snapped back, 'and I've known him most of my life. Harl wouldn't do something like that, whatever the reason.'

'And I lived with him for more than half a year,' Milena said, her voice softening. 'Perhaps I saw a side of him you never did. But if you don't want to know the truth, then leave. You know where the door is.'

'All right.' Linder seated himself again. The desire to make sense of the data was ruling him, as it always would. 'I'm listening. But I don't promise to believe you.'

'Fair enough.' Milena breathed deeply, and began pacing the room. 'I told you Harl found this place for me. Before he did, I had nothing. Literally. I'm from Vannick, and I was in one of the outhabs when the nuke went off. I'd just stepped into an underpass, crossing the Vervunhive road, at the time. A few seconds either way, and I'd have been vaporised, like everything else above ground. All my idents went up in the fireball, along with my home and my family.' She took a long, shuddering breath, and Linder found himself wondering if she'd finished.

'That's...' he began, but Milena cut him off with a sharp hand gesture.

'Eventually, I made it here. It wasn't easy, and I had to do a lot of things I never want to think about again. But without idents I couldn't find a job, or a place to live. That limits your options, believe me.'

'So what happened?' Linder asked, not sure he wanted to know the answer.

'Harl did. We got talking in a bar I used to work. Don't get me wrong, he was never a client, but he used to drink there sometimes, and we got to know each other. One night I was in a bad way, and it all came pouring out. He never said much, but he listened, and the next time I saw him he gave me an ident. Genuine. Some Spiner girl who'd picked the wrong time to visit Vervunhive and never come back.'

'I see.' Linder thought about the unthinkable. In circumstances like that, the Sitrus he remembered might have been tempted to alter the records to help the woman. It would have been easy; he could even picture the expression on his friend's face as he shuffled the requisite pieces of data round the cogitator net, the sardonic smile which never quite became a sneer. He'd seen it many times in their early years as lowly Archivists, generally directed at him, as he failed to follow Sitrus in some minor transgression of the regulations. Sitrus would have relished the challenge of getting away with it, although the risk of being caught would have been relatively low. Dealing with any hardprint copies that existed would have been a little more difficult, but not too much so; a Scribe's robe could hide a great deal more than a few sheets of paper, and once they were gone, it would be easy to ascribe their loss to the turmoil of the war. 'And something went wrong?'

'No.' Milena shook her head. 'No one noticed. Not at first.'

'At first?' Linder tried to get his reeling thoughts under control. 'What changed?'

'Harl did, I suppose. He must have got overconfident. After he helped me, he decided to rescue some of the other dispossessed.'

'Yes, he would.' Linder nodded. Once he'd crossed the line, and got away with it, Sitrus would have been unable to resist the impulse to carry on outwitting his superiors. He was constitutionally incapable of refraining from pushing his luck. Sometimes that had been an asset, propelling him up the Administratum hierarchy at a rate some of their contemporaries had been openly envious of, and sometimes a liability; Linder had seen him lose a month's remuneration on a single hand of cards before now.

'Like I said, he's a good man. And now Feris is treating him like a criminal!' Milena paced the room, her slight frame seeming too frail to contain her boiling rage.

'That must be why he wiped his records,' Linder said, considering the matter as dispassionately as he could. 'To protect you. With his access keys deleted from the system, there's no way of telling which files he accessed.'

He probably even believed that; a sufficiently devout tech-priest might be able to reconstruct them, given enough time to enact the proper rituals, but that kind of knowledge is well outside the purview of the Administratum.

'You won't tell Feris, will you?' Milena asked, twisting her hands together anxiously.

'Of course not,' Linder said, wondering if it was true. A lifetime of devotion to his calling was warring within him against the demands of friendship and compassion. It was all too much to take in.

'Thank you.' Milena smiled, with genuine warmth for the first time, the tension suddenly draining from her body. Then, to Linder's astonishment, she hugged him. 'I've been so afraid without Harl.'

'We'll find him,' Linder said, with a confidence he didn't feel, and hesitantly returned the embrace.

WHEN HE LEFT, it was close to dawn, a faint greyish glow becoming visible through the clouds of smoke rising from the manufactoria below and to the east. The rumble of industry continued unabated in the background, mere distinctions of day and night irrelevant to the vast majority of Kannack's population. Up on the Spine, though, the affluent remained more aware of the diurnal round, and the streets were accordingly quiet, which forced my observers to keep their distance; otherwise things might have been concluded a great deal more quickly than they were.

'Take this,' Milena said suddenly, as Linder turned away from the closing door. He held out his hand automatically, and found his fingers wrapping themselves around the compact weight of the miniature autopistol she'd collected from the hall table before undoing the bolt. 'I've got another.'

'No thank you.' The metal was cold, smelling faintly of lubricants, and the wooden butt felt warm where she'd been gripping it. It seemed astonishingly heavy for something so small, and Linder fumbled, almost dropping it. 'I haven't a clue how it works anyway.'

'You point it and pull the trigger,' Milena said. 'It's been blessed by a tech-priest to ensure accuracy. But you need to flick the safety off first.' Noticing Linder's blank expression, she smiled indulgently. 'That's the switch by your thumb.'

Linder almost refused again, then stuffed the little firearm into the depths of his robe. The gift was well meant, and he didn't want to hurt her feelings. 'I'll be in touch,' he said instead, 'as soon as I find out anything else.' He wasn't sure how he was going to do that, but had a vague idea of seeing if Klath remembered anything else Sitrus might have said about people or places he knew.

'I'll be waiting,' Milena said. 'But come by anyway. I don't see many people now Harl's gone.'

'I will,' Linder promised, and was rewarded with another fleeting smile.

The predawn wind was chill, unwarmed by the thermal currents rising from the industrial sectors, and Linder huddled deeper inside his robe as he hurried back towards the tunnel mouth leading to the enclosed depths of the hive below. His footsteps echoed eerily in the unaccustomed quiet, and the shadows between the waylamps seemed impenetrable pools of darkness. The tavern was open again as he passed it, if it had ever closed, the indefatigable zither player still going strong; he considered the unlikelihood of that for a moment, before realising it must have been a recording. His attention attracted by the music, he paused, considering the prospect of a reviving mug of caffeine and a warm butter roll, then dismissed the idea; he would be cutting the time of his arrival at the scriptorium fine enough as it was.

But the brief hesitation was enough. As he listened

to the echoes of his footfalls die away, another, caught
unawares, smacked into the pavement at exactly the
moment his next stride would have done.

'Who's there?' Linder looked round, seeking the
source of the sound, but the shadows between the
waylights kept their secrets. Unbidden, his hand
sought the suddenly comforting weight of the gun.
'Come on out!'

No one answered. Feeling vaguely foolish, and
inclined to blame his fears on an overactive imagination, Linder began walking again, listening to the steady
beat of echoes against the enclosing brickwork. His
hand curled round the butt of the autopistol, the small
excrescence of the safety catch snuggled against the ball
of his thumb.

Abruptly he turned, looking back the way he'd come,
and was rewarded with a flash of movement, just leaving
the pool of luminescence cast by the waylight behind
him. Emboldened by the feel of the weapon in his hand,
he took a step towards it, drawing the gun as he did so.

'Who are you?' he shouted. But the only answer he got
was the slithering of shoe soles against cobbles, as his
unseen pursuer turned and fled. A dark robe billowed
for a moment in the cone of lamplight, and the dimin-
ishing echo of hurrying footsteps rebounded from the
surrounding walls.

I suppose most men of Linder's profession would have
resumed their journey at that point, perhaps with a brief
prayer of thanks to the Throne for their deliverance, but,
as I've noted before, he could be a stubborn fellow when
the mood took him; and it took him then. Without any
thought for his safety, he ran after the fleeting shadow,
pausing now and then to catch his breath, and listen
out for the fugitive echoes. The pursuit took him away
from the thoroughfare he'd been following, ever deeper
into a maze of alleyways, and thence inside the rising
slope of the hive spine. He was vague about the details
of the route he took, but I was able to reconstruct it

later, bringing us to the market hall where he finally confronted his quarry.

At that hour it was still deserted, the stalls shuttered and empty, but the floodlamps in the ceiling had been kindled, ready for the vendors to set out their wares, and Linder blinked in the sudden brightness. As his dazzled eyes adjusted, he heard more footfalls echoing between the stands, and rounded the corner of the nearest row, aiming the gun ahead of him.

'Stop. Or I'll shoot.'

A hooded figure in a night-blue robe was crouched over a manhole cover in the middle of the aisle, frozen in the act of lifting it aside. It straightened slowly, and began to turn.

'Would you really, Zale?' The words were delivered in an amused drawl, as though the speaker was waiting for the punchline of a joke. 'You should never make a threat you're not prepared to carry out, you know. It makes you look weak.'

'Harl?' Linder lowered the weapon, stupefied with astonishment. 'What's going on?'

'I'm sure Milena filled you in,' Sitrus said, with a dismissive glance at the gun. 'You must have made quite an impression on her. She doesn't usually let other people play with her toys.'

'She told me what you did for her,' Linder said, tucking the weapon away, with a sudden flare of embarrassment.

Sitrus shrugged. 'It wasn't hard. I'd been thinking for some time about how you could match up a dormant identity with just about anyone, and she seemed the perfect person to give it a try.'

'Feris doesn't seem to feel that way,' Linder said, trying to assimilate this new and unexpected development. 'If he finds you, he'll charge you with record falsification at the very least.'

'Feris couldn't catch a cold showering naked in a blizzard,' Sitrus said, with tolerant amusement. He glanced down at the manhole next to his feet. 'But if you want to continue this conversation without interruption, we'd better get below. He's annoyingly persistent, and he's bound to have watchers trailing you.'

'Why me?' Linder asked, feeling his way down a rickety ladder. After a couple of metres his shoe soles scraped rockcrete, and he stepped aside to let his friend descend after him. The pillar of light from above cut off with a scrape and a clank as Sitrus replaced the iron cover, and the dimmer illumination of sparsely scattered glow-globes replaced it.

'Because you might lead him to me,' Sitrus said, the smile Linder had pictured so recently visible on his face as he stepped off the ladder into the gloom-shrouded tunnel. 'You really are out of your depth here, aren't you?'

'Of course I am!' Linder snapped. 'I'm a Scribe, not some dreg from the underhive! I'm not used to this kind of thing.'

'You seem to have more of a knack for it than you think,' Sitrus said. 'Which is why I took the risk of bringing you here.'

'In case you hadn't noticed, I was chasing you,' Linder said.

Sitrus smiled again. 'It saved a lot of explanation. If I'd approached you in the open, you'd start asking questions, and we'd still be talking when Feris's plodders turned up. But I had intended getting a lot closer to this little bolthole before I let you see me.' He nodded appreciatively. 'You're full of surprises, Zale.'

'Then I'm not the only one.' Linder fell into step with his friend, strolling along the dank utility duct as though they were ambling through a garden together. 'What are you going to do now?'

'Keep my head down, and wait for Feris to die of old age.' Sitrus smiled again. 'I set up a nice new life for myself before I erased the old one. I've got money, and connections, and I can well afford a juvenat or two.'

'Then why do you want to talk to me?' Linder asked, as they descended a ramp into a vaulted brick gallery lined with humming power relays.

'Because I trust you,' Sitrus said, 'and you were able to find Milena. I'd like you to pass on a message for me.'

'Of course,' Linder said. 'She's worried sick about you.'

'Then you won't mind putting her mind at rest. Just tell her I'm safe, and I've left the hive. Can you do that?'

'Consider it done,' Linder said. They were crossing a deep channel of lichen-encrusted brick, along which some thick tarry liquid flowed sluggishly into the distance, their footsteps ringing on the metal mesh bridge spanning it. 'Is there anything else?'

'I doubt it,' Sitrus said, the half-contemptuous smile back on his face. 'You're already sticking your neck out more than you're comfortable with.'

'I'll decide what I'm comfortable with,' Linder snapped. For the last year he'd been living outside the shadow cast by his friend, and he'd forgotten how annoyingly superior he could sometimes seem.

'Good for you.' Sitrus stopped walking, and looked at him appraisingly in the light from a nearby glow-globe. They'd reached a nexus of tunnels, half a dozen radiating from the circular chamber they found themselves in. When he spoke again, his voice was lower. 'There are plenty more like Milena, you know. Desperate, with nowhere to turn, and I can't help them anymore. But if you're willing to take the risk, you could.'

'Me?' For a moment Linder was too stunned even to speak. When he forced the syllable out, it sounded more like a strangulated gasp than an intelligible word.

Sitrus nodded. 'You could give them their lives back, Zale.' Then he shrugged. 'Somebody's life, anyway. It's got to be better than the one they have now.'

'Falsify records?' Linder felt nauseous at the very idea. 'No, I couldn't.'

'No, I don't suppose you could.' Sitrus gave him the look again, and a flare of resentment took Linder by surprise. It had been like that for as long as he could remember, Sitrus taking it for granted that he lacked the guts to follow where he led.

'Suppose I was able to help,' he said, surprising himself almost as much as Sitrus, judging by the unfamiliar expression of astonishment on his friend's face. 'How would I go about it?'

'You'd have to go through me,' Sitrus said. 'At least to begin with. I've got the contacts in place, and the Dispossessed trust me.' He looked at Linder appraisingly again. 'No offence, Zale, but these are damaged people, who don't give their confidence easily. You'll have to earn it.'

'None taken,' Linder said, before honesty compelled him to add, 'I'm not promising to do it, Harl. But I will think about it.'

'That's all I can reasonably expect.' Sitrus clapped him playfully on the back. 'You're a good man, Zale. I know you'll make the right choice.'

'I hope so.' Linder coughed uncomfortably. 'When I do decide, how do I let you know?'

'Ask Milena to hang something red from the second-floor balcony. When I hear it's there, I'll arrange a meeting, and we can discuss the details.'

'Something red. Right.' Linder nodded.

'Good.' Sitrus turned away, then paused, and indicated one of the tunnel mouths facing them. 'Head down that way for about three hundred metres, and you'll find a green access hatch. It opens into the tertiary storage area of the scriptorium.' Then he smiled again, the familiar mocking expression returning to his face. 'So you would have had time for that caffeine you were thinking about after all.'

Then he was gone, only the fading echo of his footsteps remaining.

'I'm a little disappointed,' I said, strolling into Linder's cubicle unannounced. 'I thought we had an agreement.'

'An agreement?' he responded, setting aside the hard-print he'd been annotating, with a deliberation which made it plain my visit was less of a surprise than I'd hoped.

I nodded, taking up my former position against the door. I didn't think he'd make a run for it, but there was no harm in closing off the option. 'To inform me if you heard from Harl Sitrus. I could count on it, apparently.'

'As you can see,' he returned, 'I'm rather busy. And I don't recall agreeing to speak to you immediately.'

'Fair enough,' I conceded. 'I should have emphasised the urgency of the matter. But you don't deny you spoke to him this morning?'

'No, I don't,' he returned levelly.

'And the substance of the conversation?'

'Was personal.' The fractional hesitation was enough to betray that he was holding something back, but they always do at first. 'He asked me to reassure Miss Dravere that he's safe and well, which I agreed to do.'

'How kind.' I shifted the focus of the questions. 'And did you discuss the charges against him?'

Linder nodded, reluctantly. 'We did. It seems I owe you an apology.'

'Accepted, of course,' I assured him. 'So he admitted it?'

'He told me he'd falsified a few records. As you can imagine, it came as rather a shock.'

'I imagine it did,' I said, trying to sound sympathetic. 'And was he any more specific than that?'

'He said he'd been giving the identities of people killed in the war to destitute refugees. I can't condone it, but he does seem to have been acting out of a misguided sense of altruism.'

'Then it seems he's been a little selective with his recollections,' I replied, wishing there was somewhere else to sit. 'Did he mention how we got on to his activities in the first place?'

Linder shifted uncomfortably in his seat. 'That didn't

come up in the conversation,' he admitted.

'No,' I said, 'somehow I didn't think it would. It was when a man named Werther Geist returned to Kannack a couple of months ago, after an absence of nearly three years. Geist's quite wealthy as it happens, with interests all over Verghast, and the last anyone heard of him, he was visiting Vervunhive. So of course he was listed among the missing.' I paused, groping automatically in my pocket for a packet of lho-sticks, before remembering I was definitely giving them up again. Probably a bad idea to light one up surrounded by a million tonnes of paper anyway. 'The thing of it was, he left a couple of hours before the Ferrozoican attack, and ended up in Hiraldi, where he got mobilised along with a whole bunch of the local auxiliaries. And once the security situation eased, he got kicked back into civilian clothes again. Are you with me so far?'

Linder nodded. 'So when he returned to Kannack, he found another Geist already living in his house?'

'Got it in one,' I told him. 'But the thing is, they could both prove they were the genuine Geist. In the end we had to run a genetic comparison to find out who the imposter was.'

'Which I take it you did,' Linder said, sounding genuinely interested.

I nodded. 'The really interesting thing was who he turned out to be. He was a refugee, right enough. But from Ferrozoica.'

I watched Linder's face crumble. He shook his head. 'That can't be right. Harl would never help one of them.'

'But he did. I can show you the transcripts if you like.' In the end I did, just to prove the point, but I could see at the time he believed me. 'Once he realised we were going to turn the case over to the Inquisition, our suspect got positively voluble. Laid out the whole thing for us step by step. What Sitrus was doing, and how much he charged for the privilege.'

'How much?' Linder was getting angry again, but it

didn't seem directed at me this time.

'Ten per cent of the assets the new identity had access to. Seems like a bargain to me,' I said.

'And how many ten per cents do you think he collected?' Linder asked, his voice thickening.

'I've no idea,' I admitted. 'I suspect his lady friend was one, but I can't prove it.'

'Then why haven't you arrested her?' Linder asked.

'Because the Arbites isn't the Inquisition,' I explained. 'We serve the law, and we operate within the letter of it at all times. Without evidence, I've no grounds to detain her. I've got a list of names as long as your arm who reappeared suddenly after being presumed dead, but I can't move against any of them either.'

'So you need Harl,' Linder said.

'I do.' I nodded slowly. 'And I'm open to suggestions.'

'THANK YOU,' MILENA said. She was smiling, but there were tears on her face. 'Just to know he's all right...'

Linder shuffled his feet, uncomfortable with the display of emotion. 'I'm sure you'll see him again soon,' he said awkwardly.

'I don't have a soon,' Milena said, matter-of-factly.

'I'm sorry?' Linder felt his face twist in a frown of confusion.

'I'm dying, Zale. For Throne's sake, haven't you worked it out? I was only a couple of kilometres from a nuclear explosion!'

'The radiation,' Linder said, with sudden understanding.

'That's right.' Milena nodded. 'I'm getting the best care money can buy, but all it can do in the end is manage the pain.'

'How long?' Linder asked, regretting the question at once. But Milena didn't seem to mind.

'Who knows?' She shrugged. 'None of us do really. But I definitely won't see the end of the year.'

'I'm sorry.' Linder took her hand, hoping the gesture

would convey what he couldn't find the words for. She smiled wanly, and returned the pressure for a moment, before withdrawing it.

'Thank you. Come to the funeral, if you can stand it. I'd like to think I'll have a friend there now Harl's gone.'

'I will,' Linder said. He probably hesitated after that, conscience, duty and friendship contending for the last time within him. Then he went on. 'Do you have something red in the house?'

SITRUS HADN'T MENTIONED how he intended getting in touch again, so when a standard missive capsule dropped from the pneumatic tube over his desk, Linder's first thought was that it was simply another piece of paperwork to deal with. Only when he unrolled the scrip inside did he discover otherwise.

Tunnels behind the scriptorium, he read. The message was unsigned, but the handwriting was unmistakably Sitrus's. His heart hammering, he left the cubicle.

It took him several minutes to reach the green access hatch he remembered; when he did so it was ajar. Pulling it open enough to admit himself, he scrambled through, then drew it almost closed again behind him, leaving only a faint filament of light to sketch its position in the wall.

'Harl?' Only echoes answered him, chasing one another down the dimly lit passageways. Then he saw the fresh impression of an arrow, scored into the crumbling brickwork opposite the hatchway. It pointed in the opposite direction to the section he'd traversed before, but the corridor was broad and high enough to walk down unobstructed, so he followed the mute instruction without hesitation.

After a few moments it opened out into a wide, circular chamber, with passageways leading off from it at the cardinal points of the compass. It was high, with a ceiling of domed industrial brick some forty or fifty metres overhead, and a series of galleries circled the walls, connected by a pair of spiralling staircases which mirrored one another all the way up the shaft. Each gallery also gave on to a number of tunnel mouths, four or six generally, although a couple seemed to have as many as eight.

'You took your time,' Sitrus said, in what seemed no more than a normal conversational tone. Fooled by the acoustics, Linder glanced around, expecting to find his friend a few paces away; only when the words were followed by a chuckle of amusement did he look up, to find him leaning casually on the balustrade of a gallery three levels above.

'I came as quickly as I could,' Linder replied, without raising his voice either. The cavernous space lent it a faintly echoing timbre, but it carried clearly. He began to walk towards the nearest staircase. 'Interesting place for a meeting.'

'It works well,' Sitrus said. 'Plenty of exits if you didn't come alone.' He was strolling casually as he talked, keeping the width of the chamber between them, and scanning the tunnel mouth behind Linder with wary eyes.

'Who would I bring?' Linder asked.

'Well, it did cross my mind you'd invite Feris,' Sitrus said.

Linder began to climb the stairway. 'He came to see me. Same old story, with a few fresh embellishments. I think he was hoping I'd turn you in.'

'More than likely.' Sitrus began to climb the steps on the other side, maintaining the distance between them. 'So you thought about what I said.'

'I did.' Linder reached the first gallery, and began to circle it, tilting his head back to keep his friend in sight. 'But I'm still a little unclear about something.'

'And what might that be?' Sitrus asked, a wary edge entering his voice.

'Whether helping Milena was really the first time you'd falsified records. I checked her new idents, and the substitution was flawless.'

'I'd massaged a few files before,' Sitrus admitted, unabashed. 'It's easy once you know how. I'm surprised everyone doesn't do it.'

Linder fought down his instinctive revulsion, keeping his voice as calm as he could, thanking the Emperor for the echoes which helped him to conceal his feelings. 'And what files would those be? Your own personal ones?' Which would explain Sitrus's rapid rise to a position of influence within the Administratum.

'Of course,' Sitrus admitted. 'You know how it is. You need every little edge you can get if you want to get on.'

'And any others?' Linder persisted.

'A few. I smoothed a few career bumps for you, for instance.'

'Me?' This time Linder wasn't quite able to conceal his shock, prompting another indulgent chuckle from above.

'You surely didn't believe you got where you are on merit, did you?'

'It had crossed my mind,' Linder said, refusing to rise to the bait. Sitrus was goading him, that was all, trying to assess his trustworthiness. 'But if you helped, I won't be resigning on principle.'

'Good man,' Sitrus said. 'Anything else bothering you?'

'Just one thing,' Linder said, starting up the next staircase. 'Werther Geist. Did you know you were helping a Ferrozoican?'

Sitrus shrugged. 'Omelettes and eggs, Zale. You know how it is.'

'Yes, I'm afraid I do.' Linder shook his head. 'You know the worst part?'

'I'm sure you're going to tell me.' Sitrus was moving more quickly now, towards a tunnel mouth. It was now or never.

'I wanted to believe you.' Linder drew the little pistol Milena had given him. 'However convincing Feris was, I kept telling myself that at least you meant well.'

'I'll take that as a no, then, shall I?' The smile was back on Sitrus's face. 'I knew you'd be too spineless to go through with it. But I let myself hope a little too. So much we could have done together, Zale; so much money we could have made.' He waved, mockingly. 'Enjoy your files; it's all you were ever really fit for.'

'Stop or I'll shoot!' Linder shouted, seeing his former friend about to flee. Footsteps were hurrying along the tunnel behind him, and with a surge of relief he realised I'd got his message after all.

'Of course you will,' Sitrus said mockingly, turning to leave.

Linder never remembered firing the gun in his hand; just a loud report, which deafened him for a moment, and a jolt as though someone had punched him in the arm. To this day I'm convinced he never intended to hit his former friend, just startle him, but the tech-priest's blessing must have been a strong one; because, when he looked again, Sitrus was staggering, an expression of stunned disbelief on his face.

'Harl!' Linder ran for the stairs, as Sitrus took a couple of steps towards the nearest tunnel mouth, and collapsed to the floor. By the time I joined them, Sitrus's face was grey, and he was fighting for breath.

'Hell of a time to grow a backbone, Zale,' he said, the sardonic smile flickering on his face for the last time.

Linder turned an anguished face in my direction. 'Call a medicae!' he implored.

'On the way,' I said calmly, although if the voices in my comm-bead were right about their location, they'd find nothing but a corpse when they arrived. I knelt on the grubby brickwork, next to Sitrus. 'How many other Ferrozoicans did you give new identities to? You know every damn one of them will be tainted by Chaos. Do you want to face the Emperor with that on your conscience?'

'You're so clever, you work it out,' Sitrus said. Then he turned to Linder. 'Tell Milena I'll see her again sooner than we thought.'

'I'll tell her,' Linder said, his voice quaking; but I doubt that Sitrus ever heard.

I COULDN'T CLOSE the case without a formal identification of the body; and as the closest thing Sitrus had to next of kin on Verghast was Milena, I had to ask her. She held up well, all things considered, only showing signs of emotion when Linder gave her Sitrus's final message. She heard him out without speaking, then nodded curtly.

'Remember what I said about my funeral?' she asked.

'Of course,' Linder said.

'I'd rather you didn't come after all.' Then she swept out of the Sector House like a mourning-clad storm front.

'What now?' Linder asked, looking faintly dazed, which I could hardly blame him for.

'Now we do it the hard way,' I said. 'Go back to our list of suspects, and pull their records apart. Check for any anomalies, however small, that might indicate they're not who they say they are.' I looked at him appraisingly. 'Your expertise would be very useful, if the Administratum can spare you.'

'I'll make sure they can,' he said. 'But what about Milena? Aren't you going to bring her in?'

I shook my head. 'She's a low priority,' I said. 'We know she's not from Ferrozoica, so she'll keep. We'll get around to her case in a year or two.' Technically, I suppose, that was Obstruction of Justice, but there was no point in prosecuting her; she'd be dead before the case came to trial. Like I said, everyone's guilty of something, even me.

Linder looked at me strangely. 'You're a good man,' he said.

A new Gaunt story from me to finish this collection, a novella, actually.

I don't want to say too much about it, because almost anything I mention will be a spoiler. All I will say is that writing this story was exactly what I needed to get me back on the horse after my Adventures in Epilepsy. It was great to engage, up close and personal, with characters who were old friends.

This story, like 'The Iron Star', fits precisely into the continuity. But I'm not going to tell you where.

Dan Abnett

OF THEIR LIVES IN THE RUINS OF THEIR CITIES

Dan Abnett

It FEELS LIKE the afterlife, and none of them are entirely convinced that it isn't.

They have pitched up in a cold and rain-lashed stretch of lowland country, on the morning after somebody else's triumph, with a bunch of half-arsed orders, a dislocating sense that the war is elsewhere and carrying on without them, and very little unit cohesion. They have a couple of actions under their belts, just enough to lift their chins, but nothing like enough to bind them together or take the deeper pain away and, besides, other men have collected the medals. They're out in the middle of nowhere, marching further and further away from anything that matters any more, because nothing matters any more.

They are just barely the Tanith First and Only. They are not Gaunt's Ghosts.

They are never going to be Gaunt's Ghosts.

* * *

SILENT LIGHTNING STROBES in the distance. His back turned towards it and the rain, the young Tanith infantryman watches Ibram Gaunt at work from the entrance of the war tent. The colonel-commissar is seated at the far end of a long table around which, an hour earlier, two dozen Guard officers and adjutants were gathered for a briefing. Now Gaunt is alone.

The infantryman has been allowed to stand at ease, but he is on call. He has been selected to act as runner for the day. It's his job to attend the commander, to pick up any notes or message satchels at a moment's notice, and deliver them as per orders. Foot couriers are necessary because the vox is down. It's been down a lot, this past week. It'd been patchy and unreliable around Voltis City. Out in the lowlands, it's useless, like audio soup. You can hear voices, now and then. Someone said maybe the distant, soundless lightning is to blame.

Munitorum-issue chem lamps, those tin-plate models that unscrew and then snap out for ignition, have been strung along the roof line, and there is a decent rechargeable glow-globe on the table beside Gaunt's elbow. The lamps along the roof line are swaying and rocking in the wind that's finding its way into the long tent. The lamps add a golden warmth to the tent's shadowy interior, a marked contrast to the raw, wet blow driving up the valley outside. There is rain in the air, sticky clay underfoot, a whitewashed sky overhead, and a line of dirty hills in the middle distance that look like a lip of rock that someone has scraped their boots against. Somewhere beyond the hills, the corpse of a city lies in a shallow grave.

Gaunt is studying reports that have been printed out on paper flimsies. He has weighed them down on the surface of the folding table with cartons of bolter rounds so they won't blow away. The wind is really getting in under the tent's skirt. He's writing careful notes with a stylus. The infantryman can only imagine the importance of those jottings. Tactical formulations, perhaps? Attack orders?

Gaunt is not well liked, but the infantryman finds him interesting. Watching him work at least takes the infantryman's mind off the fact that he's standing in the mouth of a tent with his arse out in the rain.

No indeed, Colonel-Commissar Ibram Gaunt is not well liked. A reputation for genocide will do that to a man's character. He is intriguing, though. For a career soldier, he seems surprisingly reflective, a man of thought not action. There is a promise of wisdom in his narrow features. The infantryman wonders if this was a mistake of ethnicity, a misreading brought about by cultural differences. Gaunt and the infantryman were born on opposite sides of the sector.

The infantryman finds it amusing to imagine Gaunt grown very elderly. Then he might look, the infantryman thinks, like one of those wizened old savants, the kind that know everything about fething everything.

However, the infantryman also has good reason to predict that Gaunt will never live long enough to grow old. Gaunt's profession mitigates against it, as does the cosmos he has been born into, and the specific nature of his situation.

If the Archenemy of Mankind does not kill Ibram Gaunt, the infantryman thinks, then Gaunt's own men will do the job.

A BETTER TENT.

Gaunt writes the words at the top of his list. He knows he'll have to look up the correct Munitorum code number, though he thinks it's 1NX1G1xA. Sym will know and–

Sym *would have* known, but Sym is dead. Gaunt exhales. He really has to train himself to stop doing that. Sym had been his adjutant and Gaunt had come to rely on him; it still seems perfectly normal to turn and expect to find Sym there, waiting, ready and resourceful. Sym had known how to procure a dress coat in the middle of the night, or a pot of collar starch, or a bottle of decent amasec, or a copy of the embarkation transcripts before they were published. He'd have known the Munitorum serial code for a *tent/temperate winter*. The structure Gaunt is sitting in is not a *tent/temperate winter*. It's an old tropical shelter left over from another theatre. It's waxed against rain, but there are canvas vents low down along the base hem designed to keep air circulating on balmy, humid days. This particular part of Voltemand seldom sees balmy humid days. The east wind, its cheeks full of rain, is pushing the vents open and invading the tent like a polar gale.

Under *A better tent* he writes: *A portable heater*.

He hardly cares for his own comfort, but he'd noted the officers and their junior aides around the table that morning, backs hunched, moods foul, teeth gritted against the cold, every single one of them in a hurry to get the meeting over so they could head back to their billets and their own camp stoves.

Men who are uncomfortable and in a hurry do not make good decisions. They rush things. They are not thorough. They often make general noises of consent just to get briefings over with, and that morning they'd all done it: the Tanith officers, the Ketzok tankers, the Litus B.R.U., all of them.

Gaunt knows it's all payback, though. The whole situation is payback. He is being punished for making that Blueblood general look like an idiot, even though Gaunt'd had the moral high ground. He had been avenging Tanith blood, because there isn't enough of that left for anyone to go around wasting it.

He thinks about the letter in his pocket, and then lets the thought go again.

When he'd been assigned to the Tanith, Gaunt had relished the prospect as it was presented on paper: a first founding from a small, agrarian world that was impeccable in its upkeep of tithes and devotions. Tanith had no real black marks in the Administratum's eyes, and no longstanding martial traditions to get tangled up in. There had been the opportunity to build something worthwhile, three regiments of light infantry to begin with, though Gaunt's plans had been significantly more ambitious than that: a major infantry force, fast and mobile, well-drilled and disciplined. The Munitorum's recruitment agents reported that the Tanith seemed to have a natural knack for tracking and covert work, and Gaunt had hoped to add that speciality to the regiment's portfolio. From the moment he'd reviewed the Tanith dossier, Gaunt had begun to see the sense of Slaydo's deathbed bequest to him.

The plans and dreams have come apart, though. The Archenemy, still stinging from Balhaut, burned worlds in the name of vengeance, and one of those worlds was Tanith. Gaunt got out with his life, just barely, and with him he'd dragged a few of the mustered Tanith men, enough for one regiment. Not enough men to ever be anything more than a minor infantry support force, to die as trench fodder in some Throne-forgotten ocean of mud, but just enough men to hate his living guts for the rest of forever for not letting them die with their planet.

Ibram Gaunt has been trained as a political officer, and he is a very good one, though the promotion Slaydo gave him was designed to spare him from the slow death of a political career. His political talents, however, can usually find a positive expression for even the worst scenarios.

In the cold lowlands of Voltemand, an upbeat interpretation is stubbornly eluding him.

He has stepped away from a glittering career with the Hyrkans, cut his political ties with all the men of status and influence who could assist him or advance him, and ended up in a low-value theatre on a third-tier warfront, in command of a salvaged, broken regiment of unmotivated men who hate him. There is still the letter in his pocket, of course.

He looks down at his list, and writes:

Spin this shit into gold, or get yourself a transfer to somewhere with a desk and a driver.

He looks at this for a minute, and then scratches it out. He puts the stylus down.

'Trooper,' he calls to the infantryman in the mouth of the tent. He knows the young man's name is Caffran. He is generally good with names, and he makes an effort to learn them quickly, but he is also sparing when it comes to using them. Show a common lasman you know his name too early, and it'll seem like you're trying far too hard to be his new best friend, especially if you just let his home and family burn.

It'll seem like you're weak.

The infantryman snaps to attention sharply.

'Step inside,' Gaunt calls, beckoning with two hooked fingers. 'Is it still raining?'

'Sir,' says Caffran non-committally as he approaches the table.

'I want you to locate Corbec for me. I think he's touring the west picket.'

'Sir.'

'You've got that?'

'Find Colonel Corbec, sir.'

Gaunt nods. He picks up his stylus and folds one of the flimsies in half, ready to write on the back of it. 'Tell him to ready up three squads and meet me by the north post in thirty minutes. You need me to write that down for you?'

'No, sir.'

'Three squads, north post, thirty minutes,' says Gaunt. He writes it down anyway, and then embosses it with his biometric signet ring to transfer his authority code. He hands the note to the trooper. 'Thirty minutes,' he repeats. 'Time for me to get some breakfast. Is the mess tent still cooking?'

'Sir,' Caffran replies, this time flavouring it with a tiny, sullen shrug.

Gaunt looks him in the eye for a moment. Caffran

manages to return about a second of insolent resentment, and then looks away into space over Gaunt's shoulder.

'What was her name?' Gaunt asks.

'What?'

'I took something from every single Tanith man,' says Gaunt, pushing back his chair and standing up. 'Apart from the obvious, of course. I was wondering what I'd taken from you in particular. What was her name?'

'How do you–'

'A man as young as you, it's bound to be a girl. And that tattoo indicates a family betrothal.'

'You know about Tanith marks?' Caffran can't hide his surprise.

'I studied up, trooper. I wanted to know what sort of men my reputation was going to depend upon.'

There is a pause. Rain beats against the outer skin of the tent like drumming fingertips.

'Laria,' Caffran says quietly. 'Her name was Laria.'

'I'm sorry for your loss,' says Gaunt.

Caffran looks at him again. He sneers slightly. 'Aren't you going to tell me it will be all right? Aren't you going to assure me that I'll find another girl somewhere?'

'If it makes you feel better,' says Gaunt. He sighs and turns back to look at Caffran. 'It's unlikely, but I'll say it if it makes you feel better.' Gaunt puts on a fake, jaunty smile. 'Somewhere, somehow, in one of the warzones we march into, you'll find the girl you're supposed to be with, and you'll live happily ever after. There. Better?'

Caffran's mouth tightens and he mutters something under his breath.

'If you're going to call me a bastard, do it out loud,' says Gaunt. 'I don't know why you're so pissed off. You were walking out on this Laria anyway.'

'We were betrothed!'

'You'd signed up for the Imperial Guard, trooper. First Founding. You were never going to see Tanith again. I

don't know why you had the nerve to get hitched to the
poor cow in the first place.'

'Of course I was coming back to her–'

'You sign up, you leave. Warp transfers, long rotations, tours along the rim. You never go back. You never
go home, not once the Guard has you. Years go by,
decades. You forget where you came from in the end.'

'But the recruiting officer said–'

'He lied to you, trooper. Do you think any bastard
would sign up if the recruiters told the truth?'

Caffran sags. 'He lied?'

'Yes. But I won't. That's the one thing you can count
on with me. Now go and get Corbec.'

Caffran snaps off a poor salute, turns and heads out
of the tent.

Gaunt sits down again. He begins to collect up the
flimsies, and packs away the bolter shell cartons holding them down. He thinks about the letter in his pocket
again.

On his list, he writes:
Appoint a new adjutant.
Under that, he writes:
Find a new adjutant.
Finally, under that, he writes:
Start telling a few lies?

HE PULLS HIS storm coat on as he leaves the tent, partly
to fend off the rain, and partly to cover his jacket. It's
his number one staff-issue field jacket, but it's become
too soiled with clay from the trek out of Voltis City to
wear with any dignity. He has a grubby, old number
two issue that he keeps in his kit as a spare, but it still
has Hyrkan patches on the collar, the shoulders and the
cuffs, and that's embarrassing. Sym would have patched
the skull-and-crossed-knives of the Tanith onto it by now.
He'd have got out his sewing kit and made sure both of
Gaunt's field uniforms were code perfect, the way he kept
the rest of Gaunt's day-to-day life neat and sewn up tight.

Steamy smoke is rising from the cowled chimneys of the cook-tents, and he can smell the greasy blocks of processed nutrition fibre being fried. His stomach rumbles. He sets off towards the kitchens. Beyond the row of mess tents lies the canvas city of the Tanith position, and to the north-east of that, the batteries of the Ketzok. Beyond that, the edge of the skyline flicks on and off with the unnervingly quiet lightning, far away, like a malfunctioning lamp filament that refuses to stay lit.

Slab is pretty gruesome stuff. Pressure-treated down from any and all available nutritional sources by the Munitorum, it has no discernible flavour apart from a faint, mucusy aftertaste, and it looks like grey-white putty. In fact, years before at Schola Progenium on Ignatius Cardinal, an acquaintance of Gaunt's had once kneaded some of it into a form that authentically resembled a brick of plastic explosive, complete with fuses, and then carried out a practical joke on the Master of the Scholam Arsenal that was notable for both the magnificent extent of the disruption it caused, and the stunning severity of the subsequent punishment. Slab, as it's known to every common Guard lasman, comes canned and it comes freeze-dried, it comes in packets and it comes in boxes, it comes in individual heated tins and it comes in catering blocks. Company cooks slice, dice and mince it, and use it as the bulk base of any meal when local provision sources are unavailable. They flavour it with whatever they have to hand, usually foil sachets of powder with names like *groxtail* and *vegetable (root)* and *sausage (assorted)*. Ibram Gaunt has lived on it for a great deal of his adult and sub-adult life. He is so used to the stuff, he actually misses it when it isn't around.

Men have gathered around the cook tents, huddled against the weather under their camo-cloaks. Gaunt still hasn't got used to wearing his, even though he'd promised the Tanith colonel he would, as a show of unity. It doesn't hang right around him, and in the Voltemand wind, it tugs and tangles like a devil.

The Tanith don't seem to have the same trouble. They half-watch him approach, shrouded, hooded, some supping from mess cans. They watch him approach. There is a shadow in their eyes. They are a wild lot. Beads of rainwater glint in their tangled dark hair, though occasionally the glints are studs or nose rings, piercings in lips or eyebrows. They like their ink, the Tanith, and they wear the complex, traditional patterns of blue and green on their pale skins with pride. Cheeks, throats, forearms and the backs of hands display spirals and loops, leaves and branches, sigils and whorls. They also like their edges. The Tanith weapon is a long knife with a straight, silver blade that has evolved from a hunting tool. They could hunt with it well enough, silently, like phantoms.

Gaunt's Ghosts. Someone had come up with that within a few days of their first deployment on Blackshard. It had been the sociopath with the long-las, as Gaunt recalled it, a man known to him as 'Mad'. A more withering and scornful nickname, Gaunt can't imagine.

RAWNE SAYS, 'HERE comes the fether now.'

He takes a sip from his water bottle, which does not contain water, and turns as if to say something to Murt Feygor.

'But I paid you that back!' Feygor exclaims, managing to make his voice sound wounded and plaintive, the wronged party.

Rawne makes a retort and steps back, in time to affect a blind collision with Gaunt as he makes his way into the cook tent. The impact is hard enough to rock Gaunt off his feet.

'Easy there, sir!' cries Varl, hooking a hand under Gaunt's armpit to keep him off the ground. He hoists Gaunt up.

'Thank you,' Gaunt says.

'Varl, sir,' replies the trooper. He grins a big, shit-eating grin. 'Infantryman first class Ceglan Varl, sir. Wouldn't want you taking a tumble now, would I, sir? Wouldn't want you to go falling over and getting yourself all dirty.'

'I'm sure you wouldn't, trooper,' says Gaunt. 'Carry on.'

He looks back at Rawne and Feygor.

'That was all me, sir,' says Feygor, hands up. 'The major and I were having a little dispute, and I distracted him.'

It sounds convincing. Gaunt doesn't know much about the trooper called Feygor, but he's met his type before, a conniving son of a bitch who has been blessed with the silken vocal talent to sell any story to anyone.

Gaunt doesn't even bother looking at him. He stares at Rawne.

Major Rawne stares right back. His handsome face betrays no emotion whatsoever. Gaunt is a tall man, but Rawne is one of the Tanith he doesn't tower over, and he only has a few pounds on the major.

'I know what you're thinking,' Rawne says.

'Do you, Rawne? Is that an admission of unholy gifts? Should I call for emissaries of the Ordos to examine you?'

'Ha ha,' says Rawne in a laugh-less voice. He just says the sounds. 'Look, that there was a genuine slip, sir. A genuine bump. But we have a little history, sir, you and I, so you're bound to ascribe more motive to it than that.'

A little history. In the Blackshard deadzones, Rawne had used the opportunity of a quiet moment alone with Gaunt to express his dissatisfaction with Gaunt's leadership in the strongest possible terms. Gaunt had disarmed him and carried Rawne's unconscious body clear of the fighting area. It's hard to say what part of that *history* yanks Rawne most: the fact that he had failed to murder Gaunt, or the fact that Gaunt had saved him.

'Wow,' says Gaunt.

'What?'

'You used the word *ascribe*,' says Gaunt, and turns to

go into the cook tent. Over his shoulder, he calls out, 'If you say it was a bump, then it was a bump, major. We need to trust each other.'

Gaunt turns and looks back.

'Starting in about twenty minutes. After breakfast, I'm going to take an advance out to get a look at Kosdorf. You'll be in charge.'

They watch him pick up a mess tin from the pile and head towards the slab vat where the cook is waiting with a ladle and an apologetic expression.

HE SITS DOWN with his tin at one of the mess benches. The slab seems to have been refried and then stewed along with something that was either string or mechanically recovered gristle.

'I don't know how you can eat that.'

Gaunt looks up. It's the boy, the civilian boy. The boy sits down facing him.

'Sit down, if you like,' Gaunt says.

Milo looks pinched with cold, and he has his arms wrapped around his body.

'That stuff,' he says, jutting his chin suspiciously in the direction of Gaunt's tin. 'It's not proper food. I thought Imperial Guardsmen were supposed to get proper food. I thought that was the Compact of Service between the Munitorum and the Guardsmen: three square meals a day.'

'This is proper food.'

The boy shakes his head. He is only about seventeen, but he's going to be big when he fills out. There's a blue fish inked over his right eye.

'It's not proper food,' he insists.

'Well, you're not a proper Guardsman, so you're not entitled to a proper opinion.'

The boy looks hurt. Gaunt doesn't want to be mean. He owes Brin Milo a great deal. Two people had gone beyond the call to help Ibram Gaunt get off Tanith alive. Sym had been one, and the man had died making the

effort. Milo had been the other. The boy was just a servant, a piper appointed by the Elector of Tanith Magna
to wait on Gaunt during his stay. Gaunt understands
why the boy has stuck with the regiment since the
Tanith disaster. The regiment is all Milo has left, all he
has left of his people, and he feels he has nowhere else
to go, but Gaunt wishes Milo would disappear. There
are camps and shelters, there are Munitorum refugee
programmes. Civilians didn't belong at the frontline.
They remind troopers of what they've left behind or, in
the Tanith case, lost forever. They erode morale. Gaunt
has suggested several times that Milo might be better off
at a camp at Voltis City. He even has enough pull left to
get Milo sent to a Schola Progenium or an orphanage
for the officer class.

Milo refuses to leave. It's as if he's waiting for something to happen, for someone to arrive or something
to be revealed. It's as if he's waiting for Gaunt to make
good on a promise.

'Did you want something?' Gaunt asks.

'I want to come.'

'Come where?'

'You're going to scout the approach to Kosdorf this
morning. I want to come.'

Gaunt feels a little flush of anger. 'Rawne tell you
that?'

'No one told me.'

'Caffran, then. Damn, I thought Caffran might be
trustworthy.'

'No one told me,' says Milo. 'I mean it. I just had a
feeling, a feeling you'd go out this morning. This whole
taskforce was sent to clear Kosdorf, wasn't it?'

'This whole taskforce was intended to be an instrument of petty and spiteful vengeance,' Gaunt replies.

'By whom?' asks Milo.

Gaunt finishes the last of his slab. He drops the fork
into the empty tin. Not the best he'd ever had. Throne
knows, not the worst, either.

'That general,' Gaunt says.

'General Sturm?'

'That's the one,' Gaunt nods. 'General Noches Sturm of the 50th Volpone. He was trying to use the Tanith First, and we made him look like a prize scrotum by taking Voltis when his oh-so-mighty Bluebloods couldn't manage the trick. Throne, he even let us ship back to the transport fleet before deciding we should stay another month or so to help clean up. He's done it all to inconvenience us. Pack, unpack. Ship to orbit, return to surface. March out into the backwaters of a defeated world to check the ruins of a dead city.'

'Make you eat crap instead of fresh rations?' asks Milo, looking at the mess tin.

'That too, probably,' says Gaunt.

'Probably shouldn't have pissed him off, then,' says Milo.

'I really probably shouldn't,' Gaunt agrees. 'Never mind, I heard he's getting retasked. If the Emperor shows me any providence, I'll never have to see Sturm again.'

'He'll get his just desserts,' says Milo.

'What does that mean?' asks Gaunt.

Milo shrugs. 'I dunno. It just feels that way to me. People get what they deserve, sooner or later. The universe always gets payback. One day, somebody will stick it to Sturm just like he's sticking it to you.'

'Well, that thought's cheered me up,' says Gaunt, 'except the part about getting what you deserve. What does the universe have in store for me, do you suppose, after what happened to Tanith?'

'You only need to worry about that if you think you did anything wrong,' says Milo. 'If your conscience is clear, the universe will know.'

'You talk to it much?'

'What?'

'The universe? You're on first name terms?'

Milo pulls a face.

'Things could be worse, anyway,' Milo says.

'How?'

'Well, you're in charge. You're in charge of this whole task force.'

'For my sins.'

Gaunt gets to his feet. A Munitorum skivvy comes by and collects his tin.

'So?' asks Milo. 'Can I come?'

'No,' says Gaunt.

HE'S WALKED A few yards from the mess tents when Milo calls out after him. With a resigned weariness, Gaunt turns back to look at the boy.

'What?' he asks. 'I said no.'

'Take your cape,' says Milo.

'What?'

'Take your cape with you.'

'Why?'

Milo looks startled for a moment, as if he doesn't want to give the answer, or it hadn't occurred to him that anyone would need one. He dithers for a second, and seems to be making something up.

'Because Colonel Corbec likes it when you wear it,' he says. 'He thinks it shows respect.'

Gaunt nods. Good enough.

THE ADVANCE IS waiting for him at the north post, the end marker of the camp area. There are two batteries of Ketzok Hydras there, barrels elevated at a murky sky that occasionally blinks with silent light. Gunners sit dripping under oilskin coats on the lee side of their gun-carriages. Tracks are sunk deep in oozing grey clay. Rain hisses.

'Nice day for it,' says Colm Corbec.

'I arranged the weather especially, colonel,' replies Gaunt as he walks up. The clay is wretchedly sticky underfoot. It sucks at their boots. The men in the three squads look entirely underwhelmed at the prospect of

the morning's mission. The only ones amongst them
who aren't standing slope-shouldered and dejected are
the three scout specialists that Corbec has chosen to
round out the advance. One is the leader of the scout
unit, Mkoll. Gaunt has already begun to admire Mkoll's
abilities, but he has no read on the man himself. Mkoll
is sort of nondescript, of medium build and modest
appearance, and seems a little weatherbeaten and older
than the rank and file. He chooses to say very little.

Gaunt hasn't yet learned the names of the two scouts
with Mkoll. One, he believes, he has overheard someone refer to as 'lucky'. The other one, the taller, thinner
one, has a silent, faraway look about him that's oddly
menacing.

'It may just have been me,' says Corbec, 'but didn't we
spend an hour or so in the tent this morning agreeing
not to do this?'

Gaunt nods.

'I thought,' says Corbec, 'we were to stay put until the
Ketzok had been resupplied?'

They were. The purpose of the expedition is to evalu-
ate and secure Kosdorf, Voltemand's second city, which
had been effectively taken out in the early stages of the
liberation. Orbit watch reports it as ruined, a city grave,
but the emergency government and the Administratum
want it locked down. The whole thing is a colossal waste
of time. Voltis City, which had been the stronghold for
the charismatic but now dead Archenemy demagogue
Chanthar, was the key to Voltemand. The Kosdorf
securement is the sort of mission that could have been
handled by PDF or a third-tier Guard strength.

General Sturm is playing games, of course, getting his
own back, and doing it in such a way as to make it look
like he is being magnanimous. As his last act before
passing control of the Voltemand theatre to a successor,
Sturm appointed Gaunt to lead the expedition to Kosdorf, a command of twenty thousand men including his
own Tanith, a regiment of Litus Battlefield Regimental

Units, and a decent support spread of Ketzok armour.

Everyone, including the Litus and the Ketzok, have seen it for what it is, so they've started making heavy going of it, dragging their heels. At this last encampment, supposedly the final staging point before a proper run into Kosdorf, the Ketzok have complained that their ammo trains have fallen behind, and demanded a delay of thirty-six hours until they can be sure of their supplies.

The Ketzok are a decent lot. Despite a bad incident during the Voltis attack, Gaunt has developed a good working relationship with the armoured brigade, but Sturm's edict has taken the warmth out of it. The Ketzok aren't being difficult with him, they're being difficult with the situation.

'The Ketzok can stay put,' says Gaunt. 'There's no harm getting some exercise though, is there?'

'I suppose not,' Corbec agrees.

'In this muck?' someone in the ranks calls out from behind him.

'That's enough, Larks,' Corbec says without turning. Corbec is a big fellow, tall and broad, and heavy. He raises a large hand, scoops the heavy crop of slightly greying hair out of his face, and flops it over his scalp before tying it back. Raindrops twinkle like diamonds in his beard. Despite the bullying wind, Gaunt can smell a faint odour of cigars on him.

Gaunt wonders how he's going to begin to enforce uniform code when the company colonel looks like a matted and tangled old man of the woods.

'This is just going to be a visit to size the place up,' says Gaunt, looking at Mkoll. 'I intend for us to be back before nightfall.'

Mkoll just nods.

'So what you're saying is you were getting a little bored sitting in your tent,' says Corbec.

Gaunt looks at him.

'That's all right,' Corbec smiles. 'I was getting pretty

bored sitting in mine. A walk is nice, isn't it, lads?'

No one actually answers.

Gaunt walks the line with Corbec at his side, inspecting munition supplies. They're going to be moving light, but every other man's got an extra musette bag of clips, and two troopers are carrying boxes of RPGs for the launcher. Nobody makes eye contact with Gaunt as he passes.

Gaunt comes to Caffran in the line.

'What are you doing here?' Gaunt asks.

'Step forward, trooper,' says Corbec.

'I thought I was supposed to stay with you all day,' Caffran replies, stepping forward. 'I thought those were my orders.'

'Sir,' says Corbec.

'Sir,' says Caffran.

'I suppose they are,' says Gaunt and nods Caffran back into the file. *A march in the mud and rain is the least you deserve for talking out of turn,* Gaunt thinks, *especially to a civilian.*

There's a muttering somewhere. They're amused by Caffran's insolence. Gaunt gets the feeling that Corbec doesn't like it, though Corbec does little to show it. The colonel's position is difficult. If he reinforces Gaunt's authority, he risks losing all the respect the men have for him. He risks being despised and resented too.

'Let's get moving,' says Gaunt.

'Advance company!' Corbec shouts, holding one hand above his head and rotating it with the index finger upright. 'Sergeant Blane, if you please!'

'Yes, sir!' Blane calls out from the front of the formation. He leads off.

The force begins to move down the track into the rain behind the sergeant. Mkoll and his scouts, moving at a more energetic pace, take point and begin to pull away.

Gaunt waits as the infantrymen file past, their boots glopping in the mire. Not one of them so much as glances at him. They have their heads down.

He jogs to catch up with Corbec. He had hoped that getting out and doing something active might chase away his unhappiness. It isn't working so far.

He still has that letter in his pocket.

'BACK AGAIN?' ASKS Dorden, the medicae.

The boy hovers in the doorway of the medical tent like a spectre that needs to be invited in out of the dark. The rain has picked up, and it's pattering a loud tattoo off the overhead sheets.

'I don't feel right,' says Milo.

Dorden tilts his chair back to upright and takes his feet down off the side of a cot. He folds over the corner of a page to mark his place, and sets his book aside.

'Come in, Milo,' he says.

In the back of the long tent behind Dorden, the medicae orderlies are at work checking supplies and cleaning instruments. The morning has brought the usual round of complaints generated by an army on the move: foot problems, gum problems, and gut problems, along with longer term conditions like venereal infections and wounds healing after the Voltis fight. The orderlies are chattering back and forth. Chayker and Foskin are play-fencing with forceps as they gather up instruments for cleaning. Lesp, the other orderly, is bantering with them as he prepares his needles. He's got a sideline as the company inksman. His work is generally held as the best. The ink stains his fingertips permanent blue-black, the dirtiest-looking fingers Dorden's ever seen on a medical orderly.

'How don't you feel right?' Dorden asks as Milo comes in. The boy pulls the tent flap shut behind him and shrugs.

'I just don't,' he says. 'I feel light-headed.'

'Light-headed? Faint, you mean?'

'Things seem familiar. Do you know what I mean?'

Dorden shakes his head gently, frowning.

'Like I'm seeing things again for the first time,' says the boy.

Dorden points to a folding stool, which Milo sits down on obediently, and reaches for his pressure cuff.

'You realise this is the third day you've come in here saying you don't feel right?' asks Dorden.

Milo nods.

'You know what I think it is?' asks Dorden.

'What?'

'I think you're hungry,' says Dorden. 'I know you hate the ration stuff they cook up. I don't blame you. It's swill. But you've got to eat, Brin. That's why you're light-headed and weak.'

'It's not that,' says Milo.

'It might be. You don't like the food.'

'No, I don't like the food. I admit it. But it's not that.'

'What then?'

Milo stares at him.

'I've got this feeling. I think I had a bad dream. I've got this feeling that–'

'What?'

Milo looks at the ground.

'Listen to me,' says Dorden. 'I know you want to stay with us. This man Gaunt is letting you stay. You know he should have sent you away by now. If you get sick on him, if you get sick by refusing to eat properly, he'll have the excuse he needs. He'll be able to tell himself he's sending you away for your own good. And that'll be it.'

Milo nods.

'So let's do you a favour,' says Dorden. 'Let's go to the mess tent and get you something to eat. Humour me. Eat it. If you still feel you're not right, well, then we can have another conversation.'

THE LIGHTNING LEADS them. The rain persists. They come up over the wet hills and see the city grave.

Kosdorf is a great expanse of ruins, most of it pale, like sugar icing. As they approach it, coming in from the south-east, the slumped and toppled hab blocks remind Gaunt more than anything of great, multi-tiered cakes, fancy and celebratory, that have been shoved over so that all the frosted levels have crashed down and overlapped one another, breaking and cracking, and shedding palls of dust that have become mire in the rain. A shroud of vapour hangs over the city, the foggy aftermath of destruction.

Overhead, black clouds mark the sky like ink on pale skin. Shafts of lightning, painfully bright, shoot down from the clouds into the dripping ruins, straight down, without a sound. The bars underlight the belly of the clouds, and set off brief, white flashes in amongst the ruins where they hit, like flares. Though the lightning strikes crackle with secondary sparks, like capillaries adjoining a main blood vessel, they are remarkably straight.

The regular strobing makes the daylight seem strange and impermanent. Everything is pinched and blue, caught in a twilight.

'Why can't we hear it?' one of the men grumbles.

Gaunt has called a stop on a deep embankment so he can check his chart. Tilting, teetering building shells overhang them. Water gurgles out of them.

'Because we can't, Larks,' Corbec says.

Gaunt looks up from his chart, and sees Larkin, the marksman assigned to the advance. The famous Mad Larkin. Gaunt is still learning names to go with faces, but Larkin has stood out from early on. The man can shoot. He's also, it seems to Gaunt, one of the least stable individuals ever to pass recruitment screening. Gaunt presumes the former fact had a significant bearing on the latter.

Larkin is a skinny, unhappy-looking soul with a dragon-spiral inked onto his cheek. His long-las rifle is propped over his shoulder in its weather case.

'Altitude,' Gaunt says to him.

'Come again, sir?' Larkin replies.

Gaunt gestures up at the sky behind the bent, blackened girders of the corpse-buildings above them. Larkin looks where he's pointing, up into the rain.

'The electrical discharge is firing from cloud to cloud up there, and it can reach an intensity of four hundred thousand amps. But we can't hear the thunder, because it's so high up.'

'Oh,' says Larkin. Some of the other men murmur.

'You think I'd march anyone into a dead zone without getting a full orbital sweep first?' Gaunt asks.

Larkin looks like he's going to reply. He looks like he's about to say something he shouldn't, something his brain won't allow his mouth to police.

But he shakes his head instead and smiles.

'Is that so?' he says. 'Too high for us to hear. Well, well.'

They move off down the embankment, and then follow the seam of an old river sluice that hugs the route of a highway into the city. There's a fast stream running down the bed of the drain, dirty rainwater that's washed down through the city ruin, blackened with ash, and then is running off. It splashes and froths around their toecaps. Its babbling sounds like voices, muttering.

There's the noise of the falling rain all around, the sound of dripping. Things creak. Tiles and facings and pieces of roof and guttering hang from shredded bulks, and move as the inclination of gravity or the wind takes them. They squeak like crane hoists, like gibbets. Things fall, and flutter softly or land hard, or skitter and bounce like loose rocks in a ravine.

The scouts vanish ahead of the advance, but Mkoll reappears after half an hour, and describes the route ahead to Corbec. Gaunt stands with them, but there is subtle body language, suggesting that the report is meant for Corbec's benefit, and Gaunt is merely being allowed to listen in. If things turn bad, Mkoll is trusting Corbec to look after the best interests of the men.

'Firestorms have swept through this borough,' he says. 'There's not much of anything left. I suggest we swing east.'

Corbec nods.

'There's something here,' Mkoll adds.

'A friendly something?' Corbec asks.

Mkoll shrugs.

'Hard to say. It won't let us get a look at it. Could be civilian survivors. They would have learned to stay well out of sight.'

'I would have expected any citizens to flee the city,' says Gaunt.

Mkoll and Corbec look at him.

'Flight is not always the solution,' says Mkoll.

'Sometimes, you know, people are traumatised,' says Corbec. 'They go back to a place, even when they shouldn't. Even when it's not safe.'

Mkoll shrugs again.

'It's all I'm saying,' says Corbec.

'I haven't seen bodies,' replies Gaunt. 'When you consider the size of this place, the population it must have had. In fact, I haven't seen any bodies.'

Corbec purses his lips thoughtfully.

'True enough. That *is* curious.' Corbec looks at Mkoll for confirmation.

'I haven't seen any,' says Mkoll. 'But hungry vermin can disintegrate remains inside a week.'

They turn to the east, as per Mkoll's suggestion, and leave the comparative cover of the rockcrete drainage ditch. Buildings have sagged into each other, or fallen into the street in great splashes of rubble and ejecta. Some habs lean on their neighbours for support. All glass has been broken, and the joists and beams and roofs, robbed of tiles or slates, have been turned into dark, barred windows through which to watch the lightning.

The fire has been very great. It has scorched the paving stones of the streets and squares, and the rain has turned the ash into a black paste that sticks to everything, except the heat-transmuted metals and glass from windows and doors. These molten ingots, now solid again, have been washed clean by the rain and lie scattered like iridescent fish on the tarry ground.

Gaunt has seen towns and cities without survivors before. Before Khulan, before the Crusade even began, he'd been with the Hyrkans on Sorsarah. A town there, he forgets the name, an agri-berg, had been under attack, and the town elders had ordered the entire population to shelter in the precincts of the basilica. In doing so, they had become one target.

When Gaunt had come in with the Hyrkans, whole swathes of the town were untouched, intact, preserved, as though the inhabitants would be back at any moment.

The precincts of the basilica formed a crater half a kilometre across.

They stop to rest at the edge of a broad concourse where the wind of Voltemand, brisk and unfriendly, is absent. The rain is relentless still, but the vapour hangs here, a mist that pools around the dismal ruins and broken walls.

They are drawing closer to the grounding lightning. It leaves a bloody stink in their nostrils, like hot wire, and whenever it hits the streets and ruins nearby, it makes a soft but jarring click, part overpressure, part discharge.

An explosive device of considerable magnitude has struck the corner of the concourse and detonated, unseating all the heavy paving slabs with the rippling force of a major earthquake. Gravity has relaid the slabs after the shockwave, but they have come back down to earth misaligned and overlapping, like the scales of a lizard, rather than the seamless, edge-to-edge fit the city fathers had once commissioned.

Larkin sits down on a tumbled block, takes off one boot, and begins to massage his foot. He complains to the men around him in a loud voice. The core of his complaint seems to be the stiff and unyielding quality of the newly-issued Tanith kit.

'Foot sore?' Gaunt asks him.

'These boots don't give. We've walked too far. My toes hurt.'

'Get the medicae to treat your foot when we get back. I don't want any infections.'

Larkin grins up at him.

'I wouldn't want to make my foot worse. Maybe you should carry me.'

'You'll manage,' Gaunt tells him.

'But an infection? That sounds nasty. It can get in your blood. You can die of it.'

'You're right,' Gaunt says. 'The only way to be properly sure is to amputate the extremity before infection can spread.'

He puts his hand on the pommel of his chainsword.

'Is that what you want me to do, Larkin?'

'I'll be happy to live out me born days without that ever happening, colonel-commissar,' Larkin chuckles.

'Get your boot back on.'

Gaunt wanders over to Corbec. The colonel has produced a short, black cigar and clamped it in his mouth, though he hasn't lit it. He takes another out of his pocket and offers it to Gaunt, perhaps hoping that if Gaunt accepts it, it'll give him the latitude to break field statutes and light up. Gaunt refuses the offer.

'Is Larkin taunting me?' Gaunt asks him quietly.

Corbec shakes his head.

'He's nervous,' Corbec replies. 'Larks gets spooked very easily, so this is him dealing with that. Trust me. I've known him since we were in the Tanith Magna Militia together.'

Gaunt throws a half shrug, looking around.

'He's spooked? I'm spooked,' he says.

Corbec smiles so broadly he takes the cigar out of his mouth.

'Good to know,' he says.

'Maybe we should head back,' Gaunt says. 'Push back in tomorrow with some proper armour support.'

'Best plan you've had so far,' says Corbec, 'if I may say so.'

The Tanith scout, the tall, thin man with the menacing

air, appears suddenly at the top of a ridge of rubble and signals before dropping out of sight.

'What the hell?' Gaunt begins to say. He glances around to have the signal explained by Corbec or one of the men.

He is alone on the concourse. The Tanith have vanished.

WHAT THE FETH is he doing, Caffran wonders? He's just standing there. He's just standing there out in the open, when Mkvenner clearly signalled...

He hears a sound like a bundle of sticks being broken, slowly, steadily.

Not sticks, las-shots; the sound echoes around the concourse area. He sees a couple of bolts in the air like luminous birds or lost fragments of lightning.

With a sigh, Caffran launches himself from under the cover of his camo-cloak, and tackles Colonel-Commissar Gaunt to the ground. Further shots fly over them.

'What are you playing at?' Caffran snaps. They struggle to find some cover.

'Where did everyone go?' Gaunt demands, ducking lower as a zipping las-round scorches the edge of his cap.

'Into cover, you feth-wipe!' Caffran replies. 'Get your cloak over you! Come on!'

The ingrained, starch-stiff commissar inside Gaunt wants to reprimand the infantryman for his language and his disrespect, but tone of address is hardly the point in the heat of a contact. Perhaps afterwards. Perhaps a few words afterwards.

Gaunt fumbles out his camo-cloak, still folded up and rolled over the top of his belt pouch. He realises the Tanith haven't vanished at all. At the scout's signal, they have all simply dropped and concealed themselves with their cloaks. They are still all around him. They have simply become part of the landscape.

He, on the other hand, nonplussed for a second, had

remained standing; the lone figure of an Imperial Guard commissar against a bleak, empty background.

The behaviour of a novice. A fool. A... what was it? *Feth-wipe*? Indeed.

Corbec looks over at him, his face framed between the gunsight of his rifle and the fringe of his cape.

'How many?' Gaunt hisses.

'Ven said seven, maybe eight,' Corbec calls back.

Gaunt pulls out his bolt pistol and racks it.

'Return fire,' he orders.

Corbec relays the order, and the advance company begins to shoot. Volleys of las-shots whip across the concourse.

The gunfire coming their way stops.

'Cease fire!' Gaunt commands.

He gets up, and scurries forwards over the rubble, keeping low. Corbec calls after him in protest, but nobody shoots at Gaunt. You didn't have to be a graduate of a fancy military academy, Corbec reflects, to appreciate that was a good sign. He sighs, gets up, and goes after Gaunt. They move forwards together, heads down.

'Look here,' says Corbec.

Two bodies lie on the rubble. They are wearing the armoured uniform of the local PDF, caked with black mud. Their cheeks are sunken, as if neither of them have eaten a decent plate of anything in a month.

'Damn,' says Gaunt, 'was that a mistaken exchange? Have we hit some friendlies? These are planetary defence force.'

'I think you're right,' says Corbec.

'I am right. Look at the insignia.'

'Poor fething bastards,' says Corbec. 'Maybe they've been holed up here for so long, they thought we were–'

'No,' says Mkoll.

Gaunt hasn't seen the scout standing there. Even Corbec seems to start slightly, though Gaunt wonders if this is for comic effect. Corbec is unfailingly cheerful.

The chief scout has manifested even more mysteriously than the Tanith had vanished a few minutes ago.

'There was a group of them,' he says, 'a patrol. Mkvenner and I had contact. We challenged them, making the same assumption you just did, that they were PDF. There was no mistake.'

'What do you mean?' asks Gaunt.

'I thought maybe they were scared,' says Mkoll, 'scared of everything. Survivors in the rubble, afraid that anything they bumped into might be the Archenemy. But this wasn't scared.'

'How do you know?' asks Gaunt.

'He knows,' says Corbec.

'I'd like him to explain,' says Gaunt.

'You know the difference between scared and crazy, sir?' Mkoll asks him.

'I think so,' says Gaunt.

'These men were crazy. There were speaking in strange tongues. They were ranting. They were using language I've never heard before, a language I never much want to hear again.'

'So you think there are Archenemy strengths here in Kosdorf, and they're using PDF arms and uniforms?'

Mkoll nods. 'I heard the tribal forces often use captured Guard kit.'

'That's true enough,' says Gaunt.

'Where did the others go?' asks Corbec, looking down at the corpses glumly.

'They ran when your first couple of volleys brought these two over,' says Mkoll.

'Let's circle up and head back,' says Corbec.

There's a sudden noise, a voice, gunfire. One of the other scouts has reappeared. He is hurrying back across the fish-scale slabs of the square towards them, firing off bursts from the hip. A rain of las-fire answers him. It cracks paving stones, pings pebbles, and spits up plumes of muck.

'Find cover!' the scout yells as he comes towards them. 'Find cover!'

They have jammed a stick into the ruins of Kosdorf, and wiggled it around until the nest underneath the city has been thoroughly disturbed.

Hostiles in PDF kit, caked in dirt, looking feral and thin, are assaulting the concourse area through the ruins of an old Ecclesiarchy temple and, to the west of that, the bones of a pauper's hospital.

They look like ghosts.

They come surging forwards, out of the dripping shadows, through the mist, into the strobing twilight. In their captured kit, they look to Gaunt like war-shocked survivors trying to defend what's left of their world.

'Fall back!' Corbec yells.

'I don't want to fight them,' Gaunt says to him as they run for better cover. 'Not if they're our own!'

'Mkoll was pretty sure they weren't!'

'He could have been wrong. These could be our people, come through hell. I don't want to fight them unless I have to.'

'I don't think they're going to give us a choice!' Corbec yells back.

The Tanith are returning fire, snapping shots from their corner of the open space. The air fills with a laced crossfire of energy bolts. The mist seems to thicken as the crossfire stirs the air. Gaunt sees a couple of the men in Kosdorfer uniforms crumple and fall.

'In the name of the Emperor, cease your firing,' he hollers out across the square. 'For Throne's sake, we serve the same master!'

The Kosdorf PDFers shout back. The words are unintelligible, hard to make out over their sustained gunfire.

'I said in the name of the Emperor, hold your fire,' Gaunt bellows. 'Hold your fire. I command you! We're here to help you!'

A PDFer comes at him from the left, running out of the shadows of the hospital ruins. The man has a hard-round rifle equipped with a sword bayonet. His eyes are swollen in their sockets, and one pupil has blown.

He tries to ram the bayonet into Gaunt's gut. The
blade is rusty, but the thrust is strong and practiced.
Gaunt leaps backwards.

'For the Emperor!' Gaunt yells.

The man replies with a jabbering stream of obscenity.
The words are broken, and have been purloined from
an alien language, and he is only able to pronounce
the parts of them that fit a human mouth and voice-
box. Blood leaks out of his gums and dribbles over his
cracked lips.

He lunges again. The tip of the sword bayonet goes
through Gaunt's storm coat and snags the hip pocket of
his field jacket underneath.

Gaunt shoots the man in the face with his bolt pistol.

The corpse goes over backwards, hard. Bloody back-
spatter over-paints the dirt filming Gaunt's face and
clothes.

'Fire, fire! Fire at will!' Gaunt yells. He's seen enough.
'Men of Tanith, pick your targets and fire at will!'

Another PDFer charges in at him through an archway,
backlit for a second by a pulse of lightning. He fires a
shot from his rifle that hits the wall behind Gaunt and
adds to the wet haze fuming the air. Gaunt fires back
and knocks the man out of the archway, tumbling into
two of his brethren.

The Tanith advance has been rotated out of line by
the sudden attack, and Gaunt has been pushed to the
eastern end of the formation. He has lost sight of Corbec. It is hard to issue any useful commands, because he
has little proper overview on which to base command
choices.

Gaunt tries to reposition himself. He hugs the shadows, keeping the crumbling pillars to his back. The
firefight has lit up the entire concourse. He listens to
the echoes, to the significant sound values coming off
the Tanith positions. Gaunt can hear the hard clatter
of full auto and, in places along the rubble line, see
the jumping petals of muzzle flashes. The Tanith are

eager, but inexperienced. The lasrifles they have been issued with at the Founding are good, new weapons, fresh-stamped and shipped in from forge worlds. Many of the Tanith recruits will never have had an automatic setting on a weapon before; most will have been used to single shot or even hard-round weapons. Finding themselves in a troop-fight ambush, they are unleashing maximum firepower, which is great for shock and noise but not necessarily the most effective tactic, under any circumstances.

'Corbec!' Gaunt yells. 'Colonel Corbec! Tell the men to select single f–'

He ducks back as his voice draws enemy fire. Plumes of mire and slime spurt up from the slabs he is using as cover. Impacts spit out stinging particles of stone. He tries shouting again, but the concentration of fire gets worse. The vapour billowing off the shot marks gets in his mouth and makes him retch and spit. Two or three of the PDFers have advanced on his position, and are keeping a heavy fire rate sustained. He can half see them through the veiling mist, calmly standing and taking shots at him. He can't see them well enough to get a decent shot back.

Gaunt scrambles backwards, dropping down about a metre between one rucked level of paving slabs and another, an ugly seismic fracture in the street. Loose shots are whining over his head, smacking into the plaster facade of a reclining guild house and covering it with black pockmarks. He clambers in through a staring window.

A Tanith trooper inside switches aim at him and nearly shoots him.

'Sacred Feth. Sorry, sir!' the trooper exclaims.

Gaunt shakes his head.

'I snuck up on you,' he replies.

There are four Tanith men in the ground floor of the guild house. They are using the buckled window apertures to lay fire across the concourse from the east. They'd been on the eastern end of the advance force when it turned unexpectedly, and thus have been effectively cut off. Gaunt can't chastise them. Oddities of terrain and the dynamic flow of a combat situation do that sometimes. Sometimes you just get stuck in a tight corner.

For similar reasons, he's got stuck there with them.

'What's your name?' he asks the man who'd almost shot him, even though he knows it perfectly well.

'Domor,' the man replies.

'I don't think we want to spend too much more time in here, do we, Domor?' Gaunt says. Enemy fire is pattering off the outside walls with increasing fury. It is causing the building to vibrate, and spills of earth, like sand in a time-glass, are sifting down from the bulging roof. There's a stink of sewage, of broken drains. If enemy fire doesn't finish them, it will finish the building, which will die on their heads.

'I'd certainly like to get out of here if I can, sir,' Domor replies. He has a sharp, intelligent face, with quick eyes that suggest wit and honesty.

'Well, we'll see what we can do,' Gaunt says.

One of the other men groans suddenly.

'What's up, Piet?' Domor calls. 'You hit?'

The trooper is down at one of the windows, pinking rounds off into the concourse outside.

'I'm fine,' he answers, 'but do you hear that?'

Gaunt and Domor clamber up to the sill alongside him. For a moment, Gaunt can't hear anything except the snap and whine of las-fire, and the brittle rattle of masonry debris falling from the roof above.

Then he hears it, a deeper noise, a throaty rasp.

'Someone's got a burner,' says the trooper in a depressed tone. 'Someone out there's got a burner.'

Domor looks at Gaunt.

'Gutes is right, isn't he?' he asks. 'That's a flamer, isn't it? That's the noise a flamer makes?'

Gaunt nods.

'Yes,' he says.

* * *

NONE OF THE Munitorum skivvies has the nerve to argue when Feygor helps himself to one of the full pots of caffeine on the mess tent stove.

Feygor carries the pot over to where Rawne is sitting at a mess table with the usual repeat offenders. Meryn, young and eager to impress, has brought a tray of tin cups. Brostin is smoking a lho-stick and flicking his brass igniter open and shut. Raess is cleaning his scope. Caober is putting an edge on his blade. Costin has produced his flask, and is pouring a jigger of sacra into each mug 'to keep the rain out'.

Feygor dishes out the brew from the pot.

'Come on, then,' says Rawne.

Varl grins, and slides the letter out of his inside pocket. He holds it gently by the bottom corners and sniffs it, as though it is a perfumed billet-doux. Then he licks the tip of his right index finger to lift the envelope's flap.

He starts to read to himself.

'Oh my!' he says.

'What?' asks Meryn.

'Listen to this... *My darling Ibram, how I long for your strong, manly touch...*' Varl begins, as if reading aloud.

'Don't be a feth-head, Varl,' warns Rawne. 'What does it actually say?'

'It's from somebody called Blenner,' says Varl, scanning the sheet. 'It goes on a bit. Umm, I think they knew each other years back. And from the date on this, he's been carrying it around for a while. This Blenner says he's writing because he can't believe that Gaunt got passed over after "all he did at Balhaut". He's asking Gaunt if he chose to go with "that bunch of no-hope backwoodsmen", which I think would be us.'

'It would,' says Rawne.

Varl sniffs. 'Anyway, this charming fellow Blenner says he can't believe Gaunt would have taken the field promotion willingly. Listen to this, he says, "what was Slaydo thinking? Surely the Old Man had made provision for you to be part of the command structure that succeeded him. Throne's sake, Ibram! You know he was grooming! How did you let this slight happen to you? Slaydo's legacy would have protected you for years if you'd let it".'

Varl looks up at the Tanith men around the table. 'Wasn't Slaydo the name of the Warmaster?' he asks. 'The big honking bastard commander?'

'Yup,' says Feygor.

'Well, this can't mean the same Slaydo, can it?' asks Costin.

'Of course it can't,' says Caober. 'It must be another Slaydo.'

'Well, of course,' says Varl, 'because otherwise it would mean that the feth-wipe commanding us is a more important feth-wipe than we ever imagined.'

'It doesn't mean that,' says Rawne. 'Costin's right. It's a different Slaydo, or this Blenner doesn't know what he's talking about. Go on. What else is there?'

Varl works down the sheet.

'Blenner finishes by saying that he's stationed on Hisk with a regiment called the Greygorians. He says he's got pull with a Lord General called Cybon, and that Cybon's promised him, that is Gaunt, a staff position. Blenner begs Gaunt to reconsider his "ill-advised" move and get reassigned.'

'That's it?' asks Rawne.

Varl nods.

'So he's thinking about ditching us,' murmurs Rawne.

'This letter's old, mind you,' says Varl.

'But he kept it,' says Feygor. 'It matters to him.'

'Murt's right,' says Rawne. 'This means his heart's not in it. We can exert a little pressure, and get rid of this fether without any of us having to face a firing squad.'

'Having fun?'

They all turn. Dorden is standing nearby, watching them. The boy Milo is behind him, looking pale and nervous.

'We're fine, Doc,' says Feygor. 'How are you?'

'Looks for all the world like a meeting of plotters,' says Dorden. He takes a step forwards and comes in amongst them. He's twice as old as any of them, like their grandfather. He's no fighter either. Every one of them is a young man, strong enough to break him and kill him with ease. He pours himself a mug of caffeine from their tray.

Costin makes a hasty but abortive attempt to stop him.

'There's a little–' Costin begins, in alarm.

'Sacra in it?' asks Dorden, sipping. 'I should hope so, cold day like this.'

He looks across at Varl.

'What's that you've got, Varl?'

'A letter, Doc.'

'Does it belong to you?'

'Uh, not completely.'

'Did you borrow it?'

'It fell out of someone's pocket, Doc.'

'Do you think it had better fall back in?' asks Dorden.

'I think that would be a good idea,' says Varl.

'We were just having a conversation, doctor,' says Rawne. 'No plots, no conspiracies.'

'I believe you,' Dorden replies. 'Just like I believe that no lies would ever, ever come out of your mouth, major.'

'With respect, doctor,' says Rawne, 'I'm having a private conversation with some good comrades, and the substance of it is of no consequence to you.'

Dorden nods.

'Of course, major,' he replies. 'Just as I'm here to find a plate of food for this boy and minding my own business.'

He turns to talk to the cooks about finding something other than slab in the ration crates.

Then he looks back at Rawne.

'Consider this, though. They say it's always best to

know your enemy. If you succeed in ousting Colonel-Commissar Gaunt, who might you be making room for?'

'WHERE'S THE CHIEF?' Corbec asks, ducking in.

'Frankly, I've been too busy to keep tabs on that gigantic fether,' Larkin replies.

'Oh, Larks,' murmurs Corbec over the drumming of infantry weapons, 'that lip of yours is going to get you dead before too long unless you curb it. Disrespecting a superior, it's called.'

Larkin sneers at his old friend.

'Right,' he says. 'You'd write me up.'

He is adjusting the replacement barrel of his long-las, hunkered down behind the cyclopean plinth of a heap of rubble that had once been a piece of civic statuary.

'Of course I would,' says Corbec. 'I'd have to.'

Corbec has got down on one knee on the other side of a narrow gap between the plinth and a retaining wall that is leaning at a forty-five degree angle. Solid-round fire from the enemy is travelling up the gap between them, channelled by the actual physical shape, like steel pinballs coursing along a chute. The shots scrape and squeal as they whistle past.

Corbec clacks in a fresh clip and leans out gingerly to snap some discouraging las-rounds back up the gap.

'Why?' Larkin asks. 'Why would you have to?'

Larkin laughs, mirthlessly. Corbec can almost smell the rank adrenaline sweat coming out of the wiry marksman's pores. The stress of a combat situation has pushed Larkin towards his own, personal edge, and he is barely in control.

'Because I'm the fething colonel, and I can't have you bad-mouthing the company commander,' Corbec replies.

'Yeah, but you're not really, are you?' says Larkin. 'I mean, you're not really my superior, are you?'

'What?'

'Gaunt just picked you and Rawne. It was random. It doesn't mean anything. There's no point you carrying on like there's suddenly any difference between us.'

Corbec gazes across at Larkin, watching him screw the barrel in, nattering away, stray rounds tumbling past them like seed cases in a gale.

'I mean, it's not like your shit suddenly smells better than mine, is it?' says Larkin. He looks up at last and sees Corbec's face.

'What?' he asks. 'What's the matter with you?'

Corbec glares at him.

'I am the colonel, Larks,' he snarls. 'That's the point. I'm not your friend any more. This is either real or there's no point to it at all.'

Larkin just looks at him.

'Oh, for feth's sake!' says Corbec. 'Stop looking at me with those stupid hang-dog eyes! Hold this position. That's an order, trooper! Mkoll!'

The chief scout comes scurrying over from the other corner of the plinth, head down. He drops in behind Larkin and looks across the gap at Corbec.

'Sergeant Blane's got the top end of the line firm. I'm going back down that way,' Corbec says, jerking a thumb over his shoulder. 'We seem to have lost Gaunt.'

'It's tragic,' says Larkin.

'Keep this section in place,' Corbec continues.

Mkoll nods. Corbec sets off.

'What's got into him?' Larkin mutters.

'Probably something you said,' says Mkoll.

'I don't say anything we're not all thinking,' Larkin replies.

OUTSIDE, THE FLAMER makes its sucking roar again.

All four of the Tanith men with Gaunt express their unhappiness in strong terms. Gutes and Domor are cursing.

'We're done for,' says another of them, a man called Guheen.

'They'll just torch us out like larisel in a burrow,' says the fourth.

'Maybe–' Gaunt begins.

'No maybe about it!' Gutes spits.

'No, I was trying to say, maybe this gives us a chance we didn't have before,' Gaunt tells them.

He ducks down beside Gutes again, and peers out into the mist and rain, craning for a better view. There is still no sign of the flamer, but he can certainly hear it clearly now, retching like some volcanic hog clearing its throat. He can smell promethium smoke too, the soot-black stench of Imperial cleansing.

He looks up at the ominously low ceiling bellying down at them.

'What's upstairs?' he asks.

'Another floor,' says Guheen.

'Presuming it's not all crushed in on itself,' adds Domor.

'Yes, presuming it's not,' Gaunt agrees. 'Which of you is the best shot?'

'He is,' Domor says, pointing to the fourth man. Guheen and Gutes both nod assent.

'Merrt, isn't it?' Gaunt asks. The fourth man nods.

'Merrt, you're with me. You three, sustained fire pattern here, through these windows. Just keep it steady.'

Gaunt clambers over the scree of rubble and broken furniture to the back of the chamber. A great deal of debris has poured down what had once been the staircase, blocking it. Wires and cabling hang from ruptured ceiling panels like intestinal loops. Water drips. Broken glass flickers when the lightning scores the sky outside.

Merrt comes up behind Gaunt and touches his arm. He points to the remains of a heat exchanger vent that is crushed into the rear wall of the guild house like a metal plug. They put their shoulders against it and manage to push it out of its setting.

Light shines in. The hole, now more of a slot thanks to the deformation of the building, looks directly out on to rubble at eye level. They hoist themselves up and out, on to the smashed residue of a neighbouring building that has been annihilated, and has flooded its remains down and around the guild house, packing in around its slumped form like a lava flow sweeping an object up.

Gaunt and Merrt pick their way up the slope, and re-enter the guild house through a first-floor window. The floor is sagging and insecure. A few fibres of waterlogged carpet seem to be all that's holding the joists in place.

'You're a decent shot, then?' Gaunt murmurs.

'Not bad.'

'Pull this off, I'll recommend you for a marksman lanyard.'

Merrt grins and flashes his eyebrows.

'Should've got one anyway,' he says. 'The last one went to Larkin. After his psyche evaluation, marksman status was the only special dispensation Corbec could pull to get his old mate a place in the company.'

'Is that true?' Gaunt asks.

'You ought to know. I thought you were in charge?'

Gaunt stares at him.

'I'm really looking forward to meeting a Tanith who isn't insolent or cocksure,' says Gaunt.

'Good luck with that,' says Merrt.

Gaunt shakes his head.

'I've got a smart mouth, I know,' says Merrt. 'I said a few things about Larkin getting my lanyard, earned some dark looks from the Munitorum chiefs. My mouth'll get me in trouble, one day, I reckon.'

'I think you're already in trouble,' says Gaunt. He gestures out of the window. 'I think this qualifies.'

'Feels like it.'

'So you reckon you're good?'

'Better than Larkin,' says Merrt.

They settle in by the window. The mist shrouding the concourse and the surrounding ruins has grown thicker, as though the discharge of weapons has caused some chemical reaction, and it's disguising the enemy approach.

Below, about fifteen metres shy of them, they can see the blasts of the approaching flamer, like a sun behind cloud.

'Nasty weapon, the flamer,' says Gaunt.

'I can well imagine.'

'Then again, it is essentially a can or two of extremely flammable material.'

'You going to be my shot caller?' Merrt asks.

'We have to let it get a little closer,' says Gaunt. 'You see where it burps like that?'

Another gout of amber radiance backlights the fog in the square below.

Merrt nods, raising the lasrifle to his shoulder.

'Watch which way the glow moves. It's moving out from the flamer broom.'

'Got it.'

'So the point of origin is going to be behind it, and the tank or tanks another, what, half a metre behind that?'

The flamer roars again. A long, curling rush of fire, like the leaf of a giant fern, emerges from the mist and brushes the front of the guild house. Gaunt hears Domor curse loudly.

'He's widened the aperture,' Gaunt tells Merrt. 'He's seen buildings ahead, and he's put a bit of reach on the flame, so he can scour the ruins out.'

Merrt grunts.

'We've got to do this if we're going to,' says Gaunt.

There is another popping cough and then another roar. This time, the curling arc of fire comes up high, like the jet of a pressurised hose.

Gaunt grabs Merrt, and pulls him back as the fire blisters the first-storey windows. It spills in through the window spaces, roasting the frames and sizzling the wet black filth, and plays in across the ceiling like a catch of golden fish, coiling and squirming in a mass, landed on the deck of a boat.

The flames suck out again, leaving the windows scorched around their upper frames and the ceiling blackened above the windows. All the air seems to have gone out of the room. Gaunt and Merrt gasp as if they too have just been landed out of a sea net.

Gaunt recovers the lasrifle and checks it for damage. Merrt picks himself up.

'Come on!' Gaunt hisses.

As Merrt settles into position again, Gaunt peers down into the swirl.

'There! There!' he cries, as the flames jet through the mist and rain again.

Merrt fires.

Nothing happens.

'Feth!' Merrt whispers.

'When the flame lights up, aim closer to the source,' Gaunt says.

The flamer gusts again, ripping fire at the front of the guild house.

Merrt fires again.

The tanks go up with a pressurised squeal. A huge doughnut of fire rips through the mist, rolling and coiling, yellow-hot and furious. Several broken metal objects soar into the air on streamers of flame, shrieking like parts of an exploding kettle.

Gaunt raises his head cautiously and looks down. He can see burning figures stumbling around in the fog, PDF troopers caught in the blast. They sizzle loudly in the rain.

'Let's get out of here,' he says to Merrt.

Gaunt calls to the three Tanith men below, and all five leave the guild house together and work their way back along the edge of the concourse to the advance main force, skirting the open spaces.

'I've been looking for you,' says Corbec matter-of-factly when Gaunt appears.

'Not hard enough, I'd say,' Gaunt replies.

Corbec tuts, half entertained.

'You set something off over there?' he asks.

'Just a little parlour trick to keep them occupied while we got out of their way.'

'"A little parlour trick"...' Corbec chuckles. 'You're a very amusing man, you know that?'

'Wait till you get to know me,' says Gaunt.

Corbec looks at him sadly and says nothing.

'What shape are we in, colonel?' Gaunt asks.

'Fair,' Corbec replies.

'No losses so far?'

'Couple of scratches. But look, their numbers are increasing all the time. Another hour or so, we could start losing friends fast.'

'Can we vox in for support?'

'The vox is still dead as dead,' says Corbec.

'Recommendation?'

'We pull back before the situation becomes untenable. Then we rustle up some proper strength, come back in, finish the job.'

Gaunt nods.

'There are problems with that,' he says.

'Do tell.'

'For a start, I'm still not sure who we're fighting.'

'It's tribal Archenemy,' says Corbec, 'like Mkoll says. They've just ransacked the city arsenal.'

Gaunt touches his arm and draws him out of earshot.

'You never left Tanith before, did you, Corbec?'

'No, sir.'

'Never fought on a foreign front?'

'I've been taught about the barbaric nature of the Archenemy, if that's what you're worried about. All their cults and their ritual ways–'

'Corbec, you don't know the half of it.'

Corbec looks at him.

'I think they *are* Kosdorfers,' Gaunt says. 'I think they were, anyway. I think the Ruinous Powers, may they stand accursed, have salvaged more than kit and equipment. I think they've salvaged men too.'

'Feth,' Corbec breathes. Rain drips off his beard.

'I know,' says Gaunt.

'The very thought of it.'

'I need you to keep that to yourself. Don't say anything to the men.'

'Of course.'

'None of them, colonel.'

'Yes. Yes, all right.'

Corbec's taken one of his cigars out again and stuck it in his mouth, unlit.

'Just light the damn thing,' says Gaunt.

Corbec obeys. His hands shake as he strikes the lucifer.

'You want one?'

'No,' says Gaunt.

Corbec puffs.

'All right,' he says. He looks at Gaunt.

'All right,' says Gaunt, 'if we give ground here and try to fall back, we leave ourselves open. If they take us out on the way home, they'll be all over our main force without warning. But if we can manage to keep their attention here while we relay a message back...'

Corbec frowns. 'That's a feth of a lot to ask, by any standards.'

'What, the message run or the action?' asks Gaunt.

'Both,' says Corbec.

'You entirely comfortable with the alternative, Corbec?'

Corbec shrugs. 'You know I'm not.'

'Then strengthen our position here, colonel,' Gaunt says. 'We can afford to drop back a little if necessary. Given the visibility issues, the concourse isn't helping us much.'

'What do you suggest?' asks Corbec.

'I suggest you ask Mkoll and his scouts. I suggest we make the best of that resource.'

'Yes, sir.'

Corbec turns to go.

'Corbec – another thing. Tell the men to select single shot. Mandatory, please. Full auto is wasting munitions.'

'Yes, sir.'

Corbec stubs out his cigar and moves away. Keeping his head down, Gaunt moves along the shooting line of jumbled pavers and column bases in the opposite direction.

'Trooper!'

Caffran looks up from his firing position.

'Yes, sir?'

'It's your lucky day,' says Gaunt.

He gets down beside Caffran and reaches into his jacket pockets for his stylus and a clean message wafer.

His hip pocket is torn open and flapping. It's empty. He checks all the pockets of his jacket and the pockets of his storm coat, but his stylus and the wafer pad have gone.

'Do you have the despatch bag, Caffran?'

Caffran nods, and pulls the loop of the small message satchel off over his head. Gaunt opens it, and sees it is in order: fresh message wafers, a stylus, and a couple of signal flares. Caffran has taken his duty seriously.

Gaunt begins writing on one of the wafers rapidly. He uses a gridded sheet to draw up a simple expression of their route and the layout of the city's south-eastern zone, copying from his waterproof chart. Rain taps on the sheet.

'I need you to take this back to Major Rawne,' he says as he writes. 'Understand that we need to warn him of the enemy presence here and summon his support.'

Gaunt finishes writing and presses the setting of his signet ring against the code seal of the wafer, authorising it.

'Caffran, do you understand?'

Caffran nods. Gaunt puts the wafer back into the message satchel.

'Am I to go on my own?' Caffran asks.

'I can't spare more than one man for this, Caffran,' says Gaunt.

The young man looks at him, considers it. Gaunt is a man who quite bloodlessly orders the death of people to achieve his goals. This is what's happening now. Caffran understands that. Caffran understands he is being used as an instrument, and that if he fails and dies, it'll be no more to Gaunt than a shovel breaking in a ditch or a button coming off a shirt. Gaunt has no actual interest in Caffran's life or the manner of its ending.

Caffran purses his lips and then nods again. He hands his lasrifle and the munition spares he was carrying to Gaunt.

'That'll just weigh me down. Somebody else better have them.'

The young trooper gets up, takes a last look at Gaunt, and then begins to pick his way down through the ruined street behind the advance position, keeping his head down.

Gaunt watches him until he's out of sight.

UNDER MKOLL'S INSTRUCTION, the advance gives ground.

Working as spotters out on the flanks, Mkoll's scouts, Bonin and Mkvenner, have pushed the estimate of enemy numbers beyond eight hundred. Gaunt doesn't want to show that he is already regretting his decision not to pull out while the going was good.

Against lengthening, lousy odds, he's committed his small force to the worst kind of combat, the grinding city fight, where mid-range weapons and tactics become compressed into viciously barbaric struggles that depend on reaction time, perception and, worst of all, luck.

The Tanith disengage from the edge of the concourse, which has become entirely clouded in a rising white fog of vapour lifted by the sustained firefight, and drop back into the city block at the south-west corner. Here there are two particularly large habitat structures, which have slumped upon themselves like settling pastry, a long manufactory whose chimneys have toppled like felled trees, and a data library.

The scouts lead them into the warren of ruined halls and broken floors. It is raining inside many of the chambers. Roofs are missing, or water is simply descending through ruptured layers of building fabric. The Tanith melt from view into the shadows. They cover their cloaks with the black dirt from the concourse, and it helps them to merge with the dripping shadows. Gaunt does as they do. He smears the dirt onto his coat and pulls the cloak on over the top, aware that he is looking less and less like a respectable Imperial officer. Damn it, his storm coat is torn and his jacket is ruined anyway.

They work into the habs. Gunfire cracks and echoes along the forlorn walkways and corridors. Broken water pipes, weeping and foul, protrude from walls and floors like tree stumps. The tiled floor, what little of it survives, is covered with broken glass and pot shards from crockery that has been fragmented by the concussion of war.

Gaunt has kept hold of Caffran's rifle. He's holstered his pistol and got the infantry weapon cinched across his torso, ready to fire. It's a long time since he's seen combat with a rifle in his hands.

Mkoll looms out of the filmy mist that fills the air. He is directing the Tanith forward. He looks at Gaunt and then takes Gaunt's cap off his head.

'Excuse me?' says Gaunt.

Mkoll wipes his index finger along a wall, begrimes it, and then rubs the tip over the silver aquila badge on Gaunt's cap.

He hands it back.

'It's catching the light,' says Mkoll.

'I see. And it's not advisable to wear a target on my head.'

'I just don't want you drawing fire down on our unit.'

'Of course you don't,' says Gaunt.

Every few minutes the gunfire dies away. A period of silence follows as the enemy closes in tighter, listening for movement. The only sound is the downpour. The entire environment is a source of noise: debris and rubble can be dislodged, kicked, disturbed, larger items of wreckage can be knocked over or banged into. Damaged floors groan and creak. Windows and doors protest any attempt to move them. When a weapon is discharged, the echoes set up inside the ruined buildings are a great way of locating the point of origin.

The Tanith are supremely good at this. Gaunt witnesses several occasions when a trooper makes a rattle out of a stone in an old tin cup or pot and sets up a noise to tempt a shot from the demented Kosdorfers. As soon as the shot comes, another Tanith trooper gauges the source of the bouncing echo and returns fire with a lethal volley.

The enemy becomes wise to the tricks, and starts acting more circumspectly. Unable to out-stalk the Tanith, the Kosdorfers begin to call out to them from the darkness.

It is unnerving. The voices are distant and pleading. Little sense can be made of them in terms of meaning, but the tone is clear. It is misery. They are the voices of the damned.

'Ignore them,' Gaunt orders.

They have to stick tight. The enemy has a numerical advantage. By getting out of the open, the Tanith has forced its own spatial advantage.

Gaunt wonders if it will be enough.

The ruins still feel like a grave site, a waste of mouldering funereal rot. He wonders if this place will mark the end of his life and soldiering career; a well-thought-of officer who wound up dying in some strategically worthless location because he didn't make the right choices, or shake the right hand, or whisper in the right ear, or dine with the right cliques. He's seen men make high rank that way, through the persuasive power of the officers' club and the staff coterie. They were politicians, politicians who got to execute their decisions in the most literal way. Some were very capable, most were not. Gaunt believes that there is no substitute at all for practical apprenticeship, for field learning to properly supplement the study of military texts and the codices of combat. Slaydo had believed that too, as had Oktar, Gaunt's first mentor.

The vast mechanism of the Imperial Guard, as a rule, did not. Slaydo had once said that he believed he could, through proper reform of the Guard, improve its efficiency by fifty or sixty per cent. Soberly, he had added that mankind was probably too busy fighting wars to ever initiate such reforms.

There is truth in that. Gaunt knows for a fact that Slaydo had a reform bill in mind to take to the Munitorum after the Gorikan Suppression, and again after Khulan. Every time, a new campaign beckoned, a new theatre loomed to occupy the attentions of military planners and commanders. The Sabbat Worlds, now it was the Sabbat Worlds. Slaydo had committed to it mainly, Gaunt knew, for personal reasons. After Khulan, the High Lords had tempted Slaydo with many offers: he'd had the pick of campaigns. He had turned them down, hoping to pursue a more executive office in the latter part of his life and work to the fundamental improvement of the Imperial Guard, which he believed had the capacity to be the finest fighting force in known space.

However, the High Lords had outplayed him. They had discovered his old and passionate fondness for the piety of Saint Sabbat Beati and the territories she had touched, and they had exploited it. The Sabbat Worlds had long since been thought of as unrecoverable, lost to the predations of the Ruinous Powers spreading from the so-called Sanguinary Worlds. No commander wanted to embrace such a career-destroying challenge. The High Lords wanted a leader who would stage the offensive with conviction. They sweetened the offer with the rank of Warmaster, sensing that Slaydo would be unable to resist the opportunity to liberate a significant territory of the Imperium that he felt had been woefully neglected and left to over-run, and at the same to acquire a status that allowed him much greater political firepower to achieve his reforms.

Instead, Balhaut had killed him. All he accomplished was the commencement of a military campaign that was likely to last generations and cost trillions of lives.

Thus are dreams dashed and good intentions lost. Everything returns to the dust, and everything is reduced to blind fighting in the shadowed ruins of cities against men who were brothers until madness claimed their minds.

Everything returns to the dirt, and the dirt becomes your camouflage, and hides your face and your cap badge in the dark, when death comes, growling, to find you out.

FACED ALONE, OUT of sight of the other men, the ruination of Kosdorf brings tears into his eyes.

Caffran understands the urgency of his mission, but he's also smart enough not to run. Headlong running, as the chief scout has pointed out so often, just propels a man into the open, into open spaces he hasn't checked first, across hidden objects that might be pressure-sensitive, through invisible wires, into the line of predatory gunsights.

Caffran is fit, as physically fit as any of the younger men who've been salvaged from Tanith. That's one of the reasons he's been selected as a courier.

The advance came into the grave city as a unit, testing its way and proceeding with recon. Now he's exiting alone, a solitary trooper, protected by his wits and training. There's no doubt in his mind that the enemy will have spread strengths out through the dead boroughs surrounding the fighting zone to catch any stragglers.

Kosdorf reminds him of Tanith Magna. Architecturally, it's nothing like it, of course. Tanith Magna was a smaller burg, high-walled, a gathering of predominantly dark stone towers and spires rising from the emerald canopy of Tanith like a monolith. It had nothing of

Kosdorf's dank, white, mausoleum quality. It's simply the mortality of Kosdorf that has stabbed him in the heart. Caffran knows that Tanith Magna doesn't even persist as a ruin any more, but Voltemand's second city, in death, inevitably makes him think of it, and the ruins become a substitute for his loss.

More than once, he feels quite sure he knows a street, or a particular corner. Memories superimpose themselves over alien habs and thoroughfares, and nostalgia, fletched with unbearable melancholy, spears him. He thinks he recognises one flattened frontage as the public house where he used to meet his friends, another shell as the mill shop where he had been apprenticed, and a broken walkway as the narrow street that had always taken him to the diocese temple. A patch of burned wasteland and twisted wire is most certainly the street market where he sometimes bought vegetables and meat for his ageing mother.

This terrace, this terrace with its cracked and broken flagstones, is definitely the square beside the Elector's Gardens, where he used to meet Laria. He can smell nalwood—

He can smell wet ash. Lightning jags silently.

He wipes a knuckle across his cheekbone, knowing that humiliating tears are mixing with the rain on his face.

He takes a deep breath. He isn't concentrating. He isn't paying enough attention. He stops to get his bearings, trusting the innate wiring of the Tanith mind to sense direction.

If the God-Emperor, who Caffran dutifully worshipped all his life at the little diocese temple, has seen fit to take everything away from him except this single duty, then Caffran is fething well determined to do it properly. He—

He feels the hairs prick up on the back of his neck.

The las-shot misses his face by about a palm's length. Just the slightest tremor of a trigger finger was the difference between a miss and a solid headshot. The light and noise of it rock him, the heat sears him, flash-drying the dirty tears and rain on his cheek into a crust.

Caffran throws himself down, and rolls into cover. He scrabbles in behind the foundation stones of a levelled building. Two more rounds pass over him, and then a hard round hits the block to his left. Caffran hears the distinctly different sound quality of the impact.

He thanks the God-Emperor with a nod. The enemy has just provided information. A minimum of two shooters, not one.

Caffran gets lower still. With his face almost pressing into the ooze, he repositions himself, and risks a look around the stone blocks.

Another shot whines past him, but it is speculative. The shooter hasn't seen him. A filthy PDFer is hopping across the rubble towards his position, clutching an old autorifle. He looks like a hobbled beggar. The puttee around one of his calves is loose and trailing, and his breeches are torn. His face is concealed by an old gas mask. The air pipe swings like a proboscis, unattached to any air tank. One of the glass eye discs is missing.

Behind him, a distance back, a second PDFer stands on the top of a sloping section of roof that is lying across a street. He has a lascarbine raised to his shoulder and sighted. As the PDFer in the gas mask approaches, the other one clips off in Caffran's general direction.

Caffran draws his only weapon, the long Tanith knife.

He stays low, hearing the crunch of the approaching enemy trooper. He can smell him too, a stench like putrefaction.

Another las-shot sings overhead. Caffran tries to slow his breathing. The footsteps get closer. He can hear the man's breath rasping inside the mask.

Caffran turns the knife around in his hand until he is holding the blade, and then very gently taps the pommel against the stone block, using the knife like a drum stick.

Chink! Chink! Chink!

He hears the enemy trooper's respiration rate change, his breath sounds alter as he turns to face a different direction. His footsteps clatter loose stone chips and crunch slime. He is right there. He is coming around the other side of the stone block.

The moment he appears, Caffran goes for him. He tries to make full body contact so he can bring the man over before he can aim his rifle. Caffran tries to force the muzzle of the rifle in under one of his arms rather than point it against his torso.

Locked together, they tumble down behind the block. The autorifle discharges.

From his vantage on the fallen roof slope, the other trooper hesitates, watching. He lowers his lasrifle, then raises it to sight again.

A shape pops back into view over the stone slab, a filthy shape, with a grimed gas-masked face. The watching trooper hesitates from firing.

The figure with the gas mask brings up an autorifle in a clean, fluid swing and fires a burst that hits the hesitating PDFer in the throat and chest, and tumbles him down the roof slope, scattering tiles.

Caffran drops the autorifle and wrenches off the gas mask as he falls to his knees. He gags and then vomits violently. The stench inside the borrowed mask, the *residue*, has been foul, even worse than he could have imagined. The mask's previous owner lies on his back beside him, beads of bright red blood spattering his mud-caked chest. Caffran slides the warknife out and wipes the blade.

Then he throws up again.

He can hear activity in the ruins behind him. It's time to move. He stares at the autorifle, and tries to weigh up the encumbrance against the usefulness of a ranged weapon. He reaches over and searches the large canvas musette pouches his would-be killer has strapped to the front of his webbing. One is full of odd junk:

meaningless pieces of stone and brick, shards of pottery and glass, a pair of broken spectacles and a tin of boot polish. The other holds three spare clips for the rifle, and a battered old short-pattern autopistol, a poor quality, mass-stamped weapon with limited range.

It will have to do. He puts it into his pocket.

It's really time to move.

IT'S GETTING DARK. Night doesn't drop like a lid on Voltemand like it did on Tanith. It fills the sky up slowly, billowing like ink in water.

The rain's still hammering the Imperial camp, but the dark rim of the sky makes the silent lightning more pronounced. The white spears are firing every twenty or thirty seconds, like an automatic beacon set to alarm.

The boy's asleep, legs and arms loosely arranged like a dog flopped by a grate. Dorden hates to abuse his medicae privileges, but he believes that the God-Emperor of Mankind will forgive him for crushing up a few capsules of tranquiliser and mixing them into the boy's broth. He'll do penance if he has to. They had plenty of temple chapels back in the city, and a popular local saint, a woman. She looked like the forgiving sort.

The boy's on a cot at the end of the ward. Dorden brews a leaf infusion over the small burner and turns the page of his book, open on the instrument rest. It's a work called *The Spheres of Longing*. He's yet to meet another man in the Imperial Guard who's ever heard of it, let alone read it. He doubts he will. The Imperial Guard is not a sophisticated institution.

Nearby, Lesp is cleaning his needles in a pot of water. He's done two or three family marks tonight at the end of his shift, a busy set. His eyes are tired, but he keeps going long enough to make sure the needles are sterile for the next job. Lesp is always eager to work. It's as if he's anxious to get down all the Tanith marks before he forgets them. Dorden sometimes wonders where Lesp will ink his marks when he runs out of Tanith skin to make them on.

The boy kicks as a dream trembles through him. Dorden watches him to make sure he's all right.

The doorway flap of the tent opens and Rawne steps in out of the lengthening light and the rain. Drops of it hang in his hair and on his cloak like diamonds. Dorden gets to his feet. Lesp gathers his things and makes himself scarce.

'Major.'

'Doctor.'

'Can I help you?'

'Just doing the rounds. Is everything as it should be here?'

Dorden nods.

'Nothing untoward.'

'Good,' says Rawne.

'It's getting dark,' Dorden says, as Rawne moves to leave.

'It is.'

'Doesn't that mean the advance unit is overdue?'

Rawne shrugs. 'A little.'

'Doesn't that concern you?' asks Dorden.

Rawne smiles.

'No,' he says.

'At what point will it concern you?' Dorden asks.

'When it's actually dark and they're officially missing.'

'That could be hours yet. And at that point it will be too late to mobilise any kind of force to go looking for them,' says Dorden.

'Well, we'd absolutely have to wait for morning at least,' says Rawne.

Dorden looks at him, and rubs his hand across his face.

'What do you think's happened to them?' he asks.

'I can't imagine,' says Rawne.

'What do you hope's happened to them?' Dorden asks.

'You know what I hope,' says Rawne. He's smiling still, but it's just teeth. There's no warmth. It's like lightning without thunder.

Dorden sips his drink.

'I'd ask you to consider,' he says, 'the effect it would have on the Tanith Regiment if it lost both of its senior commanding officers.'

'Please, Doctor,' says Rawne, 'this isn't an emergency. It's just a thing. They've probably just got held up somewhere.'

'And if not?'

Rawne shrugged.

'It'll be a terrible loss, like you said. But we'd just have to get over it. We've had practice at that, haven't we?'

THE EMACIATED GHOSTS of Kosdorf come at them through the skeletal ruins. They have become desperate. Their need, their hunger has overwhelmed their caution. They loom through useless doors and peer through empty windows. They clamber out of sour drains and emerge from cover behind spills of rubble. They fire their weapons and call out in pleading, raw voices.

The rain has thickened the dying light. Muzzle flashes flutter dark orange, like old flame.

The Tanith knot tight, and fend them off with precision. They fall back through the manufactory into the data library.

It's there they lose their first life. A Tanith infantryman is caught by autogun fire. He staggers suddenly, as if winded. Then he simply goes limp and falls. His hands don't even come up to break his impact against the tiled floor. Men rush to him, and drag him into cover, but Gaunt knows he's gone by the way his heels are kicking out. Blood soaks the man's tunic, and smears the floor in a great curl like black glass when they drag him. First blood.

Gaunt doesn't know the dead man's name. It's one of the names he hasn't learned yet. He hates himself for realising, just for a second, that it's one less he'll have to bother with.

Gaunt keeps the nalwood stock of Caffran's lasrifle tight against his shoulder and looses single shots. The temptation to switch to auto is almost unbearable.

The lobby of the data library is a big space, which once had a glass roof, now fallen in. Rain pours in, every single moving drop of it catching the light. Kosdorfer ghosts get up on the lobby's gallery, and angle fire down at the Tanith below. The top of the desk once used by the venerable clerk of records stipples and splinters, and the row of ornate brass kiosks where scholars and gnostics once filled out their data requests dent and quiver. Floor tiles crack. The delicate etched metal facings of the wall pit and dimple.

Corbec looks out at Gaunt from behind a chipped marble column.

'This won't do,' he shouts.

Gaunt nods back.

'Support!' Corbec yells.

They've been sparing with their heavy weapon all day. They're only a light advance team, and they weren't packing much to begin with.

The big man comes up level with Corbec, head down. He's carrying the lascarbine he's been fighting with, but he's got a long canvas sleeve across his back. He unclasps it to slide out the rocket tube.

The big man's name is Bragg. He really is big. He's not much taller than Corbec, but he's got breadth across the shoulders. There's a younger Tanith with him, one of the kids, a boy called Beltayn. He's carrying the leather box with the eight anti-tank rockets in it, and he gets one out while Bragg snaps up the tube's mechanical range-finder.

'Any time you like, Try!' Larkin yells out from behind an archway that is becoming riddled with shots.

'Shut your noise,' Bragg replies genially. He glances at Gaunt abruptly.

'Sorry, colonel-commissar, sir!' he says.

'Get on with it, please!' Gaunt shouts. It's not so much the heavy fire they're taking, it's the voices. It's probably his imagination, but the pleading, moaning voices of the Kosdorfers calling out to them are starting to make sense to him.

Beltayn goes to offer up the rocket to Bragg's launcher, and a las-bolt fells him. Gaunt's eyes widen as the rocket tumbles out of the hands of the falling boy and drops towards the tiled floor.

It hits, bounces, a tail-fin dents slightly.

It doesn't detonate.

Gaunt dashes forward. Corbec has reached Bragg too. Bragg has picked up the rocket. He taps it cheerfully against his head.

'No fear,' he says. 'Arming pin's still in.'

Gaunt snatches the rocket, and stoops to the box to swap it for an undamaged one.

'See to the boy!' he says to Corbec.

'Just a flesh wound!' Corbec replies, hunched over Beltayn. 'Just his arm.'

'Get him back to the archway!'

'I can't leave–'

'Get his arse back to the archway, colonel! I'll do this!'

'Yes sir!'

Corbec starts dragging the boy back towards the main archway. Men come out of cover to help him. Gaunt gets a clean rocket out of the box. He rolls it in his hands to check it by eye. It's been a long time since he loaded, a long time since he learned basic skills. A long time since he was the boy, the Hyrkan boy, apprenticed to war, born into it as if it was a family business.

'Set?' he asks the big man.

'Yes, sir!' says Bragg.

Gaunt fits the rocket and removes the arming pin. Bragg hoists the top-heavy tube onto the shelf of his shoulder and takes aim at the lobby gallery. Gaunt slaps him twice on the shoulder.

'Ease!' he yells.

'Ease!' Bragg yells back. The word opens the mouth and stops the eardrums bursting.

Bragg pulls the bare metal trigger. The ignition thumps the air, and blow-back spits from the back of the tube and throws up dust. The rocket howls off in the other direction, on a trail of flame. It hits the gallery just under the rail, and detonates volcanically. The entire gallery lifts for a second, and then comes down like an avalanche, spilling rubble, stonework, grit, glass and men. It collapses with a drawn-out roar, a death rattle of noise and disintegration.

Gaunt looks at Bragg. Bragg grins. Their ears are ringing.

Gaunt signals *back to the archway*.

They run in through the archway, through the smoke blowing from the lobby. They get down. Corbec has signalled a pause while they wait to hear how the enemy redeploys.

It gets quieter. The building settles. Rubble clatters as it falls now and then. Glass tinkles.

Gaunt sinks down next to Bragg, his back to a wall.

'First time that time,' says Larkin from a corner nearby.

'I know,' says Bragg. He looks at Gaunt. He's proud of himself.

'Sometimes I miss,' he explains.

'I know,' says Gaunt. The big man's nickname is *Try Again* because he's always messing up the first shot.

Gaunt sits quiet for a minute or two. He wipes the sweat off his face. He thinks about trying again, and second chances. Sometimes there just isn't the opportunity or the willingness to make things better. Sometimes you can't simply have another go. You make a choice, and it's a bad one, and you're left with it. No amount of trying again will fix it. Don't expect anyone to feel sorry for you, to cut you slack; you made a mistake you'll have to live with.

It was like failing to play the glittering game when he

had the chance as one of Slaydo's brightest; like leaving the Hyrkans; like trying to salvage anything from the Tanith disaster; like thinking he could win broken, grieving men over; like coming out with a small advance force into a city grave, just because he was bored of sitting in his tent.

He takes his cap off, leans the crown of his head back against the damp wall and closes his eyes. He opens them again. It's dark above him, the roofspace of the library. Beads of rainwater and flakes of plaster are dripping and spattering down towards him, catching the intermittent lightning, like snow, like the slow traffic of stars through the aching loneliness of space.

He remembers something, one little thing. He puts his hand in his pocket, just to touch the letter, just to put his fingers on the letter his old friend Blenner sent him: Blenner, his friend from Schola Progenium, manufacturer of fake plastic explosives and practical jokes.

Blenner, manufacturer of empty promises, too, no doubt. The letter's old. The offer may not still stand, if it ever did. Vaynom Blenner was not the most reliable man, and his mouth had a habit of making offers the rest of him couldn't keep.

But it's a small hope, a sustaining thing, the possibility of trying again.

The letter is gone.

Suddenly alert, torn from his reverie, Gaunt begins to search his pockets. It's really gone. The pocket he thought he'd put it in is hanging off, thanks to the thrust of a rusty sword bayonet. All the pockets of his field jacket and storm coat are empty.

The letter's lost. It's outside somewhere in this grave of a city, disintegrating in the rain.

'What's the matter?' asks Bragg, noticing Gaunt's activity.

'Nothing,' says Gaunt.

'You sure?'

Gaunt nods.

'Good,' says Bragg, sitting back again. 'I thought you might have the torments on you.'

'The torments?'

'Everyone gets them,' says Bragg. 'Everyone has their own. Bad dreams. Bad memories. Most of us, it's about where we come from. Tanith, you know.'

'I know,' says Gaunt.

'We miss it,' says Bragg, like this idea might, somehow, not be clear to anyone. 'It's hard to bear. It's hard to think about what happened to it, sometimes. It gets us inside. You know Gutes?'

Bragg points across at Piet Gutes, one of the men who was in the guild house with Domor. Like all the Tanith, Gutes is resting for a moment, sitting against a wall, feet pulled in, gun across his knees, listening.

'Yeah,' says Gaunt.

'Friend of mine,' says Bragg. 'He had a daughter called Finra, and she had a daughter called Foona. Feth, but he misses them. Not being away from them, you understand. Just them not being there to return to. And Mkendrick?'

Bragg points to another infantryman. His voice is low.

'He left a brother in Tanith Steeple. I think he had family in Attica too, an uncle–'

'Why are you telling me this, trooper?' Gaunt asks. 'I know what happened. I know what I did. Do you want me to suffer? I can't make amends. I can't do that.'

Bragg frowns.

'I thought,' he starts to say.

'What?' asks Gaunt.

'I thought that's what you were trying to do,' says Bragg. 'With us. I thought you were trying to make something good out of what was left of Tanith.'

'With respect, trooper, you're the only man in the regiment who thinks that. Also, with respect to the fighting merits of the Tanith, I'm an Imperial Guard commander, not a miracle worker. I've got a few men, a handful in the great scheme of things. We're never going to accomplish much. We're going to be a line of code in the middle of a Munitorum levy report, if that.'

'Oh, you never know,' says Bragg. 'Anyway, it doesn't matter if we don't. All that matters is you do right by the men.'

'I do right by them?'

'That's all we want,' says Bragg with a smile. 'We're Tanith. We're used to knowing where we're going. We're used to finding our way. We're lost now. All we want from you is for you to find a path for us and set us on it.'

Someone nearby says something. Corbec holds up a hand, makes a gesture. Pattering rain. Otherwise, silence. Everyone's listening.

Gaunt pats the big man on the arm and goes over to join Corbec.

'What is it?' he asks.

'Beltayn says he heard something,' Corbec replies. The boy is settled in beside Corbec, the wounded arm packed and taped. He looks at Gaunt.

He says, 'Something's awry.'

'What's that supposed to mean?' asks Gaunt.

Corbec indicates he should listen. Gaunt cranes his neck.

The Kosdorfers are moving. They're talking again. Their whispers are breathing out of the ruins to reach the Tanith position.

Gaunt looks sharply at Corbec.

'I think I can understand the words,' he says.

'Me too,' Corbec nods.

Gaunt swallows hard. He's got a sick feeling, and he's not sure where it's coming from. The feeling is telling him that he's not suddenly comprehending the Kosdorfers because they are speaking Low Gothic.

He's understanding them because he's learned their language.

THE BOY WAKES up with a start.

'Go back to sleep,' Dorden tells him. 'You need your sleep.'

Dorden's standing in the doorway of the tent, watching the evening coming in.

Milo gets up.

'Are they back yet?' he asks.

Dorden shakes his head.

'Someone needs to go and look for them,' the boy says flatly. 'I had another dream. A really unpleasant one. Someone needs to go and look for them.'

'Just go back to sleep,' Dorden insists. The boy slumps a little, and turns back to his cot.

'You dreamed they were in trouble, did you?' Dorden asks, trying to humour the boy.

'No,' replies the boy, sitting down on the cot and looking back at the medicae. 'That's not why I have the feeling they're in trouble. I didn't dream it, that's just common sense. They're overdue. My bad dream, it was just a dream about numbers. Like last night and the night before.'

'Numbers?' asks Dorden.

Milo nods. 'Just some numbers. In my dream, I'm trying to write these numbers down, over and over, but my stylus won't work, and for some reason that's not a pleasant dream to have.'

Dorden looks at the boy. He asks, 'So what are the numbers, Brin?', still humouring him.

The boy reels the numbers off.

'When did he tell you that?' Dorden asks.

'Who?'

'Gaunt.'

'He didn't tell me anything,' says the boy. 'He certainly didn't tell me those numbers. I just told you, they were in my dream. I dreamed about them.'

'Are you lying to me, Brin?'

'No, sir.'

Dorden keeps staring at the boy a minute more, as if a lie will suddenly give itself away, like the moon coming out from behind a cloud.

'Why do those numbers matter?' the boy asks.

'They're Gaunt's command code,' says Dorden.

'EXPLAIN YOURSELF,' THE voice demands. It comes out like an echo, from the ruins, the ghost of a voice. 'Explain yourself. We don't understand why.'

The voice tunes in and out, like a vox that's getting interference.

'We're hungry,' it adds.

Corbec looks at Gaunt. He wants to reply, Gaunt can see it on his face. Gaunt shakes his head.

'You left us here,' the voice says. It's two or three voices now, all speaking at once, like two or three vox sets tuned to the same signal, their speakers slightly out of sync. 'Why did you leave us here? We don't understand why you left us behind.'

'Feth's sake is that?' Corbec mutters to Gaunt. All good humour has gone from him. He's looking pinched and scared.

'You left us behind, and we're hungry,' the voices plead.

'I don't know,' says Gaunt. 'A trick.'

He says it, but he doesn't believe it. It's an uglier thing than that. The voices don't really sound like voices when you listen hard, or vox transmits either. They sound like... like other noises that have been carefully mixed up and glued together to make voice sounds. All the noises of the dead city have been harvested: the scatter of pebbles, the slump of masonry, the splinter and smash of glass, the creak of rebar, the crack of tiles, the spatter of rain. All those things and millions more besides, blended into a sound mosaic that almost perfectly imitates the sound of human speech.

Almost, but not quite.

Almost human, but not human enough.

'You left us behind, and we're hungry. Explain yourself. We don't understand why you left us. We don't understand why you didn't come.'

The Tanith are all up, all disturbed. Knuckles are white where hands grip weapons. Everyone's soaking wet. Everyone's watching the dripping shadows. Gaunt needs them to keep it together. He knows they can all hear it. The inhuman *imperfection* in the voices.

'I know what that is,' says Larkin.

'Steady, Larks,' growls Corbec.

'I know what that is. I know, I know what that is,' the marksman says. 'I know it. It's Tanith.'

'Shut up, Larks.'

'It's Tanith. It's dead Tanith calling to us! It's Tanith calling to us, calling us back!'

'Shut up please, Larks!'

'Larkin, shut your mouth!' Gaunt barks.

Larkin makes a sound, a mewling sob. Fear's inside him, deep as a bayonet.

The voices are out there in the dark and the rain. The words seem to move from one speaker to the next. Dead speakers. Broken throats.

'We don't understand why you didn't come. We don't understand. We don't know who we are any more. We don't know where we belong.'

Gaunt looks at Corbec.

'We getting out?' he asks.

'Through the back way?'

'Whatever way we can find.'

'What happened to holding this place until reinforcements arrive?' asks Corbec.

'No one's coming this way that we want to meet,' says Gaunt.

Corbec turns to the advance force.

'Get ready to move,' he orders.

The voice pleads, 'Where do we belong? We don't know where we belong.'

'It's Tanith!' Larkin cries out. 'It's the old place calling out to us!'

Gaunt grabs him, and pushes him against a wall.

'Listen to me,' he says. 'Larkin? Larkin? Listen to me!

Get yourself under control! Something worse than death happened here, something much worse!'

'What?' Larkin whines, wanting to know and not wanting to know.

'Something Tanith was spared, do you understand me?'

Larkin makes the sobbing sound again. Gaunt lets him go, lets him sag against the wall. He turns, and the men are all around him. Mkoll's right there, Mkvenner too, looking as if they're going to step in and pull Gaunt and Larkin apart. The Tanith men are all staring at him. No one's looking away.

'Do you understand?' Gaunt asks them. 'All of you? Any of you?'

'We understand what you did,' one of them says.

'Oh, this isn't helping anything, lads!' Corbec rumbles.

Gaunt ignores Corbec and laughs a brutal laugh. 'I'm a destroyer of worlds, am I? You credit me with too much power. Indecent amounts of it. And anyway, I don't much care what you think of me.'

'Let's go! Let's go now,' says Corbec.

'There's only one thing I want you to understand,' Gaunt says.

'What's that?' asks Larkin, his mouth trembling.

'The worst thing you can imagine,' says Gaunt, 'is not the worst thing. Not by a long way.'

In the open, the rain is heavy, like a curtain. Caffran knows he's never going to make it. The straggly figures hunting him are closing in, and they've been calling to him for the last ten minutes, using the voices of people he used to know, twisted by bad vox reception.

'We don't know why you left us,' the voices plead. 'Where do we belong? We don't know where we belong.'

Caffran's feet are sore. He's got the pistol in his hand. Its clip is empty. He's killed three more men on his way out of the ruins.

The voices call out, 'We've forgotten what we're supposed to be.'

He's reached the ramparts of the hills, with the city
grave at his back. He kneels down. The Imperial camp is
somewhere ahead, below and far away. He can't see it,
because rain and night shadows are filling the valley, but
he knows it must be there. Too far, too far.

There are signal flares in his message satchel. He's
pulling them out as the heavy raindrops bounce off his
shoulders and his scalp. Does he need to find higher
ground? There'll be obs positions looking this way,
won't there? Spotters and look-outs?

The voices call to him.

He stands and fires a flare. It makes a hollow bang and
soars up into the wet air, a white phosphor star with a
gauzy tail, like a drawing of a comet in an old manu-
script. It maxes altitude, and then starts to descend,
slow, trembling, drifting.

Caffran's watching it, the other flare in his hand ready
to fire. He knows there's no point.

The flare looks too much like the silent lightning.

There are figures on the hillside around him. They
come towards him.

They call out to him.

BONIN LOCATES THE remains of a depository entrance in
the south-western corner of the data library, and they
exit, via the basement stacks. They make their break out
from there.

The basement is flooded, up to their hips. They have
to cannibalise an RPG shell to make a charge to blow
the hatch open. Then they're out into the street, into the
rain, and they're drawing heavy fire right from the start.

Gaunt orders bounding cover, and they push along
a street from position to position. They stay in good
formation, despite the level of fire coming at them.
No one switches back to full auto, despite the temptation.

Even so, the advance is pushing the limits of the ammo supplies it's packing.

They begin to string out into a longer and longer line. They make it to the circus where two dead boulevards cross, and pick their way through the underwalks of the crippled tramway shelters to achieve the far side. Volleys of shots rain off the crumpled metal roofs of the shelters. The objective is the arterial route that joins the eastern boulevard. Gaunt and Corbec tell Blane to push ahead and edge back to bring the rear of the line up.

The advance is halfway across the circus when it's rushed by enemy ambushers. The ambushers come out of one of the underwalks that looked like it was choked with rubble. They're armed like trench raiders with clubs and mauls and butcher hooks. They hit the Tanith advance in the midsection of its bounding spread. They rush Gaunt as he's trying to direct the force forwards.

Gaunt goes down and his head strikes something. He's too stunned to know what's happened. A raider swings a hook to split his head and finish him.

Mkoll intercepts the raider, and guts him with his silver warknife. He meets the next one head-on, somehow evades a wide swing from a spiked mace, and rams the knife up through the throat so the point exits the apex of the skull.

Corbec's also been caught in the initial rush. He takes his attacker over with him, and breaks his neck using body weight and a wrestling hold he'd learned watching his old dad compete at the County Pryze fair.

He looks up in time to see Mkoll pull the knife out. Blood ribbons up in a semicircle, like a red streamer in the rain, and the raider curves backwards in the opposite direction. Through the sheeting rain, Corbec can see more raiders coming out of the underwalk at Mkoll. Corbec's lasrifle is wedged under the corpse of the man he just killed. He yells Mkoll's name. He yells *idiot* and *feth* too, for good measure. Mkoll's las is strapped over his shoulder. He's facing three men with just his knife.

There's the whine of a small but powerful fusion motor, the unmistakable whir of a chainsword firing up. Gaunt comes in beside the scout. Gaunt's got blood down the side of his face and his cap's gone missing. The three raiders are too close to Mkoll for Gaunt to risk a shot with his rifle or his bolter.

He takes a head clean off with his chainsword. The neck parts in a bloodmist venting from the blade's moving edge. Corbec can see from Gaunt's stance and the way he presents that he's been trained in sword work to the highest degree. Covered in dust and blood, on a slope of rubble, fighting feral ghouls, he still looks like a duelling master.

Gaunt lunges and puts the chainsword through the torso of a second raider, freeing Mkoll enough to tackle the last of the group in quick order. More are running in from the underwalk. Gaunt rotates, extending, and slices the chainsword around in a wide, straight-armed arc that neatly removes the top of a skull like a lid.

Corbec's on his feet. He pulls his lasrifle in against his gut and flips the toggle over. Then he rakes the mouth of the underwalk. Full auto flash lights up the rubble. Figures twist and jerk. He exhausts a power clip, and then lobs his last grenade down the underwalk to take care of any stragglers.

Gaunt looks around for his cap.

'Why didn't you do that?' he asks Mkoll.

'You wanted to conserve ammo,' says Mkoll.

'In all fairness, he probably could have taken them all with his knife,' says Corbec.

From up ahead, towards the east boulevard, they hear lasrifles starting to cut loose on full auto. The chatter is unmistakable.

'Ah. I've set a bad example,' says Corbec.

* * *

GAUNT MOVES FORWARD, shouting orders. He heads towards the front of the advance force, trying to restore firing discipline. Right away, he realises how badly broken their formation is. The ambush to the midsection of the spread has almost cut the advance in two. It's the beginning of the end. The enemy is exploiting their flaws, breaking them down, cutting them into manageable parts, reducing them. He knows the signs. It's exactly what he'd do.

It'll be over in minutes.

The back of the party is lagging too far behind. Gaunt tries to get the forward section to drop back and rejoin it, or at least hold position and not extend the break. It's still pushing ahead to try to reach the arterial route. Corbec's hollering at men, calling them by their first names, names Gaunt's never heard, let alone learned. Full auto fire is clattering away up ahead. Some PDFers loom over the rubble line, and Gaunt drops them with support fire from Domor and Guheen.

'Single shots! Single shot fire!' he's yelling.

He sees the Tanith fanning towards him, firing on full auto. At least one of his orders has got through, he thinks. At least they've swung back to keep the unit whole.

Then he's eyes-on, properly. These Tanith aren't members of the advance.

Rawne rakes a couple of bursts into the rubble line, and then approaches Gaunt as reinforcements pour in behind him.

'Major?'

'Sir.'

'Surprised to see you.'

'We ran into Caffran,' Rawne says.

'You ran into him?'

'We saw his flare. He was heading home, but we were already on our way out.'

'Why is that, major?' Gaunt asks.

'Concern was expressed to me by the medical chief

that the advance was overdue. A support mission seemed prudent, before it got dark and out of the question.'

'It's appreciated, Rawne. As you can see, things are a little lively.'

Rawne keeps looking at his timepiece.

'Let's keep falling back apace,' he says. 'Let's not outstay our welcome.'

Gaunt nods. 'Lead the way.'

Rawne turns and yells out to the men running his flanking units. Varl and Feygor get their fireteams to interlock firing patterns. They lay down a kill zone of las-fire that moves with the Tanith like a shadow. It burns through ammo, but it covers the retreat off the east boulevard and onto the main arterial route. They leave spent munition clips behind them, and the pathetic corpses of the enemy.

Adare and Meryn distribute ammo to Blane and the forward portion of the advance. Gaunt sees Caffran with Varl's squad. He tosses his rifle and his musette bag back to him. Caffran catches them and nods.

Rawne's still glancing at his timepiece.

'Let's go! Let's go!' he shouts. It's really getting dark. The fluttering, stammering barrage of the gun battle is lighting up the whole city block.

'We're going as fast as we can,' Gaunt says to Rawne.

Rawne looks at him, and sucks in a breath between clenched teeth that suggests that there's no such thing as too fast.

Gaunt hears a noise, a swift, loud, rushing hiss, the sound of a descent, of a plunge, of an angelic fall from grace. It ends in a noise shock that quakes the ground and nearly knocks him down. It feels like the lightning has found its voice at last.

Then it happens again and again.

Light blinds them. Bright detonations rip through the eastern boroughs of Kosdorf, some as close as a block or two away from their position. Blast overlaps blast, detonation touches detonation. It's precision wrath. It's bespoke annihilation.

'The Ketzok,' yells Rawne to Gaunt. 'A little early,' he admits.

Gaunt watches the heavy shelling for a moment, hand half-shielding his eyes from the flash. Then he turns the Tanith out of the zone with a simple hand signal.

It's too loud for voices any more.

DORDEN CLEANS HIS head wound.

'It's going to mend nicely,' he says, dropping the small forceps into an instrument bath. Threads of blood billow through the cleaning solution like ink in water.

Gaunt picks up a steel bowl and uses it as a mirror to examine the sutures.

'That's neat work,' he says. Dorden shrugs.

Outside, in the morning light, the Ketzok artillery is still pounding relentlessly, like the slow, steady movement of a giant clock. Munitions resupply is an hour away, the bombardiers report. A huge pall of smoke is moving north across the sky over the hills.

'Rawne says you were instrumental in urging him to mount a reinforcement,' Gaunt says.

Dorden smiles.

'I'm sure Major Rawne was simply following standard operational practices,' he says.

Gaunt leaves the medicae tent. There's still rain in the air, though now it's spiced with the stink of fyceline from the sustained bombardment. The camp is active. They'll be striking soon. Directives have come through, order bags from command. The Tanith are being routed to another front line.

He's got things to think about. A week spent getting the regiment embarked and on the lift ships will give him time.

'Sir.'

He turns, and sees Corbec.

'Caligula, I hear,' says Corbec.

'That's the next stop,' Gaunt agrees. They fall into step.

'I don't know much about Caligula,' says Corbec.

'Then request a briefing summary from the Munitorum, Corbec,' says Gaunt. 'We have libraries of data about the Sabbat Worlds. It would pay the regiment dividends if the officers knew a little bit about the local conditions before they arrived in a fighting area.'

'I can do that, can I?' asks Corbec.

'You're a regimental colonel,' says Gaunt. 'Of course you can.'

Corbec nods.

'I'll get on it,' he says.

He grins, flops back his camo-cape, and produces one of his cigars and a couple of lucifers from his breast pocket.

'Thought you might enjoy this now we're outside field discipline conditions,' he says.

Gaunt takes the gift with a nod. Corbec knocks him a little salute and walks away.

Gaunt goes into his quarters tent to spend an hour packing his kit. The rain is tapping on the roof skin.

His spare field jacket is hanging on the back of the folding chair. Someone's sponged it clean and brushed up the nap. They've taken off the Hyrkan badges and sewn Tanith ones on in their place.

There is no clue at all as to who has done this.

Gaunt takes off the muddy coat and jacket he's been wearing all night and slips the spare on, not even sure it's his. He strokes it down, adjusts the cuffs and puts his hands in the pockets.

The letter's in the right-hand hip pocket.

He slides it out and unfolds it. He'd been so certain it was in his number one field jacket. So certain.

He reads it, and re-reads it, and smiles, hearing the words in Blenner's voice.

Then he strikes one of the lucifers Corbec gave him, and holds the letter by the lower left-hand corner as he lights the lower right. It burns quickly, with a yellow flame. He holds on to it until the flames approach his fingertips, and then shakes it into the ash box beside his desk.

Then he goes out to find some breakfast.

ABOUT THE AUTHORS

Dan Abnett is a novelist and award-winning comic book writer. He has written over thirty-five novels, including the acclaimed Gaunt's Ghosts series, the Eisenhorn and Ravenor trilogies and, with Mike Lee, the Darkblade cycle. His novels *Horus Rising* and *Legion* (both for the Black Library) and his Torchwood novel *Border Princes* (for the BBC) were all bestsellers. His novel *Triumff*, for Angry Robot, was published in 2009 and nominated for the British Fantasy Society Award for Best Novel. He lives and works in Maidstone, Kent. Dan's blog and website can be found at *www.danabnett.com*

Follow him on Twitter @VincentAbnett

Hailing from Scotland, **Graham McNeill** worked for over six years as a Games Developer in Games Workshop's Design Studio before taking the plunge to become a full-time writer. Graham's written a host of SF and Fantasy novels and comics, as well as a number of side projects that keep him busy and (mostly) out of trouble. His Horus Heresy novel, *A Thousand Sons*, was a New York Times bestseller and *Empire*, book two in the Legend of Sigmar trilogy, won the 2010 David Gemmell Legend award. Graham lives and works in Nottingham and you can keep up to date with where he'll be and what he's working on by visiting his website.

Join the ranks of the 4th Company at *www.graham-mcneill.com*

Matthew Farrer lives in Australia, and is a member of the Canberra Speculative Fiction Guild. He has been writing since his teens, and has a number of novels and short stories to his name, including the popular Shira Calpurnia novels for the Black Library.

Aaron Dembski-Bowden is a British author with his beginnings in the videogame and RPG industries. He's been a deeply entrenched fan of Warhammer 40,000 ever since he first ruined his copy of Space Crusade by painting the models with all the skill expected of an overexcited nine-year-old. He lives and works in Northern Ireland with his fiancée Katie, hiding from the world in the middle of nowhere. His hobbies generally revolve around reading anything within reach, and helping people spell his surname.

Nik Vincent has more than a dozen titles to her name, mostly children's fiction, but also educational and reference books, and comics, and she co-wrote *Gilead's Blood* and *The Hammers of Ulric* with her husband, Dan Abnett. She has finally succumbed to the lure of Warhammer 40,000, and hopes to have a long and rewarding career writing about the guys and girls, and villains and daemons that play games with her imagination. Total immersion will do that to you, so, thanks, Dan.

Nick Kyme is a writer and editor from the northern wastes of Grimsby. He now lives in Nottingham where he began a career at Games Workshop as a layout designer and journalist on White Dwarf magazine. Currently walking the halls of Black Library as Senior Range Editor, Nick's writing credits include a host of short stories and novels. Principal amongst his works are the Warhammer 40,000 Tome of Fire trilogy featuring the Salamanders and his Warhammer fantasy-based dwarf novels.

Read his rambling blog at
www.nickkyme.com

Sandy Mitchell is a pseudonym of Alex Stewart, who has been writing successfully under both names since the mid 1980s. As Sandy, he's best known for his work for the Black Library, particularly the Ciaphas Cain series. Currently, he's in the final stages of a two year MA in Screenwriting at the London College of Communication, which has left far less time than usual for having fun in the 41st Millennium, but is continuing to chronicle Cain's progress at every opportunity. His most recent project as Alex was the short film *Ruffled Feathers*, a comedy about a catastrophic hen night, which premiered in July 2010.

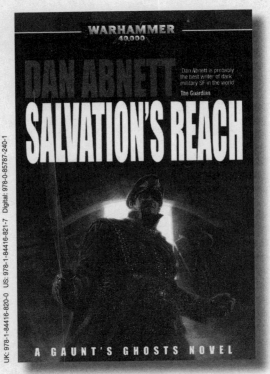

UK: 978-1-84416-820-0 US: 978-1-84416-821-7 Digital: 978-0-85787-240-1

The Ghosts of the Tanith First-and-Only have been away
from front line for too long. Listless, and hungry for some
action, they are offered a mission that perfectly suits their
talents. The objective: the mysterious Salvation's Reach, a
remote and impenetrable fortress concealing secrets that
could change the course of the Sabbat Worlds campaign.
But the proposed raid is so hazardous, it's regarded as a
suicide mission, and the Ghosts may have been in reserve
for so long they've lost their edge. Haunted by spectres
from the past and stalked by the Archenemy, Colonel-
Commissar Gaunt and his Ghosts embark upon what
could be their finest hour… or their final mission.

**AVAILABLE IN HARDBACK and EBOOK FORMATS FROM
WWW.BLACKLIBRARY.COM**

An extract from Salvation's Reach
by Dan Abnett

'YOU'VE GOT THIRTY minutes,' said one of the guards. 'That is the permitted duration authorised by your papers. You will be back here in twenty-nine minutes. If you're not, we will come looking for you and you will be considered a justified target.'

Rawne nodded.

They opened the inner cage gate. Its chain hoist clattered. He walked through the guardhouse and out onto the inner causeway of the pontoons. The tide clearly caught here between the vast stone piers of the island. There was a pronounced stink of sulphur, and a soupy mass of dissolving garbage lapped against the slimy walls of the inlet.

He left the pontoon walkway and climbed stone steps that brought him in under the archway entrance. The island was an artificial atoll of stone and rockcrete built to support a squat, formidable lighthouse tower. The bridge that had originally connected it to the shore had long since rotted away. It had been replaced by the metal pontoon and the walk span.

The lighthouse hadn't burned for a long time. Dark and neglected, the tower's thick walls and inaccessibility had been put to other uses.

Once he was out of sight of the guardhouse, Rawne stepped back into the shadows. He reached down to his left calf and removed the other Tanith warknife he was carrying. He had tied it around his shin with boot laces. The one he'd surrendered had been Meryn's. Rawne had taken it without asking. Meryn would probably be searching his billet for it already. It added to Rawne's enjoyment of the whole enterprise to think that, whatever else happened, Meryn would end up on a charge for misplacing his regimental dagger.

Rawne believed the knife would probably be enough. It certainly ought to be enough for any self-respecting Tanith-born to get the job done. But he wanted to cover all the variables.

Off to the side of the lowering entrance archway was a dim stone cistern. It had once been the chute of a garderobe, or a drain-away built to cope with heavy storm swells. The edge of his warknife, deftly applied, freed the lip of the cast iron cover. Rawne hooked his fingers around the bars of the cover and lifted it out. There was a damp stone well underneath, with water lurking in the darkness at the bottom. Other things lurked down there too, things with pincushion gums and egg-white eyes. He could hear them slopping and writhing gleefully, as if entertained by his cunning.

The cord had been attached to the underside of the drain cover, so that it hung down into the shaft of the well, weighted by the waxed burlap musette bag on the end. He pulled the line up, and the bag with it, opened the drawstring top, and took out the heavy object wrapped in vizzy cloth.

It was a collection of objects, in fact, all of them dense and heavy. Machined metal components. Rawne spread the cloth on the stone floor beside the drain, and laid the parts out on it. He slotted them together, quickly and skilfully. He'd done it a thousand times before. He could have done it blindfold. Each piece clacked or wound into place. The smell of gun oil was sweet and strong in his nostrils.

Standard Munitorum issue laspistol, Khulan V Pattern. It was one of the original stamped blanks shipped from Khulan for finishing in the armouries of Tanith, prior to issue at the Tanith Founding. The palm-spur had been fitted with a handmade nalwood grip, and age and use had lent the figuring greater beauty than any varnish or lacquer could have achieved.

The pistol had been smuggled into the lighthouse over a period of weeks, one part at a time. It lacked a power cell, a flash sleeve, and the side casings. Rawne reached into his belt pouch. Inside were two cigars rolled in black liquorice paper. The S Company sentries had taken them out, sniffed them, and given them back. Each cigar was in a little tin case. Except they weren't. One of the tin cases was actually a flash sleeve. Rawne blew out the traces of tobacco fibre, and screwed the sleeve onto the end of the barrel.

The Urdeshi had also failed to notice that he was wearing four tags, not two. Rawne unlooped the two side plates from the slender chain, dropped the tags back down under the neckline of his vest, and slotted the side plates into position.

Then he struck the tip of his knife into the back of his boot heel, and pulled the heel block away from the upper. The power cell was secured in a cavity he'd hollowed out of the heel. Rawne stamped the heel back in place, then slapped the cell into the gun. He toggled off, armed it, got a tiny green light on the grip just above his thumb. He felt the ambient hum of a charged las weapon.

He dropped the drain cover back, slipped the knife into his belt and walked up the steps from the entrance archway with the pistol down at his side in his right hand.

There was a semicircular stone chamber beyond, large and full of echoes. Munitorum-issue armoured window units had been bolted or heat-fused into the gaping stone sockets. Rawne passed on into a larger stone chamber, fully circular and three or four storeys high. It was the core of the lighthouse. In the base, dead centre, stood some of the old lampwork, a great, engineered brass contraption with a wick-mount, winding handles, and a reservoir feed from the prometheum sump below. A huge frame of gearing and chainlines surrounded it to elevate the lamp to the beacon room at the apex of the tower once it was lit.

The brass lampwork was black with age and the chains had rusted. The gears and winders were so corroded they had frozen, blotched green and white, and would never turn again. Decades of dust had accreted on the black grease of the lamp head and wick assembly in such quantity it looked like some exotic, thickly furred animal mounted on display.

Rawne walked up the stairs that ran around the curve of the chamber wall. There was no rail, and he made no sound, though the latter was not even deliberate. Like many Tanith, he had been taught, by that great educator life, not to give himself away.

He smelled caffeine and the unmistakable aroma of fried nutrition fibre. Slab, that staple of the common lasman's diet, that cornerstone of Guard rations.

Rawne reached a landing space. There was a doorway ahead. A guard, another Urdeshi man, was sitting beside the doorway on a chair borrowed from another building entirely. Rawne kept the laspistol against his hip so that the man wouldn't see it immediately. He kept walking. It was all about confidence. Confidence was the key to everything. Use enough of it and you could pull off any scam, win any fight, or bed any mamzel. The more you acted like you were absolutely supposed to be doing something, the less chance anyone would ask you what the feth you were up to, until it was too late and they were, depending on the circumstances, financially worse off, dead, or surprisingly naked.

The guard didn't spare him a second look. Rawne passed him, and went in through the doorway.

The room had originally been the tower master's chamber. It was bare boards and grilled windows, and the corkscrew staircase ran up the inside wall to the platform levels higher in the tower. The room currently contained a heavy wooden cot, a small trolley table, and an old wooden chair.

The cot was neatly made, the blanket and bedroll laid out as if for a barrack hall inspection. On the table was a small glowglobe lamp, some books, and a cookhouse tray. On the tray sat a tin cup and a flask of caffeine, a salt shaker, a mess dish with the remains of a serving of slab cake, hard biscuits and refried beanpaste and a worn metal spoon. Rawne was surprised they'd allowed a spoon. A determined man could turn a spoon into a weapon. He could sharpen it against stone, stab with it. If he didn't have time to work its edge, he could improvise. Even blunt, it could do damage to an eye or a throat if driven with enough force.

Maybe it's me, Rawne thought. Maybe I just see weapons in everything. Maybe to other people, that's just a spoon.

The books were all Imperial tracts and trancemissionary pamphlets, stamp-printed on brown, low-quality paper. It was all the monster ever seemed to read. He said they helped to settle him and fortify his resolve.

The monster was sitting in the chair beside the table, reading one of the tracts while he digested his breakfast. He was wearing unmarked black fatigues, boots and a brown hide jacket. His shaved scalp and face were covered in deliberate ritual scars, old and puckered, but the hands holding the trancemissionary treatise were soft and unmarked. The monster became aware of Rawne's approach. He stopped reading and looked up.

'Major Rawne,' he said. 'I did not expect to see you this morning.'

So fething polite. Like a real person.

'Pheguth,' Rawne replied.

The monster looked startled for a second. It wasn't just the fact that he had been called *traitor* in his own, abhuman tongue. It was the fluency of it. Rawne's time on occupied Gereon had allowed him to acquire a conversational grasp of the Archenemy language. He didn't merely know the word for *betrayer*, he could deliver it with colloquial authenticity. It was as though a part of the monster's old life had come back to threaten him.

The monster saw the weapon. He saw Rawne raising the laspistol from the guarded place beside his hip.

'Major–' he began.

Rawne said nothing else. He took aim and fired.